Praise for RAILSEA

'Miéville has an imagination of immense power . . . There
also loads of humour, plenty of action sequences, & enough
bizarre violence to keep horror fans satisfied . . . Yet for all this,
the book's chief glory is its prose. Every sentence is packed with
wit, strange but appropriate neologisms, & jostling clusters of
consonants that are there for no other reason than sheer delight
in language . . . I'll cheerfully buy a ticket for the next ride'
Guardian

Wonderful, wonderful novel . . . Miéville presents a future
world that is wondrous & believable in equal measures, while
never easing the pace of a runaway train ride of a novel'
Independent

'Miéville is a master world-builder, & never misses an opportu-
nity to hint at the nature of the surreal universe, this anything
but trackless waste, into which the reader is plunged . . . The
extended witty deconstruction of *Moby Dick* is probably the
funniest thing Miéville has written . . . a canny play of ideas
. . . Miéville's own magpie brilliance'   *Scotsman*

'Huge fun, a book that plays intellectual games . . . a rip-roaring
adventure'   *SFX*

'Miéville has imagination to burn, & his ability to conjure up
striking unreal landscapes & bizarre baroque technology is
second to none . . . *Railsea* is brilliant'   *Financial Times*

RAILSEA

CHINA MIÉVILLE lives & works in London. He is three-time winner of the prestigious Arthur C. Clarke Award & has also won the Hugo, World Fantasy & BSFA. Miéville has also won the British Fantasy Award twice. His book *The City & The City*, an existential thriller, was published in 2009 to dazzling critical acclaim & drew comparison with the works of Kafka, Orwell & Philip K. Dick. His 2011 novel *Embassytown* was a widely praised foray into science fiction, which featured on 'Books of the Year' listings for the *Guardian, Herald, Financial Times & Sunday Times*.

By China Miéville

King Rat

Perdido Street Station

The Scar

Iron Council

Looking for Jake & Other Stories

Un Lun Dun

The City & The City

Kraken

Embassytown

Railsea

CHINA MIÉVILLE

RAILSEA

PAN BOOKS

To Indigo

First published 2012 by Macmillan

This edition published 2013 by Pan Books
an imprint of Pan Macmillan, a division of Macmillan Publishers Limited
Pan Macmillan, 20 New Wharf Road, London N1 9RR
Basingstoke & Oxford
Associated companies throughout the world
www.panmacmillan.com

ISBN 978-1-4472-1367-3
ISBN 978-1-4472-2010-7 YA edition

1 3 5 7 9 8 6 4 2

A CIP catalogue record for this book is available from the British Library.

Typeset by SetSystems Ltd, Saffron Walden, Essex
Printed and bound by CPI Group (UK) Ltd, Croydon, CR0 4YY

Visit **www.panmacmillan.com** to read more about all our books
and to buy them. You will also find features, author interviews and
news of any author events, & you can sign up for e-newsletters
so that you're always first to hear about our new releases.

Part One

Great Southern Moldywarpe
Talpa ferox rex

Prologue

THIS IS THE STORY of a bloodstained boy.

There he stands, swaying as utterly as any windblown sapling. He is quite, quite red. If only that were paint! Around each of his feet the red puddles; his clothes, whatever colour they were once, are now a thickening scarlet; his hair is stiff & drenched.

Only his eyes stand out. The white of each almost glows against the gore, lightbulbs in a dark room. He stares with great fervour at nothing.

The situation is not as macabre as it sounds. The boy isn't the only bloody person there: he's surrounded by others as red & sodden as he. & they are cheerfully singing.

The boy is lost. Nothing has been solved. He thought it might be. He had hoped that this moment might bring clarity. Yet his head is still full of nothing, or he knows not what.

We're here too soon. Of course we can start anywhere: that's the beauty of the tangle, that's its very point. But where we do & don't begin has its ramifications, & this right now is not best chosen. Into reverse: let this engine go back. Just to before the boy was bloodied, there to pause & go forward again to see how we got here, to red, to music, to chaos, to a big question mark in a young man's head.

Chapter One

A MEAT ISLAND!

No. Back a bit.

A looming carcase?

Bit more.

Here. Weeks out, back when it was colder. The last several days spent fruitlessly pootling through rock passes & in the blue shadows of ice cliffs, late afternoon under a flinty sky. The boy, not yet bloodstained, was watching penguins. He stared at little rock islands furred in huddled birds plumping their oily feathers & shuffling together for comfort & warmth. He'd been giving them his attention for hours. When at last there came a sound from the speakers above, it made him start. It was the alarm for which he & the rest of the crew of the *Medes* had been waiting. A crackling blare. Then from the intercom came the exclamation: "There she blows!"

An instant frantic readiness. Mops were abandoned, spanners dropped, letters half-written & carvings half-whittled were thrust into pockets, never mind their wet ink, their sawdusty unfinishedness. To windows, to guardrails! Everyone leaned into the whipping air.

The crew squinted into the frigid wind, stared past big slate teeth. They swayed with the *Medes*'s motion. Birds gusted nearby in hope, but no one was throwing scraps now.

Way off where perspective made the line of old rails meet,

soil seethed. Rocks jostled. The ground violently rearranged. From beneath came a dust-muffled howl.

Amid strange landforms & stubs of antique plastic, black earth coned into a sudden hill. & up something clawed. Such a great & dark beast.

Soaring from its burrow in a clod-cloud & explosion it came. A monster. It roared, it soared, into the air. It hung a crazy moment at the apex of its leap. As if surveying. As if to draw attention to its very size. Crashed at last back down through the topsoil & disappeared into the below.

The moldywarpe had breached.

OF ALL THE GAPERS on the *Medes* none gaped harder than Sham. Shamus Yes ap Soorap. Big lumpy young man. Thickset, not always unclumsy, his brown hair kept short & out of trouble. Gripping a porthole, penguins forgotten, face like a light-hungry sunflower poking out of the cabin. In the distance the mole was racing through shallow earth, a yard below the surface. Sham watched the buckle in the tundra, his heart clattering like wheels on tracks.

No, this was not the first moldywarpe he'd seen. Labours, as their playful groups were called, of dog-sized specimens constantly dug in Streggeye Bay. The earth between the iron & ties of the harbour was always studded with their mounds & backs. He'd seen pups of bigger species, too, miserable in earthtanks, brought back by hunters for Stonefacemas Eve; baby bottletop moldywarpes & moonpanther moldywarpes & wriggly tarfoot moldywarpes. But the great, really great, the greatest animals, Sham ap Soorap had seen only in pictures, during Hunt Studies.

He had been made to memorise a poemlike list of the

moldywarpe's other names—underminer, talpa, muldvarp, mole. Had seen ill-exposed flatographs & etchings of the grandest animals. Stick-figure humans were drawn to scale cowering by the killer, the star-nosed, the ridged moldywarpe. & on one last much-fingered page, a page that concertinaed out to make its point about size, had been a leviathan, dwarfing the specklike person-scribble by it. The great southern moldywarpe, *Talpa ferox rex*. That was the ploughing animal ahead. Sham shivered.

The ground & rails were grey as the sky. Near the horizon, a nose bigger than him broke earth again. It made its molehill by what for a moment Sham thought a dead tree, then realised was some rust-furred metal strut toppled in long-gone ages, up-poking like the leg of a dead beetle god. Even so deep in the chill & wastes, there was salvage.

Trainspeople hung from the *Medes*'s caboose, swayed between carriages & from viewing platforms, tamping out foot-step urgency over Sham's head. "Yes yes yes, Captain . . .": the voice of Sunder Nabby, lookout, blurted from the speakers. Captain must have walkie-talkied a question & Nabby must have forgotten to switch to private. He broadcast his answer to the train, through chattering teeth & a thick Pittman accent. "Big boar, Captain. Lots of meat, fat, fur. Look at the speed on him . . ."

The track angled, the *Medes* veered, the wind fed Sham a mouthful of diesely air. He spat into railside scrub. "Eh? Well . . . it's *black*, Captain," Nabby said in answer to some unheard query. "Of course. Good dark moldywarpe black."

A pause. The whole train seemed embarrassed. Then: "Right." That was a new voice. Captain Abacat Naphi had patched in. "Attention. Moldywarpe. You've seen it. Brakers,

6

switchers: to stations. Harpoonists: ready. Stand by to launch carts. Increase speed."

The *Medes* accelerated. Sham tried to listen through his feet, as he'd been taught. A shift, he decided, from *shrashshaa* to *drag'ndragun*. He was learning the clatternames.

"How goes treatment?"

Sham spun. Dr. Lish Fremlo stared at him from the cabin threshold. Thin, ageing, energetic, gnarled as the windblown rocks, the doctor watched Sham from beneath a shag of gun-coloured hair. *Oh Stonefaces preserve me*, Sham thought, *how bleeding long have you been there?* Fremlo eyed a spread of wooden-&-cloth innards that Sham had lifted from the hollow belly of a manikin, that he should by now certainly have labelled & replaced, & that were still all over the floor.

"I'm doing it, Doctor," Sham said. "I got a little . . . there was . . ." He stuffed bits back within the model.

"Oh." Fremlo winced at the fresh cuts Sham had doodled with his penknife in the model's skin. "What unholy condition are you giving that poor thing, Sham ap Soorap? I should perhaps intervene." The doctor put up a peremptory finger. Spoke not unkindly, in that distinct sonorous voice. "Student life is not scintillating, I know. Two things you'd best learn. One is to—" Fremlo made a gentle motion. "—to calm down. & another is what you can get away with. This is the first great southern of this trip, & that means your first ever. No one, including me, gives a trainmonkey's gonads if you're practising right now."

Sham's heart accelerated.

"Go," the doctor said. "Just stay out of the way."

*

SHAM GASPED AT the cold. Most of the crew wore furs. Even Rye Shossunder, passing him with a peremptory glance, had a decent rabbitskin jerkin. Rye was younger &, as cabin boy, technically even lower in the *Medes* order than Sham, but he had been at rail once before, which in the rugged meritocracy of the moletrain gave him the edge. Sham huddled in his cheap wombatskin jacket.

Crews scrambled on walkways & all the carriagetop decks, worked windlasses, sharpened things, oiled the wheels of jolly-carts in harnesses. Way above, Nabby bobbed in his basket below the crow's-nest balloon.

Boyza Go Mbenday, first mate, stood on the viewing dais of the rearmost cartop. He was scrawny & dark & nervily energetic, his red hair flattened by the gusts of their passage. He traced their progress on charts, & muttered to the woman beside him. Captain Naphi.

Naphi watched the moldywarpe through a huge telescope. She held it quite steadily to her eye, despite its bulk & despite the fact that she hefted it one-handed in a strong right arm. She was not tall but she drew the eyes. Her legs were braced in what might have been a fighting stance. Her long grey hair was ribboned back. She stood quite still while her age-mottled brown overcoat wind-shimmied around her. Lights winked in her bulky, composite left arm. Its metal & ivory clicked & twitched.

The *Medes* rattled through snow-flecked plainland. It sped out of *drag'ndragun* into another rhythm. By rock, crack & shallow chasm, past scuffed patches of arcane salvage.

Sham was awed at the light. He looked up into the two or more miles of good air, through it into the ugly moiling border of bad cloud that marked the upsky. Bushes stubby & black as iron tore past, & bits of real iron jagging from buried antique times did, too. Atangle across the whole vista, to & past the horizon in all directions, were endless, countless rails.

The railsea.

Long straights, tight curves; metal runs on wooden ties; overlapping, spiralling, crossing at metalwork junctions; splitting off temporary sidings that abutted & rejoined main lines. Here the train tracks spread out to leave yards of unbroken earth between them; there they came close enough together that Sham could have jumped from one to the next, though that idea shivered him worse than the cold. Where they cleaved, at twenty thousand angles of track-meets-track, were mechanisms, points of every kind: wye switches; interlaced turnouts; stubs; crossovers; single & double slips. & on the approaches to them all were signals, switches, receivers, or ground frames.

The mole dove under the dense soil or stone on which sat those rails, & the ridge of its passage disappeared till it rose again to kink the ground between metal. Its earthwork wake was a broken line.

The captain raised a mic & gave crackling instructions. "Switchers; stations." Sham got another whiff of diesel & liked it this time. The switchers leaned from the walkway that sided the front engine, from the platforms of the second & fourth cars, brandishing controllers & switchhooks.

"Star'd," broadcast the captain, watching the mole alter course, & a lead switcher aimed his remote at an incoming transponder. Points snapped sideways; the signal changed. The *Medes* reached the juncture & swerved onto the new line, back on the trail.

"Star'd ... port ... second port ..." Amplified instructions lurched the *Medes* deep into Arctic wastes, tacking zigzag across wood-&-metal from rail to railsea rail, rattling over connections, closing on the mole's fast-moving turbulent earth.

"Port," came an order & a switchwoman obliged. But Mbenday yelled, "Belay that!" The captain shouted, "Star'd!" The switcher thumbed her button again but too late; the signal rushed past gleefully, it seemed to Sham, as if it knew it would cause havoc & relished the fact. Sham couldn't breathe. His fingers tightened on the handrail. The *Medes* hurtled on for the points now sending them to whatever it was that had Mbenday frantic—

—& here, Zaro Gunst, riding the coupling between fifth & sixth cars, leaned out with a switchhook & with swagger & a jouster's precision swiped the lever as it went by.

The impact sent his pole shattered & clattering across the railsea but the points slammed sideways as they disappeared below the figurehead, & the *Medes*'s front wheels hit the junction. The train continued, back on a safe line.

"Well done, that man," said the captain. "It was an ill-marked change of gauge."

Sham exhaled. With a few hours, industrial lifting & no choice you might change a vehicle's wheel-width. But hit a transition full on? They'd have been wrecked.

"So," Captain Naphi said. "He's a tricksy one. Leading us into trouble. Well grubbed, old mole."

The crew applauded. A traditional response to that traditional praise for such quarry cunning.

Into dense railsea.

The moldywarpe slowed. The *Medes* switched & circled, braked, kept a distance as the buried predator sniff-hunted for huge tundra earthworms, wary of pursuers. It wasn't only trainsfolk who could read vehicles in their vibrations. Some beasts could feel the drum & pulse of train motion from miles off. Cautiously, the traintop cranes lowered jollycarts onto nearby lines.

The cart-crews gunned their little engines, switched points gently. They closed slowly in.

"Off he goes."

Sham looked up, startled. Next to him, Hob Vurinam, the young trainswain, leaned out enthusiastically. He snapped up the collar of his battered finery with practised cockiness, his third- or fourth-hand coat. "The old velvet gent can hear them."

A molehill rose. Whiskers, a prow of dark head emerged. It was *big*. The snout went side to side & sprayed dust & spittle. Its mouth opened, very full of teeth. The talpa had good ears but the double switch-rattling confused it. It growled dustily.

With sudden violent percussion, a missile slammed down next to it. Kiragabo Luck—Sham's compatriot, Streggeye native, truculent harpoonist—had shot, & she had missed.

Instantly the moldywarpe upended. It dug at speed. Cart Two's harpoonist, Danjamin Benightly, moon-grey yellow-haired hulk from the woods of Gulflask, yelled in his barbarous accent, & his crew accelerated through the scattering soil. Benightly pulled the trigger.

Nothing. The harpoon gun was jammed.

"Damn!" said Vurinam. He hissed like a spectator at a puntball match. "Lost it!"

But Benightly the big forestman had learned javelin hunting dangling upside down from vines. He had proved himself adult by spearing a meerkat at 50 feet & reeling it in so quick its family had not noticed. Benightly grabbed the harpoon from its housing. Lifted it heavy as it was, his muscles bunched like bricks under his skin, as the cart rolled closer to the digging behemoth. Leaned back, waited—then hurled the missile right into the mole.

The moldywarpe reared, the moldywarpe roared. The spear juddered. The harpoon rope whip-unwound as the animal thrashed, blood on the soil. Rails buckled & the cart careered, tugged behind the animal. Quick—they knotted a soil-anchor to the line & threw it overboard.

The other cart was back in the game, & Kiragabo didn't miss twice. Now more anchors scraped the ground behind a bellowing hole & furious earth. The *Medes* juddered to a start & followed the molecarts.

The drags kept the burrower from going deep. It was half-in half-out of the ground. Carrion birds circled. Bolshy ones flew in to peck & the moldywarpe shook its shag.

Until at last in a lagoon of stony steppe, a dirt space in the infinite rails, it stopped. It quivered, then settled. When next the greedy railgulls landed on the furred knoll of its body, it did not dislodge them.

The world silenced. A last exhalation. Twilight was coming. The crew of the moletrain *Medes* readied knives. The devout thanked the Stonefaces or Mary Ann or the Squabbling Gods or Lizard or That Apt Ohm or whatever they believed in. Freethinkers had their own awe.

The great southern moldywarpe was dead.

Chapter Two

A MEAT ISLAND! The carcase loomed.

Molecarters snared the ropes in its skin & traintop winches hauled tons of moleflesh & a precious pelt across the ground on which no one would step. Scavenger birds at last flew home, replaced in the sky by Arctic darkbats. In waning light the moldy-warpe undertook a last, posthumous journey to the butchery wagon. & no illustrations; no flatographs; no salvaged thriddies, paintings, saltprints or liquid-crystal renditions; & certainly not the arse-achingly dull molers' reminiscences Sham had heard too many times could have prepared him for what extraordinary stinking work followed.

The mole was opened. The flatbed truck filled with its spilling remains. Sham breathed shallow at the sight. Hollow-chested. As if he was at prayer.

The crew hacked, unfolded, peeled, sawed. They grunted & sang shanties. "What Shall We Do with the Drunken Brakes-man?" they sang, & "A Life on the Open Rails". Overhead, Sunder Nabby conducted their concert with his viewscope. Sham stared & stared.

"Nothing to do?" It was Vurinam, broken off from flensing, a gory knife in his hands. "Feeling soft-hearted?"

"Nah," Sham said. Vurinam was shirtless in the tight radius of heat around the cutting & the fires, skinny & muscled & sweating mere inches from where the air would freeze him. He grinned a little crazily. Sham could suddenly believe there were only a few years between them.

No one needed first aid, but Sham knew Dr. Fremlo would not forebear lending him to the wider crew on a night like this. Vurinam's gaze went side to side as he hunted for, & found, inspiration. "Oy!" he shouted to everyone wetly unmaking what had been a mole. "Anyone thirsty?" A big tired cheer. He inclined his head & looked meaningfully in Sham's direction. "Well, you heard *that*."

Really? Sham said. He even liked Vurinam, well enough, but really? *I'm not even saying an apprentice doctor is my favourite thing to be in the world*, he said, *but hauling liquor? Don't you have a cabin boy? No disrespect, it's an honourable profession, but is it really my job to lug grog? To grog-lug? To grug?* Sham said all that but only in his head. Outside of his head, what he said was, "Yes sir."

& abruptly, Sham Yes ap Soorap was right in the middle of that moment. Quickly bloodstained. So started the longest hardest night he had ever worked. From butchery car to mess & back, again & again, running the length of the train. With drinks, with food to keep the strength up, to Fremlo's cabin where the doctor loaded him with bandages & unguents & astringents & analgesic chews for rope-burns & sliced-up palms, back again to apply them.

What reward Sham got lay in the fact that the ribaldry & jokes & excoriations of his laziness with which he was greeted by the crew unmoling the mole was more often good-humoured than not. He even, he realised, felt a bit of relief in knowing just what he was to do, the precise nature of his task, in those moments.

He snatched seconds when he could to sway in stupefied tiredness. Cutting or not, there was no avoiding the blood in that butchery wagon. So Sham became the gore-stained boy, swaying like a young tree, quite red. Not knowing what to turn his mind to. He'd been waiting for this, like all the crew, & now here he was, awed but still not knowing what it was he thought. Still lost.

He didn't ruminate on hunting. Nor on the medicine he was supposed to be learning. Nor beyond wordless aghast wonder at the scale of the mole's bones. He just endured.

Sham diluted booze—"More water than that! Not as much as that! More molasses! Don't spill it!"—snuck a couple of swigs himself. He held cups of it to the lips of those whose hands were too entrail-slippery to grip. Shossunder the cabin boy carried cups too, with poise, glancing at Sham with a nod of rare, imperious solidarity. Sham lit fires, heated metal, stoked blazes to keep trypots hot while railers took skin & fur to be tanned & cleaned, meat to be salted, strips & slabs of fat to be rendered.

The universe stank of moldywarpe: blood, pee, musk & muck. In the moonlight everything looked splashed with tar: in the train lights that black turned to the red of the blood it was. Red, black, redblack, & as if he drifted off like a paperscrap out to railsea & looked back, Sham envisioned the *Medes* as a little line of lights & fires, heard the music of its tools & train songs swallowed in the enormous southern space of ice & freezing rails. Everything spread out from the centre of the universe that at that moment was the moldywarpe face. The set snarl, the dark-furred leer, as if even in its death the great predator did not lose its contempt for those who had, outrageously, snagged it.

"Ahoy."

Dr. Fremlo nudged him & Sham lurched. He'd been asleep & dreaming where he stood.

"Alright then, Doctor," he stuttered, "I'll . . ." He tried to work out what it was he would.

"Go put your head down," Fremlo said.

"I think Mr. Vurinam wants . . ."

"& when did Mr. Vurinam pass his medical licence? Am I a doctor? & your boss? I prescribe sleep. Take one, once nightly. Now."

Sham didn't argue. Just then, for once, he knew precisely what it was he wanted: to sleep, indeed. He shuffled out of the heat, away from the empty rib-room that had been mole, into the swaying corridors. Towards his little nook. One shelf-bed among many. Through snores & farts of those who'd come off shift already. The songs of the butchers behind him were Sham's ragged lullaby.

Chapter Three

"MARVELLOUS!" had said Voam, when he got Sham the job on the *Medes*. "It's marvellous! You're not a child any more, you're quite old enough for work, & there's nothing better than a doctor. & where else are you going to learn as fast & deep as with a *moletrain* doctor, eh?"

What logic is that? Sham had wanted to shout, but how could he? Enthusiastic, hairy, barrel-shaped Voam yn Soorap, Sham's cousin or something, relative on his mother's side by a thread of unsnarlable connections, one of the two who had raised Sham, was not a trainsman. Voam kept house for a captain. The only people, however, he held in higher regard than molers were doctors. Which was not surprising, given how much of his time Sham's other cousinish surrogate parent— stooped, nervy, angular Troose yn Verba—spent with them. & they were mostly kind, too, to the boisterous old hypochondriac.

Sham could no more turn down the work Troose & Voam had arranged for him than he could have trod dog muck & railsea earth into the old men's clothes. It wasn't as if he had anything else to suggest, wrack his brains though he did. He'd been fretfully kicking his heels long enough since ending school. His time at which had also been spent, if more youthfully, kicking his heels.

Sham felt sure there was something he fervently wanted to do & to which he was excellently suited. Which made the more frustrating that he could not say what it was. Too vague about his interests for further study; too cautious in company, perhaps a little bruised by less-than-stellar school days, to thrive in sales or service; too young & sluggish to excel at heavy work: Sham's tryings-out of various candidate activities left him het up. Voam & Troose were patient but concerned.

"Maybe," he had tried to venture, more than once, "I mean, what about . . ." But the two men would always catch & interrupt his drift on that topic, in uncharacteristic accord.

"Absolutely not," said Voam.

"No way," said Troose. "Even if there was someone you could train with—& you know there ain't, this is Streggeye!— it's dangerous & dubious. You know how many beggars there are tried & failed to make that a living? You have to have a certain . . ." He had eyed Sham gently.

"You're much too . . ." Voam said.

Too what? thought Sham. He tried for fury at Voam's hesitation, but only got as far as gloom. *Too wet? Is that it?*

". . . Too *nice* a lad," Troose had concluded, & beamed. "To try his hand at *salvage.*"

Eager to give him a gently caring shove, to be an adult bird nudging a fledgling into squawking terrified first flight, Voam had pulled a favour & secured a moletrain-based apprenticeship with Fremlo for his ward.

"Life of the mind, teamwork, & a sure trade too," Voam had said. "& it'll get you out of this place. See the world!" When he told Sham, beaming, Voam had blown a kiss at the little clicking portrait of Sham's mother & father. It cycled on a three-second exposure, an endless loop. "You'll love it!"

So FAR, LOVE OF the life had been evasive. But to his own surprise, when he woke after that night of butchery, though the first noise out of him was a yelp & the second a whimper, so stiff & bone-battered was Sham, & though he staggered out of the cabin as if in rusted-up armour, when out he came & saw the grey sun through the upsky clouds & the swirling railgulls & his comrades taking hacksaws to the hosed-down pillars of the moldywarpe skeleton, even still feeling like an imposter at he knew not even what, Sham was lifted.

A kill so big, the mood aboard was good. Dramin served breakfast molemeat. Even he, ash-coloured & cadaverous, a cook who looked like a scrawny dead man & had never liked Sham at all, slopped broth into Sham's bowl with something almost like a grin.

The crew whistled as they wound rope & oiled machinery. Played quoits & back-gammony on the cartop decks, swaying expertly with the train. Sham hesitated, hankering, but blushed to remember his previous participation in the hoop-throwing. He felt fortunate the crew had let slide what had looked likely to become his permanent nickname, Captain Rubbish-Aim.

He went back to watching penguins. He took flatographs of them with his cheap little camera. The flightless charmers bickered & clattered their beaks on the islets they jostlingly inhabited. Hunting, they would dive into the inter-line ground, the earth of the railsea between the metal, & with their big shovel-shaped bills, their adapted clawfeet & muscled wings, they would tunnel aggressively for yards, burst squawking up again with some subterrestrial grub wriggling in their beaks. They might be prey in turn, chased by a fanged meerkat, a badger, predatory chipmunk packs, flurrying hunters at which Sham would stare, & which some of his trainmates strained with nets to snare.

*

THE *MEDES*'S JOURNEY was winding. Sham stared wistfully at each jag of salvage the switchers steered them past. As if one of them—that wire-wrapped stub of wheel, this dust-scoured refrigerator door, the glowing thing like a segment-missing grapefruit embedded in the shale of a shore—might wake up & do something. Could happen. Sometimes did. He thought his attentions were sneaky till he noticed the first mate & doctor watching him. Mbenday laughed at Sham's blush; Fremlo did not.

"Young man." The doctor looked patient. "Is this the sort of thing, then"—with a gesture at whatever ancient discarded object it was they left behind them in the dust—"for which you pine?"

Sham could only shrug.

They interrupted a group of person-sized star-nosed moles. The *Medes* snared two before the labour got away. Sham was bewildered that the sight of those kills, the squeals of those animals, made him wince more than the enormous slaughter of the bellowing southern moldywarpe. Still, it was more meat & fur. Sham snuck by the diesel car to see how full their holds were, to gauge how soon they would have to dock.

Fremlo gave him more doll-things to take apart & label & put back together again, to learn how the body worked. The doctor would examine the results of these macabre surgeries in horror. Fremlo put diagrams in front of him, at which Sham stared as if studying. Fremlo tested him on beginner medicine, at which Sham performed so consistently badly the doctor was almost more impressed than irritated.

Sham sat on deck, his legs dangling over the rushing dirt. He waited for epiphany. He had known soon after the journey started that medicine & he were not to be close friends. So he

RAILSEA

had auditioned fascinations. Tried scrimshaw, journal-keeping, caricature. Tried to pick up the languages of foreign crewmates. Hovered by card games to learn gamblers' skills. These efforts at interest did not take.

Northish, & the frost grew less severe, plants less cowed. People stopped singing & started arguing again. The most robust of these altercations blossomed into fights. More than once Sham had to scurry out of the path of roaring men & women knocking bells & leather out of each other at the most minimal provocations.

I know what we need, Sham thought, as ill-tempered officers ordered the perpetrators to clean the heads. He'd overheard second-hand train-lore about what to do when tensions got great. *We need some R&R.* It was not long ago he had not known what those Rs might stand for. Perhaps bored women & men, he thought, needed Rice & Remembrance. Rollers & Restitution. Rhyme & Reason.

One drab afternoon under sweaty clouds, Sham joined a circle of off-duty trainsfolk hallooing on a cartop. They gathered around a rope-coil arena in which two grumpy insects lumbered at each other. They were tank beetles, heavy iridescent hand-sized things, solitary by nature & pugnacious when that nature was denied, so perfect for this nasty sport. They hesitated, seemingly disinclined to engage. Their handlers prodded them with hot sticks until they grudgingly charged, shells clattering like angry plastic.

It was interesting, Sham supposed, but their owners' relentless provocation of their insects wasn't pleasant to watch. In cages in his colleagues' hands, he saw a burrowing lizard with anxious reptile sneer. A meerkat, & a spike-furred digging rat. The beetles were only the warm-up fight.

21

Sham shook his head. It wasn't as if the beetles were any less press-ganged or unwilling than rats or rockrabbits, but even annoyed at the one-sidedness of his own mammalian solidarity, Sham couldn't help feeling it. He backed away—and retreated right into Yashkan Worli. Sham staggered & careened into other onlookers, leaving a trail of annoyed growls.

"Where you going?" Yashkan shouted. "Too soft to watch?"

No, thought Sham. *Just not in the mood.*

"Come here! Soft belly & soft heart?" Yashkan catcalled, accompanied by Valtis Lind & a few others who could be bothered with the casual cruelties. A patter of slang name-calling, reminding Sham unpleasantly of school. He flushed beacon-bright.

"It's only a joke, Sham!" Vurinam shouted. "Grow up! Get back here."

But Sham left, thinking of the insults & those beetles pointlessly crippling each other & the scared animals waiting their turn.

THEY PASSED ANOTHER moler, diesel-powered like the *Medes*, its flags announcing it from Rockvane. The crews waved at each other. "Wouldn't know how to mole if a suicidal moldywarpe talked them through it," the *Medes* crew muttered through their smiles. Rockvane this & that, they went on, creative imprecations about their southern neighbour.

The rails here precluded an easy gam, a social meet-up, exchange of news & letters. So it was with surprise that Sham saw Gansiffer Brownall, the glum & intricately tattooed second mate, unroll a hunt-kite of the type they flew in Clarion, her austere far-off home.

What's she doing? he thought. The captain attached a letter to the kite. Brownall sent it coiling like a live thing through the air, under the roiling shadowy smear of the upsky. Two, three swoops, & she dive-bombed it into the Rockvane train.

Within minutes, the Rockvaners threw up a final pennant. Sham stared as they receded. He was still learning the language of flags, but this one he knew. In response to the captain's question, it said, *Sorry, no.*

Chapter Four

IT WAS COLD but nothing like the merciless frigidity of deep Arctic. Sham watched the rumbustious ecosystems of burrows. Peeled-looking loops of worms broke earth. Head-sized beetles. Foxes & bandicoots hurried between clots of treeroots & the perforated metal & glass of upthrust salvage. Fog closed in, obscuring rail after rail.

"Soorap," Vurinam said. The trainswain was concentrating, experimenting with a new hat. New to him, that was. Vurinam shoved his black hair beneath it, cocked it variously with & against the wind.

"Did you not hear me at the betting?" Vurinam said. "Didn't you want to watch?"

"Sort of," Sham said. "But that ain't reason enough, sometimes."

"You're going to have a hard time of it in this line of work," Vurinam said. "If a bit of animal argy-bargy upsets you."

"It ain't the same," Sham said. "That ain't it. For one, we don't go for moldywarpes for the laugh of it. & for two, they've got a good chance of getting us back."

"Allowable," Vurinam decided. "So it's about size? If Yashkan was put up against a couple of mole rats, or a thing his own scale, you'd have no objections?"

"I'd lay a bet myself," Sham muttered.

"Next time you should stick it out," Hob said.

"Vurinam." Sham made himself go on. "What was it the

captain asked the *Bagsaft*? & when we caught the big one, why did she ask what colour it was?"

"Ah," Vurinam stopped tweaking his headgear's brim & turned to look at Sham. "Well."

Sham said, "It's her philosophy, ain't it?"

"What would you know about that?" said Hob Vurinam after a moment.

"Nothing," Sham mumbled. "I just sort of supposed she's looking for something. Of a certain colour. So she must have one. She was asking if they'd seen it. What colour is it?"

"So very slow at back-gammony," Vurinam said. Glanced at the crow's nest & back at Sham. "So ill-suited to climbing." Sham shifted, uncomfortable in Vurinam's gaze. "Wistful at the sight of antique trash. Ain't much of a doctor. But that right there is a good deduction, Sham Soorap."

He leaned in. "She calls it *ivory*," Vurinam said quietly. "Or *bone-hue* sometimes. I heard her describe it once as *toothlike*. Now me I'd not backchat or argue for a treble-share of the moleprice if that's what she wants to call it but if it were *me*, what I'd say is that it's yellow." He straightened. "Her philosophy," he said, speaking into the wind, "is yellow."

"You seen it?"

"A flatograph is all." Vurinam made a humpback motion with his hand. "Big," he said. "Really ... big." He whispered, "Big & yellow."

Philosophies. Time was Sham'd wondered if that was what he wanted in his life, to surrender to a philosophy, hunt it implacably. But as he learnt more about the moletrains, it turned out they raised in him a queasiness, philosophics. A sort of nervous irritation. *I might have known*, he thought.

*

SHAM WAS RARELY tempted to do anything at night but sleep. But after that conversation, he was too jittery to surrender to his dull dreams. He sat, so far as the bed-cubby would allow. Listened to the grind & snort of wind & metal of the resting moletrain. Thought things through. At last got up.

He crept shivering through the cabin & its sleepers. Not easy in a space so intricate & equipment-cramped. Every step a negotiation of bundled rope & rags, clattery iron, tin tools, the tchotchkes by which sentimental trainsfolk made rolling stock homely. From low ceilings dangled all sorts of things on which a head could bash. But days at rail had changed him. Sham was no longer a landlubber.

Up. Night-shifts moved on other roofdecks, but Sham kept low. Into the middle of the huge cold railsea dark where nightlights swung in line, each queried by its own loyal moths. There were glints on iron lines alongside, racing shadows on the ties. Sham saw no stars.

He wanted to make a way along the traintop, to the rope-ladder, to the crow's nest. Then he wanted to make a rude gesture towards where Vurinam slept & climb into the wind, to the platform where whichever poor soul on duty crouched by a two-bar heater & stared towards the unseen horizon.

Only the maddest captain would hunt, switch rail-to-rail, at night. The lookout was watching for lights, which might be other hunters, might at worst be pirates—or just very possibly might be current-running salvage. That, Sham told himself, was what he wanted to see.

Not merely—merely!—to spot one of the looming loops of concrete-scabbed girders or a broken black dome or rubbish or plaster-glass-&-circuitry artefacts that broke the railsea. But to find one powered, running by whatever occult source ran the

26

rarest salvage. Emitting sound or light, obeying forgotten plans. He wanted that, not some captain's stupid philosophy.

Sham looked at the dangling ladder. Swore. As if it weren't too cold & he too scared. & if he did get up there & see anything, nothing would happen. Captain Naphi would mark it on a chart, to pass to others. The *Medes* would keep hunting moles.

I'd rather find nothing, Sham thought, as sulkily as a child. He crept his freezing way back to bed, refusing to feel ashamed of himself.

THE NEXT DAY when a lookout announcement made Sham's heart surge, it wasn't the call for a moldywarpe, but it wasn't really salvage either. It was something he hadn't even considered.

Chapter Five

THERE ARE TWO LAYERS to the sky, & four layers to the world. No secrets there. Sham knew that, this book knows that, & you know that too.

There's the downsky, that stretches two, three miles & a biscuit from the railsea up. That high, the air suddenly goes dinge-coloured, & more often than not roils with toxic cloud. That is the border of the upsky, in which hunt oddities, ravenous alien flyers. Mostly unseen in the dirty mist, thank goodness, except when the cover clears & makes watchers shudder. Except when their limbs & bits reach down to grab some ill-advisedly ambitious bird flying above what's sensible.

We're not talking about that. We're talking about the four-fold of the world.

There is the subterrestrial, where the digging beasts dig, where there are caverns, roots, ancient seams of salvage, & maybe the iron & wood of long-forgotten or not-yet-seen lines of railsea.

The railsea, sitting on the flatearth; that is the second level. Tracks & ties, in the random meanders of geography & ages, in all directions. Extending forever.

The lands & the countries & the continents are level three. They jut above the rails. They rise on the grundnorm, the foundation of hard earth & stone too dense for the diggers of level one to hole. That makes them habitable. These are the countless archipelagos, solitary islands, the nations & question-able continents.

& over & above all that, where the peaks of the larger lands reach, protrude through the miles of breathable downsky into the upsky, above the borderline, are the cloggy, claggy highlands. On which poison-mist-&-dodgy-air-obscured levels creep, scurry & stagger the cousins of the upsky flyers, poison-breathing parvenu predators. Like them, troublesome biology, originating elsewhere.

Of those four zones there are two & a half where human life goes on. Inland, on the islands looking over iron & ties & savage dirt of the railsea, there are orchards & meadows. There are pools & quick streams. Fertile, gentle soil full of crops. This is where farmers farm, next to where towns town. That is where the landbound, the mass of humanity, lives. Above train travels & troubles.

Edging such places is the railseaside, called the littoral zone. Those are the shorelands. Port towns, from where transport, freight, & hunting trains set out. Where lighthouses light ways past rubbish reefs breaking earth. "Give me the inland or give me the open rails," say both the railsailor & the landlubber, "only spare me the littoral-minded."

There are many such homilies among trainsfolk. They are particularly given to sayings & rules. Like: "Always do your best for those in peril on the railsea."

Chapter Six

AGAIN, THE CIRCLE OF off-duty trainspeople bickering over the odds of fighting animals. Again, the prodding & tweaking of the handlers.

The day was bright & cold & windy, & made Sham blink. He sidled up. *Oh, sneck up,* he thought, in unease he couldn't explain to himself, when he saw on what the audience was betting.

They were birds. Not indigenous to these latitudes, either— pygmy fighting cockerels. They must have been kept & coddled just for this moment. Each was smaller than a sparrow. Their tiny wattles wobbled, their minuscule cockscombs throbbed, they clucked & cawed chest-out in miniature swagger, strutted in circles, taking each other's measure. On their lower legs they wore wicked little spurs. As was traditional for the smallest fighting birds, theirs weren't metal but hardened, polished bramble thorns.

Yes, Sham could see the careful expertise with which some in the crowd were appraising the belligerents. He could appreciate the ferocity & bravery of the sudden madly fluttering assault, as bird went for tiny bird. He heard the odds, the mathematics of savagery. But strive as he did to overcome distaste, to watch with enthusiasm, or even with calm interest, Sham could only wince, & could focus only on the fact that the birds were very small.

Over slow seconds, he leaned over the fighting grounds.

What was all this, he thought? He spectated himself, as if his body was a puppet. *What is Sham up to?* Sham wondered.

Ah, there was his answer. It wasn't only mammals for which he felt sorry, it turned out. Sham was tugging his sleeves over his fingers, while the rest of the trainsfolk watched with increasing bewilderment, not even interrupting him, so methodically did he move. Now he was reaching down into the flurry of dust & feather-fluff & blood where the two tiny cockerels struggled to slaughter each other. Then right hand, left hand, Sham picked them up.

The wind, the squawks, the huffs of the engine continued, but it still felt in that moment as if everything was silent. *Ah.* That sound was in his head. It was as if he could hear the half-approving, half-disapproving amusement of Troose & Voam at his action. & behind them—a surprise to him—a whisker of the same conflicted emotion from Sham's long-gone mum & dad. Observing him.

Everyone on-deck stared at Sham. "What," said Yashkan, "are you doing?"

I have no idea, he thought. He kept watching, to learn the answer. *Ah*, again. Having rescued the birds, now, it seemed, Sham was running away.

He snapped abruptly back into his own body as if his soul was catapulted by elastic. He came to himself running full-pelt, his breath heaving, his legs drumming as the train veered. He vaulted obstacles on the cartop deck. Behind him were outraged shouts.

A glance, & Sham saw chasing him, shaking their fists & yelling vengeance & punishment, not only Brank & Zaro, the big hauler & little switcher whose birds he carried; not only Yashkan & Lind, a bit behind them, eager to get hold of Sham

31

for more vindictive reasons; but a great gathering of people who'd placed bets.

Sham was ungainly, but he jumped over chests, capstans & knee-high chimney stubs, ducked under the bars segmenting one deck-bit from another. Moved faster than he thought he could. Faster than his pursuers thought he could. & all without using his hands, each of which contained a carefully not-crushed fighting rooster. Sham ran from one end of the deck to the other, a trail of women & men behind him, shouting instructions to each other to head him off here & grab hold of him there. The birds pecked & scratched, & even tiny as they were & through the cloth wrapping his hands, they drew Sham's blood. He beat his own reflex to fling them away. He was surrounded. He scuttled up a ladder, onto a storage bin.

Nowhere to go. Brank & Zaro approached. He swallowed at the sight of their fury. But as many of his pursuers were laughing as looked angry. Vurinam was applauding. Even Shossunder the cabin boy smiled. "Well run, boy!" Mbenday shouted. Sham held out his hands full of terrified birdlings as if they were weapons. As if he would throw them, thorns & all. *What*, he thought, *am I doing?*

Desperately, he considered hurling the birds straight up, to where the wind gusted. Their wings were clipped, but flapping them frantically, they could fall in controlled feathery motion right off the deck. At least that way they'd avoid the combat that appeared to be their lot. But when they landed they would, within instants, be something's lunch. He hesitated.

There was no way he was getting out of this without a whack or two, he thought, as Brank & Zaro came at him. & then, just then as the triumphant Brank lifted his arms to pounce, there was a halloo from the crow's nest. The train was approaching something.

A frozen moment. Then Mbenday shouted, "Stations!" The crew scattered. Brank, Zaro waited, till Sham, grudging & without a choice, handed back the birds.

"Finish this later," Zaro whispered.

Whatever, thought Sham. At least the roosters had had a brief reprieve. He moved slowly again, all the energy that had hurtled him so uncharacteristically fast quite gone. Breathing heavily, Sham clambered off his little platform to find out what had been seen.

"WHAT IS IT?" Sham said. Trainsman Unkus Stone ignored him, & Mbenday tutted irritably.

They were in a stretch of atolls the size of houses. Woolly squirrels watched the *Medes* from where shoreline trees met the metal of the railsea. Across a sparsely railed stretch, Sham could see a line of much newer ruin. A crumpled silhouette.

He answered his own question. "A wreck."

A small & shattered train. An engine, lying on its side in the dust. Completely off the rails.

"SO ATTENTION THEN," the captain intercommed from her dais, in her usual mournful tones. "No flags, no activity. We've heard no maydays. No flares. We know zero. You know the protocols." Salvage, the crew of a moler was not equipped to deal with. But a vehicle in distress? All legitimate trainsfolk would drop everything for a potential rescue. That was railcode. The captain's sigh, which she did not bother turning away from the microphone to disguise, suggested she obeyed this moral obligation without enthusiasm. "Get ready." Any deviation from her own project, Sham thought—her fervour to follow, find, finesse her philosophy—she must resent.

Switchers took the train across the tracks, closer. It was tiny, that ruin, one car, one engine. It lay like a tipped cow.

Vehicles from moling nations across the railsea plied the bays of the Salaygo Mess archipelago, & of Streggeye Land his home. Sham had seen many train-shapes in his time, at harbour, & illustrations of more, in his studies. Even ruined as this one was by its damage, it looked utterly unfamiliar.

IT WAS EASIER THAN he'd thought it would be to insinuate himself onto the cart sent to investigate. Sham ran about on inventy errands as if by Fremlo's instruction, &, still buoyed up by adrenaline from his foiled animal rescue, got behind Hob Vurinam lining up for duty & jumped into the swinging cart as if ordered. Muttered something about first aid.

Shossunder, still on the main deck, raised an eyebrow, but obviously thought it beneath him to complain. Thank the Stonefaces for the cabin boy's pride, Sham thought. Second mate Gansiffer Brownall leaned from the cart as it puttered towards the wreck & yelled into a loudhailer. "Anyone there? Ahoy!"

Ain't no one alive in that, Sham thought. *That's medical knowledge right there,* he added to himself. *That's as mashed as if an angel's had at it.*

The sideways engine had no chimney: not steam-powered then. The first carriage bulged with machine remnants. It was scrunched up. Its portholes were blocked & broken. A thornbush had grown its sinewy way all the way through the carriage.

The crew was hushed. They creaked slowly closer through

flat light. Ginger-pelted & multicoloured daybats rose in congregation from where they'd been fiddling in the ruin. They circled, complaining, swept out to the nearest island.

Technically, this might be salvage. No one living on the remains? Then anything the crew found & could carry was theirs. But glad as Sham was of all the drama, that would be nu-salvage. What floated his boat, what rang his bell, what he pined for, was the glamour of arche-salvage. The most incomprehensible & ancient remains.

Little animals bustled through the grass. The *Medes* loitered in the distance, the rest of the trainsfolk staring as the jollycart ghosted to a stop, nudging the dusty engine.

"Now," said Brownall. "Volunteers." The crew eyed her. She pursed tattooed lips & pointed. "Can get in from here. No one asks you to touch the ground." They checked weapons. "Vurinam," Brownall said. The trainswain bounced on his toes & took off his battered hat. "Teodoso. Thorn & Klimy, Unkus Stone, here with me. The rest of you, double-line. In you go. Top to bottom. Anyone, anything, let's find it. Where you off to?" She said that last to Sham, as he stood with the others as if to board.

He was busy being staggered by his own uncharacteristic behaviour. "You . . . said we was going in . . ."

"Soorap, don't bugger about," she said in the melancholy accent of the island of Clarion. "Did I moan about you being on the cart? I don't notice? Didn't know you had the front, boy. Don't push your luck. Aft." She pointed. "& . . ." She put her fingers to her lips.

One by one the cautious hunt descended through a window-turned-trapdoor. "You're lucky you're not walking back," Brownall said to Sham. He gnawed his lip. She wouldn't. The very idea, though, that thought of one foot after the other, careful on the dusty ties, avoiding the terrible earth, all the way back to the train, made him swallow.

So he waited. Stared out to railsea & back at the ruin. Jens Thorn threw rusty screws at a distant signal box. Cecilie Klimy took bearings for Stoneface knew what reason with an intricate sextant. Unkus Stone sang to himself & carved at scrap. His voice was lovely: even Brownall didn't tell him to shut up. Stone sang an old song about falling on the dirt & being rescued by an underground prince.

The daybats settled. A couple of shaggy rabbits watched the crew, & Sham raised his little camera, the best that Voam & Troose could afford, that they'd presented to him with a delighted *tadah!*

"Ahoy!" Hob Vurinam's head poked from a horizontal porthole. He shook his head & dust rose from his hair.

"& so?" shouted Brownall. "Situation?"

"Well," Vurinam said. He spat over the edge of the train. "Nothing. Been here like a million years. Engine's already been gone through. More than once."

Brownall nodded. "& the last carriage?"

"Well," Vurinam said. "About that. You know you was saying Sham Soorap had to stay put?" Vurinam grinned. "Might want to rethink."

Chapter Seven

SHAM STRUGGLED through a room askew. His floor had once been a wall. He picked a cramped way past his comrades.

"See the problem?" Vurinam said. There was a door, now by the ceiling, flapping a few inches on its hinges. "It's wedged," Vurinam said. "& we're all a bit big."

It didn't seem right. Most of the time the crew kept on about Sham being big for his age, & he was. He wasn't the youngest on the *Medes*, nor the smallest, nor lightest crew-member. Yehat Borr was three foot something, muscled & bear-strong. Could do handstand press-ups. Throw harpoons almost as far as Benightly. Turn upside down dangling from a rope. But what Sham was was the smallest & lightest who happened to be right there, right then.

"I ain't even supposed to be here." Sham hated how his own voice suddenly quavered to his own hearing. But he *was* here, wasn't he? Snuck on in a sudden pining for excitement, & the universe had called his bluff. His job was to apply bandages & brew tea, thanks very much, not to haul arse into sealed-off wrecks.

Oh Stonefaces, he thought. He didn't want to go into the cabin—but how he wanted to want to.

"I told you," someone mumbled. "Leave it, he ain't going to . . ."

"Come on," said Vurinam. "You like salvage, don't you?" He met Sham's gaze. "What do you say?"

All his crewmates were looking at him. Was it shame or bravery that made Sham say yes? Ah, well. Either way.

HE GRIPPED, he hauled. He kicked. Just like exploring deserted buildings in Streggeye, he told himself. He'd done that. Not that he was brilliant at it, but he was better than you might think. He was shoved at, feet & bum, wriggled, held his breath, scraped through the gap.

Beyond the door it was dark. The windows in what was now the car's ceiling were shuttered. Rods of dusty light extended from holes, picked out patches of ground, mildew, paperscraps, cloth.

"Can't see much," Sham said. He scrabbled, bolder, was over & in & down with a thud. *Well*, he thought cautiously, wiping his hands. *This ain't so bad.*

"Here we go," he reported. "What's here?"

Not much. The back of the carriage was crushed, rammed from outside, long ago. Sham's eyes adjusted. The paper litter was still speckled with stubs of writing, too small to make sense. There were ash-piles.

"It's all rubbish," he said. The windows at his feet were open to the ground. He shivered to be so close to earth.

No surprise, of course, that this made Sham wonder about his father. Thoughts trundled as slow as an old goods vehicle through his skull. Was this how it had looked when his father's train went down? There had been no survivors & no word. Sham had imagined the train many times—an elongated, wheeled crypt. He had not, however, envisaged it on its side, like this. A failure of his imagination he now rectified. He sniffed.

Sham shuffled through junk. When he was a kid, he'd

played salvors many times. & here was, in the most trashed sense, salvage. The ruins of a chair. Shards of an ordinator. The splayed rods of a mangled typewriter. He swished his feet through debris.

Something thunked & rolled out of rags. A skull.

"What is it?" Vurinam shouted at Sham's yell.

"I'm alright," Sham called back. "Just a shock. Ain't nothing."

Sham looked at the skull, & its eyeholes watched him back. It watched him too from a third eye, neat hole bang centre of its forehead. He kicked the rag-shreds away. There were other bones. Though not enough, Sham thought with his new, very slight, insight, for a whole body.

"I think I found the captain," Sham said quietly. "& I think the captain don't want much rescuing."

An arm bone poked up from the bare dirt in a windowframe. It went deep. Near it was a broken cup, its jag filthy. As if it had been used to dig.

Sham was no baby. He knew, of course, how superstitions worked, that the earth wasn't *literal* poison. It had been many years since he'd thought it really would kill him just to touch it. But it certainly was for real dangerous. His whole life he'd been trained to avoid it, & not without reasons.

He squatted, now, though. Slowly, he reached out. Tentatively, he prodded the soil in the window, snatched his hand right back as if from a stove. It reminded him of being by the shore back in Streggeye, clustered with classmates at the island's edge, by the loamy earth of railsea where tracks tangled. Everyone goading each other to pat it.

Sham wrinkled his face, wrapped his hand in his sleeve. He tugged the arm bone from the ground & threw it from him.

He steeled himself. He reached slowly into the hole, to find what the dead person had been taking out, or putting in.

He grit his teeth. It was cold & dry within. He groped. Stretched. Felt something. He fiddled, fingertip-gripped, slowly extracted it from the earth. A plastic wafer, like the one in his camera. A picture card. He put it in his pocket, lay flat & put his hand back in the hole.

"Sham!" Vurinam said. Sham pressed his cheek to the earth. Outside the cabin, he heard wings like ruffled pages, screams of returning daybats. "Sham, get out!"

"Hold on a minute," Sham said, & stretched again.

Something bit him.

UP SHAM SPRANG like a spring-loaded toy, yelling in terror & trailing blood. Vurinam shouted, bats screamed, & from the earth came a chattering.

Sham knew where the captain's other bones had gone. He knew what had shredded all the clothes. He grabbed for the sideways door but, hurt, his hand couldn't take his weight. In the window-frames, the dirt bulged. A dreadful bony sound sounded. Sham stared into the hole. From its deeps two eyes stared back.

The thing rose. It burst from its tunnel. *Chewing its way out.* A thing of pale, wrinkled corpsy skin, appalling scissoring teeth.

The naked mole rat launched itself out of the earth.

Chapter Eight

As LONG AS HUMANITY has rolled on the railsea, the rigours & vigours & bloody triggers of the underground have been legendary. There are predators on the islands, too, of course, above the grundnorm. Hill cats, wolves, monitor lizards, aggressive flightless birds & all manner of others bite & harass & kill the unwary. But they're only one aspect of the hardland ecosystems, pinnacles on multiform animal pyramids. These systems contain vastly varied behaviours, including cooperations, symbioses, & gentlenesses.

Subterrestriality, by contrast, & life on the flatearth that is its top, is more straightforward & exacting. Almost everything wants to eat almost everything else.

There are herbivores. Chewers on roots. But they are a small unhappy minority. You might think the Squabbling Gods of the railsea, when their bickering made the world, put them there for a mean-spirited joke. Look under the tracks & ties: the beasts that make caverns, that tunnel, that steal their way into others' networks, that rise & sink above & below the groundline, that squeeze through crevices in the fractured world, that coil around roots & stalactites, are overwhelmingly, & ferociously, predators. There is something about the compact materiality of that realm, naturalists speculate, that heightens the pressures of life. By comparison, the island ecosystems are oases of pacifism.

This savage underground & flatearth does not preclude complexity. There are many ways—often ingenious—one ravenous animal can eat another, or a hapless woman or man. The beasts of the railsea give them all a try. For trainsfolk, this means a hierarchy of awfulness.

Fast flatearth-runners are bad enough, they'll tell you, of the animals that scurry with hungry intent on the surface, overleaping tracks, but what provokes the worst terror are the eruchthonous. That is a railsea word. It means *that which digs up from underneath & emerges.*

& of those eruchthonous beasts, connoisseurs of animal aggression debate the worst. Size, voracity & the sharpness of claws, while important considerations, may not define the most frightful hunter. There are other, more uncanny things to consider. There are reasons a certain animal above all, one particular tunneller more than any other, has a uniquely horrible place in the rail traveller's imagination.

Chapter Nine

WITH A SHOVE OF awful nailless hands the mole rat flew at him. Sham stumbled. A *lucky* stumble. The animal flew over him, hit the wall & slid down, dazed.

In Streggeye Terrarium Sham had seen such things. Runt, domesticated versions, chewing what scraps their keepers threw. Kept carefully apart from each other. Below him right now, the wild cousins of those prisoners used guillotine teeth to bite paths through dirt. They rose into sight. They came as a colony. Collective soldiers. Thinking with the hive mind their Streggeye keepers so assiduously kept them from attaining.

The mole rats shook off earth. Like hairless, wrinkled mammal newborn, swollen to dog-size, snapping dreadful incisors. Eyes like raisins shoved in dough. They breathed throatily. The earth growled.

Sham jumped for the door-top. He hung. The beasts gathered. Sham heard teeth.

His fingers slipped.

He fell.

Was caught.

Vurinam, just beyond the door, gripped his arm & groaned in effort. The animals leapt & bit at Sham's feet. Vurinam hauled, Sham climbed, & together they got Sham out. He fell among the crew in the sideways cabin.

"Go!" someone shouted. People jumped on what remnants of furniture there were, hammering at the earth with sticks &

weapons, as it began to move. Hoe-toothed mole-rat faces boiled the grit in the window-frames.

Clinging to walls, overleaping the snapping lurches of the colony, the trainsfolk got up & out. Sham heard shots. He ran along the skew-whiff traintop.

Bats bustled & buffeted him. Sham leaped, he pitched, he landed heavily in the jollycart among the escapees, as Gansiffer Brownall & the others clubbed mole rats breaching all around them, & fired into the moiling ground. At the cart's edge rose a flannelly animal face, all quivering whiskers & malevolent percussion. Sham grabbed for anything heavy & it was a kettle left for some dumb reason in the cart that his hand found & which he swung.

Vurinam staggered as he landed, smacked heavily into Unkus Stone. Who himself staggered to the cart's edge, tipped, toppled, fell out, between two sets of rails.

Onto the ground.

Stone floundered. He sank a clear inch into crumbling earth. Quite redundantly—everyone saw it—someone screamed: "Man overboard!"

Mole rats looked up with a simultaneous motion, puppets on one string. The capsized carriage itself shuddered, as if something big & underneath it paid sudden attention. Synchronised, the mole rats dived, bite-burrowed towards Unkus. Moving towards the jollycart, a ridge was rising in the earth.

"Grab hold!" Vurinam shouted, stretching out his hand. "Move!" Unkus crawled. Incompetent quadruped. Mole rats moved in with gusts of stygian dust. Ploughed massively from below, that big furrow still grew. Stone screamed.

Vurinam grabbed him & pulled, & others grabbed Vurinam. Agitated bats swept in chaos around Sham, making him flail.

The earth rampart rose & growled & cracked & within, Sham could see a huge hump of saggy skin, a mole-rat back twice the size of any other. The mole rats were a hive, & what was coming was the queen.

There was an explosion of dirt, a great biting down, a glimpse of great mouthness. Sham cried out, Vurinam tugged, Unkus wailed & was pulled aboard. There was a rumbling as the queen descended invisibly, preyless, frustrated. The earth settled. But Unkus still screamed. A mole rat was dangling by clenched teeth from his bloody leg. "Hit the bloody thing!" Brownall shouted.

It was Sham who did. Smacked it with his kettle harder than he'd smacked anything before. The beast somersaulted backwards into the accelerating cart's dirt.

There was one moment of exhilaration, one ragged cheer as the women & men of the *Medes* left the marauding colony. Then it was over & they saw the state of Unkus.

Chapter Ten

THE CREW OF the *Medes* crowded the edges of the cartops, in agonies at the attack they had seen but could not reach. Unkus moaned.

Sham heard a faint, pathetic beating & saw a flutter of colour. In the corner of the cart was an injured daybat. It flipped & fiddled, pitiful on damaged wings. He must have hit it when he swung. It foamed weakly from its mouth.

Vurinam went to tip it out. "No," Sham said. He lifted it gently. It snapped at him, groggily enough that those teeth were easy to avoid. When his turn came to cross the walkway between the *Medes* & the cart, Sham had the daybat wrapped in his shirt.

The doctor was waiting for him. Took hold of him brusquely, checked he was not hurt, patted his shoulder & told him to get ready. Behind him, Unkus Stone was being carried aboard.

"HOW'S HE DOING, Doc?" The questions kept coming from the corridor. "Can we talk to him?" The doctor took off the bloody apron, caught Sham's eye & nodded. Sham, still swallowing at the sight of the procedure, opened the surgery door to the crew.

"Alright," Fremlo said with the abruptness of exhaustion. "Come in. You'll not get much off him. Drugged him to the gills. & do *not* touch his leg."

"Which leg?"

"Either bloody leg."

Sham got out to give them room. He listened to them whisper.

"What did you find, Sham ap Soorap?" someone said.

He looked up. It was the captain.

Abacat Naphi. Her prosthetic arm was raised, barring his way. He stared into her dark blue eyes. They were about the same height, & he was heavier, but he felt as if he was craning back his neck to meet her gaze. Sham stammered. She had not spoken to him before, except for sentences like, "Move," "Put it over there," & "Get out." He was astonished that she knew his name.

"Answer," Fremlo growled.

Sham wondered: *Where'd the doctor come from?*

"Captain, I . . ." Sham said. His bat—no hiding it now— squeaked.

"Attention," Captain Naphi said. "Later we'll consider whether you can keep your vermin, ap Soorap. Now we answer questions. What was in the wreck?"

"Nothing, Ma'am Captain," Sham stuttered. "A skeleton I mean is all. That was it. That & only else also just rubbish."

"Is that so?" Naphi said. She closed her eyes & lowered her artificial arm, leaving a thread of exhaust & the murmur of motors. Sham watched the intricacy of its workings, the lines of its black wood.

"Nothing, Ma'am Captain, not a thing." *Are you insane?* Sham thought. *Why you lying?* & even as he thought about the little scrap of salvage he'd found that was his by finder's right, he heard himself saying, "Oh except only this," as he fished out the card from his pocket & gave it to her.

"If I might, Captain?" Fremlo was beckoning for her to

follow—who else on the train could do that? Naphi looked once more, thoughtfully, at Sham.

"Thank you for the memory," she said. She took it & followed Fremlo. Sham watched them go. Stood unmoving but for grinding jaw. Inside he was raging, demanding his tiny salvage back.

A STORM WAS COMING. Sham watched through portholes while clouds lowered, descending below the upsky & changing their nature, drawing rain across the landscape, turning the world to mud & replenishing pools & puddles between rails, speeding up the streams gushing from islands. The slick trainlines shone. The injured daybat stuck its head up from Sham's shirt, as if it, too, wanted to watch the sky. He stroked it.

"Soorap," Dr. Fremlo had said to him when they started work on Stone. "We know this is not your favourite activity. I ask only that you stay out of the way, do as I tell you when I tell you. You may not like it, you may not be very good at it—you are not, in fact, very good at it, & if *I* can tell that, that means you are very not very good at it—but you are probably somewhat better than nothing. So if I say bandage, you know what to do. & so forth. His leg's at risk. Let's do what we can."

After the whispered exchange with Naphi, Fremlo had found him again. "You do know," the doctor had said, "that you don't have to obey orders?"

"I thought that was the whole point of orders!"

"Oh yes, but no," Fremlo's voice had dropped. "I mean you are obligated to, formally, yes, but it's not uncommon to not. You really wanted that card, did you not?"

Sham, vivid red, could not tell if this was a rebuke, advice, or what.

"Good," he heard someone say, looking at the storm. "Drown the bloody things." A fine curse & worthy anger, though it wouldn't happen. Like all tellurian animals of the railsea, mole rats had strategies to avoid that fate when it rained. Airlocks, water traps, complicated tunnel shafts.

Sham saw Brank. Sham started a moment, but Brank barely looked at him. There were more important matters than briefly pilfered cockerel on the big man's mind. Even Yashkan was too distracted to glance at Sham with more than a moment's malevolence. He thought for a moment that he had escaped anger. It came for him, though, & from an unexpected direction.

"Stoneface!" Vurinam emerged from the surgery. "You had to fart around with whatever you were doing in there, didn't you?" It took Sham a moment to realise it was him the trainswain was shouting at.

"Hold on a minute," Sham said. "I never—"

"Had to prick up the ears of the bloody mole rats & was I not telling you to get out? Now look!" Vurinam stamped. He gesticulated towards where Unkus slept.

Sham tried to think of what to say.

"Steady, mate," said someone. "Sham didn't mean—"

"Well," yelled Vurinam. "'Didn't mean' never buttered no bloody parsnips, did it?"

"Attention," the captain's voice interrupted from the corridor speakers. "Unkus Stone," she said, "needs a hospital. Dr. Fremlo assures me we don't have the resources aboard. So." You could hear a big sigh down the intercom. "Detour." Another pause. "Switchers, brakers, engineers, stand by to set course," she said. "Set course for Bollons."

There were moments of silence. "Bollons?" Vurinam said.

"Stations!" the captain's voice cracklingly demanded, & everyone moved.

"Unkus can't be in a good way," someone muttered.

"Why?" said Sham to the trainswoman's retreating back. "How? How bad is it?"

"Bad enough," Vurinam shouted back, "that we're going where we're going. Bad enough that we're going to the nearest land, when it's Bollons."

He stamped away, leaving silence, a cold corridor, & Sham alone. Sham shivered. He wondered where to go. He lifted up the bat & stared into its confused animal eyes. *Don't be scared*, he thought. *You need my help.*

Part Two

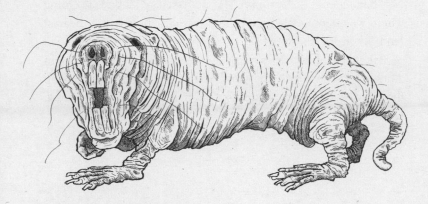

Naked Mole Rat
Heterocephalus smilodon glaber

Chapter Eleven

A MOLETRAIN on the hunt beats out one kind of rhythm. It is insistent, not too fast, stop-starting as it backs & forwards onto sidings, changes lines, trailing its prey, crews alert for give-away earthmounds.

One *kind* of rhythm: not one rhythm. The wheelbreath of hunts takes many shapes, but all instil in a moler a certainty, a calm energy, a controlled rush. They are all the default blood-quickening beats of the predator train. When old hunters hang up their trainboard gear, retire to a cottage on a crag to get up with the sun, it is one of those hunting rhythms to which their feet, unbidden & unnoticed, will move. Even in their coffins, some say, those are what the heels of a dead captain drum.

Very different is a train moving under emergency. Its rhythm is quite other. The *Medes* raced.

Chapter Twelve

THE WHEELS SPOKE mostly *radagadan*, at speed. One, two, three days after Unkus's injury, the train ground north as fast as it safely could on such wild rails. Sham brought the sick man food. He held the bowls of hot water while the doctor changed the dressings. He could see the worsening state of the wounds, the creep of necrosis. Unkus's legs suppurated.

These dusty barren stretches of plain-&-rails were near the edges of the world, & maps were contradictory. Captain Naphi & her officers annotated those they had. Kept the log up to date. The captain pored over her rumourbook. Sham would have loved a look at that.

The *Medes* headed north, but the eccentricities of rails & junctions took them briefly west, too. Enough that late one day, at the limits of vision, like a smoke wall at the horizon, loomed the slopes of Cambellia. A wild continent, a legend & a bad one, it rose from the railsea.

That would have been enough to get most of the crew out & staring at the horizon, but veering a little nearer it was clear that what might have been a line of bushes, some peculiarities of rock, was the fallen corpse of an upsky beast. Well *that* brought them all out. Muttering, pointing, taking flatographs.

It happened sometimes that those alien things fighting their obscure fights in the poisonous high air would kill each other, send each other's strange carcases plummeting to the railsea. It wasn't unprecedented for trains to have to grind slowly past or even through them, pushing impossible meat out of the way with their front-ploughs, their figureheads getting sticky with odd rot. "No flies on that, eh," said Vurinam.

Upsky things tended to decay according to their own schedules & whatever grubs they carried in them. Most made earth maggots fastidious.

This, the first upsky corpse Sham had seen, was not very comprehensible. Long, stringy, knotted strands emerging out of ooze, bits of beak, bits of claw, splayed tendrils like ropes, if they weren't bits of innard. No eyes he could see, but at least two mouths, one like a leech's, one like a buzz saw. Perhaps it was beautiful & delicate on the world on which its ancestors were born, where they had infested the ballast of some otherworldly vehicle during a brief stopoff, later to be sluiced off here on another, epochs ago.

Sham & Vurinam stood at the barrier of the forecastle, behind the howling engine. They looked away from the receding monster corpse to port at that miles-off country Cambellia. They glanced at each other. One at a time. Each only for a moment, when the other had looked away. The train's figurehead, a traditional bespectacled man, jutted over the rails, staring woodenly away from their awkwardness.

They were not so far from Bollons. From whispers, the mutterings of the crew, Sham had ascertained that it was a soulless place, too close to poisonous upland, that in Bollons they would sell everything, including secrets & their mothers, without honour or hesitation.

Every railsea nation other than Streggeye, if it was discussed by many of the Streggeye-born trainsfolk, was, Sham noted, traduced. It was too big or small, too lax or strict, too mean, too gaudy, too plain, too foolishly munificent. Lands of all dimensions & governments met with disapproval. The scholaro-cracy of Rockvane was snootily intellectual. Cabigo, that quar-relsome federation of weak monarchies, was quarrelsomely monarchist. The warlords who ran Kammy Hammy were too brutish. Clarion was governed by priests whose piety was too much, while far-off Mornington needed a dose of religion. Manihiki, by far the most powerful city-state in the railsea, brashly threw its weight around with wartrains, the grumbles went. & the democracy of which it crowed so loud was a sham, they added, in hock to money.

& on & on. Similarity to its detractors' home was no defence. Streggeye was one of several islands in the Salaygo Mess archipelago, in the railsea's east, run by a council of elders & advised by eminent captains & philosophers, but it was, those xenophobes sniffed, the only one that didn't do it *wrong*.

Sham nuzzled his recuperating daybat. It still not infre-quently tried to bite him, but the force & frequency of the snaps was decreasing. Sometimes, like now, when he swaddled it, the animal buzzed with what Sham had learned was purring. Bat happiness.

"You ever been?" said Sham.

"Cambellia?" Vurinam pursed his lips. "Why would a person go there?"

"*Exploring.*" Sham said. He had no notion what govern-ments there were on Cambellia to get things wrong & not be Streggeye. He stared towards it in fascination.

"When you've been trainsfolk as long as I have . . ." Vuri-nam began. Sham rolled his eyes. The trainswain was barely older than him. "I'm sure you must've heard stuff. Bad people, wild people," Vurinam said. "Crazy things out there!"

"Sometimes," Sham said, "it seems like every country in the

railsea's full of wild things & bad places & terrible animals. That's all you ever hear."

"Well," Vurinam said. "What if they are? The thing is with a place like Cambellia, it's the size of it. Miles & miles. Get me more than a day from the railsea lines, I get very twitchy. What I need to know's that any moment, if things gets tricky, I can run to harbour, show my papers, get on a train, hightail away. A life on the open rails." He breathed deep. Sham rolled his eyes again. "If you head northwest in Cambellia, you know where you get eventually?"

Remnants of geography lessons, remembered images from class ordinators, went through Sham's head. "The Nuzland," he said.

"The Nuzland." Vurinam raised eyebrows. "Bloody hell, eh?"

The highest reaches of Cambellia climbed past where atmosphere shifted, up higher than where the carved gods, the Stonefaces, lived on Streggeye, into the upsky. The Nuzland wasn't a pinnacle or a ridge. It was bigger by many times than Streggeye or Manihiki. Yes, Sham knew the stories, that somewhere there were whole bad plateau worlds in the upsky. Cities of the dead. Curdled high hells. Like the Nuzland, which was right over there. Sham could see its edge.

Vurinam muttered.

"What?" said Sham.

"Said *sorry*," Vurinam said. He was staring out to railsea. "Said I'm sorry for what I said to you. It weren't your fault, what happened to Stone. Might as well say it was my fault for hitting him when I jumped in the cart." *The thought*, Sham said to himself, *had occurred*. "Or Unkus's fault for being in my way. Or for not holding on hard enough. Or that captain's fault for wrecking the train, leaving it for us to see. Whatever. I shouldn't have shouted at you."

Sham blinked. "'S'alright," he said.

"Not really it ain't," Vurinam insisted. "When I'm upset I rage around. I was like a mole on the hooks." He looked at Sham at last. "I hope you'll accept my sorry." Pleasingly formal, he stuck out his hand.

Sham blushed. Fumbled & juggled with his bat. Freed up his own right hand & shook.

"You're a gent, Sham ap Soorap," Vurinam said. "What's it called?"

"Eh?"

"Your daybat."

"Oh." Sham looked at it. He spread its wings. It chittered in annoyance but let him. He'd wracked his brains for memories of Fremlo's lessons, consulted the doctor's medical textbooks with extremely uncharacteristic rigour. Fingertip gentle, he'd found the spot in the wing where bone ground against bone, & set the fracture in the multicoloured wings with a tiny makeshift splint.

"It's called . . . Day . . . Be," he said. "Daybe." The name was plucked from nowhere, in panic at the question, & he almost groaned to hear it. It was out now. Too late to take it back.

"Daybe." Vurinam blinked. "Daybe the daybat." He scratched his head. "I make no judgements. Daybe it is. It's on the mend, I hope."

"It's getting better."

"& Unkus?"

"Depends," Sham said. "Dr. Fremlo says that depends how fast we get to Bollons."

"Best get there fast then."

They were caning through diesel. Doubly desperate to get to the island now, for fuel from the town's plants, as well as for the sake of poor feverish Unkus, shivering & singing again, now, but not pleasingly. Caterwauling in delirium in the doctor's hold.

Chapter Thirteen

On a drizzly day the crew saw trains at the rain-veiled horizon. Two, three, six, amid rocklets & islets & crowning nubs a few yards across, maybe topped with scrappy treelife & halos of birds. They saw dot-dot-dot sky punctuation of steam-train exhaust. A flat-topped cold volcano, a craggy irregular mountain, on its slopes the craggy irregular town of Bollons.

The western side of the island, facing Cambellia, that farthest shore, was mostly bare but for telescopy arrays. On its eastern side were the precarious-looking concrete & wood neighbourhoods of Bollons itself. As if the town didn't want to look at the edge of the world. Houses & warehouses ran down the slope to the shore where the metal & wood & stone of the lines began, where diesel & steam trains puttered gently in the railsea bay. Sham saw the old halls his crewmates said were the guildbuildings of spies & ne'er-do-wells, where rumourmarkets were held.

"A few coppers'll get you a questionable assertion from someone drunk & past it." So Fremlo said. "A handful of dollars, something said with a straight face by one whose information has panned out more than once in the past. More than that, you're into the realm of the tempting secret.

"You won't get it from the source, I mean. The rumourmongers sell them on." They'd vouch for none of them, of course—that was the point. But if it were *them*, they'd tell their customers, they'd set more store by this story than that one—hence the higher price tag. & tell you what: buy this one, they'd throw in another—almost certainly the ravings of a feverish fantasist—free.

The *Medes* ran up flags telling any watchers who they were, & a bone-sign & red exclamation, to say there was an injury aboard. "Slow." Captain Naphi's voice on the intercom was more terse even than usual. She must be frustrated not to be pursuing her philosophy, Sham thought. They rounded harbour-edge rocks on which railgulls raucously announced themselves.

Railsailors watched them from other trains on the fanning-out rails of the inlet, each vehicle surrounded by carts, to ferry crews to land. A smokestacked steamer snorted a soot-cloud exactly as if in disdain. The *Medes* switched, backed & switch-backed towards the railfront. Veered close enough to another vehicle that it looked as if the figureheads were leaning in to kiss, short-sighted paramours. A diesel moler like the *Medes*. It was mostly moletrains there.

What were these other vehicles, though? Sham had no clue. They were smaller & stubbier than the hunters. The equipment he could see being oiled & readied was nothing he could name. It wasn't salvage, he was almost certain. On a diesel train of strange design two men vigorously hand-cranked a chugging engine on caterpillar treads, from which protruded a long coiled tube, a glass-fronted helmet & brown bodysuit, in which someone performed ponderous gymnastics.

"What the Stoneface is that?" Sham said. The pumpers had the brick-coloured skin & distinctive electronically tinkered & doohickey-enhanced goggle-glasses of Kammy Hammy, that secretive many-island nation of, supposedly, warlords.

"That?" Sham had been talking to himself, but Yehat Borr heard him, paused as he hand-scurried up a nearby ropeladder.

He swung & spun & controlled his descent, stopping in front of Sham hanging upside down. "That," Borr said, "is explorers."

Of course. It was hardly as if it was just distant-ranging molers, fuel-hungry or desperate for something to eat other than old salted burrowmeat & weevily biscuits, who stopped at the town. Bollons was the nearest port to Cambellia. To Bollons came those brave brigands, pioneers & pillagers, to buy the whispers & the stories that surrounded such continents. Stories about the terrible engined angels, monstrous cousins to the protectors & repairers of the tracks, that guarded the edge of the world. Fables of how, one day, you might get past them, out of time & history. To epochs-worth of dead & unborn riches. To all the prodigious treasures of Heaven.

Sham sniffed with what might have been desire, might have been something. In those explorers' carriages would be rations, weapons, hiking gear. Maybe an overland carriage, monitors, trade goods for the peoples of the inland. Perhaps even mountaineering gear, for the most ambitious, like that woman now taking off the helmet & gesticulating thumbs-up at the pumpers.

An updiver. She wasn't just going into Cambellia: she was going to climb. Beyond the border, roaming into uplands, to the limits of her cable, while the support crews waited below at the edge & pumped & kept her alive, or at least kept her breathing, till something other than the bad air, some bad-air beast or ghost of poisoned high ground, did for her instead.

Chapter Fourteen

A BUREAUCRAT TOOK mild pity. The *Medes* got a dockside mooring, shunting into place by the harbourmaster's offices. En route it passed a navy train all the way from Manihiki: like many of the less muscular island nations, Bollons subcontracted its defence—& attack—to that great ferronaval power. Bored-looking officers in grey uniforms wandered up & down the rooftop decks, eyed the *Medes*, oiled their guns.

Sham was in the first lot out, going with Dr. Fremlo to deliver Unkus Stone into the hands of the local sawbones. He stepped off the gangway onto solid ground, cobbles that didn't wobble, didn't rock. It was an old cliché that the first step on hardland after weeks at railsea made you stumble again, the inertness of rock suddenly feeling mad as a trampoline. An old cliché but true: Sham fell over. His comrades cackled. He started to cringe, then stopped & laughed too.

A local cart took Sham, the doctor, the captain & first mate, all fussing over the wildly delirious Unkus Stone, through narrow Bollons streets. Sham tended the wounded man as the doctor checked the dressings. He muttered in his head to That Apt Ohm, the great rotund boss-god, one of the few deities worshipped across the railsea, whatever the peculiarities of local pantheons. Bollons was ecumenical, granted church-licences to any deities whose worshippers could pay the fees. But the disrespectful worship of That Apt Ohm was taken more seriously there, pursued with more verve, than at most stops on the railsea. Sham had no idea quite what, if anything, he believed, but there seemed little harm in a quick silent word with one of the few gods whose name he remembered.

WHEN THEY MADE IT to the infirmary the doctor stayed, bickering with the local caregivers over the best course of treatment. So it was to Sham that the captain spoke, at last, on their way back to the *Medes*.

"What's your professional opinion, Soorap?" she said.

"Um . . ." Professional opinion! He could give her a professional opinion on what to carve on a wooden belly to allay boredom, if that was any use? He shrugged. "Dr. Fremlo seems hopeful, ma'am."

She looked away.

Sham was to return to the hospital the next day, for orders. For now, he was briefly free.

Now Stone was delivered, a weight & urgency dissipated. For all that they had slurred Bollons on the way, the crew were suddenly eager to explore it. They grouped according to various priorities. Yashkan & Lind sauntered off to some unpleasant gathering place the password to which, they kept hinting, they knew, to participate in something scandalous & questionably legal. The crew's devout members headed off to worship at temples to whatever. Others rubbed their hands, licked their lips for shore-food. Some were lustful.

Sham was certainly curious about that last. He watched that sniggering section of the crew making rude gestures & jokes, lascivious intimations, & muttering about to which establishment they would go. Certainly he was intrigued, but on that issue he was shyer than he was curious, so after a second Sham veered & followed Vurinam & Borr, Benightly, Kiragabo Luck, a bunch of cheerful & chatty crew whose intentions were clear from their raucous rendition of the traditional landfall shanty, "We're Going to Get Unbelievably Drunk (in a Pub)."

IT TURNED OUT, in fact, that the song was misleading: they visited not one pub but many, migrating from one alcohol-hole to the next in an increasingly bleary & beery & ultimately slobbering group like some restless migratory herd.

The first was called the Tall Bird. Its proper name was in Bollons, but it announced itself pictorially in its sign. It was lugubrious & underlit & full of muttering locals & visitors eyeing each other. Kiragabo put a small glass of something in front of Sham. It tasted like blackberries & dust.

"What was it the captain took from you?" said Kiragabo. "After Stone was bit?"

"Something from the wreck."

"Ooh, mystery man. What was it, Soorap you toerag?"

"Just a thing," he muttered, as his companions jeered & nudged him while he drank so it slopped on him, & demanded to know more, then forgot what they were talking about when Vurinam launched into some unlikely lewd anecdote. Then to the Grumpy Molly, a more flamboyant place where the walls were garish & a gleaming jukebox blared syncopated Jazzle-House that quickly had Vurinam bouncing like a fool, flirting with anyone near. He was shouting & comparing clothes with a temporary dance partner, a young woman pretty enough to make Sham blush without her even seeing him.

Benightly saw him, though, Sham realised, & laughed at him. Then Vurinam was back at the table, & there was something sweeter & darker & a lot thicker than the first drink going down Sham's throat. He pulled Daybe from beneath his shirt, let it have a sip, & his companions screamed at him for bringing the happy animal with them, then forgot what had scandalised them.

"It was a wossname," Sham said. "Little thing for a camera." It took a moment for his crewmates to understand he was answering a question from a whole pub ago.

"A memory!" said Luck. Benightly raised an eyebrow & was about to ask more, but was distracted by the insistence of a local bravo challenging him to an arm-wrestle. Then they were all at the pinnacle of a thoroughly corkscrewing path at the Clockerel, a snooty establishment signed by a hybrid timepiece-fowl, on a rock spur overlooking the raily harbour. Its staff tried for a moment to keep them out till it looked like causing more difficulties than letting them in.

"Look!" Sham bellowed. "'S the train!" Visible through the windows, it was, yes, the *Medes*. On it glimmered a few home lights. & it was Sham's round, it turned out, his trainmates helpfully informed him, & helpfully they took out his money-pouch, & helpfully emptied it to pay for jugs of Stonefaces knew what, & this time some bar snacks too, chilli-fried dustcrab & locust thing the whiskers & segmenty legs of which Sham eyed without enthusiasm but chewed on nonetheless.

"How'd you even end up on the moler?" Vurinam asked him, bewildered but not unkind. The others were leaning in with interest to hear his answer. "Was it your mum & dad?" Sham was befuddled enough that he wasn't even sure what it was he said in response.

"'Mumble mumble mum & dad mumble'?" Vurinam said. "Well, thank you for elucidating."

"It weren't me," Sham tried to explain, "it was my cousins.

I ain't got a . . ." The last four words sounded suddenly loud to him, & he closed his mouth before the words *mum & dad* could get out past his teeth & dampen the evening.

No one was listening anyway. His *Medes*-mates were all cackling loudly at Vurinam's impression of him. Vurinam who was punching him on the shoulder, now, in friendly enough fashion, telling him, "Aaah, you're alright, Soorap, just need to ease up a bit," & there was Sham thinking *ease up on what?* but that was a mystery for another time, because conversation had moved on.

Benightly was looking at him. From the sympathy on the big man's face he might even have guessed the missing words. Sham took another sip.

Then where? Some place called the Ancient Cheese, another called the Formidable, another the Drip & Doctor & Drain & Dragon or something. At what point the *Medes* women & men had started up conversations with their fellow drinkers Sham had no idea, but he was at it too.

"Wha'for the men staring?" he said to a woman with tattoos on her neck & her hair coiled like rope. She peered over her glasses. "Where you from please also?"

"Bollons men like women indoors," she said in Railcreole, the lingua franca of railsailors, with an accent Sham couldn't place. "Don't like the likes of me. From Cold Basin, me." Cold Basin! Miles & miles away, easter even than Streggeye! "Come to buy rumours. Sell them too."

"I've heard about the rumourmarkets. Where are they?"

"You have to buy rumours of where they are from street-corner rumourjockeys, hope you get lucky."

"Buy rumours about rumours?"

"How else?"

"They going to stop you doing whatever you're here t'do?" Sham said.

She shook her head. "They ain't so dumb here to tell outlanders what to do. I already done updiving on the east highlands." She teased with hinting talk about Sowmerick, a mythical upsky toxicontinent. "What was this wreck, then?"

"Oh!" Sham'd forgotten he was telling her. A garbled version of the story of, what was it? Back he set off like a train on a straight stretch, with the tale of the wreck. He gabbled through it & she stroked his daybat. Then it was another pub & she was still with him & oops, Sham was outside, puking into the steep gutter. Leaving a little bit of Streggeye behind, he thought. *You're welcome, Bollons.* More room for that schnapps, was that what they called it?

& again here he went with stories of the wreckage, of his fumbling, of the terrible mole-rat attack. "'S'why we're here. Our mate got his leg bit." *Look at me,* thought Sham, *the storyteller.* A storm of faces hanging on him & listening as off in other bits of wherever they were Kiragabo & Vurinam were dancing together, & someone gave Sham another drink, & someone said, "So what was it you found on the wreck?" & "Aaaaah," he was saying, tap-tapped the side of his nose, never you mind, secrets, that was what. That was a secret. Not that he knew, nor that he'd refrained, apparently, from mentioning that he'd found something. Hey ho, drink up. Then he was under the stars & snuggling down his head all rested on a something. They weren't so bad, he thought. They were nice, in Bollons, he thought. Giving him something to sleep on.

Chapter Fifteen

IT WAS A STONE, was what it was. His pillow.

Sham found that out gradually. Very gradually.

First a fingernail-sized rough something scratched & scratched at him. Through a very slow stretch Sham hauled himself like a hero out of the sticky slough of dreams up & oh, really very gradually, geared up the strength to reach up &, with his finger, pry open an eye.

So. Turned out he'd slept outside in the yard of some final pub. Whimpering at the assault of merciless morning light on his eyes, he blinked until he could see a few of his crewmates still snoozed in a barn, watched by contemptuous goats. Daybe the daybat was licking Sham's face. Crumbs from around his mouth. *When did I eat something?* Sham thought. Couldn't remember. Hauled himself up, froze & moaned & sat still while his head did its lurching business.

Stonefaces, he was thirsty. Was that *his* sick in a big splattery spread just beside him? No proof one way or the other. Through his fingertips, he glanced up at the sun. The upsky was pretty clear—a little fuzzing miasma, a few swirls of way-high poison camouflaging a few terrible high-fliers, but it felt as if he could see all the way into space. The sun fairly glared back down at him, like a teacher disappointed. *Oh sod off*, Sham thought, & set out for the harbour.

Past terraces where women & men were watering windowsill

plants, & cooking breakfast, or what, in fact, must be lunch, & was, whatever it was, by a long way the most unbelievably delicious-smelling food Sham had in all his years of life been privileged to sniff. Past the dogs & cats of Bollons, cheerful ownerless animals that trotted around unfussed, eyeing him sympathetically. Past the blocky rectangular churches, where the history of the godsquabble was sung. Down towards the harbour from where, over rows of houses, grocers, a statue of a sardonic-looking local godlet, he could hear the clack & smack & pistonhammer crack of trains.

It wasn't a big town, Bollons, & there was really one main thoroughfare. Up he stared at the telescopes & sensors on its roofscape, trained by way of veering tubes & wires on Cambellia. This was somewhere new, a different place. In principle he was excited. *I am getting annoyed with this*, he thought, when he wasn't sure how he felt.

He saw *Medes* comrades: Ebba Shappy at a café, waving over her chicory drink; Teodoso, who looked worse than Sham felt, & did not notice him; Dramin, the grey cook, examining odd herbs, who did see him & did not say hello.

Sham almost wept at the thought of breakfast. Bought a salty pasty from a vendor, sat on the steps of a street-pump to eat it & washed it down with the metally water. Fed finger- & thumbfuls to Daybe.

His head hurt, he ached all over, & he was sure, oh, yes, quite sure that he smelled. But whoever'd bought rounds with his money the previous night had given him back his change. He'd slept dusty but he had slept. The passersby were ignoring him or grinning at him, less judgemental than the sun. He had two or three hours before he was due back on the train.

Maybe hangovers were survivable. Whether he should or not, & despite that little flurry of familiar frustration with himself, Sham felt not too too bad.

Chapter Sixteen

AT ONE CORNER of the railseafront was the Tekniqall Nosh-house, a combination eaterie, chatterie (at its many tables the captains & officers of moletrains & explorers were doing obviously secret, muttering business), announcerie & technickerie. Sham stopped. In the shadow behind its awnings, he saw Captain Naphi talking to the owner.

She was describing something big with her hands. She handed over a piece of paper, & the man nodded & placed it in the information window, among many such flyers. Sham squinted to make out the larger words.

INFORMATION LEADING TO.

REWARD.

PHILOSOPHY.

He was about to continue. He was about, indeed, to creep away, not eager to have Naphi's imperious melancholy spoil his mood. But there was to be no creeping. She saw him & beckoned him over. Not a flicker on his face, of course, but Sham felt his heart pitch.

"One more thing," the captain said to the cafékeeper. "You have ordinators?" She pulled a handful of paper from one pocket. "I have something for you," she said to Sham. LARGE MOLDYWARPE, Sham read as he took them. UNIQUE COLOUR.

She clenched her artificial hand so a hatch opened within it. Inside was the camera memory. *That's mine!* Sham thought as she extracted it. *Finder's rule!* The café owner was nodding them towards the back. "Come. I shall check this," the captain said. "& then I'll tell you where you're going."

In the sideroom was a collection of ordinators, cobbled-together equipment, tangled tubing, jury-rigged screens from movographs, black-&-white flickering projectors, lettered keys, the hmph of a diesel generator keeping the data safely on the machines.

Sham had had a go on an ordinator once or twice, but they didn't interest him overmuch. There weren't many in Streggeye Land, & those there were, he'd been told, were not up to date. The captain cleared away wires that piled around the screen like fairytale brambles around a castle. While a glow slowly grew on the screen, she raised her left arm & with a rapid-fire *clickclickclick* different bits of it came to the fore: special machinery, magnifying glass, mini-telescope, leather-needle. It was her way of fiddling. Like someone else might drum their fingertips on a table. Sham stood politely, waited, murdering the captain in his mind. She inserted the plastic into the ordinator's slot.

Bad enough to find it & have it nicked, Sham thought. *Without you taunting me with it.* He wondered whether the memory, so long mouldering in the cold ground, nibbled by animals, would even be readable, or if there was anything on it. Then suddenly a man looked out at him from the screen.

A big, bearded man, in his fifties, perhaps. He stared at the lens full on, pulling his head slightly back, his arm jutting in perspective. The typical stance of people taking a flatograph of themselves, holding a camera at arm's length. He didn't smile, the man, but he had humour in his face.

Digitally degraded, the picture looked dirt-flecked. Behind the photographer, a woman was visible. She was out of focus, her expression unclear, folding her arms & glancing with what just might be patience, indulgence, affection.

You're the skull, Sham thought. *One of you's who I found.* He moved minutely from foot to foot.

Naphi pressed something; the image shifted. Two children. Not on a train: the backdrop was a town. Under a strange, tumbledown, unfocused arch of ill-matched white blocks. A little girl, an even younger boy. Skin the dark grey typical of Manihiki. Smiling. They stared right at Sham. He frowned. The captain glanced at him as if he'd said something.

A stern boy! A thoughtful girl! Hands by their sides, hair neat . . . but then, again, a shift. Too fast, the children were gone, & Sham was looking at a gloomy room full of junk, then almost instantly at a picture of some huge harbour, way larger than any he had ever seen, teeming with trains of countless kinds. It made him gasp, but then that went too & now an image from a traintop, rattling on the tangles of the railsea. Then the woman, again, back to the camera, standing before gauges & dials in the engine.

Clickclick, the captain scrolled. Sham was being driven crazy by her ability to sit without speaking. & on screen were images of the railsea itself & its islands. Tracks among & through thickets of old trees. A forest, no other word for it, not on any humpback island but part of the railsea itself. It had been autumn when the shot was taken, & banks of leaves piled up on the rails ahead.

A desert, flat sand, sparse tracks. Rocks like fangs under the overcast sky. Where, *where*, had these people been?

Playing moles frozen midleap ahead of the train's prow, pursuing leg-sized earthworms. The sett of a huge bull badger.

A little lake rimmed with rails. Hedgehog tangles in tree roots.
& at the very limit of the camera's capabilities, a hulking &
hermetic track-riding presence. Sham held his breath. Some
train, not like anything he had seen before but abruptly familiar
nonetheless.

He realised what the silhouette reminded him of. A fanciful
& speculative image, as all such images were, from some book
of religious instruction, of an angel. A sacred engine, rolling the
rails to save them.

Sham gaped. Wasn't it bad luck to see an angel? Some
were rumoured to maintain the rails in deep railsea reaches—
& trainsfolk were supposed to turn fast away should they ever
come close enough to see such interventions. Should he look
away now? How could he?

Wait wait! Sham thought, but the captain had moved on.
A new picture was below him now, a rearing great talpa. The
captain's turn to freeze. But the moldywarpe's fur was dark. On
she scrolled.

Where had this train been going?

Geography that made Sham furrow his brow. Strange, distinctive rock formations like giant melted candles. Overhangs
above railsea lines.

& suddenly. Railsea. But not.

Land stretched like some pegged-out dead animal in an
Anatomy & Butchery class. Flat & dusty & specked with broken
brown stones & little bits of matter that might be salvage, but
mean stuff if it was. A lowering downsky, storm clouds growling
like guard dogs. A glowing upsky above. The prow of the train
was visible like a fat arrow in the middle of the shot, pointing
at an oddly foreshortened horizon. The line it was riding was an

unnaturally straight stretch, the two rails bisecting the view all the way to where perspective knitted them together. & to either side of it—

—either side of that line the train was riding—

—was nothing.

No other rails at all.

Empty earth.

Sham leaned forward. He was trembling. Saw the captain leaning forward herself, in time with him.

Empty earth & one straight line. *One line in the railsea.* Couldn't be. *There's not nor can there be any way out of the tangle.* A single line could not be. There it was.

"Stonefaces come between us & all harm," Sham whispered, & clutched his bat, because it felt like an unholiness, all that nothing, because for goodness sake what was the world between islands but the railsea?

All that nothing. Sham got his own little camera out. Fumble, fumble, not looking at its screen, & trembling, he took a picture of that picture, the most amazing image he had ever seen.

All that nothing! It made him reel. He staggered, fell hard & loud against another ordinator. The captain turned to him as he put his camera back in his pocket. She fingerstabbed the keyboard & the image disappeared.

"Control yourself," Naphi said in a low voice. "Pull yourself together, right now."

Sham's head was still all full of that impossible rail, surrounded by all that equally impossible railless nothing.

Chapter Seventeen

AWAY AGAIN. Eating up lines, eating up the tie-&-rail miles between Bollons & the Salaygo Mess & Streggeye itself. The *Medes*, if slowly, if by roundabout routes, was going home. Without Unkus Stone.

"What d'you mean, he can't come with us?" Sham had said.

"Ah now, lad," had said Unkus Stone, & added a short scream as someone shifted where they leaned on his bed & moved his still-very-tender legs.

Sham & Vurinam & Dr. Fremlo & Yehat Borr & a few others had been in the sanatorium. The equipment around Unkus & the few other patients—here someone with injuries caused by crushing train-metal, there a blood-rabbit bite, one or two with bugs of the railsea—was battered. But it was not unclean, & the smell of the lunch the staff had brought Stone was not undelicious.

"Can't believe I'm awake," Unkus said.

"Neither can I," said Fremlo.

The laughter after that was uncomfortable.

There was no way they could wait, Sham's colleagues told him. He was being sentimental. There were moles to hunt. The bill for the sanatorium was paid for a while longer—topped up, might they point out, by the captain herself out of her own share. They had to get on.

"I really do not like it here," Vurinam said. He glanced to either side & lowered his voice. "People keep asking where we're

77

going, where we been. Bollons people are *nosy*. Someone even
asked us if it was true we was salvors!" He raised his eyebrows.
"Said they heard we'd found a wreck! & a treasure map!"

Hmmm, thought Sham, a little uneasily.

"Shouldn't just leave you," Sham had said.

"Ah now, lad." & Unkus had given Sham an awkward pat
on the arm. "I can get myself to the docks, get paid passage back
when I'm better."

"It ain't right."

It wasn't just for Unkus that he wanted to stay, though Sham
could not admit that. The longer they stayed in Bollons, he
thought, the more chance he might persuade the captain to visit
Manihiki. From where, it was his tentative judgement, the man,
woman, children in those images came. He felt uncharacteristically certain that going there was what he wanted to do—to
make that connection between those images, & that place.

He had been running through increasingly baroque ideas of
what he might say or hint to Captain Naphi to persuade her so
far out of her intended path. He had nothing. & he was still
astonished, could barely believe they were not in any case going.

He couldn't not, with an ecstasy of scandal, keep recalling
that picture. The secret of that line, that solitary line, leading, it
seemed—& it still felt like curse words even just to think it!—
out of the railsea. One of the first things he had done, back
from the ordinator room in Bollons—whatever job the captain
would have had him do forgotten by both of them—was to draw,
as well as he could, all the images he had seen, from memory.
Until he had a sheaf of scrappy ink renderings of memories of
images of unlikely landscapes. They would have meant nothing
to most who saw them, but to him were mnemonics, reminders,

to conjure the railsea flatographs he had seen, that the captain had destroyed.

Oh yes. She had, making sure he saw her do so, carefully crushed the memory in her tough, skinless hand, while Sham made an involuntary noise of protest. When she opened her tough hydraulic fingers again it was full of plastic dust. "Whatever that silliness was," she had said, "it concerned neither molers nor doctors' assistants."

Naphi had put a mechanical finger to her lips. "Be quiet," she'd said. The instruction had covered both the noise of the clumsiness of his awe, & the potential saying of what he'd seen to others.

"Captain," he'd whispered. "What was . . . ?"

"I'm a moler," Naphi had said. "You are a doctor's assistant. Whatever you saw or thought you saw, it has nothing to do with your life & aims, whatever they might be, any more than it does with mine. So we don't speak of it."

"That was Manihiki," he said. "Where they came from. We should—"

"I strongly advise," the captain had said, looking at her own hands, "that you do not now or ever tell me, or any other captain under whom you roll, what 'we' 'should' do." The quotation marks were audible. "I am considering, ap Soorap."

So Sham said nothing. The captain had led him out of the café past packs of the goats that Bollonsians let roam the streets, trained to eat rubbish & leave their droppings in alleyway compost-heaps. Slowly, heart still slamming (approximating the clattername *fudustunna*, he thought, that came with great but dogged & determined pace), he thought through what he had seen. Those pictures.

Alone at last, back on the train, he had checked his own camera. That she had not seen him use. There it was. The picture. Horribly compromised by his shakes. Off-centre. But there it was, & it was not mistakable. The single rail.

He bit his lips.

There was a family. At the centre of the railsea. A woman & man of that family had left. Exploring? The extraordinary trainless landscapes. Exploring. Past animals. Past a place where what might be an *angel* prowled. Just far enough from it to stay safe. Through areas beyond the known railsea. To (that line) . . . to (that single line) . . . to that single line. To where the railsea untangled. & out of it.

& then they had come back. By some strange route, at last via the fringes of the Arctic. Heading, surely, for home. Where those children waited.

What a journey, Sham thought, & knew that that sister & brother needed to know what had happened. Those trainsfolk had been returning for them, & it was their right to know that. *If someone found anything of the train my father'd been on,* thought Sham, *I'd want to know.*

& they would. Whatever strangeness it was, that impossible rail, it was a priceless insight. The captain, he had thought, must be desperate to get going. He thought she must be working out routes to get them to Manihiki lickety-split. Where she & her officers could do whatever it was they'd do, work out how & to whom to sell the information, reconstruct the route those flatographs represented. & meanwhile, if they weren't going to do it themselves, he, Sham, could pass on the sad news of the train's & the trainsfolks' demise to that boy & that girl.

That was what the captain must be doing.

"Your train's away soon, then," the harbourmaster said

approvingly to Vurinam, in Sham's hearing. "Good good. I hear chatter."

Chatter about what? Sham wanted to ask. But he never got that information, & in Bollons chatter itself—as currency, bait & weapon—was trouble enough. Then word of their intended route had got out, & Sham had, in disbelief, realised Naphi had meant what she first said. That it had not been a moment's reflexive denial of an underling while a plan was hatched. That Naphi was not taking them to Manihiki.

He considered saying something but, remembering her rejoinder to his first attempt, unconsidered it. Well then, he thought at last, as pugnacious as he could make his inner voice, if she really wasn't intending to go there anyway, as she bloody well should, he'd just have to persuade her.

THE BEST-LAID PLANS can go belly up, & Sham's was not even best laid. Twice he started to approach the captain, heart clatternaming on his inner rails, ready to ask her how she could do this, what this was, this refusal to pursue those images, her resolute not-talking-about-it-ness. The *Medes* set out, & headed in, as far as Sham was concerned, entirely the wrong direcion, & he couldn't think of a thing to say to her. & each time she looked at him one second too long, with very cold eyes, & he swallowed & turned away. & instead of to Manihiki, home to Streggeye Land they went.

Chapter Eighteen

ON THE DOWN SIDE, one of the *Medes* trainsfolk had been left behind, flesh & muscle gnawed off his bones, in an ether-smelling shed on the shores of a land he didn't know or like. On the up side, they'd snaffled quite the moldywarpe. Their holds were full of salted molemeat, barrels of rendered mole-oil, carefully cured skin & fur.

Between the Cape of Chatham & the questionable little hardland islands of the Leweavel Range, they snaffled two star-nosed moles. Where interline railsea earth was churned up, they would slow, & the women & men of the *Medes* cast with their rods & angled for small burrowers. They dangled wire lines, weighted & hooked & baited clockwork corkscrews that coiled & ground in the dirt, dragging snips of meat. Eventually something might grab, tug the line, & veer off through the earth. The anglers would tussle, play out wire, bring up wriggling frantic bodies at line's-end & reel them in.

They caught the smallest moldywarpes, that grew with the telling, arm-length hunting earthworms that made the crew howl in disgust, beetles as big as their heads, that, depending on their island of origin, some would eat & others throw back. Shrews, muskrats, carnivorous rabbits. Burrowing bees. This was a rich stretch of railsea. Fussy, tidying rail angels did not come here often, it seemed: there was edible weed protruding between untended rails, that the crew snatched for salad.

"Mr. Vurinam." Sham practised clearing his throat to introduce a topic. "Dr. Fremlo." He thought of those images he had seen & decided that dammit, yes, he would, he would tell them, that they were his friends were they not?

But the secrets dried up in his mouth like unloved fuel tanks. It was simply too *much*, that stretch, that solitary iron road, too impossible to be describable. He could show them the picture. But even if that shaky flatograph would mean anything to one who had not seen the original, word of his words would surely reach the captain. & that would be him committing incitement to mutiny.

It was not only that he was intimidated by her—though certainly, yes, he was. It was a sense Sham could not shake, that it would not be unhelpful to have her on his side.

TWICE, THEY PASSED close enough to trains from Streggeye that they halted & connected to each other via catapulted rope-pulley, to exchange gossip & letters. Captain Skaramash of the outgoing *Murgatroyd* visited them for tea. Over he came, sitting sedately in a dangling chair hauled & swaying across the yards of tracks.

While Shossunder & Dramin brought in the best tea & dry biscuits & silver & porcelain, Sham clambered the outside rear of the caboose—astonished by himself as he did—& hunkered out of sight, flattened at a porthole, listening, & catching glimpses.

"So, Captain Naphi," he heard Captain Skaramash say. "You'll do me a service if you can help me. I'm looking for a certain beast. A grand, big fellow." His voice took on a certain tone. "A ferret. At least a carriage long. & in his head he carries a hook. I gave him that. It protrudes out now like crooked fingers, dangling back. Beckoning me." He whispered. "Beckoning me wherever he goes. Old Hookhead."

So Skaramash had a philosophy, too, & that's what he was after. *Right then, get on with it*, Sham thought. Captain Naphi cleared her throat.

"No such animal's crossed our paths," she said. "Be assured I know now your vehicle's name, & at the first sign of that beckoning metal in a sinuate mustelid eruchthonous presence, I shall take careful notes of locations. & I shall get you word. On my honour as a captain."

"I thank you," Skaramash murmured.

"I don't doubt yours took something from you, as mine took something from me," Naphi said. Skaramash nodded, on his face an expression of speculation & grimness. Which now that he formulated that in his head, Sham realised was the expression he most usually saw on any captain's face. It was their mien.

Skaramash rolled up a trouser leg, knocked his knuckles on wood & iron beneath. Captain Naphi nodded appreciatively, then raised her light-winking arm, its intricate molebone, jet & metal. "I remember the feel as those teeth closed," she said.

"I'm grateful for your help," said Skaramash. "& for my part I will watch for the custard-coloured moldywarpe."

Sham's eyes widened.

"*Old-tooth* coloured, Captain," Naphi said harshly. "A great mole the hue of ancient parchment. Ivory-reminiscent. Lymph-like. A white stained like the old eyes of frantically ruminating scholars, Captain Skaramash."

The visitor whispered some apology.

"There's nowhere I'll go & nothing I'll not cross to reach it. My philosophy," Naphi said slowly, "is not yellow."

Her bleeding philosophy! That was why she was ignoring those pictures, Sham thought. Those proofs of—he didn't even know what of, of some grand tremendous upset to the world of the railsea, at very least. She would not spare the time out from her molehunting philosophising!

Any more than would Skaramash, it sounded like. How many of these philosophies were out there? Not every captain of the Streggeye Lands had one, but a fair proportion grew into a close antipathy-cum-connection with one particular animal, which they came to realise or decide — to decidalise — embodied meanings, potentialities, ways of looking at the world. At a certain point, & it was hard to be exact but you knew it when you saw it, the usual cunning thinking about professional prey switched onto a new rail & became something else — a faithfulness to an animal that was now a worldview.

Daybe was learning to hunt. The daybat could fly again, now, for short distances. Sham swung a bit of meat on the end of a rope, at the corner of the deck, while Daybe flapped & snapped at the whirling snack. Now that was hunting with a *point*.

Sham thought of the awe with which those very few who snared the objects of their fascination, who made it into the Museum of Completion, were held. Maybe there was competition between the captains, he thought. "Call that a philosophy?" they perhaps sneered behind each other's backs. "That prairie dog you're after? Oh my days! What is *that* supposed to signify?" One-upmanship, one-upcaptainship, of the themes some quarries had come to mean.

THEY CROSSED a ravine to get home, on one of the tangle of bridges that stretched the twenty-, thirty-yard gap. He'd known it was coming, but the view made Sham uneasy. The rails went up on raised earthworks & wood-&-iron rises, jumping pools & streams full of cramped fish.

"Hardland ho!" the tannoy announced. Then: "Home ho!"

It was twilight. Birds circled. The few interrail trees were thick & shaggy with them. The crew bustled & laughed. The local daybats were going home; darkbats were coming out. They greeted each other, handed over sky-scudding duties with chitterings. Daybe, on Sham's shoulder, chittered back. He leapt up & out. Sham wasn't worried: the daybat always came back to the *Medes*: often, as then, crunching an unlucky cricket.

Lit up by the last red blast of the sun were stone slopes. Like dark mildew, patches of jungle pelted the hilly nation they approached, & like light mildew, houses & buildings aggregated around its flanks & became the town of Streggeye. Bustling from the harbour came hardy tug-trains, to ferry goods in & out of land, to guide the *Medes* into dock.

Home.

Chapter Nineteen

THE RETURN OF any moletrain is always accompanied by delighted shrieks of husbands, wives, children, lovers, friends & creditors. Sham's heart shook happily to see Voam & Troose, on the railsea wall, waving & yelling with everyone else. They hugged him, yanked him into the air, bellowing all sorts of endearments, dragging him embarrassed & delighted home, as Daybe whirled around his head, wondering what these manthings were that were attacking its human, & why it appeared to make Sham so happy.

His cousins were unsurprised by Sham's animal acquisition. "It was going to be a tattoo," said Voam, "or jewels, or *something*, so this ain't bad."

"Lots of lasses & lads on moletrains come back with some companion," Troose said. He nodded enthusiastically. Voam winked at Sham. Troose always nodded. He always had. Including at silences, as if it was imperative that he & the world be in accord about everything, including nothing.

The house where Sham had grown up: halfway up a steep street, overlooking the railsea, epic darkness punctured from time to time by the lights of night-voyaging trains. All was as he'd left it.

He did not remember his arrival there, the first time, though he very dimly recalled moments he knew pre-dated it, the voices & solidity of his missing mother & father. Sham did not even know where on Streggeye he had lived with them. Once, some years previously, Troose had offered to show him, as they walked through an unfamiliar part of town. Sham had deliberately stamped in a puddle & got mud all the way up his trousers, begged to be taken home to change, rather than continuing wherever they were going.

His father had disappeared almost his whole life ago on some ill-fated messenger train lost to an everyday catastrophe, its specifics never known, in the wilds of the railsea. His bones doubtless gone to animals, as the bones of the train were gone to salvors. Sham's mother had taken off soon after, travelling the islands of the archipelago. There had never been a letter. Her grief was too great, Voam had gently explained to Sham, to return. To be happy. To be anything but alone. Ever. She'd hidden from her cousin, as Voam vaguely was; her son; herself. & hidden she had stayed.

"You're so big!" shouted Troose. "You've got deckhand muscles! You've got to tell me all the doctoring you've learned. Tell us everything!"

So over broth, Sham did. & in that telling he discovered himself with pleasure & a degree of surprise. A few months ago, had that stumbling young chap tripping on cables & stays on the roofdecks of the *Medes* attempted to tell a story, it wouldn't have gone well. But now? He could see Voam's & Troose's faces, agog. Sham fished for gasps & aaahs & the goggle-eyed fascination of his audience of two.

". . . so," he was saying, "I'm by the crow's nest, captain's yelling blue & bloody murder, & down comes a razory bird right at me. I swear it wanted my eyes. But up goes Daybe, right for it, & the two of them go wrestling in the air . . ." & no force on hardland, on the railsea, under it or in any of the skies would have prodded Sham into admitting, including to himself, that the bird had been not quite as low as all that, had been in fact somewhat of a speck, that it & Daybe had rather than fighting to the death perhaps been competing for the same ill-fated bug, & their wrestling match a brief bump.

But Voam & Troose enjoyed it. & there were some events he told & varnished nothing. The eruption of the mole rats from the earth; antlions gnawing prey in sight of the train; the outpost city of Bollons.

He told stories while Voam & Troose ate; he told them while the moon came up & made the metal of the railsea shimmer its own cold colour; while the night sounds of Streggeye Land rose around the house. His mouth got on with the telling, leaving him free to think about Manihiki in the centre of the world. He did not tell them what he had seen on the ordinator screen.

"You're a proper grown man now," Troose said. "You should join us. Three adults." The two men looked intense with pride as Troose said it. "Like adults like us do. We're going to the pub."

& impatient as they could sometimes make him, Sham felt that pride swell in his own chest, walking with them through the steep streets of Streggeye, kicking cobbles that bounced a long way to scuff & settle eventually, perhaps, on the railsea itself. So good was Sham's mood that it did not suffer more than a little when he realised that they had come to the Vivacious Weevil, a captains' pub, one of the most famous. Where Captain Naphi would surely be. Discussing her lemon-coloured philosophy.

Chapter Twenty

IT WAS CONTAINEDLY raucous within. Full of excited debate. People sat listening to the stars of the evening holding forth. Naphi was there, listening to the speaker, a portly, muscular man close to two metres high. Sham could tell by his cadences that he was well into his story.

"It's Vajpaz," Troose whispered. "He had another encounter."

". . . By now," the big man said, "my philosophy was coursing frenetically horizonward. You see? Carrying my leg." Oh, yes, he was missing one, Sham noticed. There were times, Sham felt, when the captains regretted there only being two types of limb they could lose to their obsessions. On the whole, you were a leg person or an arm person: had one a tail to lose, a pair of prehensile tentacles, a wing or two, it would increase the possibilities for those vivid scars of philosophising. "But I was beyond fretting. I tourniqueted my own stump & laughed. & set that jollycart after the beast. I set the course to hope. Always a few yards ahead, the rolling humps of its passage. Behind me my crew were piled onto the upturned wreck of the train, yelling for me to come back.

"The greatstoat slowed & readied itself, & burst out of the earth, looping overhead. I could have reached up & grabbed its hairs. I watched as it set forth horizonward again, underground dancing at speed. & I stopped trying to catch it, & tried only to keep pace with it, & gloried in its letting me do so. I surrendered to the speed."

Ah, there it was. So this philosophy was about *speed*. Acceleration. Captain Vajpaz theorised about a slim sinuous line of fur & savage teeth, focused on him with spike-eyes personal & full of urgency. It wanted to pass on a message. Even taking his leg had been part of its communications. "Follow me!" it had been saying. "Quick!"

So Vajpaz followed his philosophy, this greatstoat. The acceleration had become its own point, & Vajpaz's life was changing as he became a prophet of enstoated speed. & so on.

"The speed!" Vajpaz said. There was a whisper of appreciation.

In the taverns of Streggeye Land, in the books they wrote, which Sham & his classmates had sat through, in lectures public & exclusive, captains held ruminatively forth about the bloodworm, the mole rat, the termite queen or angry rex rabbit or badger or the mole, the great mole, the rampaging great moldywarpe of the railsea, become for them a principle of knowing or unknowing, humility, enlightenment, obsession, modernity, nostalgia or something. The story of the hunt as much their work as the catching of meat.

Tales told in pubs & cafés, bars & clubs of Streggeye were also of the discovery of stowaways, members of the Siblinghood of Railsea Hoboes, tucked in some hold or other. Of foreign shores. Of the imagined lands past the edge of the world. Of ghost trains, of enormous bloodworms that could emerge from the ground & wind around a train before dragging it under the ground, of the mysteries of crewless derelicts creaking on the lines, meals half-eaten but not a soul aboard, of monstrosities of the rails in secluded & terrible places, sirens, sillers, traptracks, dust krakens. But it was the philosophies that were the mainstay of these storytelling sessions.

Streggeye Land, on the western tip of the Salaygo Mess archipelago. Famous for hunters, for mole oil, for molebone art, & for its philosophers. Their texts were intellectual touchstones across the railsea.

Sham had never heard Captain Naphi talk publicly about her own quarry. He watched her stand. Sip her drink. Clear her throat. The room quieted.

But nothing had happened, Sham thought. The *Medes* had not come anywhere near the big mole she was looking for, the not-yellow thing. What was there to tell? It was tradition for any captain with a philosophy to hold forth about it at the end of any journey, but he had not until now considered what they would do had the object of their obsession not appeared. Which, now the thought occurred, must be common. Was she going to say, "Sorry—nothing to report," & sit down again?

Oh, hardly.

"The last time I spoke to you," Naphi said, "my philosophy had evaded me. Left me adrift on the railsea, without fuel or direction, with only its disappearing dust & a long road of mole-hills for my eyes. I watched him go.

"Mocker-Jack." The name rung in the room.

"You know how careful are philosophies," Naphi said. "How meanings are evasive. They hate to be parsed. Here again came the cunning of unreason. I was creaking, lost, knowing that the ivory-coloured beast had evaded my harpoon & continued his opaque diggery, resisting close reading & a solution to his mystery. I bellowed, & swore that one day I would submit him to a sharp & bladey interpretation.

"When we set out at last again, we, the *Medes*, went south. Mocker-Jack was somewhere near, surely. What confronted us first, however, was another animal, throwing itself at us. & after that, no word. No nothing. All the trains we passed I asked for help & information, but the silence about Mocker-Jack was its own taunt. His absence was a looming presence. The lack of him filled me with him, so he burrowed not only through the earth & dirt of the railsea but through my own mind, night after night. I know more now about him than ever I did before. He stayed away & came closer in one magic movement."

Ah, Sham thought. *Brilliant.* Troose was rapt. Voam was intrigued. Sham was amused & impressed & annoyed all at the same time.

"You been waiting a long time for this?" Voam whispered to a woman near him.

"I come for all the good philosophies," she said. "Captain Genn's Ferret of Unrequitedness; Zhorbal & the Too-Much-Knowledge Mole Rats; & Naphi. Of course. Naphi & Mocker-Jack, Mole of Many Meanings."

"What's her philosophy, then?" Sham said.

"Ain't you listening? Mocker-Jack means everything."

Sham listened to his captain describe her encounters & non-encounters with the quarry she'd been chasing for years, that represented everything anyone could ever imagine. "I've had my blood & bone ingested by that burrowing signifier," she said, waving her intricately splendid arm. "A taunt, daring me to ingest him back."

Naphi looked right at Sham, just then. Right at him, into his eyes. She paused just a fraction of a moment. Not long enough that anyone but him would have noticed. He smoothed down his unruly hair in blushing fluster & looked away.

I know what I want to do, he thought. *I want to get to Manihiki, whatever the captain thinks. That boy & girl deserve to know what happened.*

He looked back at Naphi, imagined her racing over junctions & the wildest railtangles, bearing down on her philosophy, the toothy giant Mocker-Jack.

Sham thought, *What will she do if she catches it?*

Chapter Twenty-One

PEOPLE HAVE WANTED TO narrate since first we banged rocks together & wondered about fire. There'll be tellings as long as there are any of us here, until the stars disappear one by one like turned-out lights.

Some such stories are themselves about the telling of others. An odd pastime. Seemingly redundant, or easy to get lost in, like a picture that contains a smaller picture of itself, which in turn contains—& so on. Such phenomena have a pleasing foreign name: they are *mise-en-abymes*.

We have just had a story of a story. Tell it yourself, again, & a story of a story in a story will be born, & you will be en route to that *abyme*. Which is an abyss.

In his first days back in Streggeye, there was, for Sham, plenty of storytelling, some of it about stories.

Chapter Twenty-Two

STRANGE TO HAVE DAYS not dictated by the clatter of wheels. To have his legs not flex & straighten in the unthinking expertise of the trainsperson, with the sway. Fremlo didn't treat patients on hardland, so Sham's duties were sweeping, cleaning, running the occasional errand, answering the very occasional telephone call, then slipping off not quite with explicit permission, but without any opposition. Scooting by pedestrians & horses tugging carts, past the horns of a few electric autos crawling up the jostling streets, to join some of the other Streggeye apprentices, snatching their own moments off from work as cooks' assistants, clerks, porters, tanners & electricians & artists, trainees of all kinds.

Many of those whose paths he crossed on the same old runs would barely have spoken to him before. Despite the years of lessons they had taken together, he knew them less well than he did his trainmates. & he was not much more smooth now than he had been while at school. But he was a traveller, who had gone out & come back, & that meant he had stories. He told Timon & Shikasta & Burbo of the mole rats & the great southern moldywarpe. & they listened, no matter that, now he spoke not to his own cousins, his delivery was hesitant. Encouraged by the attention, Sham introduced the listeners to his bat. That sealed it.

They were a temporary gang, & they trekked across the roofs of Streggeye's industrial quarter, hooting & breaking the windows of deserted halls, flirting & bickering, Daybe wheeling around them in curiosity, ducking through the forest of steam- & smoke-venting chimneys. They watched the comings & goings in markets in the busiest streets of the prosperous parts of town, & in the other places, they entered defunct warehouses, set up camps in the cold boilers of unusable ovens.

Some of the time, they talked about salvage.

STREGGEYE WAS NOT famous for salvors. Of course those searchers in old earth, those disinterrers of oddities, were from everywhere & nowhere. The various collective names they granted themselves tended to refer to that very fact: they were the Diffuse College, you might hear; they were the Scattered Siblinghood; the Antiplaced; the Universal Diggers.

Small as it was, though, Streggeye was no backwater. It provided a disproportionate amount of the molemeat & the philosophy in the railsea. It was known among explorers & updivers for its Stonefaces, the gazing rock figures that topped the island, above the treeline in unbreathable highlands air. (Sham had visited the viewing stations below the transit zone, peered through long mirrored-&-lensed periscopes at the blocky gazing heads on the island's top.) So though it was not their first port of call, salvors did, in fact, periodically visit Streggeye. More than once Sham had watched salvage trains come in.

They were like no other rolling stock on the railsea. Patchwork vehicles. Powerful engines, wicked shunters at the front, train sides riveted with cladding, bristling with the peculiar tools of the salvor's trade. Drills, hooks, cranes, sensors of various unorthodox kinds, to find & sort through the millennia of discarded rubbish that littered the railsea. Bits of salvage used & incorporated. On the topside decks salvors themselves in their distinctive clothes, tool-belts & bandoliers & stained leather chaps, snips of treated cloths & plastic feathers & showy bits & pieces pulled from the earth & miraculously unruined. Helmets of various complicated designs.

First the city authorities would come aboard & bargain for what salvage they wanted. Then high-rolling clients, the Streggeye rich. & finally, if the salvor crews were feeling generous & had a few days, they would run a market.

Their antique & reclaimed wares were set on stalls on the dockside, according to various taxonomies. Pitted & oxidised mechanisms from the Heavy Metal Age; shards from the Plastozoic; printouts on thin rubber & ancient ordinator screens from the Computational Era: all choice arche-salvage, from astoundingly long ago. & the less interesting stuff, too, that discarded or lost anything from a few hundred years ago to yesterday— nu-salvage.

There might even be a table or two of items from the third salvage category. The physically disobedient impossible scobs, that looked & behaved like nothing should. Sham remembered one such object—or was it three? A Strugatski triskele, the salvor had called it, waving it around to attract interest. Three curved black rods equidistant from each other in a Y-shape. The man had held one, & above it jutted the others, & in the centre, where they should join, was nothing. They did not touch, though they stayed together no matter how you shook them.

What that was was a piece of alt-salvage. Something made not only epochally long ago but unthinkably far away, way beyond the farthest reaches of the upsky. Brought to the railsea, used, & discarded by one of the visitors from other worlds, remnants brushed from cosmic laps, during the long-ago years when this planet had been a busy layby, a stopover point for the same brief visits that had accidentally stocked the upsky with its animals. This world had been a tip. Frequented by vehicles en route from one impossibly far place to another, with trash to dump.

The thought of striking out to salvage-reefs unknown, the burrowing, the mining, dustdiving, the picking through shore-lines of ancient trash—these activities quickened Sham's blood. But then what? He had questions. Where did salvage end up? What happened when you'd found it? Who used it for what when whoever sold or bartered it did, to whomever?

&, though it was harder to think of, a last thing gnawed at him & he could not leave it alone—when he thought of salvage, why did Sham start awed & end up deflated?

Chapter Twenty-Three

THERE WAS A WRECK in a bayful of fiddly rails at Streggeye's eastern rim, just out of town. It was a few hundred yards from shore, a stalled & rusting engine & cart that had long ago lost power—a bad captain, a drunk crew, inadequate switchers. It was too ruined to fix, worth nothing as nu-salvage. It mouldered, full of rust-dwelling birds, cawing in outrage as Daybe flew around their home.

Timon, Shikasta, & Sham were alone on the pebbly beach. They sat near a gorge where a stream of water & a railriver, a line, a long loop of track, emerged from inland & joined the railsea. They threw stones at the old engine offshore. Timon & Shikasta talked. Sham, still surprised at being in their company, watched the animal dwellers of shallow coastline earth. Meerkats, groundhogs, the tiniest moldywarpes. Shikasta, as bossy as she had been at school, but now unaccountably noticing him, looked at Sham until he blushed.

"So you going to be a moler's doctor, Sham?" Timon said. Sham shrugged. "Going to turn out like your boss? No one knowing if you're a man or a woman?"

"Shut up," Sham said uncomfortably. "Fremlo's Fremlo."

"I thought you wanted to go into salvage," Timon said.

"Talking of," interrupted Shikasta, "want to see something cool? He's right, salvage was the only thing ever made you perk up. So I wanted to show you something." From her bag she took a thing that looked somewhat like a switcher's remote control. It was black plastic or ceramic, a peculiar shape. It glimmered with lights. Bits poked from it according to absolutely no sense. It came out with a murmur as if of troubled flies.

Sham's eyes widened. "That's salvage," he gasped.

"It is," said Shikasta proudly. She brought out a box of things the size of grapes, soldered with ugly circuitry.

"That's *alt*-salvage," Sham said. Junk from another world. "How'd you get it?"

"Off a trainmate." Shikasta, like Sham, was working on the railsea—a transport vehicle, in her case. "She got it from someone else, who got it off someone else, & on & on, leading back to Manihiki. She said I could have a go on it."

"Oh my That Apt Ohm," said Timon. "You blatantly stole it."

Shikasta looked prim. "Borrowing ain't stealing," she said. "I wanted to show you," she said. "Can you make your bat come here?"

"Why?" said Sham.

"I ain't going to hurt it," she said. She held up one of the grapey things. There was a clip on it.

Sham stared at Daybe, circling in the air. Somewhere in the back of his brain were stories he'd heard, about some of the capabilities of some of the things left in some of the seams of some of the salvage. Somewhere was a little idea.

He enticed Daybe in with a strip of biltong. "You better not hurt my bat," he said.

"It ain't your bat," Shikasta said. "You're its boy." She snapped the thing on Daybe's right leg. Immediately it chirruped in rage & shot into the air, peeing on her arm as it went, to her yelled disgust.

Daybe zipped in complicated jackknifes, loop-the-loops, cork-screws, twisting its body, trying to dislodge the thing. Shikasta wiped bat wee off her hand. "Right," she said.

Her box whistled & cooed. It clicked in complicated staccato time with Daybe's ill-tempered aerobatics. The blue-lit screen glowed, an electric fog in which appeared a dot that echoed Daybe's aerial motions. The bat veered into the distance, the noise from the machine grew quieter: closer, louder.

"Is that . . . ?" said Sham.

"Yes it is," said Shikasta. "It's a tracker. It knows where the signal thing is."

"How does it work? How far?"

"It's salvage, ain't it?" Shikasta said. "No one knows."

They all three ducked as Daybe came at them. The receiver squealed, then moaned as the bat flapped away.

"Where did you—or your trainmate—get it?" said Sham.

"Manihiki. Where all the best salvage is. There's a new place in the *Scabbling Street Market*." She said that exotic name carefully, clearly enjoying it, like a spell. "These things are really useful. Like, if someone steals something & you've got one of these in it, you might be able to follow. So they ain't cheap."

"Or if there's something you're spending your life chasing . . . " said Sham slowly. Something that gets close enough to you, sometimes, for you to see. But that keeps slipping away again.

"You ain't seen one before, have you?" Shikasta smiled. "I thought you'd like it."

If you spent your life like that, chasing some taunting quarry, what wouldn't you do for one of these? Sham thought. *You'd go out of your way, wouldn't you, to get one,* he thought.

You'd go to Manihiki to buy one.

Chapter Twenty-Four

"Captain Naphi?"

If she was surprised to see Sham, she showed no sign of it. It was plausible, he supposed, that he might have simply wandered into her favourite café. That he had not tracked down several of his comrades from the *Medes* & asked them where they thought he might find her.

She was sitting at a corner table, with a journal in front of her & a pen in her hand. She did not invite him to sit nor shoo him away. She merely stared at him, long enough that his already great nervousness grew greater.

"Soorap," she said. "Doctor's aid."

She sat back & placed her hands, with a soft thump & a hard clack, on the table in front of her.

"I sincerely hope, Soorap," she said, "that you are not here to discuss—"

"No!" he stammered. "No. Not at all. Actually, there was sort of something I sort of wanted to sort of show you." Daybe scrabbled under his shirt. He pulled the animal out.

"Your beast I've seen," said the captain. Sham held out Daybe's leg, on which the tiny mechanism still protruded like a tick.

After her demonstration, Shikasta had been appalled at her inability to entice Daybe back to her, to retrieve the transmitter. She had waved, & it, of course, ignored her. "I ain't going to get that thing back!" she had shouted. & Sham had had an idea.

He beckoned the bat for her, but when it got within a few yards, he surreptitiously altered his come-here motion to a get-away one, so, wary, Daybe would spiral off up again. Sham gave Shikasta his best shrug & apologetic eyebrows. "It don't want to come," he said.

"You better hope," she said finally, all the unexpected friendliness of the last couple of days quite gone, "that no one clocks that there's one fewer of these things. I'll be in so much trouble!" Sham nodded humbly, as if it was his fault she had stolen it. "When your flying rat comes back, you take that thing off & get it back to me, alright?"

That evening, out of her ear- & eyeshot, he had whistled Daybe into his arms. Examined the clip on its leg. Whispering an apology, he had twisted it tighter. Now it would take a metal cutter to get it off. & here he was now, nervously pointing out a transceiver, or receptor, or receiver, or transceptor, or whatever the thing was called, while Daybe fiddled.

"One of my mates found this, Captain," he said. "She showed me how you work it. There's a, there's this box like a, um, & it knows where this thing is." Naphi's face gave away nothing. On Sham plunged. Talk-tunnelled through the captain's dirt-cold silence like a conversation-mole.

"I thought maybe it might interest you." He gave a rambling & rattling description of what that odd thing did. "After what I heard—I was in the pub, Captain. It's been an honour serving with you & I was hoping maybe you might let me do it again." Let her think he was a brownnoser, & ambitious. Fine. "& I thought this might be of, like of help, you know."

The captain tugged at the bat's leg, hard enough to make Daybe squeak & Sham wince. Naphi looked intent. She was breathing a little faster than a moment ago.

"Did your friend tell you," Naphi said, "where such items might be obtained?"

"She did, Captain," Sham said. "Scabbling Street Market, it's called. It's on . . ." He hesitated, but where else did one get the cuttingest-edge salvage? "On Manihiki."

Oh, she looked up at him then. "Manihiki," she said. The most gentle & sardonic ghost of a smile haunted her lips for a few seconds. "Out of the goodness of your heart, you bring me this." Still her mouth was haunted. It twitched. "How enterprising. How enterprising you are.

"This might be of use, true, Soorap," she said at last. He swallowed. "It's a possibility," she said, "to be pursued." She stared into space. Sham could almost see the train of her mind grinding over plan-rails.

"So," he said carefully, "I just thought you might want to know there are those things on Manihiki. & if you're travelling again, you know . . ."

"How did you find me, Sham ap Soorap?"

"I just heard you might be here," he said. Was she having a tryst? he thought. He had barely stopped to wonder how badly he was intruding. "Someone said you were—"

"That I was meeting someone?" she said, & with that perfect timing, a person behind Sham said Captain Naphi's name.

He turned, & it was not the secret lover he had momentarily imagined. It was Unkus Stone.

Chapter Twenty-Five

AFTER THE SHOUTS of greeting, Sham's hand still on the older man's back, he realised Stone was limping, badly. That he supported himself on sticks.

"How did you even get here?" Sham said.

"Got better," Stone said. He smiled, but it wasn't what he wanted it to be. "Thumbed a ride on a Streggeye-bound carrier. A mail-train. Legs gammy or not there are things a trainsman like me can do."

"Hello, Stone," Naphi said.

"Captain Naphi."

The silence became excruciating.

"Should I go, Captain?" Sham said. *But I've only just got started*, he thought. *I had you all interested in my salvage! We was getting somewhere! Next thing we'd have been going somewhere!*

"What are you here to tell me, Stone?" said the captain.

"Rumours," Stone said. He met Sham's eyes & glanced at the doorway, inclined his head.

Sham got the message. Despondently he turned & walked towards the door. He tried to strategise as he went. But there was a scraping sound, & the captain said his name. She had pulled another chair into place.

"If it's rumours," she said, "I'd not be so foolish as to think that any trainsperson wouldn't soon hear it anyway." She pointed, with her bone-&-metal-&-wood finger. "& I'd not be so mean-spirited," she said, "as to make her, or him, wait any longer than necessary." Sham bowed thanks, heart racing, & sat. "So. I appreciate you being the conduit of whatever it is you're conduiting, Mr. Stone."

"Well," said Stone. Coughed. "We're being followed," he said.

"Followed," said Naphi.

"Right. Well, you are. Or were. See, Captain, I was in bed for a long time, back on Bollons. But after a while, I got up." He shifted. "Did a few odd jobs. Got to know the nurses. Some of the people around. Got to hobbling myself around the area. Got to knowing the byways, & the—"

"Do please," said Captain Naphi, "expedite this journey relevance-ward."

"So one of the fruit-sellers I knew was asking me who were my friends." Stone almost stuttered in his efforts to speak quickly. "He says there's people asking about what happened to me. To us. Asking for information. Said they'd heard something from someone, from a woman who'd heard about something we'd *found* . . ." He shook his head & shrugged. Sham swallowed, & shrugged too. *I don't know anything about that either!* he managed not to yell. "They were asking about our journey. The wreck. About the crew. Asking about you, Captain. First I thought it was all nothing."

"But," Naphi said.

"But. See, when I got on that mail-train to come back, after a couple of days, there's a little train behind us. Miles off. A smart engine, a single-car, & whatever it's burning's not putting out much exhaust that I can see. Top-notch quality. I know a good vehicle when I see one, & it should've been going a mad clip. But it stayed the same distance behind us. For way too long.

"Even then, I might not have thought anything of it. It was gone after a while. Except I saw it again. & not only that.

"We were in a plain. No hills, forests, nothing. Nowhere to hide. I saw it again, & then there was another. Keeping their distance."

"Following *you*," the captain said. "Even assume that were true, surely everyone knew where you were going?"

"They knew where I *said* I was heading, Captain. & I *was* going there. But maybe they thought I was going somewhere else. Like they thought we had a plan."

"Thank you, Unkus Stone," the captain said at last. She nodded. "Well. Well, whatever our peculiar tails think they know, they're bound to disappointment. After all I've no secrets to give them.

"Well." Naphi sat up & sniffed. "Rumours must have eddied around us. Rumours & wrongnesses. If they decide to, whoever our unwanted disciples are won't have much difficulty finding out where we're going next. & going again I am. Would you like to accompany me?"

"Another voyage already, Captain?" Stone said. "It would be an honour." He swallowed. With his legs as they now were, Stone wouldn't be first choice for many crews. Naphi was going a mile for him that many would not. "So we going back down south?" Stone said. "More great southerns to find?"

"Of course. That is, after all, our job. But perhaps this will be a long trip, this one. You never know *where* we might end up, or by what route we might have to go."

But seeing her eyes, seeing how the captain stared at the mechanism clipped to Daybe's leg, Sham in fact suspected he did know. Did have a good idea of where any detours might take them. & the excitement battered on the inside of his chest. At that moment it felt in his ribs just as he imagined it would if Daybe was flying around in there.

Chapter Twenty-Six

DID WE—?

The maintenance of a log is indispensable. A good officer will be diligent, & treat any such document, whether typed into a digital machine, handwritten on fine paper, tugged into the knot-writing of the northern railsea, or whatever, like the external memory it is. Focusing on what was done & what followed should clarify causes & effects.

Alas, logging is sometimes neglected. Everyone is happy to write of encounters with predators or prey, dramatic mole chases & revelations. But the long & many days of nothing, of mere passage on everyday rails, of swabbing, seeing little of note, finding nothing, not arriving but being still a long way from where you set out? Those days, a logger can make mistakes, or not bother. & from such situations come questions like "Did we—?"

Though, sometimes, it is not inadequate attention that generates uncertainty. Even shock. The *Medes* is about to set wheel to rail. On a route very different from its initial planned. & all because of an intervention Sham very cannily made.

It seems, not at all least to him, hard to believe that is why the deviation, hard to reconstruct how he had got there. Sham's own cunning has startled him out of understanding it. He does not understand how he can be going where he wanted to go.

Chapter Twenty-Seven

BACK ON THE RAILROADS, back at railsea. Rocking on his heels on the *Medes.* Soon to remember that conversation, Unkus Stone's warning. It was amazing how much Sham felt pleasure at the slide of his feet, the rattle & tilt of rushing rails. Daybe dived & scattered the railgulls that followed them.

The captain had put together almost the same crew as before. For all her quietness, her abstraction & ponderous ruminations—the usual flaws of any captain chasing a philosophy—she motivated loyalty. Here was Fremlo & Vurinam, Shossunder & Nabby & Benightly, now blondly unshaven & still not talkative but who whacked Sham on the back with unexpected friendliness that sent him sprawling. They worked with Sham as before, with similar teasing backchat & rough camaraderie, but now drank with him too when his shifts finished, & did not seem exasperated if he was shtum, uncertain what to say.

There were more animal fights, of course. Lind & Yashkan would jeer at Sham as they put their coins down on the outcomes of awful assaults by ratlings, mice, miniature bandicoots, birds & fighting bugs. Sham stayed away from the arenas. Whenever he saw them, he would fuss with & simper over & gush attention at his surprised & gratified daybat. He did notice that Vurinam, who glanced more than once at these ministrations, seemed not to frequent the battles as once he had.

Near the upsky border was a sputtering biplane, & Daybe

spiralled up towards it. Sham could see the little source-nubbins on its leg. It had not been hard to avoid returning it to Shikasta.

The aeroplane buzzed on westward. Perhaps it was from Mornington, swish island of aviators. Perhaps a transport of rich crew from the Salaygo Mess. With the complex tech available only in a few railsea countries, the cost of fuel, the necessity of long flat runways—hard to build on steep & slopey islands—air travel was expensive & uncommon. Sham looked up at the craft longingly, wondering what its drivers could see.

They were a few days out from Streggeye, veering a good clip through forest & on undulating ground. They went through unusual railscapes. By rivers & pools, crossing the waterways on jutting mooncalf elevated tracks.

"Where we heading, Captain?" Sham heard more than one officer ask, & the question, while mildly impertinent, was not surprising. They went west, not the south or southwest or south-southwest or even west-southwest that they might have expected for a mole hunt. "We have equipment to pick up," was all the captain would say.

Sham had his duties in Fremlo's poky surgery, but he made time to explore. Found cubbyholes. Crawl-spaces. Sections of holds. He sat in a big cupboard in a storage car, put his eye to an imperfectly sealed plank & through layers of wood could glimpse the sky.

They rode tangled & intersecting bridges for yards over the yawing drops of gorges, passed small islands poking out of the endless rails, stopping sometimes to pick up provisions & stretch their land-legs.

"Morning, Zhed."

Well might Sham hesitate. He had exchanged only a few words with the harpoonist before. But he was massaging his daybat's wings, feeling its healing with fingertip gentleness, near the captain's dais, & there Zhed was leaning on the hindmost barrier, staring directly at the rails on which they had passed.

She was an odd one. A tall & muscular soldier, originally from South Kammy Hammy. She still wore the ostentatious leather of those warlike & oddball far-off islands, where wartrains ran on clockwork motors.

"Morning," Sham said again.

"Is it a good morning?" Zhed said. "Is it? Is what I wonder." She continued to stare. They twisted in the outskirts of a wood, trees rising between the tight tracks, & animals & flouncy-feathered birds screamed at them from boughs. Zhed put fingers to her lips & pointed at a spot far off above the canopy. A zipping flurry of leaves. A swirl of disturbed, rain-bloated cloud. "Look." She briefly indicated rails to either side of the one they rode.

After long seconds with only the *chukkachuchu* of the wheels, Sham said, "I don't know what I'm seeing."

"Rails cleaned like they shouldn't be if they ain't been used in days," she said. "Is what you're seeing. Things moving like they only would if something was nearby."

"You mean . . ."

"I think someone is near us." At last she turned & met Sham's eye. "For us. Waiting. Or tracking."

Sham glanced around for Stone. "Are you sure?" he said.

"No. Not at all. I said 'I think.' But think it I do."

Sham looked into the dark the racing trees shed as shadow. "What might it be?" he whispered.

"I ain't a psychic. But I am a trainsperson & I know how the rails go."

THAT NIGHT, Sham swayed in his bunk to the *Medes*'s rhythm, & the motion of the carriage through the dark translated itself into unhappy dreams. He was walking across rails, long steps tie to tie, shuddering & fear-stiff so close to the earth. The earth that boiled, that oozed with life, ready to take him at his first stumble. & behind him something was coming.

It chased him out of a fringe of trees. It was something, oh, it was certainly something. He tried to hurry & stumbled & glimpsed & heard a snort & felt the rails shake & saw something both train & beast, a snarling thing pawing the rails as its wheels ground at him. Grunting. A goblin of the railsea, an angel of the rails.

When he woke Sham was not surprised to find that it was still deep night. He shivered & crept deckward without waking his comrades. Stars or little lights winked far out to railsea, miles & miles from safe hardland.

"HAVE YOU EVER seen an angel?" Sham said to Dr. Fremlo.

"I have," Fremlo said, in that voice both low & high. "Or I have not. Depends. How long does a glimpse have to be to count as a 'see'? I've travelled longer than anyone else on board, you know." The doctor smiled sharply. "I shall tell you something, Sham ap Soorap, which, while not a secret, is not generally admitted. Trains' doctors—we are awfully much more exciting than your sawbones is at home. But mostly, we're not nearly such good doctors.

"Can't keep up with the research. We're years out of date. & what gets us into this line is that we want to think about things other than medicine, sometimes. Which is why I'm not wholly stricken by your variable interest." Sham said nothing. "Now, don't get me wrong: I'll do for most of the things likely to afflict a traincrew. I am at worst a mediocre doctor, but I'm an excellent tracksperson. & I'm the only person—& yes, I think that includes the captain—who's seen an angel.

"But if you've come to me for ghoul stories I'm afraid you'll be disappointed. It was a long time ago, it was far away, & it was a moment. They're not invisible, whatever you've heard. But they move fast. By byways & switchways no one else knows."

"What did you see?" Sham said.

"We were off the coast of Colony Cocos. Treasure hunting." Fremlo raised an eyebrow. "By a right tangle of rails, some rock teeth. We knew something was watching us. & then we heard a sound.

"A little way off, no more'n a couple of hundred yards, a clot of the rails tangled together, crisscrossing back & forth & merging into a tunnel into cliff."

"The tracks went in?" said Sham.

"It had a lot of dark in it. It was full up with shadow. & something else. Something that, blaring that noise, suddenly & loud & awful, came out."

Sham started as something gripped his shoulder: Daybe, dropped from the air, to perch on him.

"I won't call it a train," Fremlo said. "Trains, in all their varieties, are machines made for carrying us. This was for nothing but itself. It came out of that hole in silver fire.

"D'you think we stuck around to see it get closer? We hightailed it back out into the known railsea. & luckily it let us go. Went back for more orders from the great director in the sky."

The way Fremlo said it, Sham could not tell if the doctor was a believer, or merely citing folklore.

*

AN INVISIBLE CLOUD squatted above the train. To Sham, everyone seemed contained, oppressed. No one said a word, but everyone seemed to agree that something was definitely following the damned train. Be it for angels, hungry monsters, pirates, marauders or imaginaries, the train was a quarry.

So it was almost a surprise that they made it anywhere. When, late on a beautiful evening in a stretch where the ground between the rails was thick with wild grass & tall weeds that rippled at them in wind-driven welcome, they saw a set of islands. Rocks where gulls fluffed their bums in scrub & eyed them with interest.

The *Medes* came closer, past larger landings, signs of habitation, more switches, electrical wires, lighthouses warning of weak-railed patches, & nasty rocks & reefs & pylons spreading & electrifying certain rails for trains that could run by that current, & then trains themselves, suddenly, shuffling or motionless, trains of every possible kind ranged around a great rocky land. On its shore a city. A place of towers & an architecture of scrapyard ingenuity & awe.

"Land!" announced the tannoy, someone from the crow's nest, wildly redundantly. Everyone knew by then where they were.

Manihiki City.

Part Three

Burrowing Tortoise
Magnigopherus polyphemus

Reproduced with permission from the archives of the
Streggeye Molers' Benevolent Society.

Chapter Twenty-Eight

So this was the centre of the world.

Sham did his best not to gaze like a greenhorn. Manihiki didn't make it easy, though: the spectacle started before they'd even pulled into the sidings in the largest harbour in the known world.

They came through an endless chaotic catalogue of vehicles. Past crews that ignored them, crews that stared at them, crews in outfits that marked them out as Streggeye's neighbours, & those dressed like illustrations or dreams. & the engines. Or, to be more precise—because not all the trains were engined—the means of locomotion.

Here a small train, three carriages only, manoeuvring the rails of the harbour at the end of great thrumming cables, tugged by two great birds. Well: a buzzard-train, emissary from the Teekhee archipelago. Wooden trains decorated with masks; trains coated in die-cast tin shapes; trains flanked with bone ornaments; double- & triple-decker trains; plastic-pelted trains stained in acrylic colours. The *Medes* passed the clatter & clank of diesel vehicles like their own. Past the shrill fussy shenanigans of steam trains that spat & whistled & burped dirty clouds, like irritating godly babies. & others.

The railsea: a vast & various train ecosystem. They passed under wires, for the few juiced-up miles of coastal rails. Here a stubby vehicle of scrubbed steel, its few windows tinted, & turning its wheels were back-curved pistons jutting from its sides. What were these grim faces from Fremlo, from all Sham's crew? This controlled disgust Captain Naphi showed?

Oh. That was a galleytrain. In its hot bowels scores of slaves were strapped in rows, hauling on the handles to turn the wheels, encouraged by whips.

"How can they allow it?" Sham breathed.

"Manihiki calls itself civilised," Fremlo said. "No slavery ashore. But you know how port-peace works. On each harboured train the laws of home." There were as many laws among the railsea lands as there were lands. In some were slaves.

Sham imagined kicking down doors & racing through the train corridors, shooting dastardly guards. His impotence embarrassed him.

& solar trains from Gul Fofkal; lunar ones from who-knew-where?; pedal trains from Mendana; a rococo clockwork train that made Zhed smile & salute as its crews sang the songs of winding & twisted their great key; treadmill trains from Clarion, their crews jogging to keep them moving; little trains tugged by trackside ungulate herds able to fight off the burrowing predators of shallow railsea; one-person traincycles; hulking invisibly powered wartrains; electric trains with the snaps & sparks of their passing.

Manihiki.

SHAM'S FIRST TASK at port was not, as he'd expected, to wind bandages, nor to clear up Fremlo's cabin, nor even to go shopping for whatever doctorly bits & pieces were needed. Instead, to Fremlo's narrow-eyed fascination, the captain herself ordered Sham to accompany her on what she called "her errands" in Manihiki town.

"You've never been here before," she said, pulling on her gloves, the left one altered to fit her inorganic hand, checking the buttons & fastenings of her dress coat, sweeping dust from her stiff pantaloons.

"No, Captain." Sham wished he had good clothes into which to squeeze.

By the jollycart, with the putter & grind of displaced earth, the curious snub faces of local moles & baby-sized earthrats, semi-tame & well fed on thrown scraps & organic rubbish, poked their heads up. Blind or not, they seemed to meet Sham's gaze. Daybe gripped his shoulder all the way to the harbour. Until they disembarked.

Into a city that, Sham's limited experience with alcohol suggested, was as giddying as being drunk. Raucous docks, a tight-packed, polyglot crowd. Catcalls, laughter, the shouting of wares. Sham saw people in clothes of all designs & colour & every tradition, beggarly rags through rubberised jumpsuits to the top hats of priests of That Apt Ohm, mimicking the dandy dress of their god. & — Sham stared — the rugged crazy costumes & makeshift uniforms of salvors.

Scholars from Rockvane watched Tharp conjurors; Cabigo emissaries swept their robes out of Manihiki puddles; hunters in Pittman overalls swapped maps & banter with updivers from Colony Cocos. The quaysides were haunts of pickers of pockets, players of rigged games, shake-lurks, fake survivors of fake train wrecks, asking for alms. Sham had no money to protect.

History seemed meaningless here, or at least bewildered. This building was grandly new, with steel in its plaster. This next was older by hundreds of years, & shabby. A mongrel place. Animal-tugged landcars, rickshaws, combustion engines growled past street furniture in endlessly different styles, houses made from what looked nothing like building materials. As if they'd been used as part of a bet.

Manihiki naval officers lounged in uniform, half on duty, half on display, half flirting with passersby. Yes, the maths was correct: such swagger could only be made up of three halves. They might bellow an instruction to a passing kid, or intervene in some minor altercation with tough, sanctioned panache. Imagine them at rail, Sham thought. A ferronaval train grinding down on pirates, guns going, rescue missions & defence-for-hire.

Off went Daybe into the low sky, investigating eaves, carvings, the gargoyles cobbled, Sham realised, out of salvage. "Careful," he called to the bat. Maybe there were arm-sized flying scorpions above Manihiki. He'd no clue.

He followed the captain, squeezing through the throng. By shops, stalls & hawkers selling bottles & magnets. Flowers & cameras. Illustrations of beasts & angels punishing the hubristic, sneaking out at night & fixing rails, of swirling-winged birds from beyond the world.

Into a region of bookshops, with, Sham realised, a broad view of what made a book a book. Dark rooms full of paper & leather, disks for ordinators & spools of film. Captain Naphi was greeted with courteous recognition. At more than one stand, she said her name & the seller would check a ledger or pull up a file on a glowing screen.

"The Unknown," they would murmur. "Is that correct? General theories. Also Floating Signifiers, Asymptotic Telos, Evasive Purpose. Loss. That's what we have you for." They cross-referenced her on-record tags with texts newly acquired. "Sulayman's *On Hunting Philosophies* has a new edition. & there was an article, let me see, 'Catching Quarries' in the last-but-three issue of *Captain-Philosopher's Quarterly,* but you've probably seen it." & so on.

What am I doing here? thought Sham. *If she needed a dogsbody, why ain't she brought Shossunder?*

As if she heard that thought the captain muttered, "Come now, Soorap, eyes up. Your suggestion brought us to Manihiki. Well done. Would you waste these sights?"

She considered the merits of various offerings. Those texts she bought she passed wordlessly to Sham. His bag grew heavy.

At an enormous, shabby & tumbledown warehouse, from within which came raucous bickering, Daybe investigated roofs. Naphi watched it go. "Tell me again," she said, "the places your friend thought the tracker might be found."

"Scabbling Street," Sham said. "The market. She said that's where the best salvage is."

She pointed at a sign on the wall. Scabbling Street Market. Sham gaped. Naphi knew, no question, what sort of artefacts it was he hankered to see. After schlepping through all the bookshops, was this a reward for telling her about the tech?

"So," Naphi said. She indicated, with a sudden lovely sweep of her hands, that he should enter before her. "I am going salvage shopping."

Chapter Twenty-Nine

"YOU HAVE THE BOOKS?" the captain said. "Your job is to get them back to the train. I won't need you, Soorap, for a while."

"I've to go back?" *You only just* brought *me in here*, he thought.

"Indeed. I want my books by nightfall."

"By . . . ?" That was hours away. He had hours. She was giving him hours! Hours to find his way through the streets of Manihiki. Through this market. Naphi was holding out a note. Money, too? "Lunch. Consider it from your share." He stammered a thanks, but Naphi was gone.

Well here I am, Sham thought languidly. *Amid the salvage.*

The market was in an arcade. Above, levels of busy walkways reachable by spiral stairs. Around Sham, stall after stall of startling found detritus. Absolutely ringing with the noise of attempted sales, arguments, singing, the declaration of wares. A little band accompanying all the business with guitar & oboe, a woman overseeing strange sounds emerging from what looked like a bone box.

People smart & scruffy, businesswomen & -men, tough-dressed mercenaries & buyable thugs. Trainsfolk. Bookish types. Dignitaries & explorers in the sumptuous or strange or barbarian clothes of their homelands. & everywhere salvors.

I know, I know, Sham thought in answer to the correctives & the warnings levelled by Troose & Voam. I know they're showoffs. Still though!

124

The salvors yelled at each other in slang. Slid layered visors into use & out of it again, pressed studs & extrusions on their protective overalls, their leather butchers'-style aprons & many-pocketed trousers. They prodded & finger-tinkered with odd boxes, with bits & pieces of salvage that threw colours & images into the air, that sung & dimmed local lights & made dogs lie down.

His curiosity overcame Sham's awe. "What's that?" He pointed at a rust-deformed wedge of iron. The salesman looked wryly at him.

"A wrench," the man said.

"& that?" Some rot-mottled square in various colours, stamped on by tiny statues.

"A children's game. So scholars say. Or a divination kit."

"That?" A filigreed arachnid nub of what looked like glass, leg-things drumming in complicated articulation.

"No one knows." The man handed Sham a bit of wood. "Hit it."

"Eh?"

"Give it a whack." The man grinned. Sham walloped the salvage. It did not break as it looked like it should. Instead the stick itself coiled in on itself like an injured tentacle. Sham held it up. It was a tight spiral, now, though it still felt hard in his hand.

"That's offterran, duh," the man said. "That's alt-salvage, that curlbug. From one of the celestial stopoffs."

"How much are they?" Sham said. The man looked at him gently & said a price that made Sham clamp his mouth shut & turn away. Then he turned back.

"Oh, can I ask you . . ." He glanced around to make sure Naphi wasn't in sight or earshot. "Do you know some, some kids? A family? They have an arch, that looks like it's made of some old salvage."

The man stared at him."What are you after, boy?" he said at last. "No. I don't. I have no idea who they might be & I suggest that you don't either." He ignored Sham's consternation & started up again with his barking, singsonging announcements that he was selling tools & curlbugs & fine cheap salvage.

Sham tried a woman haggling with an ill-tempered buyer over antique ordinator circuitry; to a pair of men who specialised in offterran alt-salvage, their cubbyhole full of thoroughly discomfiting nuggets of strangeness; to a purveyor not of salvage but of equipment for its extraction: lodestones, gauges, telegoggles, shovels, corkscrew drillboots, air pumps & masks for total earth-submersion. A group of young men & women about his age watched Sham. They snickered & whispered to each other, picked their fingernails with foolish little knives. They dispersed as a sharp-faced ferronaval officer glared at them, gathered again when he passed on.

A table of dolls. Old dolls, salvaged dolls. No matter how cleaned they had been, the dust in which they had lain for so many lifetimes had permanently coloured them: whatever tone their skin had been supposed to be, it looked ensepiaed, as if seen through dirty glass. Mostly they were shaped like people, mostly like women or girls, though of deeply questionable physical proportions, with thickety knotted & scrambled hair where it remained at all. A few were grotesques, monsters. Many were limbless. They needed the ministrations of a dollmaker.

Everywhere Sham went the responses to his question, his description of the arch & the two children, were either sincere-seeming ignorance, or guarded recognition followed by lies &/

the lookout for certain things. The *Medes*, is it? Isn't that your train?"

"Yes," Sham said. "How did you know?"

"It's my job to pick through things thrown out there, & that might include things said. The *Medes*. Made an unexpected stop in Bollons." Sham's gasp was awfully eloquent. "Ah, it's not so much of a thing," Sirocco said. "I can tell you the same sort of snippets of likely wholly boring such stuff about plenty of recent arrivals." She smiled.

"If you say so," he muttered.

"Still wishing things had gone another way?" She inclined her head. "I'd stick with your crew if I were you." She did not say it unkindly.

"Well . . . thank you."

"I think your friends are waiting for you." Sirocco nodded at the still-watching gang.

"They ain't my friends," Sham said.

"Hm." The woman frowned a little. "Watch yourself, then, won't you?"

He would. Sham was already ready.

There were occasions he'd been accused of being a bit dozy, had Sham ap Soorap, but not this time. He hefted the bag of books onto his shoulder, thanked Sirocco again, left the building. & it really did not come as a huge surprise to him, when he emerged into the afternoon light of Manihiki, that the ganglet bundled out of the hall after him & rushed him, grabbing for his bag, his money, came with their fists swinging.

or suggestions that he leave it alone. Mostly it was the salvors who displayed the former, the local merchants the latter.

What did he know of this family? Older sister, younger brother. Messy house. With vigorous & far-travelling parents. Who, the bones said, had died.

Which thoughts, inevitably, took Sham to thinking of his own family. He did not often ruminate on his mother & father, lost by him to heartbreak & accident. It was not that he did not care: certainly he cared. It was not that he did not suspect their not-there-ness was important. He was not stupid. It was, rather, all but unremembering their ministrations, cared for as he had been throughout his life by Troose & Voam—who *were* his parents, really, no two ways about it. The care Sham felt for his mum & dad was care for lost strangers, dwelling on whom might feel disloyal to those who had raised him.

But he was abruptly aware that he seemed to share with these two children in the image the fact that he was, technically, to be exact about it, an orphan. Well there was a word to sit in the throat. So. Were this girl & this boy also doctors' assistants, dissatisfied, salvage-pining, missing something? Sham doubted it.

There were clocks all over the hall in a thousand designs. Some were modern, others obviously salvage, proudly rejigged to work again, extruding little birds at set moments. Some were blue-screened, glowing with digits. All showed Sham how fast time was going.

"How did you become a salvor?" The tough-looking woman to whom Sham spoke looked up in surprise. She was sipping tarry coffee, had been exchanging dig-anecdotes with colleagues. She laughed at Sham, not unkindly. She flipped a coin at a baker at her stall & indicated that Sham should take a pastry.

"Dig," she said. "Find a piece. Take it to a salvage train. Dig more. Find another piece. Don't be a . . ." She looked him up & down. "A dogsbody? A cabin boy? A steward? A trainee moler?"

"Doctor's assistant," he said.

"Ah. Well yes, that too. Don't be that."

"I found a bat," Sham said through a mouthful of his sticky bread present. "I suppose that ain't salvage, though. It's my mate."

He was still watched, he realised, by the little gang. & they, he saw, were watched by another young man, a wiry & quick-moving lad Sham wondered if he'd seen before.

The salvor rummaged below her table. "I need more Smearing Widgets," she said.

"Thank you very much for the cake," Sham said. The woman was splendid-looking. He blinked & tried to concentrate. "I don't suppose—have you ever seen two children? They live near a . . ."

"An arch," she said. Sham blinked. "A salvage arch. I heard someone was looking for them."

"What?" said Sham. "Since I came *in* you heard that?"

"Word travels. Who are you, lad?" She tilted her head. "What do I know about you? Nothing yet. You know I'm not from here. But these salvage-surrounded siblings, they ring a bell."

"You must come here all the time," Sham said. "Maybe you heard of them once."

"Of course. This is Manihiki. It sticks in the mind, that sort of architectural detail you describe, don't it? I was here, it would be a couple of journeys ago, which would be a few months, I suppose? Selling direct. Anyway." She nodded slowly at the memory. "There were two here like the ones you're describing.

Young! Young young, but calm as you like." She [...] eyebrow. "Prodding, picking, asking questions. & th[...] their salvage."

"You think it was the ones I'm looking for?"

"I could hear this lot whispering." She twirled her h[...] indicate the stallholders: not salvors, but local agents, the[...] chants. "Talking trash about them. & trash is my business[...] smiled. "They bought a load of stuff from me." She clicke[...] fingers. "Talking of which, I really must get on."

She lifted up a little box of alt-salvage things. Thumb-si[...] each shaped unlike any of the others, each a green-glass sha[...] each hairy with wires. & each slid side to side as if alive on t[...] tabletop & spread behind it a snailtrail of what looked like blac[...] ink, that disappeared after a few seconds.

"Smearing Widgets," she said. "I'd give you one," she said[...] "except that I'm not going to."

"I need to find those children," Sham said, staring acquisi[...] tively at the offterran refuse.

"I can help you. They bought too much to carry, arrang[...] for delivery."

"To where?" Sham's voice came quick. "Their house?"

"It was in Subzi. You know where that is?" She drew a [...] in the air with her fingers. "North of the old city."

"Do you remember the street? The house number?"

"No. But don't worry about that. Just ask for the ar[...] do you. It's been a pleasure chatting." She held out he[...] "Sirocco. Travisande Sirocco."

"Sham ap Soorap." He started at the expression [...] provoked. "What?"

"Nothing. Only—I think perhaps someone men[...] Soorap." She cocked her head again. "Chap about [...]

Chapter Thirty

A FIGHT, THEN.

What kind?

Fights are much taxonomised. They have been subject over centuries to a complex, exhaustive categoric imperative. Humans like nothing more than to pigeonhole the events & phenomena that punctuate their lives.

Some bemoan this fact: "Why does everything have to be put into boxes?" they say. & fair enough, up to a point. But this vigorous drive to divide, subdivide & label has been rather maligned. Such conceptual shuffling is inevitable, & a reasonable defence against what would otherwise face us as thoroughgoing chaos. The germane issue is not whether, but *how*, to divide.

Certain types of events are particularly carefully delineated. Such as fights.

What ran towards Sham, announcing its presence with throaty jeers, was incipient fightness, carried in the vectors of eight or nine aggressive young men & women. But what kind of fight?

Let fight equal x. Was this, then a play x? An x to the death? An x for honour? A drunken x?

Sham focused. Hands & boots were incoming. One of those hands, in fact, was grasping for his bag, & in doing so answering that question.

What this was was a *mugging*.

Chapter Thirty-One

Two big lads coming for him. Sham ducked—he moved quick for a heavy young man. He was ringed, his attackers shouting, & here they came again & now *he* was kicking, & he could be proud of that one, but there were too many of them & something hit his face & *wow* hurt & he tried to pull hair but someone hit his eye & he was all rocked for a second—

Something interrupted. A sound high-pitched & not even distantly human. Enraged vespertilian lungs! *Oh*, Sham thought, you *beauty*. From his undesired vantage point, flat on his back, hands up to block a blow, what he saw framed in backlit clouds with wings spread & wingskin taut, descending like a small furry avenging ghost, was Daybe.

& there came another voice. A boy. "Oy, bastard!" Behind the tallest & heaviest of the muggers was the young man Sham had seen watching his own watchers. Here he came, shoving hard & hands up. A gust of blows from the newcomer & a skirr of bony-&-leathery wings from Daybe. The boy's attacks were, to Sham's bruised eyes, more enthusiastic than effective, but the muggers scurried out of his way. & they were genuinely terrified by Daybe, small but so demoniac in chattery-toothed appearance.

It was a mad gush rush. Sham was struggling shakily to his feet, the attackers were suddenly scarpering away fast, the boy who'd come to his aid was yelling imprecations as they went, & Daybe brave & splendid mouse-sized bodyguard, Stonefaced gods of Streggeye bless & keep it—still chased them as if it would catch them & eat them, as if they were flies.

"You alright?" His rescuer turned & helped Sham brush himself down. "You're bleeding a bit."

"Yeah," said Sham. Dabbed at his face with his finger & checked the flow. Not too bad. "Thanks. Yeah. Thanks a lot."

The boy shook his head. "Sure you're okay?"

Was Sham sure he was okay? What scraps of doctorliness he had bobbed to the top of his brain. He was mildly surprised to find them there at all. Teeth? All present, only slightly bloodied. Nose? Not loosened, though sore. Face abraded, but that was all.

"Yeah. Thank you."

The boy shrugged. "Bullies," he said. "They're all cowards."

"People do say that," Sham said. "I think there must be a few brave bullies out there & everyone's going to be in a bit of a shock when they meet them." He checked his pockets. Still had his coin. "How did you know they were going to attack me?"

"Oh." The boy waved vaguely & grinned. "Well." He laughed a bit sheepishly. "I've done enough ambushing in my time to know when I can see someone else about to have a go."

"So why'd you stop them?"

"Because eight against one ain't fair!" The boy blushed & looked away a moment. "I'm Robalson. Where's your bat gone?"

"Oh, it's always off. It'll be back."

"We should go," Robalson said. "The navy'll be here soon."

"Isn't that good?" Sham said.

"No!" Robalson began to tug at him. "They ain't going to help. & you don't want to get mixed up with that sort of so-&-so."

Sham went with him a way, confused, then abruptly raised his hands & squeezed shut his eyes. "They got my bag," he said. "My captain's stuff. I'm bloody for it."

He looked vaguely about him. He wanted the bag back, he wanted to punish those muggers, he wanted to track down the children of the wreck, but, lungs full of dust & defeat, he felt suddenly quite deflated. *Come on!* he tried to think. He tried to think himself into energy. It didn't go well. "I better go," he muttered.

"Is that it, then?" Robalson said, to Sham's back. "Come on, mate!" Sham didn't answer. Didn't look back. Began the miserable trudge back to the harbour.

He slowed as he went. Began to feel the ache & scrape of all those injuries. Down the hill he went, through streets & by landmarks he'd not known he'd noticed on the way. Sham dragged out the journey. He more than took his time. He was thinking about the books. He'd clocked how expensive & rare some were.

A figure emerged from an alley ahead, cutting off his morose descent. He stopped. It was Robalson. "Books?" Robalson said. Meeting Sham's eye, holding out the bag in which was every one of the texts he thought he'd lost.

"How did you find them?" Sham's question came after a flurry of gratitude & astonishment.

"I know Manihiki better than you. I've been here a few times. Second of all I thought I saw your bat circling over something, so I went to check it out. Well, it was: it was over this. That lot who went for you ain't interested in stuff like this."

"But these are precious."

"They ain't master criminals, they're just out for a quick dollar. They slung them."

"& you found me again."

"I know where the harbour is. It was obvious you were having a bad day, figured you'd head home. So." Robalson raised his eyebrows. They stared at each other. "Anyway, so," Robalson said. He nodded. "Glad you got them back," he said at last. He turned to go.

"Wait!" said Sham. He jiggled the coin in his pocket. "I owe you big-time. Let me . . . I'd like to say thanks. Do you know any good pubs or whatever? "

"Sure," said Robalson. He grinned. "Yeah, I know all the best Manihiki places. Near the harbour? We've both got trains to get back to."

Sham thought. "Maybe eight o'clock tomorrow? I have to do something now."

"The Dustmaid. On Protocol Abyss Street. Eight o'clock. I'll be there."

"& what's your train?" Sham said. "Mine's the *Medes*. Just in case there's a problem I can find you."

"Oh," said Robalson. "My train's—something I'll tell you later. You ain't the only one with secrets."

"What?" Sham said. "What is it? Is it a moler? A trader? Railnavy? Fighter? *Salvor?* What are you?"

"What is it?" Robalson walked backwards & met Sham's eye. "What am I? Why'd you think I want to get away from the navy?" He put his hands to the sides of his mouth.

"I'm a pirate," he said, in an exaggerated whisper, grinned, turned, was gone.

Chapter Thirty-Two

DAYBE CAME BACK. It looked pleased with itself, lazily snapping at local beetles more on principle than out of hunger.

"You're *such* a good bat," Sham cooed. "Such a good bat." It nipped his nose & drew a blood bead, but he knew it was in affection.

Sham followed the salvor's directions. "Why'd you want to go there?" the locals asked, but they pointed the way. Through noisy machine- & navy-filled streets, into grubbier areas full of rubbish & quivering dogs eyeing Sham & making him nervous.

"He says he's a pirate," whispered Sham to Daybe. Images came to Sham—how could they not?—of pirate trains. Devilish, smoke-spewing, weapon-studded, thronging with dashing, deadly men & women swinging cutlasses, snarling under crossed-spanner pendants, bearing down on other trains.

"'Scuse me," he asked stoop-sitters, hawkers, builders & loungers-by-roadsides. "Where's the arch?" He could feel the streets descending. They were nearing railsea level. "Can you tell me where the arch is?" he asked a street-sweeper who leaned amiably on his shuddering cleaning machine & pointed him on.

This was a region of building sites, rubbish sites, drosscapes. & right there in among them—"How'd I miss that, Daybe?" Sham whispered—was the entrance to a lot. & over it, announcing it, was that arch.

Eighteen yards tall, triumphal & oddly blocky as if it were

pixelated, it looked as if it had been cut, *hewn* as the captain might have had it, from cold white stone. But those weren't stone slabs Sham was looking at. They were metal. They were salvage.

The arch was salvage. Arche-salvage, too—but not of mysteries. The nature of this had been long-established by scholars. The arch was mostly made of washing machines.

He'd seen a demonstration of one once. At a fair on Streggeye, a show of restored findings. Hooked up to chuggering generators, a whining thing like a needy animal prince issuing stupid orders: a fax machine. An ancient screen on which enthusiastic badly drawn figures hit each other: a vijogame. & one of these white things, used to clean ancients' clothes.

Why would you use arche-salvage for something it clearly wasn't for? When there were much bloody easier things to build an arch out of?

"Hello?" Sham knocked on it. His knuckles made the hollow machines boom.

Beyond the arch was a bony-looking leafless tree, a big garden, if he could call the tangles of bramble & wire that, if a scrubland free of plants but for exuberant weeds was gardeny. What the land seemed really to be was a resting place for endless bits of salvage, odd-shaped metal, plastic, rubber, rotted wood, festooned with sludgy ruins of old advertisements. There was a patch of scratched-up plastic telephones. Their wires jutted up, stiffened. At the end of each was a coloured receiver like a recurved plastic flower.

"Hello?" A path led to a big old brick house, with extra rooms constructed, Sham saw, of more washing machines, of the old ice makers called fridges, of antique ordinators, of black-rubber wheels & the hulking fish-body of a car. Sham shook his head.

"Hello?"

"Leave it at the end of the path," someone said. Sham jumped. Daybe jumped too, from his shoulder, & kept going, circled a tree. Watching Sham from a branch, a security camera winked. "What have you brought? Leave it at the end of the path. We're in credit," said a crackling voice from a speaker, that had been crooked so long in the V where a bough met the trunk that the tree had grown around it, embedded it in its skin, so it protruded like a bubo.

"I . . ." Sham stepped closer & talked into it. "I think you've got me mixed up. I'm not a delivery man. I'm looking for—I don't know their names. I'm looking for a girl & a boy. About . . . well I don't know how old the pictures are. One's about three or four years older than the other, I think."

Sham could hear distant bickering from the speaker, voices muttering at each other, disguised by static. "Go away," he heard; then in a different voice, "No, wait." Then more murmurs. & at last, to him, the question, "Who are you?" Sham could hear the suspicion. He ran his fingers through his hair & gazed into the clouds & the discoloured upsky above.

"I'm from Streggeye Land," he said. "I've got some information. From a lost train."

WHAT OPENED the door to him was a stamping figure covered completely in a dark leather costume, eyes obscure behind flinty glass, uniform strapped all over with charcoal filters & water bottles, bits of equipment, tubes & nozzles, shaggy & swaying like a fruit tree. Sham didn't blink. The figure raised an arm & ushered him ponderously in.

The house didn't even surprise him. After that arch & the

garden he fully expected it to be the mix of sumptuous decay, jury-rigged half-fixes, splendour, & grubby salvage it was. Past all kinds of strange stuff, salvage stuff, the silent guide took him into a kitchen. Also crammed, every surface covered, in bits of everything. Junk covered the huge table like unappetising hors d'oeuvres. Trash sat under dust on windowsills.

Behind the huge table, looking at Sham with his arms folded over his denim overalls, was the boy from the flatograph. Sham exhaled.

The boy was perhaps two years older than in the picture. Maybe ten? Dark skin, short dark hair jutting straight up like hedgehog bristles. Brown eyes full of suspicion. He was stocky, compact, his chest broad like a tough older boy's. He stuck out his chin & his lower lip as if pointing at Sham with them, & waited.

The person who had led Sham in peeled off the strange outer clothes. From the helmet fell shoulder-length dark coils of hair. It was a girl who shook them from her face, the other child from the lost picture. She was close to Sham's age. Her skin was as dark & grey as her brother's, though dotted with rust-coloured freckles, her face as fierce & furrow-browed as his, her lips as set, but her expression not quite so forbidding. She wiped a sweat-wet fringe of hair out of her eyes & looked at Sham levelly. Under the outerwear now puddled at her feet she wore a grubby jumper & longjohns.

"Had to test it," she said. "So."

"So," the boy said. Sham nodded at them & soothed Daybe, wriggling on his shoulder.

"So," the girl said, "You have something to tell us."

*

& SLOWLY, STOPPING & starting, not very coherently but as thoroughly as he could, Sham went over it all. The ruin of the strange train, the debris. The attack of the mole rats.

He did not mention skeleton nor skull, but, looking away, he said that there'd been evidence that someone had died there. When he looked up, the siblings were staring at each other. They made no sounds. Both of them kept their bodies still; neither of them said a word. Both of them were blinking through tears.

Sham was appalled. He looked urgently from one to the other, desperate for them to stop. They did not sob, they made very little noise. They only blinked & their lips trembled.

"What are you, can you, I didn't," Sham blurted. Desperate to make them say something. They ignored him. The girl hugged her brother, quickly & hard, held him at arm's length & examined him. Whatever it was that needed to pass between them did so. They turned at last to Sham.

"I'm Caldera," said the girl. She cleared her throat. "This is Caldero." Sham repeated the names, keeping his eyes on her.

"Call me Dero," the boy said. He did not sniff, but he wiped tears from his cheeks. "Dero's easier. Otherwise it sounds too much like her name, which can be confusing."

"Shroake," his sister said. "We're the Shroakes."

"I'm Sham ap Soorap. So," he added eventually, when they showed no inclination to speak. "It was your father's train?"

"Our mother's," said Caldera.

"But she took our dad with her," said Dero.

"What was she doing?" Sham said. "What were *they* doing?" Perhaps, he thought, he should not ask, but his curiosity was too strong to resist. "Way out there?" The Shroakes glanced at each other.

"Our mum," Dero said, "was *Ethel Shroake*." As if that was an answer. As if Sham should recognise the name. Which he did not.

"Why did you come, Sham ap Soorap?" said Caldera. "& how did you know where to find us?"

"Well," Sham said. He was still troubled, far more than he understood, at the sight of the Shroakes' grief. He thought of that side-slid train, the dust & bones & rags that filled it. Of travellers & families & adventures gone wrong, & trains turned into sarcophagi, with bones within them.

"See, there was a time I saw something that I don't think I was maybe supposed to see." He was talking quickly, & his breath came in a shudder. "Something from that train. A memory card from a camera. It was like . . . they knew everything was going to get stripped, but they found a way to hide that one thing."

The Shroakes were staring. "That would be Dad," Caldera said quietly. "He did like that camera."

"There were pictures on it," Sham said. "I . . . saw you. He took one of you two."

"He did," said Caldera. Dero was nodding. Caldera looked up at the ceiling. "It's been a long time," she said. "We always knew they might . . . & as it went on, it got more & more likely." She spoke Railcreole with a lovely strange accent. "Truth is, I thought, if anything happened, we'd never know. That we'd just wait & wait. & now, you come here with these stories."

"Well," Sham said. "I think if someone in my family never came back . . . Which actually, sort of . . ." He took another breath. "I think I'd like it if someone told me if they found them. Later." Caldera & Dero stared levelly at him. He thought of the pictures, & his heart sped up with excitement; he couldn't help it. "& also," he said, "because of what else was on them pictures. That's why I wanted to find you. What were they looking for?"

"Why?" said Dero.

"Why?" said Caldera, her eyes narrowing.

This is something, Sham thought, & excitement filled him right up. He took out his camera. He told them, one by one, about the images he had seen. He thumbed on the tiny screen that showed his own, scrolled through one by rubbish useless one of rails & penguins & raildwellers & weather & the *Medes* crew & not much at all, until he reached *that* picture. The picture of the last shot Caldera's parents had taken.

His camera was cheap, his focus was off, he had taken it as he fell. It was a poor effort. But it was just clear enough, if you knew what you were looking at. An empty plain & a single line. Rails stretching out to nowhere. Alone.

"Because," he said, "they were coming back from this."

Chapter Thirty-Three

THERE WAS A TIME when we did not form all words as now we do, in writing on a page. There was a time when the word "&" was written with several distinct & separate letters. It seems madness now. But there it is, & there is nothing we can do about it.

Humanity learnt to ride the rails, & that motion made us what we are, a ferromaritime people. The lines of the railsea go *everywhere* but from one place straight to another. It is always switchback, junction, coils around & over our own train-trails.

What word better could there be to symbolise the railsea that connects & separates all lands, than "&" itself? Where else does the railsea take us but to this place & that one & that one & that one, & so on? & what better embodies, in the sweep of the pen, the recurved motion of trains, than "&"?

An efficient route from where we start to where we end would make the word the tiniest line. But it takes a veering route, up & backwards, overshooting & correcting, back down again south & west, crossing its own earlier path, changing direction, another overlap, to stop, finally, a few hairs' widths from where we began.

& tacks & yaws, switches on its way to where it's going, as we all must do.

Chapter Thirty-Four

"I can't help wondering," Sham said, "what they were doing."

"You're a moler?" said Dero. Sham blinked.

"Yeah."

"You hunt moles?"

"Well, me, no. I help a doctor. & sometimes I clean floors & pick up ropes. But I do that on a train that hunts moles, yeah."

"You don't," said Dero, "sound happy."

"About moling? Or doctoring?"

"What would you rather be doing?" Caldera said. She glanced at him, & something in her look rather took his breath away.

"I'm fine," Sham said. "Anyway, look. This isn't why I came here, to talk about this."

"No indeed," agreed Caldera. Dero shook his head, then nodded, then shook it again, stern-faced as a little general. "Still though. What *would* you like?"

"Well," Sham said. "I mean . . ." He was shy to say it. "It would be good to do what your family does. To be a salvor."

Dero & Caldera regarded him. "You think we're *salvors*?" said Dero.

"I mean, well, yeah," said Sham. "I mean—" He shrugged & indicated the house, so full to brimming with found technology & reconstructed bits & pieces. "Yeah. & where they were going." He shook the camera. "That was salvage hunting. Far off. Weren't it?"

"What do your family do?" Dero said.

"Well," Sham said. "My, it's my cousins, sort of, they do bits & pieces, nothing like this. &, but my mum & dad were—well, my dad was on the trains. Neither of them were salvors anyway. Not like yours."

Caldera raised an eyebrow. "We've *been* salvors, of sorts," she said. "I suppose. Mum was. Dad was. Once. But is that what you think would get you up in the mornings?"

"We are not salvors," Dero said. Sham kept looking at Caldera.

"I said we were," she said. "Not we are. What we are is salvage-*adjacent*."

"I mean, all the searching, though," Sham said, his voice coming quicker the more he spoke. "That's got to be exciting, ain't it? Finding things no one's found before, digging down, finding more, uncovering the past, making *new* things, all the time, learning & that."

"You're contradicting yourself," Caldera said. "You can't find things no one's found before by uncovering the past, can you? Searching for something. I see the appeal." She stared at him. "But you don't *uncover the past* if you're a salvor: you pick up rubbish. The last thing I think you should think about's the past. That's what they do wrong here."

"Here?"

"Here, Manihiki." She shrugged a big shrug, to indicate the island beyond her walls.

"Why you here?" Dero said.

"Yeah, why are you? In Manihiki?" Caldera said. "Your crew. No moles here."

Sham waved his hand. "Everyone always ends up in Mani-hiki at some point. Supplies & whatnot."

"Really," Caldera said.

"Salvage," Dero said. "You here for salvage?"

"No," Sham said. "Supplies. Whatnot."

He walked with Caldera & Dero through their house. It was so rambling & tumbledown he called it, in his head, ramble-down. Up stairs, down again via elevator, escalator up, ladder down, past all sorts of odd spaces like sheds indoors.

"It was good of you to come tell us," Caldera said.

"Yeah," said Dero.

"I'm very sorry about your dad & your mum," Sham said.

"Thank you," Caldera said.

"Thank you," Dero said solemnly.

"We're sorry about yours," Caldera said.

"Oh." Sham was vague. "That was *ages* ago."

"It must've been a massive effort to get here," Caldera said. "To tell us."

"We were coming anyway," Sham said.

"Of course." She stopped at a door. Put her hand on the handle. Looked at her brother, who looked back at her. They seemed to draw strength from each other. She breathed deep. Dero nodded, she nodded back, & led them into what had once been a bedroom, now had two walls removed so it opened onto the low sky of the garden. Daybe chirruped at the smell of fresh air. The space contained as much mould, ivy, old rain stains & outside air as it did furniture & floor. Caldera ran her fingers over damp dust.

Sitting at a desk, facing out into the hole, was a man. He was writing, skipping between pen & paper & an ordinator. He was writing almost alarmingly quickly.

"Dad," said Caldera.

Sham's eyes widened.

The man looked around & gave them a smile. Sham stayed at the door. The man's eyes looked not quite focused. His pleasure at seeing them was a little desperate.

"Hello there," the man said. "A guest? Please please do come in."

"This is Sham," Caldera said.

"He came to do us a favour," Dero said.

"Dad," said Caldera. "We've got some bad news."

She came closer, & trepidation went across the man's face. Sham backed quietly out & closed the door. He tried to move a good distance away, but after a minute or two, he did think he could hear crying.

& a minute or two after that, the sombre-faced Shroake children came back out.

"I thought, you said that was your dad who . . . that that was who I found," Sham whispered.

"It was," said Dero. "That's our other one."

There were almost as many kinds of families as there were rock islands in the railsea—that, of course, Sham knew. There were many disinclined to take the shape that their homes would rather they did. & in those nations where the norms were not policed by law, if they were willing to put up with disapproval— as, it was clear, the Shroakes were—they could take their own shapes. Hence the Shroakes' strange household.

"There were three of them," Caldera said. "But Dad Byro . . ." She glanced in the direction of the room. "He didn't have the same want to go gallivanting that Dad Evan & our mum did."

"Gallivanting," Sham said, hopeful for more.

"He keeps house," Dero said. Behind him, unseen by him,

his sister met Sham's eye &, silently, mouthed the word *kept*. "He writes." Caldera mouthed *Wrote*. "He's . . . forgetful. He looks after us, though." Caldera mouthed, *We look after him*.

Sham blinked. "There's no one else here?" he said. How could they be looking after that lost man & themselves, all alone? A thought struck him.

"You know what I heard," he said. "I heard there was ways of building artificial people. Out of this stuff." He indicated the salvage. "That could walk around & think & do things . . ." He looked around as if expecting such a trash-coagulation, a junk nanny powered on strange energies, to appear, cooing at her charges.

"A salvagebot?" Dero said. He made a rude noise.

"Myths," Caldera said. "No such thing." The metal-rubber-glass-stone figure in Sham's head disappeared in a puff of reality, leaving Caldera & Dero looking after themselves, & their lamenting second father.

Chapter Thirty-Five

DESPITE THE ODD TUG of community he felt to the Shroakes in their newly certain two-thirds orphanhood—a bond he had not expected—& despite his frustration at not understanding more of the elder Shroakes' story, Sham could not stay. Time was doing what time always does, going faster & faster as if downhill. & in truth, Sham admitted to himself, he was not sure the Shroakes did not want him gone. Did not want to be alone with their remaining parent.

Dero ushered him from the house as Caldera checked again on Dad Byro. As he retraced his steps out of the garden, under the arch of washing machines & back into the streets of Manihiki, Sham thought about the duty roster, about Dr. Fremlo & whoever else might be around, about whose instruction he could & whose he could not evade, in his eagerness to slip away, revisit the Shroakes. Perhaps it was because he was thinking about authority & unwanted attentions that he noticed the man outside the Shroake house.

He stood leaning against a wall, swaddled in a long grey coat larger than the temperature would seem to warrant. Under the wide brim of his hat, it was impossible to see his face. Sham frowned. The man might be staring right at him. He certainly seemed to be looking in the general direction of the Shroakes' house. & as passersby passed by & the light continued to leak from the sky, Sham was certain the man's presence was not coincidence.

The watcher, as Sham anxiously gazed, began to saunter across the street. Sham played for time. Knelt for a moment & fiddled with his shoes. The man was approaching him. As casually as he could manage, Sham started to walk away. He willed himself not to look over his shoulder, but the two eye-sized spots on his back where he imagined the man's gaze landing itched, & he could not help a quick glance. The man was closing on him. Sham sped up. Still looking backwards, he walked straight into someone.

He was gabbling an apology before he even saw who he had hit. It was a woman, tall & broad enough that despite Sham being a heavy boy, impact with him had moved her not at all. She was staring at him with concern. She put her hands on his arms.

"Hey," she said. "You alright?" She saw his backwards glance. "Is that man giving you trouble?"

"No, I, yes, no, I don't know," Sham said. "I don't know what he wants, he was watching—"

"Watching?" said the woman. The man had stopped. Appeared suddenly interested in a wall. The woman narrowed her eyes. "You came from in there?" she said, indicating the Shroakes'. Sham nodded.

"Don't worry, son," she said. She put an arm around his shoulder. "Whatever it is he wants, we'll keep you out of his hands."

"Thanks," Sham muttered.

"Don't you worry. We take care of visitors in Manihiki." She led him away, towards better-lit parts of town. "As, I'm sure, did the Shroakes. What was it you were talking to them about?" The question came out of her mouth without the slightest change of tone. Still, though, it made Sham look up. To see that she was staring, in that instant, not at him, but at the man behind them, & that she was looking at him not in suspicion but unspoken communication.

Sham's very throat began to pulse, so fast did his heart slam at that sight. His rescuer who was not his rescuer looked at him, her face hardened & her hand closed tight on Sham's shoulder. Options for subtlety & subterfuge removed from him, Sham took the only other path he could see. He stamped on the woman's foot.

She howled & swore & hopped & bellowed, & the dark, shadow-faced man behind them started sprinting after Sham. He was fast. His coat gusted around him.

Sham ran. Opened his shirt & released Daybe. The bat dive-bombed the man, but unlike the young bullies, this enemy was not so easily cowed. He swatted at Daybe & continued running, closing in on Sham.

"Up!" shouted Sham. "Get away!" He flapped his arms & the bat rose.

Had it been decided on speed alone, Sham would have been in custody within seconds. But he felt possessed by the souls of generations of young people chased through neighbour-hoods by adults for reasons unclear or unfair. He channelled their techniques of righteous evasion. None-too-fast as he was, still he veered with the zigzags of justice, scrambled low walls with the vigour & rigour of unfairness-avoidance, reached a street still full of catcalls & the noise of late-afternoon commerce & traffic & rolled in the waning light below low-chassised vehicles with valorous discretion. To lie very still. He held his breath.

Daybe, he thought, ferociously attempting to project his mind, *stay away*.

Among the percussion of urban footfall, the disembodied

steps tramping by him, the grind of wheels & the curious noses of cats & dogs, Sham saw two black leather boots pound down the middle of the street. Stop. Turn. Run a few steps in this direction, a few in that, take off finally in a third. When they were out of sight, Sham burst out, wheezing, hauled himself out from under the cart.

Muddied, shaking & bloodied. He looked up, raised his arms, & here came Daybe, out of the sky & back into his shirt. Sham swayed. Stood mostly ignored by Manihiki locals, until he croaked a question to one of them, got directions back to the docks & skulked, by as roundabout routes as he could manage, back to the *Medes*.

THE WAY TO the docks took Sham under disorganised street-lamps, electricity, gas, glowing sepia. Through places where those lights were salvage from humanity's past, bright, historically misplaced colours; & even some alt-salvage, for show, turning footprint-like shapes, or unfolding swirls within containment fields.

His bruises were puffing up. A jollycart, its lamp swaying, shedding shadows as it rolled between snoozing trains, took him to the *Medes*.

"Late night, was it?" shouted Kiragabo. Sham cringed & stumbled over deck stuff.

"I'm late," he said. "Captain'll flay me."

"She will not. She's got other stuff on her mind."

& indeed, when he made his way belowdecks, he didn't just creep his way to Naphi's cabin to drop the texts into her lockbox, but was distracted by & went to investigate the noises he heard from the officers' mess. *Oohs, ahs, goshes* of impressedness.

The captain & her officers were crowded around something.

"Sham," someone said. "Get on in here, look at this." Even the captain beckoned him. The officers made space around the table. On which were artefacts.

Sham thought his appearance, the muck & fight-residue on him, would necessitate an explanation. But no one cared. Sham had never heard the captain so voluble. Clickety-glimmer went her arm, the lights on it, the tripping of her fingers faster than flesh fingers could go.

"& look, this. You see here." She was fiddling with a receiver. It winked & made henlike sounds. It showed lights in combinations. So she'd found the receiver-seller, then.

"Range of—well, miles, they tell me. Perhaps as many as a hundred. & it can pass through feet of earth."

"They go deeper'n that, Captain," someone said.

"Yes & they come up again. No one's suggested it'll take us to the moldywarpe's door, Mr. Quex. No one claims the receiver will let us in & make us tea. We will still have a job to do. You'll still be a hunter. We still even have to learn how to read this thing. But." She looked around. "Get this—" She held up a little transmitter. "Get this in its skin—it will change things."

Bozlateen Quex shifted his dandy clothes &, with Naphi's permission, picked up the receiver. It was cobbled together. More cobbled than together, really—a mess poised at the point of collapse. Made from arche-salvage & alt-salvage. It whispered like a live thing. Odd little circuit. Antiquity & alien expertise mashed into one ugly astonishing machinelette.

Sham moved for a better look. Quex twirled dials & the lights changed. Changed colour, position, velocity. Sham stopped moving a moment, then continued, & as he did so, so did those lights. Everyone looked at him. He blinked & moved again. The lights' shenanigans continued with his motion.

"What the hell?" said Quex. He prodded a button, the glow grew in his hand. The instrument was paying attention to Sham. Daybe poked its head up from his shirt.

"Ah. It's the animal," said the captain. "It has the thing still on its leg. This one is picking up something from that, some backwash signal. Quex, you'll have to adjust it. Make sure it's looking for these ones, instead." She shook her handful of receivers. As they rattled, the receiver barked like a duck & its light changed again.

"As I say," the captain said, "there is some learning to do. But still. This changes things, does it not? So so so." She rubbed her hands. She looked at Sham, the source of this idea, to seek out this mechanism. She did not smile—she was Captain Naphi!—but nod at him she did. Which was enough to fluster him. "Check what details we have, work out where last there was sign. Where we might find good molegrounds. That is where we're heading."

Chapter Thirty-Six

"I KNOW, but we can't just leave him," Dero said.

"We ain't just leaving him," Caldera said. "It ain't like we haven't got people coming to take care of him. You think I won't miss him too? You know he'd want us to go."

"I know, but *I* don't want us to go. Not with him here. He needs us."

The siblings Shroake had retired to another room to have this argument, but if they'd thought it removed them from Sham's earshot they were mistaken.

"Dero." Caldera's voice was subdued. "He'll forget we're gone."

"I know but then he'll remember & be sad again."

"& then forget again."

". . . I know."

When the Shroakes came out, into the corridor where he waited, Dero, red-eyed, stared at Sham as if in challenge. Caldera stood a fraction behind her brother, hand on his shoulder. They met Sham's gaze.

"He's why we haven't gone looking for them," Caldera said. "It's been a while. It's not like what you told us was a big surprise. But him."

"He's been waiting," her brother said.

"Byro's been waiting to hear," Caldera said. "That's what he's been writing. Letters to them. Are you a letter-writer, Sham?"

"Not as much as I should be. With Troose & Voam—" Sham stopped, aware, suddenly, of how long it had been since he'd sent them word. "Last night," Sham said. "When I was here before. When I came out, I saw something. Someone. Your house." He looked grim. "It's being *watched*." The Shroakes stared at him.

"Well, yeah," said Dero. He shrugged.

"Oh," said Sham. "Well. As long as you know."

"Of course," said Caldera.

"Well, obviously of course," Sham said. "But, you know, I just wanted to make sure. So, why? Why is it of course?"

"Why's it watched?" said Caldera.

"'Cause we're the *Shroakes*," said Dero. He jerked his right thumb at himself as he made the announcement, used his left one to snap his braces. Raised one eyebrow. Sham could not help laughing. Even Dero, after a moment of glowering, laughed a bit, too.

"They were sort of salvors, like I said," Caldera told Sham. "& sort of makers. & investigators. They went places & did things this lot would love to be able to do. They want to know where they went, & why."

"Who does?" Sham said. "Which lot? Manihiki?"

"Manihiki," said Caldera. "So of course, when they didn't come back, Byro couldn't go to the navy. Search & rescue ain't their priority. Oh, they came offering to *search*, asking what maps we had, where they'd been going."

"As if we'd tell *them*," Dero said. "As if we knew."

"They didn't keep logs of their route on the train," Caldera said. "That's why they hid that memory. Even wounded, one of them made sure to bury it in the ground. They must've realised there were hints on it about where they'd been."

"They took windabout ways where they were going & windabout back again," Dero said.

"Dad Byro might have been getting a little . . ." Caldera's voice petered out & picked up again. "But he wasn't so gone as to trust the navy. Nor tell them what he knew of the route."

"So there *was* a chart?" Sham said.

"Not on the train. & none that you or they could read. Manihiki wanted to find them, but for their reasons, not ours. The Shroakes never gave them what they wanted." She sounded proud. "All manner of engines & machines made that no one else could make. What they wanted wasn't Mum & Other Dad back—it was whatever they might have with them. What they might have made or found."

"They'll have been looking for them for ages," Dero said. "Since they were gone."

"But now you're here," Caldera said, "they'll be whispering for the first time in years, 'We have a lead!'"

"They had me hiding in a gutter," Sham said. "Takes more than a bit of whatever-they-are to get hold of a Streggeye boy."

"Wanted to know who you are," Caldera said. "& what you know. About where the *Shroakes* are." Sham remembered the caution with which Caldera & Dero had greeted him, when first he had arrived. No wonder they had been suspicious. No wonder they had no friends: even had they not been looking so carefully after Dad Byro, & pining for the return of their other parents, they had to assume everyone who visited was a potential spy.

"Till you came," Dero mumbled to Sham, "I still always thought they might come back."

"It was the longest time they'd been away, but you don't stop wondering," Caldera said. She inclined her head in the direction of the room where Dad Byro confusedly grieved. "& how could we leave him when we weren't sure? Go off in one direction, have them come back in the other?"

"We're sure now though?" Dero said. It sounded like a statement until the very end, when it tweaked suddenly up into a question, a moment's hope for uncertainty, that twanged on Sham's heart.

"We're sure now," Caldera gently said. "So we have to do right by them. Finish what they started. It's what Mum & Other Dad would've wanted. & it's what he'd want too." She looked at the door again.

"Maybe," Dero said.

"He might be writing to them again," Caldera said.

"If he's going to forget," Sham asked, "why did you tell him they were gone?"

"Well he loves them, don't he?" Caldera said. She led him to the kitchen, brought Sham a cup of some oily-looking tea. "Doesn't he deserve to mourn?"

Sham stirred the drink dubiously. "Whenever I mention this place to anyone," he said, "I get looks. It's obvious people talk about your family. & I saw the wreck. I ain't never seen a train like that. & then there's that picture." He looked up at her. "Will you tell me? What were they doing? Do you know?"

"Do we know what they'd been up to?" said Caldera. "Where they were going, & why? Oh, yes."

"We do," said Dero.

"But then, you do too," Caldera said. She glanced at her brother. After a second, he shrugged. "It's not very complicated," Caldera said. "Like you say, you've seen the picture."

"They were looking for something," Sham said.

"Found," said Caldera, after a moment. "They were looking

for something & they *found* something. Which was . . . ?" She waited like a schoolteacher.

"A way out of the railsea," Sham said at last. "Something beyond the rails."

Well of *course*. Sham had seen that one line. So he had sort of known that. Still, to hear it! He had a delight in the blasphemy. Spouting heresy, it turned out, was invigorating as well as nerve-wracking.

"There *is* nothing beyond the rails," he squawked. Annoyed by his own voice.

"Looks like we've got work to do, Dero," Caldera said. An edge of seriousness, an effort, had come into her voice. When her brother spoke, it was in his, too.

"There's some stuff in Dad Byro's room," Dero said. "I'll bring it down when I get him his supper."

"There *is* nothing beyond the rails," Sham said again.

"Can we seriously leave him?" Dero said. He glanced back at the door where their remaining father waited.

"We aren't going to leave him," Caldera said gently. "You know that. We'll take care of him." She came closer to Dero. "All that we've been putting away for the nurses—you know they'll look after him. You know if he could he'd go himself. He can't. But we can. For him. For all of us."

"I know," Dero said. He shook his head.

Sham started to give it one more try. "There *is* . . ."

"Oh, will you stop it?" Caldera said to him. "Obviously there is. You saw the picture."

"But everybody knows—," Sham said, then stopped. He exhaled. "Alright," he said. There were no certainties. He itemised what he knew. "No one knows where the railsea came from."

"Well, no one *knows*," Caldera said, "but they've got a sense of the possibilities. What do they say where you come from? Streggeye, you said? What do you think? Were the rails put down by gods?" Her questions came faster. Were they extruded from the ground? Were they writing in heavenly script, that people unknowingly recited as they travelled? Were the rails produced by as-yet-not-understood natural processes? Some radicals said there were no gods at all. Were the rails spit up by the interactions of rock, heat, cold, pressure & dirt? Did humans, big-brained monkeys, think up ways to use them when the rails emerged, to stay safe from the deadly dirt? Was that how trains got thought up? Was the world an infinity of rails down as well as around, seams of them through layers of earth & salvage, down to the core? Down to hell? Sometimes storms gusted off topsoil & uncovered iron below. The most excavation-gung-ho salvors claimed to have found some tracks yards underground. What about Heaven? What was in Heaven? Where was it?

"I think—what we were told—you know," said Sham. He tutted at his own incoherence. "It all comes from That Apt Ohm."

"Ah, right," Caldera said. Of all the gods worshipped, feared, scorned, placated & bickered with, his influence was the most widespread. Great chimney-headed controller in dark robes. He protected & controlled the railsea, its nations, its passengers. "There might have been one some time," Caldera said. "Years & years ago. A boss. Where do they go? The rails? What's at the edge of the railsea?"

Sham twisted in discomfort.

"Sham," Caldera said. "What's the upsky? Don't say it's where the gods put poison. Where do the rails come from? What's the godsquabble?"

"It's when at the start of the world all the gods were fighting to make the earth, & That Apt Ohm was the strongest, & in their fighting the railsea rose out of the earth. "

"It was a fight between different railroad companies," Caldera said.

Sham had heard that theory too, he conceded, nervously.

"It was after everything went bad, & they were trying to make money again. With public works. People paid for passage, & rulers paid for every mile of build. So it went crazy. They were competing, all putting down new routes all over the place. Ruthless, because the more they built the more they made.

"They burnt off years of noxious stuff—that's where the upsky comes from—& ended up chugging stuff into the ground, too, changing things. They could jury-rig the whole world. It was a company war. They laid traps for each other's trains, so there's trap-switches, trap-lines, out there.

"They made the lines," Caldera said. "They destroyed each other. But they couldn't stave off ruin. & all they left were the rails. We live in the aftermath of business bickering." She smiled.

"Our mum & dad were looking for something," Dero said. "They knew the history. Stories about dead treasure, history, angels, a vale of tears."

"I've heard all that!" Sham said. "'The ghost of all the riches ever born & yet unborn live in Heaven'!" He recited words from old stories. "'Oh, shun the vale of tears!' You telling me they was chasing myths?"

"What if it isn't?" said Caldera. "Heaven might not be what everyone thinks it is, but that don't mean it's a myth. It don't mean the ghosts of all the riches *ain't* there, either."

With an abrupt digital blare, one of the wall clocks demanded Sham's attention. *Not now!* he thought. He wanted to hear these salvage stories, to rummage through this house.

"I . . . have to go," he said. "Got to meet someone."

"That's a shame," said Dero, politely. "We have to go, too."

"What? Where? When?"

"Not quite now," Caldera said. She closed her eyes.

"Soon though," Dero said.

"Not quite now," Caldera said. "But now we know what happened, now you told us, we have a job to finish. Don't look surprised, Sham. You heard what we been saying. You knew we'd have to. I think that's why you came to show us the picture.

"You didn't think we'd leave Mum & Dad's work unfinished, did you?"

Chapter Thirty-Seven

THE DUSTMAID WAS as crowded as most dockside drinkeries, loud with the electronic chirps of games. Sham watched the salvors gathered by the bar. They weren't wearing their salvaging clothes, but even their downtime outfits marked them out— reconstructed finery from ages of high fashion up to which humanity had long since failed to live. He got close enough to hear them spouting their Salvage Slang—they called each other *Fren & Bluv*, they talked about *Diggiters & Spinecandy & Noshells*. Sham mouthed the words.

"So," Robalson said. "Your captain like her books, then?" He swigged from the drink Sham had bought him. It was called Trainoil—a concoction of sweet whiskey & stout & molasses that was simultaneously disgusting & rather nice.

"Yeah," Sham said. "Thanks again for, you know, yesterday."

"So, what's your story, Sham? How long you been at rail?"

"This is my second trip."

"There you go, then. People like that, they can sniff noobs. I don't mean no offence, it's just how it is."

"So," said Sham. "Are any of your crew here?"

"This ain't the sort of place they drink."

"They go to special pirate bars?"

"Yeah," said Robalson at last. He said it quite deadpan. Raised an eyebrow. "Special pirate bars."

*

MUCH LATER THAN he had intended, when the frenetic drumming of the song "Jump Up All You Train Ruffians" came on the jukebox, Sham shouted with pleasure & joined in the rumbustious chorus. Robalson sang too. Other customers watched them with combined disapproval & amusement.

"Disapprovesalment," Robalson suggested, when Sham pointed this out.

"Amduseapproval," said Sham.

"Sham," Robalson said. "If you keep up like this you'll get us kicked out. What is it with those salvors, anyway? Ever since you come in you been eyeing them like they're worm meat & you're a badger."

"I just, you know," Sham said. He wriggled in his chair. "The way they dress, the way they talk. What they do. It's— Well, it's cool, ain't it? I wish . . ."

"You was talking to one in that hall, weren't you? That woman."

"Yeah. Something Sirocco. She was lovely. Bought me a cake." Sham grinned.

"Don't you think," Robalson said, "there's someone out there on the railsea on a salvagetrain, & all the time when they pass moletrains they're like, 'They do such more exciting stuff than me.'"

"Don't know," Sham said.

"They're like, 'Oh, imagine being a doctor's assistant on that train.'"

"Give me their address, I'll call them to swap."

"Plus, didn't I hear that your captain has a philosophy?" Robalson said.

"So?"

"So ain't that something to aspire to? I bet salvors are probably a boring bunch."

A man & a woman in the corner of the bar were watching the two young men. Sham eyed them. Not salvors, he thought. They saw him see them, looked away. His whole body froze up, stiff with a sudden memory of hiding under the cart.

"I met a couple of people who I think might be," he said. "Salvors. *Sort of* salvors." He narrowed his eyes. "They weren't boring. Believe me. A brother & sister."

"Oh, that rings a trainbell," Robalson said. "The Shoots? The Shrikes? Soaks?"

"How d'you know?"

Robalson shrugged. "I listen to stories. There's enough of them about. There's one about an oddball brother & sister heading out on some hunt to the land of bleeding Green Cheese or whatever, Engineday next. Whispers are that someone wants after them. On the lookout for imaginary treasure."

Sham had crept away from the Shroakes, this time, by routes they had suggested, that took him away & back into the town without drawing the attention of the watchers that were undoubtedly there. He blinked at what Robalson was saying. Robalson himself seemed uninterested in the rumours of state attention he was, unthinkingly, recounting.

"I just don't see it," he said. "About you, I mean. You *think* you want to be a salvor, but I'm not even sure you do."

"Funny," said Sham. "That's what they said. & what about you, then? What do you even do, Robalson?"

"What do I do? Depends on the day. Some days I wash decks. Some days I clean the heads & oh my oily hell I'd rather get smacked into the godsquabble. Some days I do better things.

Know what I saw today? Something from the upsky fell, about a month ago. Onto a beach in the north. They keep it in a jar, charge a few coppers to see it."

"It's alive?"

"Sham. It fell out of the upsky. No it's not alive. But they keep it in vinegar or something."

"But anyway you know that ain't what I meant," Sham said. "Which is your train?"

"Oh," said Robalson. "Never you mind."

"Yeah," Sham said. "Whatever." Fine. Let him play his mystery-boy games. "The upsky," Sham said distractedly. "The grundnorm. The horizon. All these edges. What stories d'you know about, y'know, the edge of the whole world?"

Robalson blinked. "Stories?" he said. "You mean, like, Heaven? Same as you, probably. Why?"

"Wouldn't you like to know if they was true?" Sham said, with sudden fervour, an intensity that took him quite by surprise.

"Not really," said Robalson. "For a start, they ain't, they're just stories. For a second, if they *are* true, some of them you don't want to be. What if it's true that you *should* shun it? What is it they say's there? A universe of sobbing, is it? Or, a crying treasure?" He shook his head. "It don't have to make much sense to know it ain't good. Angry ghosts? Crying forever?"

Chapter Thirty-Eight

THE OWNERS OF the *Medes* wanted the coin & credit that molemeat & fur & oils would bring. They didn't care whether or not Naphi caught this, that, or the other particular mole. Except just perhaps that certain events would mean an increase in the power of her name, & that kind of brand recognition might mean income for them.

They were passing rare, captains who not only had their ultimate quarries, their nemeses, but who actually snared them. Like all Streggeye youth, Sham had been to the Museum of Completion, seen the famous flatographs of women & men standing on the mountainous carcases of philosophies: Haberstam on his beetle; ap Mograve on her mole; Ptarmeen on the sinuous mutant badger Brock the Nihil, beaming like a schoolchild with his dead nothing-symbol under his foot.

The *Medes* crew had three days to turn a middling moletrain into a travelling fortress of philosophy-hunting. Hammers hammered, spanners spanned. The trainsfolk ran tests on the engines & the backup engines. Sharpened harpoons, stocked up on gunpowder. They patched up leaks in the cladding. The *Medes* hadn't looked so good for years. It hadn't looked this good when it was first made.

"You know what the stakes of this are," Naphi said. She wasn't much of a one for speechifying, but she couldn't not. As her officers had told her, the crew needed to hear something. "We may be at railsea a long time," the captain said,

167

voice cracking through the tubes. "Months. Years. This hunt will take us far. I am prepared. Will you come with me?" *Ooh, nice touch*, Sham thought.

"There are no trainspeople I'd rather have with me. We hunt for the glory of Streggeye, for the owners of this fine train." A few knowing smirks at that. "For knowledge. & if you will, you hunt for me. & I won't forget it. We go south—& then we go where knowledge takes us. Gentlemen & ladies of the rails— shall we?"

The crew cheered. They raised raucous support for the hunt, for the end of the uncertainty. "For the captain's philosophy!" The shout was taken up across the decks, from every carriage of the train. *Really?* Sham thought.

"Sham," said Dr. Fremlo as the crew went to their tasks. "The harbourmaster delivered this." The doctor handed over a sealed letter, at which Sham stared in consternation. He muttered thanks—not every crewmember would have handed it over, certainly not so honourably refusing to read it first. *Sam Saroop*, the letter said. Close enough, he supposed. Honourable or not, the doctor was not uncurious, & waited while Sham split the seal.

SPECIAL OFFER! Sham read. TO THE VISITOR TO THE SHROAKES. GOOD RATES PAID FOR INFORMATION ABOUT THEIR PLANS! VISIT HARBOURMASTER TO FIND OUT MORE. ACT NOW TO RECEIVE FREE GIFTS!

"What is it?" Dr. Fremlo said, as Sham scrunched the paper up & curled his lip.

"Nothing," Sham said. "Junk mail. Rubbish."

"I DON'T KNOW what's wrong with me," Sham said, "that I just don't feel it." He'd been telling the Shroakes of Naphi's rhetoric, her galvanising the crew.

Caldera shrugged. "Neither do I," she said. "But maybe you're lucky."

"Lucky?"

"Not to want to throw your hat in the air." Caldera was counting what looked like pins or screws or something on the kitchen table. Dero was packing tins into suitcases.

Sham was getting better at sneaking away from the *Medes*. When he had turned up at the Shroake house, the siblings had greeted him without surprise.

"Come in." Caldera smiled. "We're just at the end of lessons."

"Lessons" turned out to be Dero & Caldera sitting opposite each other in the library, amid a scree of books, ordinator tablets & printouts. On the shelves around them were as many bones & bizarreries as books. Dero was sorting & stashing the materials of learning, according to some incomprehensible system. "What are your lessons like in Streggeye?" Caldera said. "What's your school like?" She blinked under Sham's gaze. "Don't know that many people your age here, let alone elsewhere," she said. "I'm curious." Was she blushing? Well, no. But she was a bit bashful.

"We went to Streggeye," Dero said. "Didn't we?"

"Oh, they took us all over," said Caldera. "But I can't remember. I can't say we *know* anywhere."

So Sham told her a little about Streggeye Land. He was blushing, even if she was not. He stumblingly turned an anecdote or two from his quite ordinary childhood into stories of an exotic land, while Dero finished putting away the bits & pieces.

Sham continued, & Caldera listened without looking at him, & Dero left the room. Sham heard the door to Byro's room open & close. & he kept talking, & after a minute it opened again, & Dero returned. His face was set & his eyes red. Dero stood between Sham & Caldera. Sham's stories faltered at last. The young man from Streggeye & the quasi-salvors' daughter turned away from each other.

"My turn," said Caldera, & slipped out of the room.

"Turn for what?" said Sham. He did not expect Dero to explain, & Dero did not. He just stood with his lip out as if ready for a fight, in increasingly lengthy & uncomfortable silence, until Caldera came back. She carried a picture of Dad Byro, a scarf, a battered old foldable ordinator from his desk.

Her face was as stricken as her brother's, but when she spoke, she made her voice sound normal. "Where's your bat?" she said.

"Hunting somewhere." Sham steepled his fingers thoughtfully. "Someone sent me a message," he said. "Offering me stuff if I'd tell things about you."

"What did you say?" Caldera said.

"What do you think? I threw it away. & I came here the back ways you told me. But seems like there's more & more rumours about you. & I know there's rumours about the *Medes*."

Caldera put a fingertip thoughtfully to her lips. "There are lots of rumours about your train, yes," she said. "Rails & rumours. How you got here, where you're going, what you've found on the way."

"I been asking people what they think of when they hear about this end-of-the-world stuff," Sham said, "& I have to tell you, it don't sound pretty."

"Are you coming with us, Sham ap Soorap?" Dero said.

"Wh-What?" Sham said.

"Not now, Dero," Caldera said.

"Wait, what does he mean?" Sham said.

"Not now," Caldera said again. "What is it you were saying about your captain's speech, Sham?"

"Oh, well. Just that it didn't . . . work on me. I really don't think I want to get on another moletrain." Sham looked around the house, at all the salvage.

"There are people," Caldera said, "who say all of us have a Task—they'd say it like that, they wouldn't say *task*, they'd say *Task*—& you'll know what it is when you hear it. That it's out there, waiting for you."

"Maybe," Sham said thoughtfully.

"I think that's rubbish myself," Caldera said. Dero giggled. Sham blinked.

"So *none* of us have tasks," Sham said.

"I didn't say that. Did I say that? I said maybe *you* don't have a task. My task right now is to carry stuff." She lifted various bits of luggage. "No, Dero, your task right now is to stay here & sort through this all. What do you think yours is, Sham?"

Dero tutted & grumbled as Sham followed Caldera, past boxes tied with string & strapped into place, past trunks distended from within like glutted snakes, out into the drossland garden. In sight of the landmark white metal arch, she placed a key in a coffee tin, under a polished tortoise-shell, under a bucket.

"I'm glad it was so important to you to find us & tell us," Caldera said. "What was it happened to *your* parents?"

Sham looked up at her. "What?" he said. "Why?" She looked at him until he slumped. Sham pushed after her through the salvagey garden, & muttered a brief version of the story of his father's disappearance & mother's grief. "Voam & Troose look after me, though," he said.

"I believe you," Caldera said.

"They're well pleased I got to work on a moler," he said. "Get to see the world."

"Some of it," she said. "I knew what you were going to tell us the moment I opened the door, you know. I mean about our parents. & I hadn't known until then how much I'd been waiting. I wish someone could've found your dad's wreck. Or where your mum is. Told you. Done that for you, like you done for us."

She smiled at him. Very quickly & kindly. It was gone almost immediately. Caldera held ragged weed aside for him. "The world's fine," she said. "But you got to wonder what comes after it."

They were, Sham realised with a start, on the shore. The earth a few yards off became flat & dusty & abruptly less fertile, crammed with intertwined rails. A wooden walkway extended some yards over the rails, at its end a jollycart. Big slabby rock teeth shielded the garden from sight.

"You have a private beach?" Sham said.

Caldera walked onto the jetty. The slats were old, & through their gaps Sham could see paint flakes falling onto earth churned by ferocious little mammals.

"Out there," she said, "there's so many things. There are people miles out who roll with the wind, you know, on trains that ain't changed for centuries. Our parents found their hunt-grounds, & found them. They went with them, learned from them. How to travel without engines. All their stories about the railsea & heaven & how to get there & the weeping. Everything. Everyone knows something worth learning."

"Not everyone," Sham said.

"Alright, not everyone. Most people, though."

Clouds momentarily parted, & Sham glimpsed the yellow upsky. He heard a plane.

"Do you believe there's all them riches?" Sham said. "Is that what you're looking for?"

Caldera shrugged. "I don't know if I believe it or not. But it ain't why we're going."

"You're *exploring*," said Sham. "You just want to know."

She nodded. "We were waiting for them," she said. "& as much as you could, you brought them back. What else would we do but go where they went? & it ain't just duty. I promise you that. You showed me a picture. Well, I'll show you a picture back."

Caldera took a print from her pocket. Rock weathered into snarls, hillocks supporting scraggy hardland animals, cactus & ivy. Railsea miles. & a staircase.

A staircase. It emerged from the ground, as high as a house, jutting at 45 degrees, ending in the air. A salvage overhang! Sham stared.

"It's an escalator," Caldera said. "Way out there." She pointed to railsea. Below the apex of the stairs' rise was a cone of dirt & rubbish. What fell from it was not even salvage, but true useless rubbish, rejectamenta beyond reclamation, hauled up out of the innards of the world.

Chapter Thirty-Nine

"Oh my Stoneface," Sham said. "Where is that?"

Caldera glanced back at the house. "Dero'll be going spare, me leaving him there like that. I just needed a moment." She looked at Sham. "Just listen. Let me tell you about what's under there." She cleared her throat. Caldera told him:

The stairs keep grinding. They move up, all the time. So when you land on them—& the rails don't go that close, you have to jump!—you have to race down against the motion so the old escalator powered by who knows what current down there doesn't deposit you with the garbage—

"How do you know?" Sham said. Caldera blinked.

"They took me once," she said. "My parents. They were changing their plans. They knew how to use salvage, they just . . . took me there when they didn't love doing it any more. To tell me why. Shhh."

Caldera continued:

—with the garbage.

So down you run against it carrying your pack, down the metal stairs, into the darkness under the railsea. I know what you're thinking: that's where the animals live, & why would you ever do that? But mostly they don't come into these tunnels &

no I don't know why. So don't think about burrowing predators, toxic earth, rockfalls, grizzly chthonic deaths.

There are electric lights down there. In the salvage mine.

Don't think about burrowers. Don't think about seeing a bulge in that garbage wall, as you walk hunched to get under the beams of the supports, past the trolleys & wagons & discarded tools; don't think about that bulge roaring into a split into the shadows under the world & onto a snuffling, blind, toothed face.

Just look at this passage. Between layers of pressure-hardened earth & shaley rock, an archaeology of discards, centuries layered. Extruded edges of junk, shards, glass, bits & pieces, faint stretching fronds of ripped-up plastic bags. A greening layer: tiny cogs from a clockwork epoch; crushed plastic; the scintilla from an era of glass; rag-seams of degraded video tape; a gallimaufryan coagulum of mixed-up oddness.

There are places where the pressures of ages & the jostling of continents against each other like slow uncomfortable bed-fellows shoves such motherlodes airward, & the railsea is broken by the dangerous jags of salvage reefs, full of trash treasure. & there are these tunnels. Just like there are tunnels where trains can go. You know there are.

What the scholars want to do is work out what these things *were*. Salvors want to know what they were if & only if it helps sell them. & if it doesn't, they don't care. People who want to use them want to know what they were if it means they can be used. Although they'll work out something to do with them one way or another. They'll take some reclaimed thing & hit nails with it & call it a hammer if it comes to that.

*

"What's wrong with doing that?" Sham said.

"Wrong?"

There's nothing wrong with that. There isn't anything right with it either. There's only one thing that everyone agrees on about salvage. Whether you're digging it out of the ground or selling it or buying it, or studying it, or bribing someone with it, or wearing it, or looking for it, it catches the eye. Like foil for magpies.

Salvors don't *have* to dress like they do. They want to. Those are their peacock feathers. That's the one thing you can always say for salvage. It looks cool.

& really, who cares?

Who cares? Say you're a salvor, or a pair of salvors, who doesn't or don't love salvage any more. Maybe you don't have to cast about to find out what it is you want instead. It's enough, maybe, to know you don't want what you thought you did. That's enough to be getting on with.

"The question is," said Caldera, "this—" She shook the picture. "—the stuff you want to chase? Buried rubbish? Maybe there's something better than that. Or maybe there's something just else. Think about it. You've got an hour or two."

"Till what?" Sham said. "What happens then?"

"Then we go. So by then you have to decide if you're coming with us."

Chapter Forty

DAYBE FELL FROM NOWHERE onto Sham's shoulder. Caldera jumped. Sham didn't even glance at the animal, humming & whickering in his ear.

"The key you left," he said.

"For the nurses," Caldera said. She headed back for the house. "They're good people. We looked a long time. There's money. Dad Byro'll be taken to the sanatorium." She closed her eyes. "Because we've got stuff to do. So."

"You don't even know where they went!"

"Byro did," she said. "However confused he got, that he never told. We have his machine. It's got secrets. & there's what you told us."

The Shroakes bustled from room to salvage-filled room, from room to open-to-the-sky-&-wall-less room, from room to whirring-clockwork-&-diesel-instrument-mazed room. They gathered things, pulled them on carts, lined them up in the kitchen. They pulled clothes from closets, tugged them to test for strength, fingered them to test for warmth, sniffed them to test for mildew.

"But wait," Sham said. "I heard, someone told me, you're going on *Engineday*. That's not for ages!"

"That worked, then," Dero said.

"Engineday," said Caldera, "is when we *put it about* that we'd be going. Should give us a little while before anyone thinks to look, or comes after us."

"Comes after you?" Sham said. "You really think . . . ?"

"Indubitably," Dero said.

"Yes," Caldera said. "They will. Too many rumours about what our parents were looking for." She rubbed her finger & thumb in a money motion.

"You said that weren't it," said Sham.

"It weren't it. But rumours don't care what was it or not. So—" She put her finger to her lips.

Sham's mind was going like train wheels at their fastest. "Why do you want to go?" he said.

"Don't you?" Caldera said.

"I don't know!" Exploring. Finding something new. All that way. "But what about my, my family," Sham said, then stopped. Hold on. Would Troose & Voam mind if he went?

Yes, they would mind. But not as much as if he were a miserable bad doctor for years.

"I think," Sham said slowly, trying to think it through, "they wanted me to do well, maybe even get my own philosophy."

"I thought it was just captains did that," Dero said.

"You could be a captain from being a doctor. Although I don't know if they thought it through that much." What Troose & Voam knew well was that he'd had a space to be filled, Sham thought with a little ache for them.

"Dero," said Caldera. "Go get it. Do you want to philosophise?" she said to Sham when her brother left. "Get obsessed with an animal? Give it a meaning? Make that your life?" There was nothing snide in her tone. She staggered under the load she carried. "There are places," she said, "where rails go up off the beach into uplands."

"Railrivers, yeah," he said.

"Yes. Some go up the mountains. Right into the uplands."

"& loop down again somewhere else. They all merge back into the railsea."

"Some of them go into old dead cities up there."

"& out again," Sham said. Caldera looked at him.

'This is heavy," she said. Her burden, not the story. Sham took it from her, carried it to the jetty. Where he stopped, & stared.

Something was approaching from between knolls in the railsea. The earth around it breaking with curious moles' snouts. Here came Dero, in—well. In a train.

The engine was a snubby, tough-looking thing with a few small carriages behind it. There were glass portholes in its flanks. Daybe raced through the intervening air to investigate. The engine was armoured & chimneyless. There was no telltale exhaust at all, that Sham could see or smell. & these were not electrified rails. "How does it run?" he whispered.

Dero leaned out of the oncoming vehicle. He looked up at Daybe, who dipped in his turning & angled his wings. "Caldera," Dero shouted.

She stood by Sham. "We're off, then," she said to him. She looked through gaps in the surrounding rocks, into the railsea. A complicated tangle of gauges, here, a tricksy piece of switching, there. "So. Would you like to come, Sham?"

& Daybe cawed, an uncharacteristic crowlike sound, just as if it had heard the idea & got excited. & Dero shouted, "Caldera, come *on*."

"What if it's terrible?" Sham blurted out. "What if it all ends in tears? It ain't like there's no warning. You were the one reminded me we're supposed to shun it!"

Caldera did not reply. She & her brother turned, in the

same moment, & stared at the house. Sham knew they were thinking of Dad Byro. Tears came up in Caldera's eyes. They stayed there a moment. Then, without a word, she pushed them down again.

Sham could be with them. & while he wouldn't be a salvor, nor would he be a train doctor nor a moler either. He'd be something else.

But he wasn't saying anything, & then it was a moment later & still he wasn't saying anything. He heard himself saying nothing. Caldera looked at him, a long, a *long* moment. Then at last gave a sad shrug. The train approached. The switches on its route switched. Caldera turned away from Sham towards it.

The train accelerated faster than Sham would have imagined. It turned more tightly too. He, contrariwise, was still.

"Wait," he shouted. He ran at last forward. But he was slow, & the train was fast, & here it was at the jetty's end, opening a door, & Caldera was jumping on & getting in, not looking at him, determinedly not looking at him, & the train was moving again. How did that happen so quick? What crazy cutting-edge & salvage-cobbled equipment were they driving?

"Wait!" Sham shouted again, reaching the edge of the wood, jumping in the glints off the tracks below, but time had moved on & the Shroakes were receding.

Sham sat. Just collapsed on his bum. Watched the rear end of a train move at an amazing rate.

The light was going. When the sun went down it went down fast. As if giving up all the effort with a flop of relief. The Shroakes' train was away in the dusk.

Leaving Sham to pick himself up when all sight of it was gone. He looked into the shallow coastal rails. Made his way through the garden, past the house, under the washing-machine arch, back into bloody Manihiki. Where his moletrain waited.

Stupid, useless. That's what he kept saying to himself, all the way.

Chapter Forty-One

ROBALSON WAS IN the pub again. "What got hold of you?" he said, at the sight of Sham's face.

"I'm stupid & useless."

"Blimey," Robalson said.

"You know I said I was going to see some people? Well, they gave me the chance to go somewhere with them. They wanted me to go with them, I think. One of them. & I wanted to go with her. But I bottled it. & I don't even know why! I think I did want to go. But I can't have done, can I?"

"Who were they?"

"Just a family. I found something of theirs. A sort of a treasure map. Sort of. & they've gone off to find out if it's right."

"This is them Soaks. & you didn't go?"

"I didn't. Because I'm stupid . . ."

"Whoa, hush. Look. Tell me about it. I don't think you're stupid or useless. You're no one's fool, Sham."

Nice to have someone think so. It was a scrappy version of the story that Sham told. He rambled about the wreck, spoke in vague terms of "evidence", of "something", of a secret that the poor dead prospectors appeared to have managed to keep, that the Shroakes had the right to know.

Robalson was rapt. "I heard Engineday they was going!" he said.

"That was . . . disinformation."

"No!" Robalson said at last. He looked thoughtful. He looked grim. "I think I understand. The rumours are right!"

"Eh? What rumours?"

"The rumours about you."

"What?" breathed Sham. "What are you talking about?"

"You made the right decision not to go, Sham." Robalson spoke tensely. "I have to tell you something." He was glancing side to side.

"What is this? What do you mean?"

"Come outside," Robalson said. "I'll explain. Wait. Don't make it look like we're going together. You've got to be careful." He was not looking at Sham as he spoke. "Outside, left, there's a little alley. I'll go first. Five minutes, follow me. & Sham— don't let anyone see you leave."

& he was gone, & Sham was bewildered & not unafraid. He waited. He swallowed. He felt his blood rush. At last—head whizzing & not from booze—he stood. Was he watched? He glanced at the drinkers in the dim light. He had no idea.

Into the grey of local streetlamps, the Manihiki night. He crept round into shadows. Daybe came out of the sky & landed on him. He nuzzled it. There was Robalson, slouched by the wall, waiting by a trash bin.

"You got your bat with you?" he whispered nervously.

"What's the big secret?" Sham whispered.

"The big secret." Robalson nodded. "You remember when you asked me what my train was? Asked me what I did?"

Sham shivered. "Yeah," he said. "You said you was—well, you made a joke."

"Yeah. You remember. The secret's this." Robalson leaned closer. "I wasn't lying. I *am* a pirate."

& Sham discovered—as he was grabbed roughly from

behind & gripped so he couldn't move, as his unseen assailant shoved a fumey cloth up against his mouth & nose so great gusts of bleach-&-menthol-smelling stuff went into his lungs & made his head corkscrew into dark, as he heard Daybe shriek a bat shriek—Sham discovered that he wasn't really surprised to hear it.

Part Four

Antlion
Myrmeleon deinos

Chapter Forty-Two

WHAT CAN WE get on with while our consciousness rests? A researcher into the mind, a psychonomer, a thought-mapper, might claim this is a meaningless question: that we are nothing without our consciousness. When it rests, so do we.

Conversely, others might see this as a kind of paradox that gives rise to critical thought, to mental innovation. Provocations do not have to be sensible to help our minds rise to an occasion. What if ridiculous questions are an indispensable philosophical tool?

Our minds we salvage from history's rubbish, & they are machines to make chaos into story. This is the story of a bloodstained boy. It is his mind that renders it down. But in such rendering we might defy paradox, perform the cheeky escapology of narrative, & thus the resting of that crucial particular consciousness might not detain us. Asked: *What should the story do when the primary window through which we view it is shuttered?* we might say: *It should look through another window.*

That is to say, follow other rails, see through other eyes.

Chapter Forty-Three

LATE EVENING, into the gloaming, through its descent into night & that night itself, the Shroakes' train went. It went untroubled by the darkest of the darkness.

The Shroakes checked expensive maps, used their fine & cutting-edge sensors, which surrounded the vehicle in a fringe of sensitivity. In those lines close enough to shore that Manihiki's government claimed them as their own, the Shroake train, as much as any train could ever be said to, crept. It whispered along unlit.

The Shroakes wore their best clothes. Though the day was a secret, & though they had packed almost nothing but rugged, ugly items chosen for practicalities, each had made one outfit's-worth of an exception. A few miles beyond the shoreline of Manihiki, where their journey could be said to have started for real, they had changed.

Dero wore a fancy lapelled suit in blue cotton, only very slightly too small for him, & had parted his disobedient hair in the middle. Caldera wore loose burgundy trousers & a froufrou shirt that made her brother raise his eyebrows, & that she was not wildly fond of herself, but that was without question her smartest thing. She & Dero stared at each other with their identically brown eyes.

"There," Dero said. It was a formal occasion, this, they had decided.

In the distance, the lighthouse of the main harbour shone,

its beam rotating, a sweep of glimmering across the miles as the illumination touched thousands of rails in its passing. The train's engines & equipment, its charts & intentions, were matters of interest, its passengers knew, to the government. So they rode darkly, days before they had claimed, to escape attention.

Eventually, beyond their nation's immediate purview, they kicked up the levels of their strange engine, accelerated, & turned on their lamps. From its front the locomotive was a light-cyclops, its blasting ivory beam flooding the iron tangle before it, sending startled burrowing beasts out of its way. The train went east, north, east, north, north, north. Whole generations, whole civilisations of moths hurtled at this luminously exciting thing &—so cruel a fixation!—were swiftly splatted on the light they loved.

If any had made it past that unforgiving glow, entered, what would they have seen? The foremost carriage shared something of the character of the Shroake house. More compact & cleaner, but its bunks, chairs, table, desk, discreet commode were, too, hemmed in by paperwork, books, tools & salvage.

In the uppermost bunk slept Dero, swaying with the vehicle's motion. He woke occasionally & abruptly—such had been the shape of his sleep a long time, since two-thirds of his parents had disappeared. When wake he did, he would sit up & stare, as if through the metal ceiling, as if he were the train's eyes. His gaze was the same as the one his mother had had when she grew tired of salvage, of piecing together & making things, & had looked, instead, beyond. Dero was too young to remember his inherited expression on she who had bequeathed it to him, but when his sister saw it on his face, she gasped, because she was not.

Caldera, tired but wired, watched the screens her mother & fathers had taught her to read. Prodded the controls they had taught her to control. She sat in the middle of a nest of avant-garde tech & salvage combined. A tweak of a mechanism & her chair went roofward, so she could peer through a high ribbon of window; then she took it back down to pore over various camera-feeds on screens around her.

Over the *raskaba* of the wheels & the whooshing of the fusion engine, Caldera hummed. Did she stare with the same hankering for distance & something-or-other as did her brother & as had her mother? Perhaps. Something like that.

She thought about Sham, with gratitude for his information, for the picture that he had shown them. She tapped keys on Dad Byro's ordinator. Extracted information. Collated it with their other information, including Sham's descriptions. Began to build a route.

With distant affection Caldera regretted that Sham had not come. She took bites from a sandwich, sang.

An alarm bleated, glowed red. She checked her clattering information. A change of gauge was coming.

She prodded buttons. How much would this particular technology have excited the burghers, the salvors, the privateers of Manihiki! she thought.

Raskaba-tak, the train slowed but not by very much—a tug or two of levers, a switch set, & the engine shuddered exactly like a troubled animal; braces emerged from its underside, took its weight as it rolled, raised it an instant, mechanisms wound, the wheels on the momentarily suspended vehicle slipping closer together to return & to land *snikt* into these new narrower rails.

There were no hours of complicated rail-&-wheel-side shenanigans, only seconds with the gauge-slip. Caldera inserted words of salutation & praise for her family into her song.

She did not wake Dero when she passed a hunk of metal that she suddenly suspected was one of her parents' carriages. Discarded by them so early in their trip, for reasons unknown. She said nothing.

When she had to sleep she stopped the train & armed its defences. The ordinator would probably have been able to continue the journey unwatched, but she would rather avoid any risk. It would soon be 5, & Dero's turn.

& on the day that followed, & for days after that, the Shroakes continued their single-minded drive through hostile country. They traced creative routes through the railsea towards its most arcane & neglected places, following their family's secret route, looking for whatever it was their mother & father had found.

Chapter Forty-Four

WITHOUT QUESTION, the most important science is ferrovia-oceanology, the study of the railsea's iron lines themselves. This is boss, nexus of investigations. Done right, it extends, rail-&-tie-like, across ruminations of all fields. To study the rails means not only the metallurgy of their substance, but the applied theology of their maintenance, sustained, cleaned & fixed as they are by the secretive ministrations of the locomotive-angels. It means the study of biology, to hypothesise the relationship between the lairs of all the burrowers, those eruchthonous & those eternally underground, & the tangled lines above them.

It means the study of symbology. Ever since the god-squabble, since the rest of the world was brought into shape & existence to serve the aesthetic & symbolic needs of the railsea, we—cities, continents, towns, trains & you & me—have been functions of rails.

Travel far enough, a trainswoman will find worshippers of gods of all sizes & shapes, all powers, persuasions & proclivities. & not only gods—uplifted mortals, ancestor spirits, abstract principles. In North Pittman is a particularly striking theology. There, one church memorably teaches that if all the trains were to be still, together, for one moment, if there were no wheels percussing the iron road, all human life would wink instantly out. Because such noises are the snoring, the sleep-breathing of a railsea world, & it is the rails that dream us. We do not dream the rails.

Chapter Forty-Five

IN VERY OTHER parts of the railsea, a much older, much more traditional train, ground south. Its passage was less strange than the Shroakes', its route on one gauge only, but it travelled with no less urgency.

Thus the *Medes*. Chased again by an eager coterie, a squabbling comet's tail of railgulls chowing on the scraps the trainsfolk threw. A day was all it took, a day's quick determined driving, & Manihiki, its outliers, a hundred rocklets prodding out between the ties, were gone. Wide-open rails, & southward ho. With perhaps a certain melancholy.

On the *Medes*'s last day in Manihiki, several people, of course, had been late to arrive back on-deck. One by one they returned, & one by one were punished. Nothing too severe— this was typical minor transgression.

& ap Soorap?

Sham ap Soorap?

Where was Sham ap Soorap?

He didn't answer *any* calls. He did not return.

The captain herself even asked where he was. Preparations continued. The captain herself paced & asked again if there was word of the doctor's assistant.

Until at last the harbourmasters arrived, bearing a letter to Fremlo, which the doctor read, swore at & read to the captain, leaving the door open a crack. The doctor was too experienced for that to be an accident. It was the technique known as *trainboard telegraph.* Minutes later the whole crew knew the message's contents.

" 'To Dr. Fremlo & Captain Naphi & the officers & all my friends on the train *Medes*. I am sorry to be not there but I cannot do this job any more I have a new crew they are salvors with T Sirocco. They will teach me to be a salvor I was never a person who wanted to be a molehunter nor a doctor so I will go with them. Please tell my family thank you & sorry. I am sorry for this but I have always wanted to be someone who finds salvage & this is my chance good luck & thank you. Yr obedient servant Sham ap Soorap.' "

THEY RACED INTO winds that whipped with less & less mercy. The heads, the bodies, of animals that broke subterranean cover grew larger as the *Medes* came to wilder, colder lands. Older hands marked the change in wheelcalls & clatternames as the iron cooled.

On the fourth day they rolled in the shadow of an old pumping rig crowning above a copse, still extracting oil though near its life's end. A labour of moldywarpes, grey beasts of moderate size & quality, surfaced near them, playing & puffing dust. Three were swiftly skewered, roped, dragged to the butchery wagons, reduced to components.

"Hey, d'you remember," Vurinam said abruptly to no one in particular, "how that Sham ap Soorap brought the grog when he had to?" He cleared his throat. "Couldn't work out if he liked doing it more or less than his usual doctoring, weren't that so, Fremlo?"

There were a few laughs. Were they happy or sad that Vurinam had mentioned their runaway? Yes. They were happy or sad.

"Shut up, Vurinam," Yashkan said. "Nobody cares." But his heart wasn't in it.

"Didn't know he had it in him," Fremlo muttered to Mbenday when they drank bad smoky tea late that night. "He was hopeless, though you couldn't but like the lad, but I'd never have thought he'd have the oomph to go be a salvor, no matter how mooningly he stared at them."

The *Medes* passed a slave-powered train from Rockvane, which the captain would not hail. Shossunder & Dramin the cook stared out to railsea, as in their wake a big old bull armadillo, like a grunting armoured cart, groped up into the air, sniffed for prey, & ground below again.

"He was funny with his food," Dramin said.

"Odd having him not around," the cabin boy said.

They reached a huge & clanking wartrain from one of the Cabigo monarchies. They approached the double-decked wheeled fortress, porcupine-spined with guns, howling sooty smoke, on its manoeuvres & reconnaissance.

Admiral Shiverjay received Naphi, & after niceties & a cup of cactus tea, after paying sufficient polite attention to his ill-tempered train-cat, in the halting combination of languages with which they could get by, she asked him if he had any news of a large, pale moldywarpe.

& he only bloody *had*.

MANY TRAINS KEPT records of overhearings like sightings of megabeasts, of any talk of sports & monsters they encountered, knowing molers they met might be searching. Shiverjay ran a finger down a rumour-list, past tales of the largest badger, albino antlions, aardvarks of prodigious size. Some had the names of captains marked alongside. Some had more than one: oh, those were awkward occasions, clashes of hunt. *What to do when more than one philosopher sought the same symbol?* It was notoriously embarrassing.

"Ah now," Shiverjay said. "Here's a thing." He had a superb stock of stories. "You know where the Bajjer roll?" Naphi nodded a vague nod. The sail-nomads gathered & hunted across great swathes of the railsea. "A deep-railsea spearhunter, back from their grounds, she told me something that she'd heard from a furrier who'd been trading with a salvor crew—"

The lineage, the genealogy by which the story was delivered at last into Captain Naphi's ears, was convoluted & not important. What mattered was this: "A solo trainsman saw our quarry," Naphi said, back on her own vehicle. She controlled herself, stiff & upright & careful, but she was all-but bass-string vibrating at the news. "He *ain't too far.* Switchers, south-southwest."

& still there was that sniff of loss about the *Medes.*

A PECULIARITY OF geography had the railsea dipping into a sheltered declivity that thronged with rabbit. There a light steam train all the way from Gulflask passed on stories they too, like the wartrain, had heard about the jaundiced-looking *Talpa rex.* They directed the *Medes* west, to where the earthworms were huge & sluggish & the largest moldywarpes fed.

Three days, following earth-trails of ever-increasing sizes, & the *Medes* saw two great southern moldywarpes. One sleek young male too far to chase; the second, a grizzled sow, they might have been able to run down. But Naphi told the harpoonists no.

As the sun dropped & the cold went vicious, they reached a dangerous intricate knot of rails, of manifold gauges. It would need charting for passage. The captain was untouched by any tiredness. She stared rapt & intently through her telescope, into the last of the light.

Abruptly she volunteered Mbenday, Brownall, Benightly & Borr to go with her. The crewmembers were like inflated people, so bundled were they in fleece & fur. The captain herself wore only a moderately quilted jacket.

"She don't need no furs, she's warmed by her crazy," Borr whispered to Benightly as they took the jollycart slowly forward. They mapped & took careful notes, prepared switches for the *Medes* that would follow. They glanced longingly at the receding warmth & light of the train.

Slowly they rounded a patch of bushes metal-coloured in the twilight . . . steered between trees thin & gnarled as pained skeletons . . . knocked stones from the rails with their trainhooks . . . They moved at a creeping pace in thickets of tough vegetation, in a range of dense rails, broken by spare patches of ground & the curve of a hill towards which they steered.

"Stop here," Naphi said, her voice trembling. She stood, ready to disembark. "Let's see what we can see from the top." They rolled closer to the pale hill. The shaggy bone-coloured hill.

The hill covered not in pale freeze-bleached grass but in hair.

The yellow hill rumbled. It shuddered.

The hill growled.

A twitch, a switch, & stubs & tufted nubs on the hill moved. Moved as a chewing sound sounded, as there came from all around them a slam of teeth & a throaty animal exhalation.

The hill opened wicked eyes.

"Oh my good gods!" someone screamed. "It's him!"

& with violence & suddenness the earth shook & birds were calling as loud as the crew & the hill was not a hill, was the colossal humped flank & back of Mocker-Jack the pale mole. & there was throating & a snarl of tree-sized slaver-spattering tusks & a plunging with appalling motion so enormous that the world itself, time itself, seemed to buckle, & countless tons of meat & malevolent muscle & dead-hued fur moved. & with a red stare near-sightless but quite terrible the beast rose an instant then plunged straight, straight down, leaving ruination, buckled rails, splintered ties, a quivering-edged pit.

A gun fired, a flash in the dark. The earth shuddered again. Benightly, Brownall, Borr were falling & clinging to the cart's sides as the world pitched. Someone braked hard to stop them following the beast into the below. From which came a dust-choked roar.

Oh, so appalling a timbre.

ONE BY ONE the crew on the cart opened their eyes. They coughed in the clouds left by Mocker-Jack's passing. Checked their cuts & bruises & that they were not dead.

They looked up one by dizzy one. To see, standing, unruffled, indeed exultant, the captain. She held a rifle against her hip. Smoke from its muzzle fingered the air.

Naphi was leaning towards the new hole, peering into the new shadow. In her artificial hand was the mechanism she had bought. Lights flashed upon it. She shook the gun, the electric box, & smiled. It was a chilling smile. "Now," she said. "We will just see."

"Lizards," Mbenday whispered at last, a curse to the strange iguana gods of Mendana, his home. "You *knew* what it was. But you knew we wouldn't come if *we* knew. You *saw* it. This was the plan. Phase one. Is that not it, Captain?" There was as much admiration as anger in his voice.

198

The captain said nothing. She pressed a button on the box she held, & read the lights. The scanner in her hand traced the sub-dirt passage of her nemesis. It sent back information from the tracer she had shot into the giant mole's flesh.

Chapter Forty-Six

THESE WERE the railsea's middle reaches: not yet the deepest open rail, far from hardland, nor the bays & heavily patrolled inlets & railrivers of territorial stretches. The lines & the train upon them wound through stunted hardy forests.

"Ooh ooh," said Dero. He steered the Shroake train a good decent distance from the barricaded buildings of some tiny rock-perching hamlet, peered again through his lever-side windows at the community of small simians that watched him from the trees. He tried, once more, to imitate them. "Eeh eeh," he said. He jumped up & down.

The monkey family watched the train go, prim & glum. The older female sniffed & peed. The others wandered off, on their branches, hand over hand.

"Tchah," said Dero. "Stupid animals," he said. "Ain't they?"

"Whatever you say," Caldera said. She was writing in the Shroake train journal & log.

"Come on, Cal. This is supposed to be fun."

"Fun?" she said slowly. She put the book down. "Fun? You know where we're heading? Course you don't. Neither do I. That's the whole point. But you know this ain't going to be a joke. This is a promise we're making, that's what. For them. So let me ask you again—you think it's supposed to be fun?"

She stared at her brother. He met her gaze. He was littler than her, by a good ways, but he stuck out his chin & furrowed his brow & said, "Yeah. A bit."

& after a second, Caldera slumped & sighed, & said, "Yeah. I suppose it should be a bit. Tell you what." She glanced in the direction of the copse they had left. "Next one we pass, we'll throw fruit at the monkeys."

ANOTHER CHARACTERISTIC of these inner-outer stretches— given the reefs of rock, fields of scattered salvage dispropor- tionately jagged with metal, the trees & narrow straits between hardland islands—was that they were dangerous. Look to your charts, drivers. & it was so much more dangerous if you were determined to roll at night.

The Shroakes were determined to roll at night. Their instru- ments on, they sat in a winking cave of diodes as their train progressed. It was dimmer even than usual that starless evening, but for the soundless sweeps of far-off white beams from another light-tower ahead.

"Careful here," Caldera muttered to herself, checked the chart that warned of dangerous proximity of the rails to rockfalls & quicksand.

"Drattit," she murmured, slowing & backing up. "I'm taking us that way," she said. "That must be the Safehouse Good Beacon." She checked her chart again. "So if we go this route . . ."

She worked her remote control on switches & picked them slowly towards the lighthouse. The wheels whispered on the iron. The light fluttered with tiny shadows, as nightbirds & darkbats bickered in its beam for hunting rights.

"Where is it we are?" Dero said. Caldera pointed at the map. Dero frowned. "Really?" he said.

"I know what you're going to say," Caldera said. She gritted her teeth & wrestled with the controls. "I know, I know, from the direction of the line, you'd have thought we were closer north a bit, right? Well." They rumbled over unsteady ground. "Well, these aren't the most up-to-date charts. They must be wrong."

"If you say so," Dero said doubtfully. "I mean . . ." He squinted into the night.

"Well, there's not much else it can be, is there?" Caldera said. She adjusted, switched. "I mean look at the lighthouse. They ain't going to have built a new one, are they?"

But of course by the time that last word was out of her mouth, Caldera had answered her own question in her head. Dero was staring at her, uncomprehending but horrified by her look. Glinting outside took his attention. Glinting much too close. "There's something," he said, "on that beach."

"Stop!" Caldera shouted. Hauled hard, hard on the brake, & the train's wheels screamed in resentment as it grudgingly halted. Dero staggered & fell. "Back back back!" Caldera shouted.

"What are you . . . ?"

"Check the rear!" Above them the light beam went by. The train slowly began to move again, backed up, away from one bit of darkness among many.

"What am I looking for?" Dero said.

"Anything behind us."

"There ain't nothing."

"Perfect then!" Caldera said, & accelerated in reverse. "Keep watching! We'll turn around when we can."

& with a lurch of the retreating train, the vivid glare of its headlamp swung a few yards, & Caldera saw how close to either side of the route they'd been taking were rises of flint. She had been a breath away from steering her train into a pass. On the edges of which, overlooking them, poised with great rocks ready to roll in to derail her, silent figures watched.

She caught her breath. She bit her lip. Another light swing showed the pale faces of the ambushers. They stared at her retreating vehicle, stared right through the glass, through the cameras & at her.

Calm-faced men & women. Armed. Carrying tools, the equipment with which to take an errant train apart. They lay where they had been hiding, their expressions betraying no shame nor any aggression: only mild disappointment as their prey escaped.

"Of course someone built a new lighthouse," Caldera whispered.

"What's that?" Dero said. "I can't hear you. What is going on, anyway?"

What was going on? People had smashed the lights of the real & automated tower, that must, Caldera thought, be standing to useless dark attention on a nearby beach, not at all where she thought she had seen it. Locals had by careful reference to railsea charts lit a fake beacon at a place chosen to appeal as a reference in the darkest nights, that would lure the unlucky in to a terrible impassable part of the rails, where the crews who had built that false light would be waiting, to do what was necessary to travellers, to scavenge the scrap their intervention left behind. The cruellest kind of salvage. Train-ghouls, derailers & thieves.

"Wreckers," Caldera whispered.

Chapter Forty-Seven

A RED SIGNAL at this junction of the story-train's route.

Generations of thinkers have stood with notebooks open on coastlines, the endless spread of ties-&-iron before them — countless junctions, switches, possibilities in all directions — & insisted that what characterises rails is that they have no terminus. No schedule, no end, no direction. This has become common sense. This is a cliché.

Every rail demands consideration of every other, & all the branches onto which that other rail might switch. There are those who would issue orders, & would control the passage of all such narratives. They may, from time to time, even be able to assert authority. They will not, however, always be successful. One could consider history an unending brawl between such planners, & others who take vehicles down byways.

So, now. The signal demands the story stop. With diesel wheeze & wheel complaint, our train reverses. With a whack of trainhooks a story-switch is thrown, & our text proceeds again from days ago, from where it had got to. To answer a question bellowed, we might imagine, by moldywarpe critics as we took routes where the Siblings Shroake drove & the *Medes* hunted. Curious & impatient mole listeners raised heads from earth & shouted across the flatlands of untold things. Demanding attentions elsewhere.

Chapter Forty-Eight

SHAM THEN.

What happened miles, days ago, was that Sham wobbled slowly up from the deeps of unconsciousness until he popped right into his own head. & into a headache. & winced & opened his eyes.

A room. A tiny train cabin. A cold line of light from a porthole. Boxes & papers wedged into shelves. Footsteps above him. The light wavered & swayed & dragged across the wall as the train changed direction. Sham could feel the shuddering now, through his back. He could feel that he was travelling fast.

He could not sit up. Was trussed on a bunk. He could just about see his own hands clutching at nothing. He tried to shout & discovered that a gag was in the way. Sham thrashed, but it was no good. He panicked. The panic was no good either. It gave up at last & left. He stretched each muscle that he could.

Vurinam? he thought. *Fremlo? Captain Naphi?* He tried to say the names out loud, & made muffled noises. *Caldera?* Where *was* he? Where was everyone else? An image of the Shroake train took him. Could he be on the Shroake train? Minutes, or hours, or seconds, passed. The door at last opened. Sham strained, turned his head, croaking. Robalson stood in the doorway.

"Ah ha," Robalson said. "At last. We didn't give you that much. I thought you'd wake up ages ago." He grinned. "I'm going to untie your hands & mouth, let you sit up," he said. "Your end of the deal is you're not going to be a pain in my arse."

He put down a bowl of food & loosened Sham's bonds, & Sham began to shout even as the dirty cloth left his mouth. "What the hell are you doing my captain's going to find me you're going to pay for this you crazy pig," & so on. Sham had hoped it would sound like a bellow. It came out more like a loud whine. Robalson sighed & tugged the gag back on.

"Now is that being not a pain in my arse?" he said. "Goat porridge for non-arse-painery. That's the deal. There's worse things I can do than put a gag on."

This time when Robalson relaxed the mouthpiece Sham said nothing. Just stared at him in cold fury.

He also stared at the porridge. He really was hungry.

"What the bloody hell do you call this?" Sham said through a mouthful of the delicious stuff.

Robalson rubbed his nose. "A kidnapping, I suppose. What do you call it?"

"It ain't funny!"

"It is a bit."

"You . . . You're a *pirate*!"

Robalson shook his head as if at imbecility. "I *told* you I was," he said.

"Where are we going?"

"That depends."

"Where's my bat?" Sham said.

"Flew off when we took you."

"Why are we going so fast?"

"Because we want to get there quickly, & because we're

pirates. We ain't the only ones heard things. Salvors've been asking after you. & what with us up & suddenly buggering off like that, you can bet a bunch of other people are curious & looking our way."

"What do you want with me?"

"What we want," said a new voice, "Sham ap Soorap, is information." In from the corridor came a man.

He wore an engineer's boiler suit. His hair was short & greased. He held his hands together gently, he spoke quietly, & his bloodshot eyes fixed on Sham's with intelligence. "I'm Captain Elfrish," he said gently. "You are, I haven't decided yet."

"I'm Sham ap Soorap!"

"I haven't decided what you are, yet."

The captain of the pirate train did not wear a greatcoat in which lived polecats & weasels. He did not have a beard woven with smouldering twists of gunpowder to surround himself with a stench & demonic aura. He did not cock a tricorn hat or have handprints in blood on his shirt. He did not dangle a necklace of bones & flesh-scraps. All these were things of which Sham had heard, ways in which railsea pirates spread the terror on which they relied.

This man wore large glasses. He had what Sham would, had circumstances been otherwise, have said was a kind face. He couldn't help thinking it, & then he couldn't help a miserable little laugh.

The man folded his arms. "Your situation amuses you?" he said. He sounded like an office manager asking someone to clarify a row of figures.

"No," Sham said. It was, to his own surprise & grim pleasure, anger more than fear that swept him. "You're in so much trouble, don't you even know? My captain's going to come for you. She's going to—"

"She's going to nothing," said the captain. He cleaned his glasses. "She got your message. The one about wanting to be a salvor? The one about rolling off with them? Full of details only you'd know? Wishing her good luck & goodbye? Telling her you were seeking your fortune? She got it."

He put his spectacles back on. "Everyone knows you've been with those Shroakes. It's not as if your aspirations come out of the blue. Your captain knows you've gone, are following your dream. She's not coming for you, boy."

All those things, Sham thought. All those stories, those secrets, those desires, the sense of adventure, the pining after the vividly dressed salvors, that he had harboured, that he had confessed to Robalson—used against him.

"What do you want?" he croaked. "I ain't got no money."

"No indeed," Elfrish said. "& our train's short of space. If you've no purpose, there's no point keeping you, you see? So it might be worth your while to think about what you can offer instead of coin. To be indispensable."

"What do you want?" Sham was whispering now.

"Oh, I don't know." Elfrish said. "What might one want? My decks are swabbed. We have cooks, we have crew, we have everything we could need. Oh, but wait a minute." He looked thoughtful. "There is one thing, though. That's a thought. How about you show us on a map where you found the wreck. Of which none of your crew were supposed to speak. While you're at it, you tell me what you found on it. Stories have been after you since, ooh, Bollons. About where poor old Captains Shroake ended up. How about you tell me everything, & I do mean everything, that you brought with you to give those Shroakes.

"We on this train have a little bit of a vested interest. These are names not wholly unknown to us. Names I wasn't expecting to deal with again, though of course one keeps a little ear out for what the oh-so-clever second-generation Shroakes are up to. Plenty of people do, of course, but some of us have more *investment* than others.

"Experiments don't interest me. Journeys, however, especially journeys in response to secret posthumous messages, journeys after absolutely unique treasures, now they *do*. Apart from anything, it makes a person think they missed something, & that's never a good feeling, now, is it?"

"What?" said Sham. "Missed what?" But Elfrish did not answer. Instead, from his pocket, he pulled Sham's little camera.

"There's a picture on this I'm particularly interested in," he said. "Par, tick, you, lairly. & I don't mean your penguins. See, I had no idea they'd be leaving yet, those Shroakelets. Or we'd have gone after them our own selves. Caught us on the hop. But we know you've been chatting to them.

"& if," he said, & his voice was suddenly chill & bony & metal & like the scuttling of a very bad insect, "you'd like not to be cut open & dangled over the side of this train & dragged along with your legs on the ground spilling blood everything under the flatearth can smell while we go slow enough for long, long miles that they can rise & eat you from the toes up & from the inside out, you know what you could do for me, Sham?

"Tell me where the Shroakes are going."

Chapter Forty-Nine

"So what do they do?" Since their close escape from the light-deploying wreckers Dero had become obsessed with them, with whatever the Siblings Shroake had just avoided.

"I told you, I don't know," Caldera said. "Release some of that pressure—we've got a buildup in the port engines. They lure stuff in, smash them up, & take them apart, I suppose."

The train arced over a rise—here, the flatearth was not quite, well, flat. They passed little streams & ponds, shaggy trees sprouting right between the rails. Sometimes there would be a rattling as branches knocked the side of the vehicle, as if something was asking for entrance.

"That's what they do to trains," said Dero. "What about people? In the trains? What about if they'd got us?"

"What's that?" Caldera said. The iron rails ahead looked as if they were spreading out *from* something. Specifically, from a hill, it looked like, a stub island of the railsea. But you shouldn't be able to see through an island. It should not have a silhouette like filigree, an island should not *glint*.

"It's a bridgeknot," Dero said.

The rails thicketed together, clumped, clotted, weaving over & under each other on girders & supports, on buttresses & poles in an absurdly tight snarl. It could have been the iron skeleton of a quite impossible behemoth. Within it at various heights, the Shroakes could see two, three old trains. Cold, deserted, of old design. Lifeless as husks & long abandoned.

"Go round it," Dero said.

"It ain't as simple as that," Caldera said. She switched, line to line. "The rails everywhere round here are coming off it. Like wax off a candle. It's going to take hours 'n' hours to plot a route around it. We want to be right on the other side." She pointed.

"So?"

"We go through it."

THE NOISE OF their passage changed on the footrails. Suspended suddenly on rickety rattling rises, the percussion went from heartbeat to performance, tinnier & more resonant. Raised rails made temporary little skies. The Shroakes passed into shadows, & through the patterings of moisture dripping from the lines' undersides.

Rails below, rails above. They were six, seven yards up, shaking the strut maze, switching switches, pushing through the heart of it all. They looked uneasily at each other as the tracks wobbled.

"Is this thing safe?" Dero whispered.

"Angels will've kept it alright," Caldera said.

"We hope," Dero said.

"We hope."

Sunlight dappled them through the old lines. The Shroake train was speckled as if they were deep in a hedge.

"Who gets wrecked in the middle of a thing like this?" Dero said, looking at the deserted vehicles embedded in the structure. One was close. They were approaching it.

"Careless people," Caldera said. "Unlucky people." She looked at the antique outlines of the train. "They weren't wrecked, anyway. They were . . . becalmed." The vehicle was heavy & huge & designed according to outmoded aesthetics. It

211

had no chimney nor any exhaust: from its back jutted a huge lever. Clockwork.

"Maybe that's why," Caldera said. "I think that's from Kammy Hammy. They got halfway up, wheels ran out. That bar you wind it up with—you can't twist that in here, there's no space to turn the key."

It loomed over them on a steep side rail, as if watching as they passed. From every one of its windows billowed clouds of ivy & wiry bramble. In which, from the front-most window at least, they could see tangled-up tools, rain-ruined helmets, & bones. The exuberant flora hogged the space, crowding out the dead.

"A few more switches," Caldera said, "& we'll be coming through to the other side." Through the mossed & windblown palimpsest of crossbars ahead she could see the open railsea.

"We've got an amazing view," Dero said. They pitched. Their passage shook the lines. The railknot swayed. Caldera gritted her teeth. Behind her there was a resonant crack. The sound of metal snapping under strain. A groan. & the trembling of the rails grew.

"What," said Caldera, "was that?" She checked her mirrors. "Oh," she said.

That old train was not used to this shaking. Bolts had shaken, strained & sheared. Old brakes were long atrophied. Once-taut metal wheel-locks had given abruptly up under the vibrations. Blocks & chocks crumbled & the clockwork train was slipping from its position, & was rolling onto their track, following them. Accelerating.

"Oh . . . my . . ." said Dero.

"Quick now," Caldera muttered. "Quick, quick, chop chop,

on we go." She yanked her controls, sped the Shroake train up. Their cold accidental pursuer accidentally pursued.

A working train versus one long ruined unto scrap? Quite foregone which would be faster, no? But Caldera had a grave disadvantage. She was alive. & she wanted to keep it that way. She had, then, to exercise care. The fossil that pursued them had no such restraint. Where she slowed at branches, it did not. Where she sought the best route out of the girderweb, it did not care. Where she strove to ensure that she did not send her brother & herself hurtling to their doom, doom had long ago claimed their hunters, who strove deadly for nothing but speed.

The old train was accelerating. Following them junction for junction, switch for switch, shaking the whole railknot & making the Shroakes scream. It roared after them, carried by gravity, gathering momentum, sending struts & supports of the strange structure scattered like spillikins behind it.

"Go faster!" Dero shouted.

"Oh, thank you!" shouted Caldera. "I hadn't thought of that! Here I was going half speed!" They rolled towards the light, a dead crew close behind them. Only yards now to the flatearth where they could veer out of the path, but the clockwork was too close, too fast, was seconds from shunting them violently off the line.

"Purge!" shouted Caldera. Dero hesitated only one instant, then obeyed.

He stabbed at keys. Caldera listed what they would lose. *I left my jumper in that carriage*, she thought giddily, *I left my second best pen, there's all the liquorice*, but no time for regrets, as with a last yank, Dero shouted "Purging!" & the rearmost carriage on the Shroake train was decoupled & blown backwards with percussive bolts, to slide right in the path of what came for them.

The dead train slammed into the retreating carriage. There was no way the discarded Shroake cabin could stop that hefty skeleton, but it did not need to. All it needed to do, & what it did, with a scream of wheels, was momentarily slow it. Long enough, those few seconds, that Caldera & Dero & their little train, lighter & faster now, hauled away & out, & were back at railsea again, whooping with the whole being-alive-ness of it.

They switched, & were a way away on sidelines of the route they had been taking, rushing to the windows to watch. As it howled out into the bright sun, the carriage slowing it, the pursuing engine shook with the percussion of the bridgeknot. Which creaked, which swayed, until with thunderous clatter & the rush of air, the whole precarious rusted mass of the structure began to collapse.

As if staggering, the clockwork train-tomb flipped, sending the brake that had until moments ago been the Shroakes' sleeping cabin screeching off the line into the wilderness. The old engine somersaulted horribly & mightily, coming apart as it flew, spreading debris & disgruntled ivy & the bones of dead explorers far across the rails.

FOR A LONG TIME dust kept pluming. The cacophony of falling bridgeknot continued. Piece by agonised piece it fell, until at last it was still, its broken silhouette emerging from dirt clouds. Bits of shattered train rolled across the railsea.

Long after the awful sound, at very last, rodent curiosity got the better of rodent caution, & the burrowing beasts of the railsea peered up from scrubby grass. A breeze pushed Caldera's & Dero's hair this way & that. They leaned out of their window, gaping at all the collapse, at the second death of the clockwork train.

"& that," said Caldera, "is why we never leave anything essential in the last carriage."

Chapter Fifty

"I DON'T KNOW! I don't know! That's the whole point! I don't know where they've gone!"

Elfrish had not even touched him, had just put his face very close to Sham's, stared at him with eyes that no longer looked mild. That looked like poison & ice. Behind his captain, Robalson looked uncomfortable.

"I swear," Sham babbled, "I don't know nothing, I just saw the pictures & thought they should know . . ."

"Pictures," said Elfrish. "As in . . ." He shook the camera.

"Pictures! From a camera! They were in the wreck!"

"You're lying, boy." Elfrish's voice was frosty & certain. "They were not."

"They was! Only in the ground! In a hole!"

The captain cocked his head. "A hole?" he said.

"One of the Shroakes dug it! Where the window used to be. Shoved it inside."

Elfrish gazed thoughtfully roofward, scrunched up his eyes in thought or memory. "A hole," he breathed. "A hole." He looked at Sham. "If there *were* pictures," he said, "perhaps someone might use them to reconstruct just where the Shroakes had been. They were always assiduous about not disclosing their itineraries. Whatever the encouragement."

"Yeah!" said Robalson. "We should totally do that!" He nodded nervously at his captain.

"But," whispered Elfrish to Sham, "you don't have those pictures any more."

& though he wanted more than anything to say, "Yes I do," Sham, after he had stalled as long as he dared, had to whisper, "No I don't."

With a bellow like an animal, Captain Elfrish dragged Sham abruptly out of the room & into the corridor. Down the hallways, past pirates at their tasks. They looked like other trainsfolk. Only the furnishings were more random, their clothes more varied, & every one of them was armed.

Into a room where scarred officers were waiting. Sham saw through the windows that they were racing through lush lands, overbent by mottled boughs & climbing flowers & trees that seemed to scream, so full of bright birds & startled marmosets were they. Sham could feel the train judder over junctions, pass signal boxes & switches, as lines veered from their own.

So they were heading north, then. Someone was holding Sham down in a chair. He shook & yelled but could not break free. On the table in front of him, someone laid out thick paper. As if to protect the table from spills. Sham yelled again. An officer was slowly unrolling a leather pack containing glittering sharp things.

"I don't know nothing!" Sham shouted. What ghastly instruments were these? "I told him!"

"Juddamore," Elfrish said. "Begin."

The big man took a wicked grey spike from the pack. Licked his thumb & pressed it to the point. Winced his appreciation. Sham screeched. The man lowered it until it pointed at Sham's face.

"So," said Elfrish. "You said you found pictures. That would be these." He held up scraps—the greasy, now-torn & well-worn images that Sham had scribbled for himself, the remembrances of what he had seen on screen. "& culminating in this." Sham's cheap little camera. On its screen that single line. Even so small & ill-focused, it hushed the room.

"Know where this leads?" Elfrish whispered. "No. Neither do I. But I am, as you know by now, very much of a one for stories. & such intimations as there are for people to hunt the let-me-stress-it legendary, mythical, obviously-not-at-all-real places beyond, revolve around money. A lot of it. You see my point.

"Oh, people'll go after those Shroakes. It's hardly just me. With their train, that won't go well, I suspect. But followed as they know they are, they'll wind their route. What I want to do is *head them off*. Which means knowing where they're going.

"Now, your well-being is up to you, Sham ap Soorap. These—" He shook the images. "—may make sense to you. To me, not so helpful. To me they are scrawls. So, the things you saw?

"Describe them."

The man called Juddamore lowered his sharp point to the paper. It was a pencil. He began to draw.

HE TRANSLATED SHAM'S gabbled descriptions into images. Juddamore was talented. Even in his wash of fear & relief, Sham was impressed to watch the pictures emerge from scrawled grey lines as tangled as the railsea.

Someone'll run come save me, he thought, & described his pictures & memories, in case they did not, in fact. In the days & weeks that he had prepared his trip to Manihiki, formulating his plan, Sham had gone over those images in his mind, leafed through his scrappy redrawings, more than once. They were vivid in his mind.

"& then in the third one there's, yeah, that one . . ."

"What is that?" some deep-voiced pirate muttered, staring at Sham's original. "Is that a bird?"

Sham. Never an artist.

"No, it's, it's like, a sort of, a sort of overhang, like, like . . ." & with frantic hand-motions Sham described the rock angle, & so on. To stay alive. Juddamore drew what he described, & Sham would pass comment & correct him like some lunatically agitated critic. "Not like that, the little forest was a bit more, lower trees, like . . ."

Each of these scenes had originally been chosen & frozen because it was a sight, after all. Each of them had some quality, some feature, something to distinguish it from the everyday railsea, to make it worth recording. For hours, Juddamore drew pictures of descriptions of memories of glimpses of digital images of sights once long ago seen. The pirate officers looked, heads cocked, rubbing their chins. Debated what they saw.

"& this is the order?"

"Look. That bit there sounds like the corner off the coast of Norwest Peace."

"There's rumours about rail shenanigans up Kammy Hammy way, & couldn't that be the cut in the mountains that gets you up by its western islands?"

They traced a route. With maps beside them, they ruminated. Over a long time, guessing where they had to, putting to one side controversies, the best brains of the pirate train reconstructed a dead explorers' route. Until, astoundingly, they had decided they knew—more or less, roughly, in broad sweeps—where they were going.

This is not what I ever had in mind, Sham thought. *I ain't even a pirate. I'm a pirate-abetter.*

Chapter Fifty-One

BUT WAIT. Students of the railsea, of course you have questions. You are likely to narrow in on uncertain & mysterious questions of iron-rail theology.

You wish to know which is the oldest civilisation in the railsea, which island state's records go back furthest, using which calendar? What do they tell us about the history of the world, the Lunchtime Ages, prehistory, the times before the scattered debris from offhand offworld picnicking visitors was added to aeons of salvage? Is it true the upsky used to be full of the same birds as now fly the down? & if so, what was the point of that?

What of the decline & fall of empires? Human empires & godly ones? & what *about* those gods—That Apt Ohm, Mary Ann the Digger, Railhater Beeching, all that brood? What, above all, about *wood*?

That is the key mystery. Wood makes trees trees. Wood is also what makes ties—those bars crosswise between railsea rails—ties. A thing can have only one essence. How can this, then, be?

Of all the philosophers' answers, three stand out as least unlikely.

—Wood & wood are, in fact, appearances notwithstanding, different things.

—Trees are creations of a devil that delights in confusing us.

—Trees are the ghosts of ties, their gnarled & twisted &

dreamlike echoes born when parts of the railsea are damaged
& destroyed. Transubstantiated matter.

All other suggestions are deeply eccentric. One of these
three is most likely true. Which you believe is up to you.

We have pirates to return to.

Chapter Fifty-Two

GENERALLY IT WAS Robalson who brought Sham his food. It was Robalson who waited around after Elfrish left, on his brief visits to double-check on picture descriptions, that left Sham quivering. "Yeah," Robalson would say, as if agreeing with whatever terror Elfrish had instilled. He'd twist his face into a sneer, undermined only somewhat by his visible discomfort at Sham's fear.

One time he came alone, & led Sham upstairs constrained, with his wrists shackled to a belt itself attached to a pole that Robalson held. It was a modern train. Diesel. They were moving faster than the *Medes* could have. They were on a strip of pondside rail star'd, with quicksand to port, from which muck-worms poked bleached eyeless faces.

Sham took stock. You never knew. Seven, no, eight carriages. Two double-decker. Crew everywhere. A conning tower. Not as high as the crow's nests he was used to, but the telescope jutting from its viewing slit looked powerful. The *Tarralesh* was not in pursuit, did not fly the notorious skull-&-spanners flag. But it bristled with barrels. From specialised portholes & little holes poked cannons & machine guns. & there was Elfrish. Sham shivered.

"Well?" Elfrish shouted. The captain pointed. Dead ahead a scrappy forest gave way to sand, brick-coloured in the odd light. "Was that what you saw?"

This was why they'd brought him out—not for his comfort,

but to verify the landscape. Elfrish & his officers were gathered around Juddamore's pictures.

Should Sham lie? Tell them to go to airy hell? Tell them this was not the place when—he looked, & oh, it was. He caught his breath. This was the first image he had seen over Captain Naphi's shoulder. He should lie. Tell them no, you should be somewhere very else. Get them off the Shroakes' tails?

A *rumour & a picture?* Sham thought. What kind of crazy person was Elfrish, that that was enough to send him halfway across the railsea, into unknown stretches, on the off chance of who knew what? Evil & cold & terrifying & all that he might be, but Elfrish never seemed crazy—

& he wasn't. It hit Sham abruptly. The captain talking about missing something previously. The certainty in his voice when refuting Sham about the wreck's contents. The sense, in all his talk of the Shroakes, not only of greed, but of work unfinished.

It was him, thought Sham. *It was him took them before. It was this train wrecked the Shroakes.*

Oh, Caldera, Sham thought. *Dero, Caldera.* He imagined the *Tarralesh* bearing down on what must have been a severely battered Shroake train. Grappling hooks fired across cold rails. The boarding, attackers sweeping through the tiny vehicle, swinging cutlasses, firing guns. *Oh, Caldera.*

A chance encounter on the Shroakes' carefully roundabout voyage home? Elfrish must've found hints of the journey. Evidence of the astonishing feats of engineering & salvage. & realising these were not just any nomads, remembered stories of the heaven the evasive coded logs hinted they'd approached, full of endless riches, the ghosts of money born & died & not yet made.

How the pirates must've hunted for hints as to the route. Stripped & ripped & wrecked the wreckage. Brutally demanded answers, if any Shroake then still breathed. Neglecting that frantically dug hole. No wonder Elfrish was obsessed. All possible rewards aside, those pictures were a rebuke to him. Evidence of his piracy fail.

Sham shivered at the sight of the captain. He should, he decided grimly, looking out to railsea, he definitely should lie.

"Let me tell you why you definitely shouldn't lie," Elfrish said. "Because what's keeping you alive is your directions. It's like a checklist. You get one mark for each picture. We have a rough idea where we're going, but we need to double-check with you. Twelve checks & you win, we get to the end. But if it's too long between one mark to another, you don't win, & then you stop. Dead . . . Stop." Sham swallowed. "So. If this is not where we need to be, you better tell us, so we can rethink & get where we're going fast, because you *need* your first checkmark.

"I just know," Elfrish said, "you don't want to die, do you?"

Really not. Even so, there was a part of Sham that wanted to simply tell some ludicrous untruth, have them roar off in thoroughly the wrong direction as long as he could sustain it. Would that be a glorious death?

"I can see you thinking it over," Elfrish said kindly. "I'll give you a minute or two. I quite understand. This is a big decision."

"Come on," muttered Robalson. He jerked Sham's chain. "Don't be stupid."

Sham came close. Had given up hope, & why not, why not mess with them? He came close. But at that moment he looked into the little storm of railgulls arcing around the train & saw the silhouette of quite un-avian wings.

Daybe! Lurching with a frantic bat flap, a careering pell-mell motion nothing like birds'. Sham kept himself still, did not show his excitement.

The bat had definitely seen him. Sham's chest swelled. How far had Daybe come? How long been following? It was that, the sudden not-being-alone-ness, the presence of even an animal friend, that changed Sham's mind. For reasons he couldn't have put very clearly into words it was abruptly important to him that he keep himself alive, which at the moment meant useful, as long as possible. Because look, there was Daybe.

"Yeah," he said. "That's what was in the picture."

"Good," said Elfrish. "There really wasn't very much else that first picture you described could be. If you'd told us no, I'd probably have had to chuck you off. Good decision. Welcome to staying alive."

As he turned, Sham glimpsed Robalson's face. To his shock, the pirate boy was staring at the bat in the air. He knew! He'd seen it! But Robalson looked at him, & said nothing.

He led Sham back to the cell, checked they were alone, then eagerly winked. "No harm in having a friendly face around," he whispered, & gave Sham an uneasy smile.

What? thought Sham. *You want to be* friends?

But he would not risk his daybat's freedom or life. Swallowing distaste, Sham smiled back.

He waited until the sound of his young jailer's footsteps had disappeared, then quickly Sham opened the tiny window of his cell & shoved his arm out into the gusts, as far as it would go. The angle was awkward, the pain in his limb not inconsiderable, the flying specks as random-looking & momentary as soot in a storm. Sham waved & whispered & made noises that must have been snatched by the wind & track-clatter, but he made them anyway. & after mere moments of this he let out a cry of triumph, because swooping down, landing heavy & warm & shaggy on his arm, was Daybe, snickering in greeting.

Chapter Fifty-Three

"THEM ANGELS CAN'T have done much of a job on that bridge-knot," Dero said.

"Celestial intervention." said Caldera. "It ain't what it used to be."

"Look!" Dero pointed. Smoke. In the distance. Dirty smudgy smoke—the breath of a steam engine burning something not clean—that tickled the underside of the upsky, which was roiling & hazy that day.

"What is it?" Caldera said. Dero checked & rechecked, gazed through far-seeing scopes & persuaded his on-train ordinators to extrapolate & best-guess.

"I dunno," he said. "It's too far. But I think—I *think* . . ." He turned to his sister. "I think it's pirates."

Caldera looked up. "What?" she shouted. "Again?"

AGAIN. THEIR SUBTERFUGE had lasted as long as it had lasted, the Shroakes' misleading rumour-mongering about their intended journey. But now everyone in Manihiki who cared must know they'd gone, & that meant stories & grapevines, & that was why they had started, as the days went on, glimpsing pirate trains.

These were not undangerous railsea stretches. There were a plethora of islets, here, & ill-charted woodlands & chasms in which a skilful captain might hide. It was no surprise buccaneers favoured them. They had not, though, expected quite how many would be looking for them.

A few days previously they had had the first of them. It could still have been a random encounter, they had thought. A jumped-up little beast-train had emerged from low trees remarkably close to them, & charged. The captain had cracked his enormous whip—it had been close enough with the wind going the right way for the Shroakes to hear—& goaded his snorting six-animal gang, three to each side of the rail, into massive gallops, while the small & vicious-looking pirate crew jeered & sneered on the ornate battledeck.

"Ooh look," Dero had said. "Rhinos. Never thought I'd see rhinos."

"Mmm-hm." Caldera had given a contemptuous little kick, a little lick of speed, & they had left their pursuers coughing in their exhaust. The Shroake train, driven as it was by a hermetic engine, emitted no smoke: it did, though, have tanks of specially synthesised filthy fumes that could, with a button-push, be spurted out backwards to make a point.

"I liked them rhinos," Dero said. "Did you? Caldera?" She said nothing. "Sometimes you wish I wasn't with you, don't you?" he muttered.

Caldera had rolled her eyes. "Don't be absurd," she'd said. Just occasionally it would have been nice to have someone else around, was all. "Enjoy that rhino-sighting while you can, Dero, because you ain't going to see any more."

"Why?"

"There ain't many places a beast-train can relax about what pulls it," she said. "& there's things here'll take a rhino *no* problem. They ain't going to last long. They're a way from home. Must be looking for something."

The siblings had glanced at each other when she said that, but had still not assumed they were the target of these pirate forays. Until two days later, when a gang of small vehicles, each armoured like a dark tortoise, nearly caught up to them in the night, with surprisingly skilful switching. As their alarms sounded & the Shroakes powered away, they heard the lead dieselpunk shouting, "That's them!"

Since then they had sped up to get themselves beyond any danger of detection. "You know," Caldera said, "there are trainsfolk down south who get called 'pirate' all the time, & all they do is look after their coasts, 'cause for years trains of all the other places just dump junk there. Mum told me that. Loads of the people we call pirates aren't doing anything bad at all."

"These ones ain't them," Dero said, watching the progress of their pursuers.

"No," said Caldera. "These ones seem to be the other ones."

Their way was plotted from a combination of what their parents had told them before they left, what they had been able to glean from the notes left behind & their remaining father's confused reminiscences. Those & the ordinator files, & the descriptions Sham had given them, from that old screen.

They were approaching a river. "Bridge?" Caldera asked the world. She could not see any.

"Um." Dero checked the chart. "I think if we go star'd for— well, for ages—we'll get to one." Caldera calculated time in her head. "Know what?" Dero said slowly. "We can be quicker. What about if we take a tunnel?"

"A *tunnel*?" Caldera said. "You think?"

Underground was never a preferred route. There seemed something unholy about the passing, on rails, below, like some deep-digger heading home. Tunnels made the devout grumble. Usually trains would switch out of the way of such stygiana. Usually.

"Save us time," Dero said. He was excited.

"Hmmm," Caldera said. There were, it did look like, routes directly under the water.

The rails took them down, past a fringe of tough shrub, a mouthlike ring of rocks, into a concrete shaft. Some such were even lit, Caldera had heard. This was not. They travelled behind the fierce glare of their own bulb, the tracks, the damp-mottled cement & riblike reinforced supports of the underground passage flitting in & out of pitch as they passed.

"It sounds *weird*," said Dero, his eyes wide. They were cocooned by echoes, every snap & clatter up close & reverberating against the metal of the train. "How far, do you think?"

"Shouldn't be far," Caldera said. "So long as we keep going roughly in this direction."

Out of the shadow loomed more tunnels veering from their own, a submerged maze. At each they slowed, checked the switches. Went on.

They were shocked by a sudden unearthly sound. A quavering, hooting shriek that made the tracks rattle, the ground around them shake. Caldera hit the brakes.

"What was that?" she said. Her own voice was strangulated. Dero stared & clutched her arm.

It came again. More aggressive this time, & closer. A coughing, swallowing, hollow screaming gasp. & now a faint clapping.

Staggering out of dark into the glare of the train lights, something came. It lurched. It staggered & flailed its limbs. Its great trembling throat glistened. A bird. A bird, its eyes sealed closed, covered in fluff, a bird taller than the tallest woman or man. It shook stubby wings, that could never have taken its weight, & tottered. Behind it came others, staggering into sight.

"Look at them!" shouted Dero. "What they *doing* here? They're, they're babies!" He smiled. "What are you doing, Cal?" His sister was scrabbling with the controls, checking the radar, moving fast & gritting her teeth. "Cal, they can't get in." The chicks could barely walk. They fell over as they came, trod on each other, eliciting squawks & pathetic little trills.

"That right there," Caldera said, "is a nest. Those right there are the chicks of a burrowing owl that's been too lazy to dig its own hole. Just moved in here. That noise they're making . . ."

Dero gasped as realisation took hold. ". . . is an alarm call," he said. He fell into his own seat, clicking through controls. They backed up. The newborns staggered after them, sounding piteously.

From behind the train came a much deeper, much louder call. It sent frost down Caldera's bones. They heard a grating step.

Swinging side to side, eyes like giant lanterns hypnotic with rage, recurved beak an evil hook, an owl parent stepped into their hindlights. Its claws were out & ready. It rushed in to protect its babies.

"I'd go the other way," Dero said in a choked voice.

The owl was taller than their train, hunched & stooped to scratch its way through the tunnels, filling the shaft with its wings. Its eyes shone like the worst moon. It screamed. Those claws would rip the Shroake train apart. To get at the soft Shroake grubs within.

Switch, clickety split. Caldera was getting good at these abrupt & sudden line changes. Back past the junction while the chicks stumbled & the terrifying adult closed in, forward again down a sideline, accelerating out of that predator's burrow.

"It's still coming," said Dero

"I know," Caldera said. Switch, forward, star'd, fast.

"It's still coming!" Dero shouted.

"Wait!" Caldera shouted. "I think we're—"

With a rush & the merciful dissipation of all the close-up noise, they burst out again, into the day. On the far side of the river. The raging owl stamped out after them, almost at their speed, opening wings & lurching on stilty legs, half flying, half running, fast, but not as fast as a fleeing Shroake train zipping through grass.

"& farewell to *you*, angry owl," said Caldera triumphantly.

"No! More! Quick routes! Through weird things!" shouted Dero.

"Ah, hush. It was your idea. We made it, didn't we?"

"Yeah, but now I'm just wondering . . ." said Dero.

"What?" Caldera said. "Don't I even get any well-dones for having got us out?"

"It's just . . . doesn't it take two big owls to make little ones?" said Dero.

A colossal noise above, a thunderclap of wings.

In this case, they learnt, as a shadow blotted out the sun beyond the upsky, it took one big & one very, very big owl. Which, that latter, descended, with a bass hoot that made the Shroakes' bones & their train vibrate. Which swooped down towards the rear of the rearmost carriage, clenched claws like dockyard machines that split & splintered the vehicle's roof, &, wings hammering again, ascended. Still gripping. So that one by one, from the back of the train forward, the cars of the Shroakes' train uncoupled from the rails, began to rise.

Chapter Fifty-Four

ELSEWHERE IN the railsea, the ties were stone-hard, the iron of the rails was a black no amount of train-wheel polishing could make shine, & the ground beneath & between them was very cold. Over such tracks came the *Medes*.

Had it been observed by a sky-dwelling god with any knowledge of moling, such a watcher would have been struck by the vehicle's speed. The *Medes* raced on the icy railroad in *shekkachashek*, a rhythm suited to hot pursuit, not to these conditions. No moldywarpe was visible: the train would, the imagined watcher might have presumed, been better suited to prowl at lower speeds & slippery wheelbeats.

At the *Medes*'s prow, the captain, her tracer in her mechanical hand, looked up & down between screen & the horizon. The latter was all grey air & baleful clouds: the former a dancing dot of red, a complaining diode.

"Mr. Mbenday," Naphi said, "it's taken a turn star'd. Switchers to switch." Switch they did, curving through a sequence of points, until the scanner light was again nearly straight ahead.

When she did not track on that relentless screen, the captain retired with books of philosophies. Reading memoirs & thoughts & speculations of the rare completers. She made notes in the margins. What happens when the evasive concepts you hunt, get found?

Three times the devilish fast beast they followed dug too far, too fast, too deep to be followed, dragged its glimmer-self beyond the range of Captain Naphi's reader. Each time, within a few days of roaming, scanner at maximum power, drawing on more traditional techniques of moleground deduction, she found the signal again.

The second time they lost & found the blip that meant great talpa, they had seen, far, far off, a molehill born. An eruption of dust that silenced them with awe, & left a truly prodigious mound behind.

"Wish the lad could see this," Fremlo had muttered. "I heard it was him got her the scanner. He'd have liked this." No one answered.

There was still a chase; they were still molers, tracking & inferring & judging on their hunterly insights. But now Captain Naphi's philosophy left an electrical spoor. Perhaps once or twice the captain looked like she was whispering, muttering something that might have including the word "thanks" as she fiddled with her receiver.

Mocker-Jack did not travel like a moldywarpe should travel. "How does it *know*?" Vurinam demanded of the world. "How does it know we're on its bloody tail? How come it keeps trying to get away?" That was how he interpreted the creature's unusual evasive speed & motion.

It's always taunted the captain, some crewmates whispered back. That's why it's her philosophy.

Hob Vurinam had another question. As they circled a stretch of ice, in the very bloody light of evening, as he turned his pockets inside out & right-way round again in fret, he said to Dr. Fremlo, "D'you ever feel like it might be cheating?"

The doctor was watching groundhogs bicker by their holes. Fremlo said nothing.

"If Naphi gets Mocker-Jack like this," Vurinam said,

"mightn't it be cheating to complete your philosophy that way? Can you shortcut an insight-hunt, do you think?" Fremlo threw scrunched-up paper into a groundhog squabble as the train passed. "Wonder what Sham would think," Vurinam said.

"Not much," Fremlo said. "It isn't salvage, is it? It's just a big mole."

The sun went down on the two of them talking about Sham, while the vehicle to which they owed temporary paid loyalty described raggedy spirals in intersecting rails, closing in on its captain's obsession.

Chapter Fifty-Five

THE FIRST FEW TIMES he enticed it from the sky, Sham just stroked Daybe & took heart from the presence of something that liked him & didn't care if he could verify that a piece of railsea was a particular piece of pictured railsea. Those duties continued. He said yes to a petrified forest; a glacier creeping at them, its slowly incoming edge already eating railsea rails; a particular patch of distinctive hillocky ground. "Is that what you saw?"

Each time Sham was out there to check, Daybe circled. Each time Sham said yes—until that last one, when, after a hesitation, he told the truth: no. & after another hesitation, Elfrish nodded & altered course.

Daybe wouldn't enter Sham's dreary cell, but it perched on the rim of the tiny window. With outswept arms & exaggerated pointings Sham would encourage it out to local islands, to disrupt railgulls & to pick up snacks of grubs. With swoopy beckonings he'd entice it back. He saw it flit under the clouds & upsky, above a ragged reef of salvage.

Where were they?

Sham was at the mercy of a man he knew to be wholly ruthless. Of murderers who would throw him overboard or spit him on a trainhook for the laugh of it, if the thought appealed. But as long as he was alive & making himself useful, he was somewhere he had never been. Neither doctoring nor pining, but somewhere quite new, doing something new, & with that came—whatever the danger—excitement.

Robalson visited him at all hours & would go on about nothing. Would start halfheartedly taunting Sham, until that was done & he'd just sit, uneasily. "There's so many stories going round," he said at last. "If whatever it is the Shroakes are after, that their family found, is even half as good as people think it might be, we're going to be . . ." He made lip-smacking noises. "They say you can't even imagine it. So we got to keep moving before anyone else gets smart. Course, they ain't got your pictures, have they?"

No, thought Sham, but they'll be after the Shroakes. He bit his lip.

A WHISTLE SOUNDED, & there came the heavy beat of running. The train accelerated, skewed away from the direction it had been going. This was skilled switching. The swift manoeuvres continued, these sudden changes of direction, abrupt speedings-up & slowings-down. Robalson leapt up.

"What is it?" Sham shouted. His jailer took a moment to shoot him a very nervous grin, then was gone & turning the key. Sham stared from the little window & caught his breath. The *Tarralesh* was racing after another train. Some small merchant vehicle, plying goods between railsea islands, now gusting at the limit of its steam strength. "Get out of here!" he shouted across the miles, & as if it heard him, the littler train tried.

There was a booming. A fusillade of missiles arced with dreadful laziness from the pirate train, over the rails, to rainbow down in a succession of withering explosions that sent ripped-up rail shreds & ties in all directions. One of the flying bombs hit the rear of their quarry.

Sham moaned. The caboose exploded, sent flames & metal & wood in a big splash, as well as, oh my Stoneface, little pinwheeling figures. They landed scattered. & near those who still moved, now fitfully, injured, the earth erupted, as carnivorous burrowers smelled person-meat.

Another flurry of shots, & the train was immobilised. Over horrible minutes, the *Tarralesh* came closer. Sham could hear the crew catcalling & arming themselves. On the deck of the immobilised train the men & women waited with swords, guns, & terrified expressions. They may not have been soldiers or pirates, but they would fight.

NOT THAT IT DID them overmuch good. The *Tarralesh* bombed them some more, spilt defenders like spillikins onto the awful ground. Elfrish's vehicle came alongside, to an adjacent rail, & snagged the crippled merchant with grappling hooks. Hallooing to some aggressive pirate god, the fighting crew of the *Tarralesh* swept aboard, & the hand-to-hand melee began.

Sham couldn't see much. A blessing. He could see enough. He saw women & men shoot each other at close hand, send wounded & dead flying off the train. Some fell near enough that he could hear their cries, see them crawling on broken bones, clutching at wounds, scrabbling to get back aboard.

The sandy soil began to churn. To swirl & sink. A circle slid down into a cone. A man slid down too, crying out. From the base of that pit scissored two great chitin mandibles, beetle-coloured scythes. Compound eyes.

Sham looked away before the antlion's jaws closed on its meal & a scream abruptly ended. He flattened himself against the wall below his porthole. He felt as if his heartbeat was fast & hard enough to shake the train. When he looked again, the predators were fighting between themselves, & the ground churned not only with men & women but with the squabbles of giant insects & mole rats, shrews & moles. While in the ruined train, pirates took control.

Those pirates overboard & still living were rescued. The merchants on the earth were left to scrabble their own way back to their wreck, around antlion pits, the loose earth of hungry badgers.

Elfrish's crew hauled goods out of the holds, craned & grappling-hooked & pulleyed them across to the *Tarralesh*. Watching them under armed guard were the last dejected & sobbing merchants. Sham couldn't hear what Elfrish was saying, but he saw two or three of the defeated crew pulled out—the best dressed, it looked like, the captain & officers. They were dragged onto the pirate train, out of his sight. Sham could hear scuffs above him. A groan of horror from the other merchants, all staring at whatever was occurring above Sham's head.

When at last the *Tarralesh* pulled away, it left behind it an empty & immobile train, a big chunk of nu-salvage for someone to pick clean. On its roof the last of its crew, allowed by laziness to live, mourning, cold, marooned.

"What a day, eh?" Robalson said.

"What'll happen to them?" Sham could not turn to look at him.

"Someone'll probably come for them, maybe, when they don't turn up where they're expected," Robalson said. He shrugged. He wouldn't meet Sham's eye. "Don't look at me like that," Robalson muttered. Sulkily put down a bowl.

"What did you do to those last ones?" Sham said. "I could hear . . ."

"Plank," Robalson said. He made walking-finger motions. "They was the officers. I said don't *look* at me like that. You know we lost six people? If they'd just surrendered we wouldn't have had to do any of that."

"Right," said Sham, & turned back to the window. He felt like crying. He shivered. "What was under the plank? Where'd you do it?" When there was no answer, he said, "It was more antlions, weren't it? Centipedes?" Robalson was already gone.

Sham hunted for paper as carefully as once his crew had hunted moldywarpes. Found a scrap of drawer-liner. Kept looking. Found at last a discarded pencil stub. Had to chew-sharpen it. He wrote:

"Please! I am a captive in the train *Tarralesh*. It is pirates. They have guns. They are a pirate train. They are making me show them the way to a secret if I don't do it they will drop me into the railsea & maybe an antlion trap or something. My name is S. a. Soorap training under Capt. Naphi of the *Medes*. Please can you help me. Please also tell Troose yn Verba & Voam yn Soorap of Streggeye that I have not run away & that I will come back! The *Tarralesh* wants to Do Harm to two young Manihiki travellers & also to me please help!! West & North is all I know where we are going. Thank you."

Sham leaned into the dark, chattered, beckoned until Daybe came in. Sham twisted up the paper very tight & tucked it into the tracer still secured to the daybat's leg.

"Listen," he said. "I know this is going to be hard. You came to find me. & you don't know how much that meant. But you know what I need you to do now?" He swept out his arm, hard, in the direction they had come. "I need you to go back. Fly back. Find someone. Find anyone."

The bat stared at him. Intimidated by the night. It huddled, licked him, met Sham's eyes. His heart breaking, Sham started the long process of persuading it, intimidating it, frightening it if he had to, into flying away.

Chapter Fifty-Six

ANOTHER CARRIAGE was gone, taken skyward in vengeful & tremendous owl claws. Caldera had pressed the release, as the owl had flown. Just in time but at the right time, restraining herself until those strigine talons were directly over the track on which the Shroakes' engine had still raced, the last to be dragged up, gunning it so the train lurched forward as the carriages fell & with sparks & terrifying bangs slammed wheels-down back onto the rails. One more moment, they'd have been too high, or too far to one side or the other, & the whole vehicle would have been lost.

The Shroakes, gasping & owl-eyed themselves, had watched the metal tons of what had been their rearmost carriage hauled off into skyborne silhouette, viciously pecked as it went, & shedding shredded metal. It looked like straw & gossamer as it fell, & landed with booms & made the earth shudder.

At last they pushed on, under a huge night, in the deeps of which upsky predators made sounds. The Shroakes—

—but wait. On reflection, now is not the time for Shroakes. There is at this instant too much occurring or about to occur to Sham ap Soorap.

Look: Sham has just sent away his own, furred, little-winged friend. Once bloodstained, a poor tryer at medicine, an aspirer to salvage-hunting, & now a locked-away captive in a pirate train.

This train, our story, will not, cannot, veer now from this track on which, though not by choice, Sham is dragged.

Later, Shroakes. Sham is with pirates.

Chapter Fifty-Seven

"WHAT'S THE MATTER with you?" Robalson was always shirty with Sham when Sham was sad. & the morning after Sham had finally persuaded Daybe off into the dark, he was very sad.

They were in wildlands now, oddlands, & the railsea was punctuated with anomalies. Hillocks of bridges, rotators to swivel an engine amid a starburst of rails, a multiply holed island. Salvage. & not all old arche-salvage. Wrecks. Ranging in size from tiny scout carts to large, now-skeletal vehicles. Overgrown, weather-stripped, rusted, cold. A train boneyard.

"Someone'll probably come for them," Robalson had said about those stranded merchants. Sham wondered. You never knew. That night, alone, he watched the birds, none of which would come to him when he waved. He had a bit of a sniff because his heart hurt that Daybe had gone, & now he had not a single friend on this train.

& then the next morning, he looked out again & gasped. Sham held his breath, he bit his lip so that he wouldn't scream in delight. Because at the horizon, like a miracle, as if he had conjured it, called for it, which perhaps his beautiful bat friend had, he saw a Manihiki ferronavy train.

It moved hard, fast & well. These were some railsailors. It was perhaps three miles off. Approaching on interception course. It ran up pendants, that Sham, a trainsman now, could read. *Prepare*, they said, *for Inspection.*

*

AMONG THE FLURRY of feet & anxious preparations, Robalson stuck his head around the door.

"You," he said. "Shtum. Not a word. I'm right outside. You make a sound . . ." He shook his head. "The captain's waiting for an excuse. So you make a sound &—all sorts of stuff'll happen." He made a close-your-mouth motion & went.

"Attention *Tarralesh*." An amplified voice boomed from the Manihiki train. "Prepare to receive visitors." Sham watched it draw near on close rails, set down a cart of splendid speed & modern appearance, full of uniformed officers. He leaned, he waved, he yelled, out of the window.

Had they seen him? What cock-&-bull story was the captain offering? Had they swept away all the appurtenances of the pirate's life? Sham heard stamping on the deck above. He did not know when he would be safe to yell. Someone was approaching down the corridor. He hesitated. He could hear a roaring argument. Sham could not make out anything, until the shouters stopped outside his cabin & his heart went into his throat & abruptly the door flew open & a tall officer in the Manihiki navy, a captain in smart black uniform, brocaded & gilded & polished-buttoned, was standing before him, yelling back at Elfrish & Robalson. The officer pointed at Sham & yelled, "*That* boy, that's who I'm talking about. So bring him out. You have a lot of explaining to do."

"THEY BEEN KEEPING me prisoner!" Sham shouted as he ran after the officer. "Don't be fooled, sir, they're pirates! Sir! Thank you for rescuing me!" Elfrish struggled to shut him up, to put a hand over his mouth, but Sham was moving too fast. "They want me to lead them to a secret, sir & I don't even really know what it is or where, but they think I recognise things & they've had me here for days & they're breaking the law—"

They were outside, in creepier railscape still than Sham had seen. Ahead, the rails wove between scrubby rock hills, & into them, into brief dark tunnels overlooked by leafless trees. There were other Manihiki officers on the deck. "Captain Reeth," they barked as Sham's rescuer appeared.

Reeth made some imperious gesture. He was tall & looked down at everyone. He gestured for Sham to come closer. Sham breathed out, shuddering, in relief.

"You really shouldn't listen to this idiot boy, sir," Elfrish said, & cuffed at him. "He's our cabin boy."

"You said this was your cabin boy." Reeth pointed at Robalson.

"They both are. Never have too many cabin boys. Except this one, this Sham. He's been trouble since he joined us."

"So you can have too many." The officer put his hand on Sham's shoulder.

"Certainly you can, Captain Reeth. We had him in the brig for, for thieving, sir. He stole food."

"They're lying!" In confused but exhaustive detail, interspersed with expostulations of ostentatious disbelief from Elfrish, Sham jabbered his story. "You got to arrest them all!" he said. "They done all killings & robbings & they're going to kill me! He killed the Shroakes! Smashed their train ages ago. You heard of them?"

"He's a fantasist," sneered Elfrish.

"He may be," said Reeth. "But unfortunately for you we know it's perfectly true that two young Manihikians called Shroake have departed the city. We've heard word that the remains of their long-disappeared family were in fact found. & these youngsters have left in a train that we are eager to find. This we also know. Now, Captain. Do you think, do you *really* think, we've heard nothing of the young man whose visit spurred a new generation of Shroakes to their annoying aspirations?"

He must have made some flickering signal with his eyes. His subordinates raised their weapons, simultaneously. Sham held his breath.

"If I were to check your hold, Captain Elfrish," Reeth said, "what goods would I find?"

There was a silence. The *Tarralesh* crew fingered their weapons. *He's got them!* Sham thought.

Elfrish sighed. "Alright then," he said. "Yes," he said. "It's sort of like he says."

"You see?" Sham shouted. "Arrest them!"

"But," Elfrish said. With reassuring this-is-not-a-weapon motions, he withdrew from his pocket a leather wallet, held it up open to a silver stamp. "My letter of marque. I'm licensed. Manihiki seal. All official."

A—what? Sham thought.

"Why didn't you just say this from the start?" Reeth said.

"Say what?" said Sham.

"Well . . ." Elfrish said. He grinned sheepishly.

"Tax?" Reeth said. "As a privateer, twenty per cent of everything in your hold belongs to Manihiki. You're a bloody tax avoider."

"When you going to *arrest* him?" Sham shouted. Elfrish cuffed him, & Reeth did not stop him.

"See," Reeth said, "here's the thing. If his story's true, he & you are going to the same place these young Shroakes are going.

244

& I like the sound of the technique you're using." He considered.

"Arrest them?" said Sham. No one did a thing.

"I'm claiming him," Reeth decided. "In lieu of your tax. See what I can get out of him."

"What?" shouted Sham.

"What?" shouted Elfrish. "You can't do that!"

"Certainly I can," said Reeth.

This wasn't between police & criminal, Sham realised. His insides felt like dust. The dead & robbed they'd left behind weren't *Manihiki* merchants, after all, not the navy's charges. He did not think it was—he hoped it was not—his daybat who had called them. Elfrish wasn't freelance. He was a sanctioned pirate, under the purview of a government, a Manihiki agent as much as Reeth. This was an argument between colleagues. Departmental politics.

"You know," Elfrish said, "what's beyond the railsea? Neither do I. But you know & I know, Captain, that there's an inverse correlation between proximity & pecuniary recompense, vis-à-vis treasure. To put it another way, the further out the hoard, the bigger. So. What d'you suppose is *beyond the railsea?*"

"No such place as beyond," Reeth said carefully.

"Beg to differ." Elfrish raised his gun, carefully, even as Reeth's men eyed him, their weapons up. It was as if he moved so slowly they were somehow paralysed, watching. He pointed it at Reeth. Some of his crew raised theirs, too.

"The boy's mine," Elfrish said.

Reeth laughed. "Well done," Reeth said. "You just lost your licence. So far I count obstruction of an officer, threatening behaviour, & illegal piracy."

"But," Elfrish said, "I'm willing to bet—& look, so's my crew—that what's at the end of the world makes all that worth it."

It was quiet under the sun. The birds circled. The wind pushed Sham's hair around. Reeth, at last, said one word: "Fire."

Whatever frozen moment had taken them, his officers were back in control. They were unafraid, & efficient. They fired.

The pirates fired back. Everyone fighting over Sham. Who dropped.

It went haywire on that deck. Shouting, shots, running feet. People scrambled for cover. There were screams. Reeth, still firing, dragged a wounded comrade across the deck, shouting a signal into his shoulder-mic. The wartrain's huge-bore guns swivelled. Reeth & his officers hunched & scrambled back for thier own jollycart.

"Holy flaming hell," Elfrish shouted. Even so weapon-bristling a train as the *Tarralesh* had little chance against a Manihiki wartrain. "Full power! Full power! Go go go go! Get away from them!"

They shot forward. The vehicle lurched, powering on into that merciful maze of hills & tunnels.

Sham had a plan. If you could call it that. He crawled; the chaos continued. He reached the base of the crow's nest & quickly started to climb. The wartrain still approached. "Get him down," Elfrish shouted. The *Tarralesh* powered towards a tunnel.

The naval train fired. Now that, *that* was an explosion. A whole mountain of boom grew out of nothing. The *Tarralesh* swayed, seemed to gust on a shockwave. Here came a wartrain.

Sham tried to work out trajectories. He could see, very calmly, suddenly, what was going to happen, where, when. "Get him!" Elfrish was yelling, waving his weapon in Sham's direction, but his crew were scattering. Robalson was right below Sham, staring up at him with a look of miserable astonishment.

& the wartrain arrived, hard & fast, firing again, & an explosive came down, & the rear of the *Tarralesh*, accelerating without control, exploded.

A chorus of wails. Pirates flying through the air, scattering across the railsea. The bulk of the train itself shoved brutally forward by the impact, hurtling out of control towards & into that tunnel, that cut-out route through a rock hill ahead.

As Sham stared down, the explosion snatched Robalson away. Sham gasped.

The *Tarralesh* was shattering as it moved, Sham saw. Sham watched, aghast, as the train plunged into the dark, as the very crow's nest he climbed slammed into the side of the island & tottered like a cut-down tree. He was prepared. He rode it. Down it came, slowly, it seemed, taking him clear of the snaggliest rock teeth. Falling down towards whatever isolated island this was that wrecked them.

Pirates were scattered & wailing in the dirt & the railsea. There was Elfrish, staring up at Sham from a dark hole in the earth, where he had fallen, all rage & hatred. Staring as up from below some unseen underground thing disturbed in the burrow rose, jostled, snarled, came up to take him. Elfrish did not take his eyes from Sham as it grabbed him. As it sucked him down.

Then Sham could see no more.

Down he came. Aiming for a bush he knew would hurt but less than the stones & a great slamming *huff* & crack of metal & he was right *ow* it did hurt, but he was rolling & on hardland now & breathing & shaking & lying very still, partly out of pain but partly because he couldn't believe he'd done it, & because he knew he was still hunted.

Sham lay & listened to the wartrain approach, & the cries for help from the ruins of the *Tarralesh* & the terrified pirates in the predator-thronging ground.

THERE ON THE top of the hill, on an island in a vehicle grave-yard in the wild reaches of the railsea, Sham lay.

Part Five

Burrowing Owl
Athene cunicularia trux

Chapter Fifty-Eight

INVESTIGATE A MAP. Look for the least-charted, least-visited, wildest, most strange, most dangerous, all-around particularly problematical parts of the railsea.

A fringe of unknownness spreads from a point at the northwestern edge of the world. There are patches of troublesome sparsely sketched-out rails eastward of that mountain & highland & monster-bounded place. The darkest polar iceholes of the south have their terrible aspects. & so on. At these wild parts the rails seem drunk on rarities. The rails misbehave. Switches do not do as they are bid, ground is not so strong & stable as it appears, there are chicanes & trouble, the iron itself has been made to mess with trains. A most scandalous wrongness.

Here, deities tinkered with each other's rails, warring sisters & brothers, to ruin each other's plans. Such stretches have been there as long as there has been a railsea, & will remain as long as it remains.

It would be foolish to say any such place was *impassable*. History is long; there are, have been & will be many trains. Most things eventually happen. Less controversial, however, not even controversial at all, is the assertion that such stretches are at least *horribly difficult*.

Chapter Fifty-Nine

SALVORS SALVAGED—one in particular. Pirates pirated. Naval trains hunted & claimed islands for Manihiki. & animals?

Talpa ferox. Never the most predictable mole. Its rapacity & power made it subterrestrial king. & now?

There was no remaining doubt that Mocker-Jack, the captain's philosophy, had changed its behaviour. Was tunnelling more quickly, zigging less & zagging not quite so much as it had once done, straight-lining more. You might almost have called what it was doing "fleeing".

The captain's thing for the moldywarpe had infected her crew. Enthusiasm is a virus, as is curiosity, as is obsession. Some are immune: a few spat disgustedly as they raced, their gob disappearing into the dirt; some lobbied the officers as subtly as they could to encourage a turnaround, a more traditional hunt. Vurinam was troubled. But they were the minority.

Naphi's officers took turns reading the little scanner, & the train did not stop, no matter if it was night. They roared on past isolated communities, clots of lights like firebugs, past rocks. Mocker-Jack went north. Veering from the usual haunts.

"You'd have liked this," whispered Dr. Fremlo, on the deck, watching the nothing of night, watching the train's narrow lights unzip the darkness & zip it up again. "I hope life as a salvor's treating you well."

ON A REEF OF salvage were remnants of rust-ruined trains, scattered bones of trainsfolk. The windblown carapace segments of great boring bugs, beetles, recoiled centipedes many people long. Birds avoided that sparsely railed place, but circling it right then at least one thing was flying.

The rubbishy earth churned. Something rose. With a whine, a fussing, a spray of dust & the shards of refuse, up came a metal-flanged spinning spire, a machine a carriage long that reared up out of the below & slapped down skew-whiff across the rails. A subterrain of sleek intimidating design. The dust of its passage sank around it, its hatch opened, a head poked out. The subterrainer scanned her surrounds. She lowered her eye-piece from a face so filthy it looked more oil & grease than skin.

"Alright then," she muttered to herself. "We're clear." She clicked her fingers. With serial clanks & gusts like sulky breaths, the digger's chassis began to unfold into many-segmented arms, mechanical grabs. Travisande Sirocco looked out on the rubbishscape with professional detachment. En route to where rumours had a merchant train newly smashed to scavenge. Sirocco pursed her lips. You might have thought that she was estimating prices of what junk she saw & you would have been right.

Something dived & yawed above her. Agitated in the air.

"Hello," Sirocco said. Up went her goggles, a whir & click of zooms. "Hello indeed," she said. "You're not from around here." She pursed her lips again, & this time it had nothing to do with money.

"Some meat," she said. "& a rope. Looks like I'm going sky-baiting. I have a guest."

Chapter Sixty

SHAM HID. For hours, that was more or less all he did. He did it hard, he did it with all his energy.

After that crazy leap to rock-strewn freedom, there he was, exploded pirate train behind him, scattered & slid across the rails, the Manihiki navy powering in, survivors shrieking, the sounds of the last bits of battle, the snarls of predators. The haul of prisoners.

Sham had slid down the scree, into a steep slope hidden from the wind. Into the shadow of stones, shivering as the cold of that isolated islet hit him. Sham scootched into a hollow & hugged his knees. & waited. Both the fighting forces wanted him, & he wanted neither of them.

What was he supposed to do?

The noises didn't last very long. He heard the last of the pirates wait until the last of the navy had investigated the last of the audible sounds. Hunting, among other things, for him. He heard the great train go back the way it had come. He heard the jollycarts, which in some patrician mercy the Manihiki forces used to pick up the pirate wounded, putter away.

Sham tried not to think about the fact that he could not stay like this forever. He closed his eyes, & tried to stop the image looping in his head, the sight of Robalson gusted away in smoke & fire.

In the second or third hour after the last skirmish, long after

there were no more sounds, he listened to the absolute trainless-
ness of the island. He heard railgulls, wind, dust sandpapering
stone. He searched his pockets as carefully as any explorer on
the wrong bit of a map ever did. Found some nuts & the stump
of a block of tacky. Ate a miserable meal.

& then it was dark. How & when did it go dark?

& then he slept.

Without much else to do, stripped of options, exhausted,
fearful, hungry, thoroughly & utterly alone, Sham retreated out
of wakefulness &, surprised that he even could, slept.

HE WOKE VERY EARLY with flinty cold going through him &
the sky light but not bright. He was stiff like a miserable puppet,
like a bundle of damp twigs. Sham hugged himself a while &
listened to the wolflike snuffling of his stomach. Eventually what
got him up was that he was bored of being terrified.

That day he explored. On the railsea off the coast he saw
the remains of the pirate train. & here & there the grisly remains
of those pirates dead & not taken.

His island was perhaps a couple of miles round. Its sides
were absurdly steep, shagged in ivy & vines of various scrubby
kinds, from some of which hung little nodules of fruit or
something. Gingerly he nibbled at them. Horrible, bitter, sappy
grossness he spat out. His stomach yowled. There was water,
though. It dribbled down from some on-high aquifer. Sham put
his lips into the streamlet & slurped, not even minding the cold
& mineral bite of it.

The island was full of noises. The rustlings of birds, the
chatterings of other things, that went silent when he approached
only to sound off again behind Sham's back. He climbed as far
as he safely could & stared at the upper reaches where, maybe,

the peak prodded into the upsky. He descended to the pebbled shore, where the island met the dark & ancient rails.

A few scrips & scraps of stuff lay near the shoreline. Stuff he could maybe even get hold of if he went for it with a stick. Things lost from pirate pockets, the debris of trainsplosions. Stuff too small for salvors, too drab for glint-loving birds.

Thinking of salvors made Sham think of the Shroakes. Though they were not salvors, of course. Perhaps that's why he had thought of them. Minds, he thought, can be funny that way. Sham considered Caldera, only a little younger than he, commanding her impossibly advanced train. She would not stop for sloughed-off junk like this.

There were many words for what she had. Oomph, verve, drive, élan. Caldera & Dero seemed full of all of them. It was as if there was none left for anyone else. Sham sat on the shore. Sort of fell onto it, cross-legged. He picked up a bit of wood. He picked at it with his nail.

This must be a notorious clutch of train-wrecking islands. He could see others, out to railsea, beyond the shells of carriages & engines. The mashed-up *Tarralesh* was just the latest. Even so close to maps' edges, salvors had come, cleared out the worst or best of the ruination. But there was plenty of unreclaimable junk out there.

Sham looked down. He realised that he had been using his thumbnail to give the old wood he carried a face.

The nearest island to his, he saw, was lusher, lower, flatter. Covered with trees. Maybe they grew fruit. Sham licked his lips. Between this beach & that one were perhaps two miles of rails. Between each of those rails were stretches of rumbustious earth. & motion. Animal motion. Sham shivered.

A spine of stony offshoot islands trailed from the shore, on each of them weeds & squabbling birds. Stones bent up broken-tooth-style between ties to send trainsfolk to the ground. Sham could see remnants from cargo holds spilled & mummified or rotted; a rust-clogged handcart; a cairn of ruined engine parts; a crushed caboose.

His stomach muttered, impatient little animal. *What do you want from me?* he asked it, & tried to keep his panic under control. A wodge of birds came at him, & for a moment he imagined it might be Daybe at their head, come to snap affectionately at his face. It wasn't. It was just some anonymous, ill-tempered, guano-bombing gull.

That other island looked increasingly delicious. *I'm not a kid any more*, Sham thought. *Shouldn't take anything for granted.* A big bird cawed as he thought that, & Sham took it as applause. *All my life*, he thought, *they've told me about the dangers of the earth. Maybe it's true. But* . . . He kept his eyes on the foody island across the narrow railsea strait. *But maybe it's also useful for them if everyone believes it. If people are too scared to just go.*

Without giving himself time to think, Sham set out walking.

He stuck out his chest, kept his stare ahead. He marched off the edge of the rock shore. Stepped over the closest rail, put his foot between ties & iron, & continued.

I'm walking, he thought. *I'm on the earth.* He kept going, crossing rail after rail. He laughed. He sped up. He whooped. He tripped. He sprawled. He thumped the ties. The earth jiggled.

Oh. Yes, the earth definitely moved. Sham rose, no longer laughing. There he was, stopped, looking back at the shore. Which looked an awfully long way away.

It wasn't a jiggle any more, what was going on in the ground, it was a full-blown shudder. Again. He watched aghast as a ridge came up. Something moved underground. It was coming towards him. *Experiment fail*, Sham thought, turned & ran.

He ran, & behind him there was a boom, a crash, the grind of the ground. Muck showered Sham as whatever that was coming burst the earth from below. It closed on him, clattering.

Sham wailed & accelerated. With two last huge leaps he made it back to the baked, rocky earth, almost blown by a howl from his pursuer, something like a kettle screaming & an electrical short, all at once. He stumbled, rolled, turned to see.

Shiny segmented shell, scissoring pincer on its rear, bumjaws. It wriggled down again out of the light. He just glimpsed it. An earwig. Oh Stonefaces. Sham was lucky. In a different mood it might have come up onto the shore after him.

He picked up a big rock, chucked it onto the disturbed earth of the earwig's wake. Another rumbling, & he saw the head of a meat-eating worm. A flurry of fur & metal-hard claws as a vicious digging shrew came just up enough to yank it down.

Everywhere Sham looked, the ground between ties, the dirt around rails, the muck shoring up stays, seethed. He yelled at the excited birds, as the little ones laughed at him & the bigger urged him to get further back. "Albloodyright," he yelled at them. "The earth *is* dangerous!"

Chapter Sixty-One

AT THIS POINT, the intention had been to say that it was such slippery western terrain as few trainsfolk ever see, such strange wrong rails, that the Shroakes, by then, had reached, & in which & on which they travelled. But the time is not yet right.

The instant it is feasible, the Shroakes will be found. It's Caldera & Dero, after all: as if they could be ignored.

There are monsters under the earth, & in the trees above it, & swinging from those trees to the rooftop decks of trains, & there are creatures that can barely be called animals watching from the upsky, & any of them might find, might sniff for, might zero in on the Shroakes. It would be wrong to leave them forever. But though the rails themselves are everywhere in profusion, fanned out & proliferating in all directions, we can ride only one at a time.

This is the story of a bloodstained boy. The Shroakes deserve their own telling, & will get it. Though their things & Sham's are plaited together now, inextricable.

Chapter Sixty-Two

COULD IT BE? Oh, they thought it could. They began to believe that they, the crew of the *Medes*, would make it into the Museum of Completion.

Once again, as the *Medes* continued across the railsea, zeroing in on Mocker-Jack, they talked of Shedni ap Yes, who'd caught an elusive meerkat commensurate with playful pointlessness. Hoomy's prey, the desert tortoise known as Boshevel, a dome-shelled symbol of tenacity. Guya & Sammov, who had sought & found a termite queen (doubt) & a bull-sized bandicoot (prejudice).

It was common to insist that the worst thing that could happen to a person was to get the wisdom for which they strove. "Feh," said Dr. Fremlo. "Believe me, most people really do want what they want. Downsides there may be to getting it, but they're heftily outweighed by the up, & by the downs of *not* doing so."

There was no pretence any more that this was any kind of regular hunt. Whether out of fidelity to Naphi, excitement at what they might achieve, or the suddenly-less-unthinkable possibility of riches that a finishing train would accrue, most of the crew were content to ignore other moldywarpes & follow the transceiver. Into scrappy corners of the railsea where great southern moldywarpes had no business burrowing, that should have been too warm, with ground too hard or too soft, too marbled by too many salvage seams, like fat in a steak.

In a tiny townlet the *Medes* was gouged by diesel-merchants who correctly gauged that they were in too great a hurry to barter. They surprised the burghers of Marquessa by waving at the gravelly shore but not stopping. Beyond all but the most speculative maps they went. Into badrail. Wild shores where trees shook with the movements of animals of the interior. A nameless atoll from where the train was shot at by small-arms fire. The bullets only ricocheted with dramatic pings, but it was a scare.

"Not long now," they reassured each other. But all of them feared the malevolent cunning that Mocker-Jack, great & terrible but dumb beast, should not possess. But seemed to. It led them to where the rails were stained dark.

"Been a while since anyone came this way," Dramin said.

& across an empty reach of sky came a roar, a bass boom like the declaration of a storm. It shook the hair on the crew's heads, made the train vibrate, gusted them with wind & dust. The silence in its aftermath was silenter than any silence had been for a long time. Yashkan tried to snigger, but nerves meant it did not take.

"What in the Stonefaces' name . . ." Vurinam started to say, as if it was a mystery. The captain herself answered him.

"Mocker-Jack."

She leaned over the rails. "Mocker-Jack," she shouted. "Mocker-Jack, Mocker-Jack." She turned at last & bellowed at no one in particular & at everyone, "Make—this—train—go—*faster.*"

The train accelerated towards the sound, into dangerous railsea strewn with rubble. The unseen moldywarpe called again.

"Blimey," someone whispered. The way ahead was blocked

by huge rock pillars. To port was an enormous declivity. A hole in the fabric of the earth, miles across, hundreds of stomach-dropping yards deep. Lines reached its edges & jutted & were broken. The sinkhole was scattered with ties & ruined rails. It hurt to see it. Rails beyond the reach of angel or salvor. There were the ruins of trains down there.

Mocker-Jack called a third time. It was near. The *Medes* headed for a passage between a gnarled-up spire & the great canyon.

"Switchers," Mbenday shouted. "Ready." They lined up with remote controls & switchhooks. "Come now, gentlemen & ladies. Let us show this beast how molers move." Ebba Shappy threw her lever, & the junction ahead clicked smoothly into place as the *Medes* approached.

But then, audibly & terribly, with their front wheels scant feet from it, it switched again, reverted, unbidden, & the *Medes* passed over it & veered to port, heading straight for the gorge.

Chapter Sixty-Three

PANDEMONIUM. The void was close. The captain was yelling, & with the quickest of quick thinking, the most vigorous button-pushing & lever-smacking on the part of the most heroic switchers, another gauge turned them from immediate disaster. Jens Thorn was leaning out, prodding buttons to take them star'd. "They won't stay, Captain," he yelled. The switches were switching *back*, junctions conspiring to tip them into the pit.

The switchers strained with the mechanisms, defeated the junctions straining one by terrifying one to send them port. They veered star'd towards the rock pillar, fighting to keep going. "A godsquabble booby-trap," Mbenday shouted.

"Captain?" said Vurinam. "Is everything alright?"

"No," Naphi said. "It's something . . ." She stared at the shaft near which they had to pass, that cast an immensely long shadow across the world. They were in that shadow. The captain lifted her microphone & said, "To arms." For seconds, the crew did not understand. "To arms!" she said again. Then came screams.

Uncoiling from where they had lain disguised with stone-grey skins, emerging suddenly from cave-holes in the stiletto-island's sides, came snakelike things.

"What," Vurinam whispered, "in the name of That Apt Ohm . . . ?"

There were three, there were five, there were seven of the

things. Swaying, flailing, eyeless but not mouthless—on each was a circle rimmed with oozing gums & chitinous teeth.

"Weapons!" Someone was shouting. Someone was firing. Molers raced to get guns. "Weapons now!" The wavering things drew themselves up. Their pulsing mouths drooled, then spat, leaving gluey spittle where they struck. The trainsfolk shot, & the attackers were harried by bullets like frenetic flies. The tentacular things drew back, then, whip-quick, struck.

One closed with a terrible sucking noise on Yorkaj Teodoso's chest. He screamed. It tugged him from the traintop deck, dangled him, reeled him in to the island they passed. "Fire! Fire!" Captain Naphi shouted. Trainsfolk were screaming Teodoso's name. Where shots hit the attacking things' skins they sprayed dark blood. They recoiled, but not far, not for long; they came down blindly grubbing, their mouths moistly smacking.

They launched themselves at the crew. Yashkan howled. Fired the pistol he held blindly behind him as he ran. He almost hit Lind. Mbenday ducked under one of the looping coils, leaped another, smacked at a third with a machete. The slippery thing spasmed & oozed great slopping dollops of slime.

"Fire & drive!" the captain shouted. "Accelerate! On, will you?" Down came the coils again, & again found prey. One grabbed Cecilie Klimy by her left arm, one by her right. Her crewmates howled her name. They ran for her, they grabbed for her, Lind & Mbenday & even gibbering Yashkan pawing to try to get hold of her, but with awful collaboration the two mouth-things moved in concert, hauled her shrieking off as the train moved. The crew were firing now with purpose, were slashing with something other than utter panic. "Klimy!" they shouted. "Teodoso!"

Their colleagues were gone. Pulled out of sight, into the

rock. Tendril-beast after tendril-beast tried to grip the train as it went, suckering onto the grinding wheels, the splintering deck.

"You will not!" It was Naphi herself shouting. Not standing back, right there, shooting with a weapon in one hand, swivelling through a succession of spikes & blades in her left limb until she fixed on a nastily serrated edge & slashed at a coiling enemy.

"We have to go back!" Vurinam shouted, but the train kept moving, accelerating, as the creatures tried again. "We have to go back for them!" Benightly roared & fired a big rapid gun & the monsters shuddered. A ripple corkscrewed around & went the height of the island.

"Oh my god!" said Fremlo. "It's all one thing!"

On the stone the necks conjoined into a single thick ropy body that wound into the upsky. At the landform's very top, at the level of the toxic clouds, was the creature's diffuse gas-filled body. It was like the canopy of a great tree all fruited with watching eyes.

The mountainside shook, the shoreline curved away. The *Medes* reached a safe distance from the hole on one side & from the monster on the other. It stopped in the sunlight. The bewildered & battered crew gathered. Some were crying.

"What in the name of holy bloody hell?" someone said.

"Siller," Fremlo said. The doctor looked at the captain. At the thing behind them. They couldn't see its tendrils any more. They'd retreated & lay still. "It's called a siller. Breathes up there, dips its feeding toes down here. & that . . ." The doctor pointed at the canyon. "That's the Kribbis Hole. That's why that siller hunts here. Because to stay out of the hole, you have to get close to it."

"Those rails!" Vurinam shouted. "That shunt you into the damn hole! Why don't the angels fix them?"

"They aren't broken," said Dr. Fremlo. "In this place, that's how the rails are supposed to be. This place is an old, old, old trap."

"Captain," Vurinam said. "We have to go back." Captain Naphi was examining her tracker. She didn't speak. "I thought this place was a bloody legend," Vurinam gabbled. He stared at Naphi & abruptly stood straighter. "You knew," he said.

There was silence. Naphi raised her head to meet his eyes. She did not look cowed. She put the scanner down. Spread her artificial fingers.

"Don't shilly-shally, Mr. Vurinam," she said. "Make your accusation."

"You knew where we were," he breathed. "But because your damned moldywarpe's nearby, you said nothing. Couldn't be bothered to have us go the long way round." He choked up & stopped. The crew were all open-eyed & staring.

"Anyone else?" Naphi said at last. "Anyone similar accusations? Speak freely." Nothing. "Very well. I've heard of this place, as have you. & it is true that when Mr. Mbenday said the switches were misbehaving, a possibility occurred to me. So if you arraign me before your court accused of having half-held notions, fleeting recollections, then I plead guilty.

"If, however, you claim I deliberately allowed my crew to steer themselves into danger, then sir how dare you?" She walked towards Vurinam. "I did not hear you complaining about our route nor our objective. I haven't heard you declining your share of whatever comes should we be successful in this endeavour."

Vurinam wriggled under her gaze. "You *still* keep checking

that scanner," he said. "You still want to know where that bloody mole is, more'n anything."

"Yes," Naphi shouted. She raised her hand. Her louder, clattering one. She shook it. "I do. That's what we *hunt*. That's what we're *doing here*. If anything's going to provide for Klimy's family now, to keep alive her memory & that of Teodoso, to ensure that this terrible moment has a purpose, it is *bringing the beast down*. Snaring the philosophy. So, yes, Mr. Vurinam. I want Mocker-Jack."

The captain still clenched her fist at him. Its lights winked, it rattled. But—wait. "Your arm," Vurinam said. "Captain. That thing hurt you, you're—bleeding?"

Her constructed limb had cracked. &, what made no sense, the split was oozing blood.

"How can she . . . ?"

"Where's it . . . ?"

The captain herself stared, as fascinated by the red drips as anyone else. Fremlo was there in a moment, prodding & squinting at the damaged limb. Naphi seemed to wake, tried to shake herself free, but the doctor was having none of it, kept on with the examination.

"You're cut rather badly, Captain," Fremlo announced at last. With scorn, the doctor released the arm as if it was hot, turned to face the crew, & continued. "Your arm, Captain. The one that appears to have been encased in metal & molebone, all this time. That is in fact not missing at all, only hidden. Your still-present left arm is injured, Captain."

Silence spread like a slick. Naphi drew herself calmly up. Not an instant of embarrassment crossed her face. Slowly, with ostentation, refusing to flinch from her crew's gazes, she held up the bleeding limb.

"Indeed," she said at last. "I will require you to take care of this for me."

"All this time," Vurinam whispered. Mbenday was staring at Naphi, back at his friend Vurinam, back & forth. "You were lying!" Vurinam said. "It was like some game! Oh, I get it. It was so they'd take you serious." Vurinam shimmied pugnaciously in his dusty coat, his eyes wide. "So you didn't get left out."

It had been a badge of intensity, of honour, that pretended lack. Had Naphi feared that fully in possession of her original body, she would not possess some requisite rigour? Certainly it looked that way.

She drew herself up. "There are those," she said. She was using her most splendid voice. "Whose faith. In their philosophies. Follows from something being taken from them. Who need that terrible bite & rupture to spur their fascination. Their revenge.

"It is weak of them," she said. "I would not so wait. Nor, however, would I fail to know what it is to suffer those agonies for a philosophy. & so. & hence." She raised her mechanical limb-glove. "I fail to see your point. My rigour, Mr. Vurinam, is such that I have both made & refused to make a sacrifice."

It was a good line. One by one, the crew looked back at Vurinam. He stamped in frustration.

"That don't even bloody *mean* anything!" he despaired. "It's complete bloody gibberish!"

"Something occurs to me," said Dr. Fremlo. "Arguably, right now it ain't where Mocker-Jack is that should concern us. Forget for a moment our captain's skin, bones & circuitry." There was a noise, an engine grind, from somewhere. "Let's focus on what's important. We've just lost two friends." The doctor let that sit with them a moment. "The issue is not so much where the moldywarpe is, as what it's doing."

Fremlo pointed at the pass through which they'd come. "Do you think it lay just so, sounded off like it did, just at this point, when we were where we were, by chance? It *wanted* us to go through there. It was sending us into the trap."

"Don't be crazy," someone started to say.

"It's leading us into danger," Fremlo interrupted. "The mole is trying to kill us."

Only the wind spoke, for a long while. It seemed as if Mocker-Jack might laugh, as if they might hear a booming moldywarpe snigger, but no.

"Oh, Stonefaces help us," said Zhed the Yimmer at last. Captain Naphi moved her fingers like horse's hooves. "What do we do?" Zhed said. "Things couldn't get any weirder."

It would have been simply rude for reality not to respond to a challenge like that. As that last word came out of Zhed's mouth, there came the whistling noise of something plummeting, & a small, firm, heavy body fell out of the air into Vurinam's hands.

Everyone yelled. Vurinam yelled, he staggered back, but what had landed held him tight, & Vurinam saw its jabbering little face. Sham's bat. Daybe, the transmitter still winking on its leg.

Chapter Sixty-Four

Time for the Shroakes?
Not yet.

Chapter Sixty-Five

SHAM ROLLED UP his sleeves, went to the shoreline, & looked out at the ruined trains.

With care, effort & bravery, he was able to brace himself on the iron, the ties, the various bits of natural & wrecky business he could reach. He even walked the earth where he had to, dragging a makeshift cart. Sham made it at last to the ruin of some once-grand cargo train, stripped it of fittings. He dug into the ground & hauled out debris.

Dangerous work, but he got on with it. He dumped his finds on the shore. Gathered junk. A few more trips out to the wreck & Sham had a yard-load of nu-salvage. As night fell he began to cobble it together. When the sun came up he was standing, proudly, in a hut.

He made it into the old train's hold where he discovered that, by happy chance, it had been carrying seeds. These he planted. He continued building until he had made a small township of corrugated iron. His crop grew. Sham collected rainwater & wove flax. He tamed local animals & got more stuff from the train. Sham made bread.

In the second year he got a bit lonely & then luckily he found the footprints of another human being on the island. He followed them & met a native, who was astonished but impressed by him & became his happy servant. Together they continued building, & after a few more years Sham managed to build an actual train, & he left the new country that he had founded with the handy discards of his old, & he set out on a journey back to Streggeye, the wind in his hair.

That didn't happen.

Sham sat, cold, frightened, starving, on the beach. Staring at nothing. His fantasy hadn't made him feel any better. It hadn't been convincing at all.

He chewed at the . . . well, it was a sort of leaf that he had found.

"Mmmm," he said. Out loud. "Piney. You're the first ingredient for a new drink I'm going to make." He grimaced & swallowed. "I'm going to call you fizzboont."

He had, in fact, built a shelter out of rubbish, but he would hesitate to say he had "salvaged" it: it was only trash lying at shoreside. & he would hesitate to say he had "built" it: he had really sort of leaned it up one bit against another. & he would hesitate to call it a "shelter". It was more of a pile.

"Troose," he said. He sniffed. "Voam." Their hopes for him—were they so foolish? Did their ultimate aim, that he might at least abut a philosophy, seem quite so terrible now?

The wind blew on him, & it felt like it was mocking him. Like it was saying *Pfffft*, disdainfully, at this almighty castaway failure. Whatever, the wind said, smacking him on the head. He could have cried. He did, a bit. Just a little bit in the corners of his eyes. It was just because he was staring into blown grit, but then again it wasn't just that really.

Sham did spend a lot of time looking out at the salvage, like in his daydream. He was very hungry. It had been two days. He was *very* hungry. He spent his time looking at ruined trains, at spread-eagled bonelike stubs of cranes, at scattered carts, bruising & bloodying his thumb by using it like a crude chisel or awl on his slowly enfiguring stick. He wondered what would happen to him.

Scattered carts. Some were bust up, some upside down. One, half-hidden in a thicket a few score yards offshore, right-way-up, was on its wheels.

On its wheels. On the rails.

Sham got slowly up & walked to where the rails started. It wasn't even a jollycar. No motor. It didn't even have sides. It was an ancient, tiny, flat handcart. A tabletop, basically, with a crank like a seesaw, for two operators to pump up & down, to make the wheels turn.

A two-person pump that, in a pinch, one person could use. Actually—

Actually, thought Sham, *enough.*

Looking straight into the wind that rushed across the railsea, blinking from its gust-borne dust, & in the flurry of his own resolve, too, Sham felt something catch inside him. Long-stalled wheels strained for purchase. Straining to pull himself together.

Sham swallowed. Like the crew-member he was, with the skills into which he had been trained, he traced a rail-route to the cart with his eyes. He threw his unfinished nail-carved figure away.

SHOULDN'T YOU JUST STAY?

Sham heard that voice in him more than once. As he gathered his useless stuff, a few odds & ends of rubbish on the shore. As he stretched & psyched himself up. A fearful bit of his head asked him if he was quite sure he wouldn't rather wait a bit? That, you never knew, someone might turn up.

Enough. He shut it up. He surprised himself, battening

down that little whine as if it were something troublesome rolling on a deck in a gale. *No I should not wait*, he thought. *Will not.*

He had to go. Sham didn't stop to think about what the stakes were—he simply knew he would not stay & wait. He wanted food, he wanted revenge, he wanted to find his old crew. & he was worried for the Shroakes. Their enemies still hunted.

He stood on the beach & swung his arms. Sham stripped to the waist. He'd lost weight. He threw a handful of rocks, in diversion. Another. Then while his missiles still settled, he jumped onto the nearest tie. He walked the rail. Balanced on the iron, jumped from plank to plank. Threw another bunch of distracting stones. He veered at a junction, & jumped across a couple of yards of unbroken earth, & onto another rail.

Sham rolled, Sham staggered, Sham threw more stones. He was walking on the rails! He was in the railsea! The only thing worse would be if he was on the actual earth.

Hush, don't think about that. He ran fast, & ever faster, his heart hammering, taking the route he had planned until with an almighty jump & a gasp of triumph he leapt, & landed on the handcart. He lay still.

"How about that, Daybe, eh?" he gasped. "What d'you say, Caldera?"

He wasn't losing his mind. He knew the bat was elsewhere, that the older Shroake was countless miles away. He just wished that wasn't so. He remembered the colours in the former's pretty pelt, the latter's frank stare, the one that flustered him. He rose. Standing there on his new perch, Sham was overwhelmingly bored of feeling overwhelmed. The more he worked, he realised, the quicker he worked.

✳

OF COURSE THE handle was solid with rust, but he worked at it, hitting it with a stone. Tried to spread what grease remained on the mechanism around. Again & again & again. Hit, smear.

His percussion went on so long the railsea, the railsea animals, began to ignore it. Slowly, the fauna emerged, as Sham continued his cack-handed engineering. The twitching-nosed face of a moldywarpe broke ground nearby, a specimen about his size. It sniffed & made dry-throated noises & he paid it no mind. A shoal of arm-sized earthworms churned amid the ties. There was the plastic-on-plastic rattle of scute: a buried bug, a glimpse of its mandibles telling him it was a good thing he was on the platform. Bang, smear, clang, smear. & now it was evening, & Sham was still banging & smearing.

& then the handle moved. It moved, & Sham whooped & leaned on it with all his weight, his feet dangling, & over the crunch & gristly grumbling of surrendering corrosion, it slowly sank, & screaming their own complaint, the cart's wheels began to turn.

It was a vehicle made for two. Having to haul up as well as to shove down was exhausting. Very quickly, Sham's arms & shoulders hurt. Soon they were hurting a lot. But the cart was rolling, & with each foot it moved, it moved faster, its old cogs remembering their roles, its scabs of oxide falling away.

Sham, giddy, sang shanties & pumped his way into—lord, it was late—the railsea twilight.

HE HAD NO LIGHT but he could see. There were not many clouds, & the moon did its best, all the way through the upsky. Sham couldn't go fast. He stopped & started, rested his poor limbs. He slowed at junctions. Mostly he stuck with his existing trajectory: only occasionally, according to whims he did not question, would he effortfully smack or kick old switches until they changed, & veer off on a new siding.

Sham had no idea where he was going. But though he was cold & moving at a punishing slow pace, he was peaceful. Not tired, though Stonefaces knew he should have been, but calm. He listened to burrowers lowing, the call of nocturnal hunters. He saw brief bioluminescence from a predator in the upsky, something that looked like a colour-winking thread of nerves or lace. Up close it must, he knew, be the most monstrous thing, that tangling beast, but that didn't stop it being wind-gusted silk just then, & beautiful.

Perhaps he slept. He opened his eyes & it was washed-out daylight & he was still pumping. The creak & creak & whine had become the sound of his life. Hours of pumping & stopping & starting again, & there was another shoal. Grubs, the size of his feet, surfacing & tunnelling & moving en masse & as fast as he was on his old cart.

What now? A scrap of hook protruding from the jaw of one of the grumbling beasts. Someone had tried to catch that one, once. He followed them. Sham watched his own long shadow lurch up & down pumping its own long-shadow handcart. He made for churning earth beyond a copse where the bugs were playing.

Were they? Why had they stopped? The animals were corralled. Tangled in fine mesh nets. Sham was waking up. The panicked grubs wriggled, thrashed & sprayed dust. It really wouldn't be so hard to catch one now, Sham thought, & almost fainted with stored-up hunger.

He wondered what he would do to snare one, how he might cook it, whether he could bear to eat it raw, & as the shifting of his stomach told him, yes, he rather thought he could, Sham heard sounds other than the scratch of the disturbed earth.

Looked up. Billows were coming his way. Sham stared. Licked dry lips with a dry tongue. At last let out a quavering cracked halloo.

Those were not mirages. These were sails. They were approaching.

Chapter Sixty-Six

IT RAINED & MADE the railsea mud & slick metal, the ties slippy. The venting clouds obscured the upsky. The *Medes* seemed to hunker in the pouring wet.

Beside it, not hunkering, thrusting rather from the muck, was the subterranean digger, the *Pinschon*. Captain Naphi stood with her officers around her, the crew around them, & beside her in the middle of the circle on the rooftop *Medes* deck was Travisande Sirocco, the salvor.

WHEN DAYBE HAD dropped onto the deck, the crew had done a quick recce of the surrounds, & seen a pipe jutting from the ground in the middle distance. Swivelling to watch them, dragging through earth. A periscope. The ground had upfolded & fallen away, & "Ahoy!" a voice had boomed from the speakers of the tunnelling machine. "Sorry to interrupt you. There's something you ought to know."

"Look at that," Sirocco said when she came aboard the *Medes*, & stared at the monster-rooted siller in the distance. "Haven't seen one of them for, oh. & that's the Kribbis pit, ain't it? Would that I could get down there. All that salvage. But the rock's too hard, & there are ticks down there you wouldn't believe. Anyway, I'm one for arche-salvage myself."

Sirocco had put up her hand. Various of the trash nubbins on her protective suit had raised as if in echo. "Let me explain why I'm here. I met your young man in Manihiki. We had a chat. He seemed a good lad."

"He's with you, ain't he?" someone shouted. She rolled her eyes.

"You know what I told him?" she said. "When he was going on about salvors this & salvage that & such the other? *I* told him to stay with his crew. Which is why it raised my eyebrows to hear word a bit later that he was with me. Because he ain't."

So she'd been heading in a certain direction, she said with some vague evasion, to strip what—she'd got word back in Manihiki—might be a new ruin after the intervention of a particular train. A train that might even have something to do with their missing young man. So there she'd been, heading, when this peculiar little bugger had dropped from the sky.

"There was a message," she said. "I *thought* I remembered Sham saying something about a bat. It had a message on it that I thought you'd want to see. So I've been asking around. You leave a trail, you know. A moler in the wrong part of the world. A moler going for the biggest game, a long way from where it should be." She smiled. "I've been trying to find you. Then suddenly, in the last couple of days, this one"—she indicated Daybe—"went nuts. Went zooming off. As if it heard something. I've been following it."

How could the bat have known where the *Medes* was? Sirocco shrugged. "Do you think I'd follow it across the railsea for the good of my health? I'm in business, & my business is salvage. I've no call to gallivant off on wild-bat chases."

"So?" said Captain Naphi. "Why did you?"

Sirocco held up a message written in Sham's hand. Naphi snatched for it, but Sirocco stepped back & read it aloud, herself, to the listening crew. "'Please!'" she began. "'I am a captive in the train *Tarralesh* . . .'"

WHEN SHE HAD FINISHED there was another long quiet. The crew, the salvor, the bat & the captain stood sodden on the *Medes* deck, ignoring the rain & watching each other. Everyone was staring. At Sirocco, at each other, at the captain.

"Oh my Stoneface," someone said.

"This is absurd," the captain said. She grabbed the sheet. Despite the blood, her artificial arm seemed to be working as well as ever. The pencil marks on the paper were softening in the rain. "It's impossible even to tell what this says," she said. "Let alone who wrote it. This is very possibly some elaborate trick being played for I do not know what reason."

"Really?" It was Dr. Fremlo. "Does anyone here seriously want to pretend we think Sham would have let go of Daybe by choice? This is the very salvor with whom he's supposed to have gone. Yet here she is, Shamless to her core. & there his beloved aerial vermin, to which we know out of whatever misplaced sentimentality he was devoted, & which reciprocates that affection, is here, frantically eager for us to follow it somewhere. Wherever our trainmate is, he is there not of his own choice."

"This, makes, no, sense," Naphi said through her teeth. "I don't know why someone wants to keep me from—" She glanced in the direction of Mocker-Jack, then stared at Sirocco. "What is your agenda? You're asking us—"

"I'm not asking you anything," Sirocco said. "I'm just delivering a bat's message. & my job's done." She sauntered to the rail.

"I've no idea how this animal happens to be here," the

captain said. "For all we know it could have escaped, lost Sham. Not one part of this story makes any sense."

The crew stared. Captain Naphi closed her eyes. "As we told him, once," Naphi said, "sentiment & moletrains don't mix."

"There is nowhere," Fremlo said, "more sentimental than a moletrain. Thankfully."

Vurinam looked from one side of the deck to the other with sudden cocky urgency, met as many eyes as he could. He cleared his throat. Sham. Worst assistant train doctor ever. Couldn't play quoits. The crew stared.

"I wish him the best," said Yashkan suddenly, "but we can't—"

"The best?" Vurinam said. "You?"

"The reputation of salvors precedes them," Naphi said. She looked at Sirocco. "We have no idea why she is here. For what she's searching. What is her agenda. Mr. Mbenday. Set course." She pulled out the scanner. She waved it for a signal, shook it twice. The proximity of Daybe's leg transmitter appeared to be interfering with it. Daybe squeaked & shuddered. There was a fingertip drumming of rain. Nobody went anywhere. The crew were looking in every direction.

"Mr. Mbenday," the captain said. "You will plot us a course. We are scant miles from the greatest moldywarpe you or I or any of us have ever seen." The captain reached quickly & grabbed Daybe with her uncovered flesh hand. It fluttered, & Sirocco hissed & caught its other outstretched wing. They stretched the bat between them. It squeaked. "A beast," Naphi said, "that I've been hunting since I was little more than a girl. A beast desperate for us to catch it." Her voice was rising. "We are a harpoon's throw from a *philosophy*. I am your captain."

The trainsfolk watched Captain Naphi pull & the salvor pull back. They spread Daybe's wings. It made frightened sounds.

Vurinam muttered, "Sham," looked as if he would say more, but at that moment Dramin coughed. Everyone looked at him. The cook held up a finger, seemed to be thinking.

"The boy is," he said at last, audibly surprised at his own words, "in trouble."

"What?" said Yashkan, but even as he spoke, Lind, his companion on more than one Sham-baiting escapade, put her finger to Yashkan's lips.

"Mr. Mbenday," Vurinam said. "May I suggest we set about & encourage this daybat to fly? Bet it'll go back to him. Maybe we can ask this salvor where she arrived from?"

"Good idea," Mbenday said. "I think that's a *fine suggestion*." He looked at Naphi. "Captain? Will you issue the order?"

Captain Naphi looked from one face to another. Some looked longingly in the direction of the *Talpa ferox*. Some looked stricken. You could all but hear flapping wings as the money they had imagined into their pockets from their imaginarily successful hunting of Mocker-Jack took imaginary flight. But more—the captain visibly, carefully tallied—did not. Beyond Mbenday's courteous request lay mutiny.

The captain looked down. From deep inside her came a sound. An exhalation. She raised her head, started to keen, looking up & up until she stared right into the tipping-down sky, & was howling. A long, loud wail. A moment of lament for a moment lost. The crew gave her that. She was, for all of it, a good captain.

She finished. Looked down. Released the bat into Sirocco's arms.

"Mr. Mbenday," she said. Her voice was perfectly calm.

"Find us a junction. Switchers, ready. Ms., Lady, Sirocco, salvor, person." She didn't pause. "The bat, we think, remembers the direction it came from. & it trusts you, now?"

The salvor shrugged. If Sirocco smiled, it was so subtle as to be hard to see. "I'll stick around," she said. "There's bound to be some salvage on the way."

"Stations," the captain shouted. The train shuddered as engines fired. "Find us a way around this sinkhole. We hunt one young trainmate, name of Sham ap Soorap."

Chapter Sixty-Seven

TACKING, SWITCHING EXPERTLY with & against the wind, sliding from rail to rail with quick touches of the points, came the travellers. A community of trainsfolk in single-carriage vehicles. Each was light, made of fire-hardened wood. None encumbered with an engine, they gusted, were masted, complexly patchworked with triangular sails. Their canvas boomed as the wind yanked. The wind-powered trains hauled a zigzag way across the railsea. Standing at the prow of the front-running vehicle was Sham.

He still marvelled at the quiet running. (Even as he was willing them to get a bloody move on.) His vocabulary of clatternames was unhelpful for these nomads: their very wheels were wood, & the vibrations they sent his feet were softer & more whispered than any he had known. He would have to introduce new words when he made it back to Streggeye. The *hrahoom* of a skilfully executed line shift, the *thehthehtheh* of a long straight.

His rescuers, the Bajjer, followed a labour of moldywarpes: red-furred horse-sized moles, fast-moving, cantankerous by nature & made more so by the dive-bombing of the Bajjer's domesticated hawks & the snaps of the dogs that ran with them trackside, by the harassment of the hunters who harried them with javelins to wear them down. The carts weaved across the animals' paths, moving in concert, their sails swinging.

This hunt was opportunistic, chances taken en route to &

from the net traps where the Bajjer gathered most of their meat. It was at one such that they had found Sham, hallucinating with hunger & exhaustion.

Over the last few days, he had grown used to the spices with which his rescuers cooked & the air-dried gamey molemeat with which they had coaxed him back to health. He wore what of his old clothes he could save & that were not so big they fell off him, together with the fur & skin vestments of the Bajjer.

A man only a little older than Sham came up behind him. What was his name again, Stoffer or something? He was one of those who spoke a few words of Railcreole, & he was keen to learn more. With several of the Bajjer, Sham was able to make halting conversation in simple mixed-up tongue.

Sham knew his urgency was beginning to annoy them. "So . . ." he said. "When? When Manihiki?" The young man shrugged. Sham did not even know for certain that that was where they were going.

The Bajjer had undoubtedly saved his life. Sham knew he had little right or reason to expect them to disrupt the rhythms of their own lives, too. But he was desperate & impatient & he could not stop asking. The rail-nomads' travels took them, he understood, to trade points, every so often, where they might drop him. Mostly these were tiny market villages & isolated hunting communities in the railsea. Pirate towns, maybe, too. Well, that would be interesting. Whatever. Sometimes, though, they'd take their business to one of the larger hubs — very occasionally Manihiki.

So far as he could tell, Sham's fervent campaign of begging had persuaded the Bajjer to make that city a stop on their unending journey slightly sooner than it might otherwise have been. Dangerous as it undoubtedly would be, it was his best chance of finding a way to get home, or to follow the Shroakes. All he could do meanwhile was console himself with two facts: one, that he was travelling much faster than he would have done alone; & two, that he was not dead.

Sham tried to learn to sail. He could not stop worrying about Caldera & Dero. The navy would be hunting for them. He consoled himself with the knowledge that if there was ever, anywhere in any of the railsea, a pair better suited to escaping even so total an enemy, it was Caldera & Dero Shroake. That put a smile on his face.

It was those thoughts, of that family, that reminded him of something. Sham had told his rescuers what little he could of his story. They had not seemed entirely surprised. Which in turn surprised him. Maybe they were forever rescuing castaways & playing host to fascinated travellers, he thought.

& a memory stirred in him then. Something Caldera had said in her salvage-cluttered kitchen, about her parents' preparations, their researches. They were railseaologists. They had got ready for their journey assiduously. They had, Sham abruptly recalled, sought out & investigated the particular expertises among the railsea nomads.

"Shroakes," he demanded. "Know them? Shroakes? In a train?" *Shrood?* the Bajjer muttered to each other. *Shott? Shraht?* "Shroake!" Ah. One or two remembered that name.

"Years gone," one said. "Learn rails."

"What did they ask you?" Sham said. Another round of muttering.

"Heaven," they said. Heaven? "Stories. Of the . . ." Mutter mutter mutter, the Bajjer debated the best word. "Shun it," someone said. "Angry angels." *Right,* Sham thought uneasily.

Shunning again. "Weeping," the Bajjer said. "Weeping forever."
Yes, he'd heard that before. Shun the weeping. No matter how
you interpreted it, Sham thought, it does not sound much like
Heaven.

Chapter Sixty-Eight

MOST EVENINGS the Bajjer of this troupe would find a place where the rails gathered & circle their rolling stock as best they could, build a fire on the ground of the railsea itself. Cook & debate things. Let the semi-wild dogs that hunted alongside them into the light & heat.

As a guest—initially honoured, now, he feared, becoming a bit of a bore—Sham was given decent cuts. Another time, he would have been fascinated by the specifics of this lifestyle: he would have learnt to rod-cast, to net fleeing bugs, to sing the songs, to play the dice games, call the calls that summoned the hunting birds. It was just very not the right time. Every morning he woke early, looked to the horizon, past molehills & termite mounds, straight across & ignoring the occasional grots of salvage.

When Sham's Bajjer crew saw the sails of another group they veered off to meet them. He could have wept as they took their time, collected carts together over convivial suppers, exchanged news & gossip, which various enthusiasts would whisper-translate into Sham's ear.

"Oh—they say this person die, was eatted by antlion." A pause, a moment's mourning. "This other group found, um, hunt place . . . is good, they say we should go." Oh bloody *hell* please not, Sham thought. "They want to know who is you. How we finds you." The Bajjer told that story, of Shroakes & pirates & Sham & the navy.

That night there was more jumping from cart to cart than usual. Sham was flushed & startled by the frank attentions of a Bajjer girl about his age. After deeply flustered hesitation, he avoided her & fled to bed, where he thoroughly unsuccessfully attempted sleep. *Another time*, he thought again, oh were it only another time.

The next morning the groups parted with ceremonial valedictories, & Sham realised that they had swapped a few members. The whole convivial, he supposed, had only cost a half-day or so. But a couple of days after that he saw more rapidly approaching sails, & Sham thought he might cry in frustration.

This time, though, there was to be no relaxation, no nattering or supper. The newcomers were blowing alarm trumpets & waving flags. When they came close enough, he saw they wore expressions of misery & rage. They were waving flags & pointing. They were pointing right at Sham.

HIS RESCUERS STRUGGLED to explain. Somewhere, something the Bajjer treasured had been attacked. In a place they went to hunt & harvest. It was not an accident. & it was something to do with Sham.

"What are they *talking* about?" Sham said.

They were not accusing him, though they stared in suspicion & anger. It was more tenuous than responsibility. Nothing was certain; these travellers had seen nothing at first hand, were passing on garbled information as it had been passed to them. But even as details faded further from the source, the whispers that raced along rails & among traveller bands linked whatever it was that had been perpetrated—some abomination, committed by ferocious pirates, the slaughter of some band & the poisoning of their runs—to the story of Sham's grub-trap rescue.

The few survivors of the onslaught said their onslaughterers had been looking for someone, demanding information to stop what they were doing. A lost boy. A Streggeye boy lost & got away from pirates.

"We go." Everyone readied their carts & weapons. "See. All the Bajjer go." East. Towards wherever it was that had happened had happened. Away from Manihiki, & from any direction the Shroakes might have taken.

"But . . ." Sham half wanted to beg. "We can't lose any more time." But how could he? These were their people. How could they not go?

NOTHING PREPARED THEM. Three days into their eastward trek, the two bands sailing together, they reached the outskirts of the tract where the attack had happened. Where Sham had thought they might find injured escapees, perhaps dead remains, a battered sail-cart band.

There was a stink in the air. Chemicals, worse than any factories Sham had ever sniffed. They rolled towards smoke. "Look." Sham pointed. A stench came up from below. Sham's eyes widened. Oil & effluent, on the ground between the rails, on the roots of trees, dripping from the branches, on the rails themselves. The trainsfolk switched, swung, steered, their faces grim.

A grieving silence descended. Even the wheels seemed muted, as they reached splintered & scattered remnants of Bajjer craft. At the limits of his vision Sham saw a tower, a huge engine, of the type that dotted the railsea, drawing energy from deep below the flatearth. It was motionless, burning off no excess.

"Is it a spill?" Sham said. "Have they had a blowout? Is that what happened here?"

Other sails were approaching. Bands were converging as word spread. With signals, with coloured flags, they swapped what little they knew, going further, slowly, in more disgust & misery, into a zone that seemed almost to be dissolving, sopping & destroyed with industrial slop, defoliant & toxin.

"This ain't no broken rig," Sham said. This was thuggery, a carnage of landscape. Someone was sending the Bajjer a message. No wild crops would grow here now. There was nothing to hunt, & would not be for years. The earth was motionless, animals all rotting in their holes.

Among the vehicles approaching, Sham saw one much larger than the rattling wooden crafts. All around him, the Bajjer stared at this act of oily war. Sham narrowed his eyes. The big train came out of the distance, venting diesel fumes.

Despite the depredation around him, the despondency & anger of his companions, Sham's whole body lurched with shock, because the train approaching through the trashed-up hunt-grounds, escorted by scudding Bajjer-carts, cutting through the newly ruined railsea, was the *Medes*.

Even as the Bajjer gazed helplessly at the catastrophe, Sham let out a whoop of joy. & then another as, like a nuzzling thunderbolt, streaking out of the sky into a heavy sniffing kiss in his arms, came Daybe, the bat.

Part Six

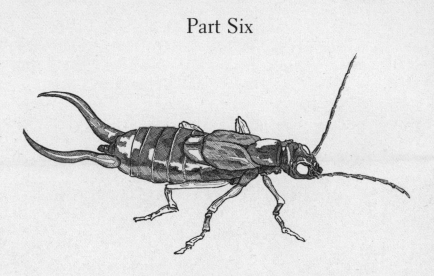

Earwig
Dermaptera monstruosus

Chapter Sixty-Nine

IT WAS BADLY BATTERED, a brutalised & creaking train in which the Shroakes passed beyond any horizon most trainsfolk would ever see. & here their troubles began.

Actually—

It is, in fact, not time for the Shroakes. Not quite.

That phrase—here the troubles began—is ancient. It has been the fulcrum of many stories, the moment when everything is much bigger & more vertiginous than anyone thought. This is in the nature of things.

Technically, our name, to those who speak science, is *Homo sapiens*—wise person. But we have been described in many other ways. *Homo narrans, juridicus, ludens, diaspora*: we are storytelling, legal, game-playing, scattered people too. True but incomplete.

That old phrase has the secret. We are all, have always been, will always be, *Homo vorago aperientis*: person before whom opens a vast & awesome hole.

Chapter Seventy

OUT OF THE east & south the train came. It howled, it whistled, en route through & out of the known railsea. It breathed diesel breath. An everyday moletrain, transmogrified by urgency & peculiar direction into something more than itself, something grander, buckling of more swashes.

The *Medes* was not alone. It came as part of a multitude.

Syncopating with the staccato of its iron wheels was the hard wood rush of a Bajjer war party, windblown in the *Medes's* wake. Like a huge semi-trained predator, the subterrain *Pinschon* grumbled fast into the light where rails allowed, submerged again to tunnel alongside & below the hunters.

Leaning from the *Medes*, Sham was at the head of an armada. *Don't dwell on that*, the voice in him said. *Don't even think about it. You have a job to do.*

It had been a bittersweet reunion, in the mashed-up Bajjer grounds. Of course, the eruption of welcome from his train-mates had made Sham cry happy tears. The tears had stayed & the happiness gone when he heard what had gone down, of the loss of Klimy & Teodoso to a monster out of the bad sky.

"Someone punished us," a Bajjer warrior said, staring at pools of scummy offrun in what had been fertile soil. "Who? For what?"

"Who," Sirocco said, "is easy." She had leaned on the sub-terrain's hatch.

"You!" Sham said.

"Good to see you again, young man." She touched the brim of an imaginary hat.

"What are *you* doing here?"

"Sham!" It was Hob Vurinam. Arms outstretched, vaguely dandy threads even more battered than usual by the remorseless journey, tiredness making him look much older than he was, but his lined face wide in delight. He grabbed Sham & they pounded each other's back in greeting, & Vurinam scruffed up Sham's now-shaggy hair for longer than you would have thought, only becoming embarrassed after a few seconds.

& there was Mbenday, jumping from foot to foot, almost as vigorous in his welcome, & Kiragabo Luck, more restrained but not by much, Shappy, all his trainmates, suddenly Dr. Fremlo to Sham's happy squawk, giving Sham a huge & lengthy hug, then holding him at arm's length & shaking his hand.

"If it weren't for her we wouldn't have ever found you," Mbenday said, pointing at the salvor. "She knows how to follow trails, & she was watching the bat, & then there were rumours that someone had you, & then that there'd been something terrible. But it was her."

"Me?" Sirocco said. She glanced down into the bowels of the *Pinschon*. "I'm just here for the salvage."

People lined up to greet the returned boy. Even Lind & Yashkan shook Sham's hand, surly but not wholly ungracious. & then, suddenly, there was Captain Naphi.

She stood back. Sham hesitated. Was he happy to see her? Unhappy? He could not have said. She looked a little lessened. Diminished? She wore—Sham blinked at the sight—a bandage wrapped around her artificial arm. He bowed, & the captain bowed back. "Ap Soorap," she said. "I'm pleased to see you're alive. We've worked hard. We've given a lot to find you. A *lot*."

"How did you know where I was?" he said. "Why did you break off hunting? &—" He stared at the stink all around. "& who then?"

"Who did this?" Sirocco said. "Who do you think?"

"Pirates!" someone shouted. Sirocco shook her head.

"That? See that?" She pointed at a particular ditch of sump. "That oil—you'll excuse me but as you can imagine I know my effluent & runoff—that particular oil . . ." She wafted the air towards her & sniffed like a connoisseur. ". . . is used almost exclusively by one force. The Manihiki ferronavy."

There was a silence. "That—" She pointed at a bush not merely killed but dripping with the remains of leaves enzymatically degraded into slop like a salted slug. "—is their favourite unleafer."

"I heard it was pirates," the same voice as before said.

"They may have driven under the skull-&-spanners flag," Sirocco shrugged. "But . . ." She performed a mocking salute.

"What do they *want*?" Sham said. Then looking across the acres of miserable Bajjer, he said, "I know why. They were looking for information. & punishing the Bajjer because of who they once helped."

"What?" said Vurinam. "Who did they help?"

"They want information about me," Sham said. "& the people I'm trying to go after. & they're punishing these people. Because of who they taught about the railsea."

The Bajjer who could understand him nodded. "Shroakes," someone said.

"The Shroakes," said Sham. That little bit of history! That investigation, by Caldera's & Dero's parents, the meeting of those minds. All these years later, this deadened land was what it had cost the Bajjer, to have helped the Shroakes find a way to Heaven & the eternity of tears. To have helped them, & now to have helped him.

"Would someone," Fremlo said, "& by 'someone', Sham ap Soorap, I mean you, please explain what in the name of the Stonefaces & Their Stern Gaze you are *talking* about?"

So, rushing the details for now & promising to come back to them, Sham told the gathering about the Siblings Shroake, about their family & their family's work, of their odyssey towards something of which they were quite unsure, & of what & who was hunting them.

The Bajjer had no loudspeakers, but Sirocco had three. "Can't believe she came for me," Sham whispered to Vurinam, as the equipment was checked & walloped into working. He stared at Captain Naphi on her dais.

"Well . . ." Vurinam said, & shrugged. "Tell you later."

Sham saw the captain check the scanner again, again & again, but such glimmers of nostalgia for the hunt she almost made were surely forgivable. When she spoke, her voice was firm.

"May I suggest," she said, "that we come to some sort of order?" & one by one, across all the vehicles, loudhailers sounded in repetition, translation & debate, until everyone there understood the shape of this. That, when you got down to it, Sham was looking for a hunted girl & boy.

"& whatever the rest of you decide," Sham said, "I'm going after them. I've got to. They need help."

The Bajjer were raging. The dead & the land, they said, whispering translations to Sham between exhortations, demanded revenge. "Don't think who did this is finished with you," Sham said. "Until they get what they want."

"Punish." That word was fast translated, & more & more Bajjer began to say it, in Railcreole.

"Plus also," Sham said after a decent pause, "where we're going there's an X. X the unknown. Off the edge of the map. Figuratively speaking. You know what X means." He rubbed his fingers together.

Night reached them. Tumbleweed tumbled, investigating the gathering while a consensus emerged in shouts & declarations.

Sham listened. He was slowly staggered. He had to bite his lip. Whether out of a sense of justice at the thought of young Shroakes chased by armoured trains, out of a hope for treasure, out of fury at this despoliation, solidarity with him, or some combination, an astonishing number of those present were ready to come with him.

"But come where?" Mbenday said. "The whole *point* of this—" He indicated the poisonous slurry. "—is that no one knows where the Shroakes've gone."

During the silence that followed that, Sham thought. A strategy he could not have followed on his own might not, in company, be closed.

"The Bajjer go all over, yes? All over the railsea? & Sirocco?" She was moonbathing on the hull of her digger. She looked up politely. "You must've travelled a lot, there's salvage all over. & us." Sham looked at the *Medes* crew. "We got people from Streggeye, from Manihiki, Rockvane, Molochai, from all over. We're trainsfolk. What we don't know about the railsea ain't worth knowing. Between all of us," he said, "we'd surely recognise pretty much anything out there.

"Captain," Sham said, & gave up the last secret. Rumbled her. "A long time ago, you & me saw some pictures." Everyone turned to her & stared. "I want you to help me, because you saw them too. If we want to find the Shroakes," Sham said, "we have to find where they're going. So everyone listen. Tell me where you think this stuff is. I'm going to describe some places to you."

Chapter Seventy-One

Now. At last. Surely.

This must be the moment to return to the Shroakes & to their rail. Surely.

It is, in fact, yes, Shroake O'Clock.

The strange train managed. How battered it was. How shortened, how patched where glass had broken, beasts had snatched, where the frustrated fire of pirates had worn down armour.

Where the gauges narrowed, their mechanism still—just—worked. Where the pitch of rising tracks would have been impassable to most vehicles, the Shroakes'—just—coped. Event after brutalising event.

Pirate biplanes, very far from home, breaking the prime rule of exploratory flying, which was "Don't." Blitzing them from the air till they hid under overhangs. Railtracks through rock, into darkness, swaddled in silk, tunnels made lairs by train-eating funnelwebs. Shedding more rear carriages, distractions, like a lizard sheds its tail. Once above a beach of cracked helmets they watched a tussle between two specklike upsky monsters, until one must have glanced their way, & showered them with caustic spittle as they raced away.

Caldera, as bruised & tired-looking as her train, read from what screens still operated.

"So," said Dero.

"So what?" said Caldera. Her voice cracked.

"Wait. I'm thinking."

"If this is another not-very-disguised one Mum & Dad brought back from the Bajjer that I remember from when we were little, you forfeit ten million points," Caldera said.

"Shut up."

"You're already on minus seventeen million."

"Shut *up*," Dero said. "There was a mouse. Who lived in a hole." Mostly it was Caldera who told stories as they drove, but not this time.

"Where?" said Caldera. "Between the rails?"

"Stupid. She'd get et up. A hole in a wall. & she could do magic."

Caldera checked some notes. "What sort of magic?"

"Magic to do with sticks," Dero decided. "She could make sticks come alive."

Then the Shroakes gasped. The air outside the train was suddenly hammered by noise. In their nook, an alarm sounded, as if there weren't enough cacophony already. Above them flew something nothing like a plane. An insecty thing that juddered & dangled from a patch of blurred air.

"What is that?" whispered Dero.

"What's it doing?" said Caldera. Then—

"Oh my lord," whispered Caldera. "It's an angel."

Not one of the great & terrible driverless heavenly trains, wheeled angels shoring up foundations. A watcher. A getterbird. It scudded above them. Faced its bulbous dark sheen their way, regarded them flatly. They held their breath. It brought its own cloud with it. Venting filth. It was close enough that they could see its carapace. Scabbed with dirt & rust. Scratched & battered. The thing lurched in the air.

At last it turned & dipped its head with the hammering clattering &, faster than any bird or bat, was gone in a burst of soot.

"That," said Caldera at last, "was a bit of an anticlimax."

"You disappointed?" Dero said.

"Hardly. Just not used to seeing things that ain't trying to kill me."

"Oh," Dero muttered. "Give it a minute."

THE SHROAKES WERE down to the last of their equipment. They lived crammed & cramped in the engine room. They took it in turns to sleep, one diagonalwise across the floor while the other drove the train.

Dero rubbed his eyes, drank water, ate a snack from their (dwindling—hush) supplies.

"Why we going so *slow*?" Dero said. He sniffed. "We smell," he said.

"You smell," Caldera said. "I'm like a flower."

"We have to go quicker," Dero said. "We must be nearly there." He rocked back & forwards, as if he would lend his momentum to the train. He turned & looked from the rear window.

"I'm being careful," Caldera said. "I thought I heard something. This is as fast as I think's safe."

"Well," Dero said. He spoke very precisely. "Well, I think you should maybe consider that going a bit faster might be a bit safer than not going so quick. See, because there's a train behind us."

"What?" It was true. Their scanners must be on the fritz, but there it was, visible to the naked eye. "Where did they *come* from?" she breathed.

"Behind that little forest," Dero said, "I think."

"But there's nothing there! Pirates again," said Caldera, but then she gasped. It was getting closer. & it was not what she had thought. It was a Manihiki ferronaval train. Definitely. That was a whole other thing.

The Shroakes looked at each other. "They got us," Dero whispered. "At last."

"At last," said Caldera. "Or maybe—maybe they been behind us for ages. Maybe they been following us all this time." She swallowed. "They know the way, now. Maybe we showed them the way."

"Cald," Dero said firmly. "We still got a chance. Get us out of here. Top speed. *Now!*"

Caldera didn't move.

"Now," Dero said, "would be good."

"Can't." Caldera bit her lip.

"Engine?"

"Engine."

"Buggered again?"

"Again."

He stared at her, she stared at him, the Manihiki officers got closer.

"You said you'd been going slow deliberately," Dero said.

"I was lying."

"I thought you was lying."

They knew how to make the Shroake train go when it was in the mood to work, but not to tweak something wrong in the strange metal hearts & tubes their parents had built. The vehicle sputtered at pitiful speed.

"So what," Dero said, "d'you propose we do?"

Caldera leaned out of the window. "You know," she said at last, with rising excitement. "I don't know that they've actually seen us. Look at how they're switching. They know we're round here somewhere, but . . ."

She steered with renewed energy. Took them over points that veered lines close to a looming cliff. Thickly, richly vegetational. Their long journey had already sprayed their train's flanks with dirt & dust. "Right," Caldera said. She slowed them yet slower, & stopped the train in the shadows. "Quick," she said. Climbed out of the roof hatch, & with hook & hands snatched plant matter from the overhangs. Dero did the same, until they stood under a wodge of richly smelling sappy green stuff. They draped their vehicle in the creepers.

"This is a *rubbish* plan," Dero said, as they crawled back inside.

"I await your improvements eagerly. & complaining is *awesomely* helpful."

Up close, the Shroake train was an absurd, green-pelted, unconvincing thing. But perhaps, in the stark light contrasts of the railsea, over miles, at motion, their poor battered conveyance might pass for some ignorable viney nothing. Dero & Caldera waited. They watched the incoming train through dirty glass & now, too, from behind a green fringe.

"Always knew Mum & Dads had annoyed them," Dero said. He & Caldera held hands. They waited. The naval train came closer. It approached, closer, closer, it was abreast of them, only a few rail-widths away.

It passed on again. At last, the Siblings Shroake breathed out.

"This thing is barely even going," Dero said at last. He kicked the inside of the carriage. "What are we going to do?"

"They're going to find us again, you know," Caldera said. "I just don't think we can get by them. They probably will."

"Yeah," said Dero. For just a sad & terrible second, he looked like he would cry. "So what we going to do?"

"What can we do?" Caldera said at last. "Keep trying. Do our best."

She shrugged. After a minute, her brother shrugged too.

Chapter Seventy-Two

THE DETAILS ARE DISTINCT, the specifics specific, but the trend clear. Event, encounter, pushing on, the slow degradation of the Shroake train, an against-the-odds continuation. That is what has been.

The train is such a battered shade of itself. But this is the railsea. A greater surprise is surely that the Shroakes are still here at all.

What Dero would admit to, who can say? But Caldera, certainly, is astonished.

"WELL YOU'VE DONE IT NOW!" Caldera didn't even know who she was talking to any more.

It was the purest & most undeserved luck that the Manihiki train had not wheeled round, come back & found them. Someone else, however, was after them.

The Shroake train, coaxed to a last life lease, was hauling rail to rail. There was no hiding now. Nothing in this outermost railsea—not landscape, fauna, flora, the rails themselves—behaved as it ought. They passed bridges from & to nowhere, that doubled back at the apex of their curves; lines that spiralled into sinkholes. Birds much bigger than they should be, perhaps a little too limb-encumbered, flew high enough to tickle the upsky.

"Maybe," Dero whispered, "out here all the lines are blurry, & maybe birds in the sky & really bad things in the upsky are making babies."

Caldera & Dero pored over charts & teased their dead parents fondly for their scrawls. They configured plans. They blinked too much & missed food. Dero snapped at Caldera & Caldera said less & less, sometimes nothing for hours.

Now here came a train, racing for them with clear intent. "You've done it now!" Caldera repeated. Local brigands, she thought, a ferocious compact battletrain from insular nearby islands full, myth had it, of monstrosities & prodigies, trains that ran backwards through time. & who, it seemed, had either heard of the Shroakes, or greeted all incomers in so pugnacious a fashion.

"You've been & gone & done it now!" Caldera shouted, & shoved forward the levers, which did nothing any more.

Once they would have outrun such an enemy without bothering to break off from sandwiches & backgammon. Now their locomotive wheezed & lurched like a moribund mule. Dero switched & the pursuers gained. Their diesel growl grew louder.

A last push, another throttle. Caldera held her breath.

She heard a cannon fire. She closed her eyes. But nothing hit them. The train drummed under a rain of earth.

"Cal," Dero said.

A fusillade of missiles was slamming into the attack-train on their tail. Rocks, arrows, small-arms fire. Nothing devastating, but enough to mess with, to confound & hurt the wildland attackers, who scrambled to turn their weapons towards this new threat.

Windblown carts! Switching & track-riding with skills a delight to see; tacking in gusts from line to line; firing catapults, slingshots, crossbows, pistols; in & out again. & here, bearing down by its sailing companions, on the brigand-train switching lines, came a moletrain. A moletrain, miles, miles & miles from any moldywarpe runs.

The sailing carriages scattered, firing as they went. The moler came in fast. Its harpoon guns were levelled. It faced the attacker, on the same track, heading straight for them. Caldera shook her head. "What are they *doing?*" she whispered. Even a moler in top shape was no match for these local warlords. *Thanks very much for saving us,* Caldera thought. *I wish you weren't about to die.* She counted down seconds till impact. *Ten,* she thought. *Nine. Eight.*

But no: it was a well-judged challenge. The brigands flinched. A switch & they were slaloming out of the moler's path. To where ground suddenly jumped like an animal provoked.

Up came a grinding machine. Breaching all manner of railsea taboos, a subterrain smashed through the *ties themselves,* buckled the rails & sent the pirate train into the air & crashing down.

The moler slowed. The trainsfolk watched. The pirates wailed. Dust was spraying. There was a silence. Then: "Come on, we got 'em!"

The Shroakes knew that voice. Caldera grabbed Dero's arm. On the roof of the moler's engine a young man stood.

"Wait now," Dero said, "is it, you don't know . . ." But Caldera was whooping. The figure hefted a clumsy pistol. He waved at her.

He stared through yards of air over yards of rails through the window of her own poor battered vehicle, right into Caldera Shroake's poor tired eyes. With another whoop like a siren, like a train sounding triumph at a journey well done, at an arrival, Caldera leaned out & waved back. At the same moment, each on their own train, she & the newcomer, Sham ap Soorap, smiled.

Part Seven

Blood Rabbit
Lepus cruentus

Chapter Seventy-Three

"NONE OF YOU HAVE TO," Sham said. "I don't even expect any of you to. I don't deserve you to. But yeah, of *course* I'm going on." He smiled. "With them."

Caldera smiled too. *Thanks*, she mouthed at him.

Of those Bajjer who had stuck the journey this far, most took their own leave after the Fight of the Rescue of the Siblings Shroake. Now the Shroakes were—temporarily at least—saved. A quest, for something that lay beyond pictures the Bajjer & their companions had never even seen, was the only reason to go on. Most of the Bajjer had little interest in quests. There were exceptions. & there were those insistent on revenge on the Manihiki navy train the Shroakes told them was close.

The crew of the *Medes*, which had once been a moletrain & was now who-knew-quite-what, having performed the rescue they had promised to Sham, were no more obliged to continue than the Bajjer. The captain, if such she still was, fiddled with her tracker.

"I'll stick with you a bit, though, if you've no objection," Sirocco said.

"Ah," said Vurinam. "We're so near now. Why not let's just see what we find?"

He spoke for the bulk of the crew. Those for whom he did not joined the mass of Bajjer carts, complaining at the unorthodox conveyance, to start a slow way back east to the known world.

"Captain Naphi?" Sham said. She looked up, startled. She still prodded at her tracking mechanism, with a tool extruded from her arm. The one her crew now called her artificial artificial one.

"Should throw that bloody thing to Mocker-Jack," Fremlo muttered.

"I stay with my train," Naphi said at last, turned back to what she was doing. So there was that.

Those heading back & those going on separated with camaraderie & without rancour, waving as they parted. The flotilla of sailtrains scattered back towards distant mountains.

The investigators argued over their clue-map. "What's this sound like?" someone would shout, & yellingly repeat the description Sham, with muttered help from the captain, had given. Then debates: that looks like such-&-such a place; no, you're mad, that's wossname; & wasn't there a story about these or those hills? Bajjer scout-carts would beetle off in candidate directions, until forward motion was agreed, & the *Medes*, the remaining Bajjer vehicles & the *Pinschon* hauled on.

Dero & Caldera watched their own train disappear behind them. Their rolling-stock home for so long. "You had to," Sham said quietly. "It was falling apart." For a while, neither Shroake said a word.

"Thanks for letting us carry on," Dero said at last. "For using your train." *Ain't really mine*, Sham thought. He left the Shroakes to their goodbye.

The captain, at the *Medes*'s rear, intent in her strange work, gave a *hm* of triumph. Daybe veered overhead. The air so far out seemed to confuse it. It arced, abruptly curved back towards the train. Heading not straight for Sham but for the last carriage. Circled Captain Naphı, standing staring back the way they had come, towards her lost philosophy, like some befuddled anti-figurehead. No one bothered her. No one minded her in her backwards command. She fiddled with her machine while the bat circled.

There was salvage even here, & once or twice they saw the remnants of ruined trains. They made slow progress—there were days when they decided they'd taken a wrong move, & the whole group would reverse, or grind on to where junctions allowed them to turn. But they grew better at unpicking clues. Their false starts grew fewer.

They had, after all, a method for knowing when they'd gone right: with a hush & increasingly uncanny sense, Sham would find himself, with a sudden turn of the rails, staring at an exact scene he remembered from the screen. Only the sky would be different, the clouds & upsky coilings. They progressed through old pictures.

The further they travelled beyond the trade routes of the railsea, filling in specifics on charts marked only with the vaguest rumours, the sparser the railsea, the larger the stretches of un-broken land, the fewer the rails. There was a winnowing of iron possibilities.

The other thing that made them certain they were en route to something hidden, at the edge of the railsea & therefore of the world, was that they were harassed by angels.

Chapter Seventy-Four

IT WAS NIGHT. Still they travelled. A Bajjer scout reported something in the distance. The explorers woke as the air shook.

"What . . . ?"

"Is that . . . ?"

They came on deck, rubbing their eyes & looking up at the lights low in the sky. In came a flock of flying angels.

"Oh my Stoneface," Sham whispered.

The crew watched the air-chopping investigators. They could not make much out: swaying lights, reflections on recurved shells, stars glimpsed through their shimmering. Fables! The watchers at the edge of the world. The heralds of the godsquabble. Getterbirds, utterers in air. They had as many names as most holy things do.

The crew cringed, kept weapons in their hands, whispered to switchers to get ready, anticipating attack. Which did not come. At last the whirling-winged things scattered. Some back the way they had come, back towards the world's edge, others east, & south.

"Where they going?" said Caldera. "If only we had a plane to see."

Sham looked at her thoughtfully. "That we don't," he said. "But we do have something."

He scaled the crow's nest. *Remember when I couldn't do this?* he thought. Into the gloom & freezing air. Telescope in hand, Sham waited. He looked for flying lights & considered. If he tried to think full on about where he was, what he was doing, how he had got there, it was all a great deal too much. So he simply didn't. Sham just thought of stories about what was ahead. The end of the world, ghostly money, endless sorrow. Sham strained his eyes.

It was not deep night. It was dark but not quite dark. The stars were hidden but not wholly. By sitting still & staring a long, long time, Sham could make out textures in the black. The edge of something, approaching. A horizon. That's what it was. Dark on dark. A horizon that was definitely, without question, closer than it should be. He caught his breath.

Mountains, rocks, a split, gaps, & foreshortened earth.

& then a rush, a whir of lights, & another angel rushed into view. It roared around him, filling the air with dust & noise. He clung to the ladder & gritted his teeth. He could see his crewmates shouting below, could of course hear nothing. When at last the angel careered off eastward, Sham trained his lens on it.

Daybe gusted off, following it. As if the bat would grab it out of the air & crunch it down. Sham watched the winking diode light from Daybe's leg. Daybe was no daybat now, staying up all hours, like Sham himself. It did not fly straight, still obviously confused. It veered again for where the captain stood, even so late, alone & left behind by events.

Daybe swooped around her & the mechanism she endlessly probed. Sham stared.

"Captain."

Naphi turned. The crew were ranged behind her. For a while there was only the noise of the train. Everyone swayed with its motion.

"Captain," Sham said again. He stood with a Shroake to either side. "What are you doing?"

She met his stare. "Keeping watch," she said.

"But for what, exactly?" said Caldera Shroake.

"You know what's ahead of us, Captain?" Sham said. "An edge. The end of something. I saw it. But you're looking the other way. What are you watching for? What's *behind* us?"

The captain stared at him, & he held her gaze, & as planned Vurinam suddenly blindsided her. The young train-swain stepped in &, gentle enough not to hurt, he grabbed her mechanism. "No!" she shouted, but Vurinam wrested it from her, threw it to Sham. "No!" the captain said again, stepped forwards, but now Benightly was ready. She struggled as he restrained her.

Daybe landed on Sham's arm. The bat nuzzled the receiver. "You will let me go!" the captain shouted.

"Mbenday," Sham said. "What does that mean?" He pointed at a blipping & winking & whistling.

The man stared at it. "That little light there?" Mbenday said at last. He looked up. "That's your little friend. But there's another one *there*." Mbenday pointed at another light, & swallowed. "A big one, it looks like. Coming towards us. Fast."

Captain Naphi stopped struggling. She stood tall & straightened her clothes.

"How long have you known, Captain?" Sham said. "How long have you known what was coming?" He raised the receiver. "*Mocker-Jack*."

There was a collective gasp. "Mocker-Jack the mole," Sham said. "& we ain't going after it any more. It's coming after us."

*

"IT WAS NEVER going to let us go," the captain said. "We had the hubris to think we were hunting it. *We* were never hunting *it*." She did not sound mad. "Now the gloves are off. The boot is on the other foot." She smiled. "Mocker-Jack is my philosophy. & I am its."

"Sirocco," Sham said. He fiddled with the mechanism & watched Daybe move again. "Signals like this, do they work both ways?"

"Ah," Sirocco said slowly. She nodded thoughtfully. "Could be. Could be made to."

"You see Daybe," Sham said. He wiggled the receiver & the bat bobbed.

"It ain't tuned to him," Caldera said. "It's a different frequency. How come it shows him?"

"Salvage," Sirocco said. "It's always a bit iffy. There's bound to be bleed. Especially when, like right now, that thing you're holding must be kicking out a lot of power. Ain't it, Captain? When did you learn to reverse its field?" Sirocco said.

"Sham," said Vurinam. "D'you think you could please tell the rest of us what the bloody hell you lot are on about?"

"She *flipped the signal*," Sham said. "This . . ." He shook the receiver. "It ain't *finding* Mocker-Jack any more. It's *pulling*. The moldywarpe's finding *it*."

The crew stared. "Turn the bloody thing off, then!" Vurinam squawked. Sirocco took it from Sham & hurriedly fiddled.

"How'd you even learn to do this, Captain?" she said.

"You salvors," Naphi said. "You'll tell a person anything with the right blandishments. If you can show off about it."

"Why do you think she stuck with us?" Mbenday said, frantically pulling at his own hair. "She wasn't going to let us take the *Medes*. She needs a moletrain."

"Can we outpace it?" Sham said. "The mole?" Mbenday read the screen, carefully.

"Yes," he said.

"No," said the captain.

"No," said Mbenday. "I don't know."

"I don't know if I can reverse this," Sirocco said.

"Much too late. Do you really think," the captain said, "that Mocker-Jack can't sniff us now? Can't feel us? That it doesn't know the signature of our wheels? It's coming. *This is what we've wanted.*"

"No, Captain," Sham shouted. "This is what *you've* wanted. The rest of us been wanting *other, bloody, things!*"

"It's really coming quite fast," Mbenday whispered, staring at the display. "I mean, it's a few hours away at most. It's really coming at *quite a clip.*" He swallowed.

"Wait," Sham said, slowly. "Sirocco, leave it on."

"What?" said Vurinam. "Are you crazy?"

"Mocker-Jack's going to find us anyway now. At least this way we know where it is."

They stood, on the deck, staring, unsure, where they were going, what there was to say. Sham hunted an idea. It teased him. "We're so close," he said. He pointed in the direction of the dark edge he'd seen approaching.

"Ahoy!" To their star'd flank, two Bajjer scouts approached swinging lanterns in semaphore. They came closer, shouting in every language they knew. They yelled with bullhorns, struggling to make themselves heard & understood.

"What is it?" Sham loudhailered back. "We're sort of in the middle of something."

"Is reason is why angels go over there," one shouted, & pointed east the way they'd come.

"Looking for the mole, yeah?" yelled back Sham.

"No! What? Mole what? Is more."

"More what?"

"More trains."

"Pirates?" Sham shouted, & the Bajjer wagged their fingers no.

"Navy," they bellowed. "Manihiki navy is coming."

Chapter Seventy-Five

THE RAILSEA SHRUGGED off the night, & uncovered the ruins of many ancient trains. What graveyard was this? A macabre scene of failed ventures.

Coupled to the back of the *Medes*, where the captain still stood—what point was there to incarcerating her when all she did was stare, in the direction of her incoming philosophy?— the *Pinschon* rode the rails on its own stubby wheels. It could not have kept up by tunnelling at this speed. Beyond it, coming for them, the navy was now a visible cloud. Exhaust, fumes, the dust of travel.

"They were never going to let us go," Caldera said. She turned her charts, looked at them from all angles. "We're close. To something. I can see where my mum & dad were going, & I can see . . . I think it looks like we're heading for somewhere they were trying to *avoid* . . ."

"Something got these trains," Dero said. "Look at them all."

"We have to think," Sham said. "We have to think this through."

They did not have time to investigate, to weave & switch between discarded train shells. But as they emerged from that shatterscape, Dero pointed. A way beyond the thickest thickets of wreck-matter, flipped upside down by some strange catastrophe, balanced on its roof on a makeshift flatbed truck with its wheels still to the rails, was a weirdly battered carriage. Its skyward-pointing floor was tarpaulined, its front buckled into an ugly wedge. Dero & Caldera both gasped. Sirocco eyed the carriage appraisingly.

It had been, Sham realised, part of their parents' train, part of the first Shroake exploration. "What happened to it?" Sham said.

"They purged them, sometimes," Dero said. "They taught us that. But that looks . . ."

"I don't know what that looks like," Caldera said.

"Look." Sirocco pointed to where the navy were becoming visible. "They're going faster'n us."

"It's that same one again," Dero whispered. "Found us better'n anyone else. It's like they were here before us."

"Some of them," Sham said carefully, thinking of Judda-more's pictures, "might've had information. About where you were going."

Through the best of the *Medes*'s scopes, Sham could still see only malicious smudges. Sirocco passed him her own salvaged-up mechanism, nu-salvage & arche-salvage combined. He put his eyes to that & jumped with the bright up-closeness of the quarry. That great navy wartrain, skewering the sky with guns.

"Reeth," he whispered. Who was it, he wondered, which pirate snatched from railsea death had remembered the pictures well enough to give Reeth clues? Juddamore? Elfrish was gone. Robalson was horribly gone.

The rails grew sparser. The *Medes* & its companions raced towards a line of rock, a crag-curtain broken by slits as if peered through by some impatient actor. "We have to box really bloody clever," Sham said. "Really, bloody, clever."

The last Bajjer windcarts began to pull away. There were not enough lines to either side of the *Medes*, now, for them to keep up. "Wait," Sham shouted across to them. In the rudiments of their language, more than he thought he'd picked up, he begged them not to go. "Come aboard! We're close!"

"To what?" someone shouted back.

There were arguments on some cars. They lurched line to line in disputation. Sham watched agog as a Bajjer warrior shook her fist at her fellows, turned & leapt magnificently from her cart, across yards of railsea, to slam into the *Medes*'s side & grab & grip its rail & pull herself aboard as her vehicle veered away. A few brave others did the same, those who were in this for the end. They jumped rapidly increasing gaps.

"Quick!" Sham shouted. But a nearby trainsman mistimed his bound. He leapt & his fingers slipped without purchase on the moler's flank. A gasp, a scream, a thudding, & he was dashed horribly into railside rocks.

Everyone stared aghast. Even the captain looked up in shock. The Bajjer carts receded. It was too late now for any more. None of the warriors still readying themselves to join that fight could do anything but look up at Sham, from already distant rails, & raise hands in inadequate farewell.

They became specks. Sham hoped they had seen his own hand raised, in response & thanks.

"CALDERA HAS—" Dero started to say.

"Go there," Caldera said. She showed Sham a place on her chart. Pointed at it. She looked at him intently. "*There.*"

"—an idea," her brother finished.

Sham wasted not a second. Did not demand clarification. Did not question Caldera Shroake. Just yelled at the switchers, who in turn switched as he demanded without quibbling or enquiry, on these last scattered yards of points, veering a mile or more into a little snarl of lines, a route near mounds & mounts.

You could see the wartrain easily now without fancy salvage business. "Get us over *there*," hissed Caldera. She gave more directions & the *Medes* shuddered.

A getterbird overflew them to investigate the navy, but as it approached, with an abrupt gush of fire a missile roared skyward from the guntrain. The angel exploded in a great flaming yelp, scattering debris.

"Oh my bloody Stonefaces!" Vurinam yelled. "They're *insane*! They're firing on *Heaven*."

"They're going to catch us," Fremlo said. "There's no way they're not."

There were but two trains, now, in the whole landscape, for all the gnarled derelicts in rust. The wartrain was close enough to see its trainsfolks' sneers. Molers took positions at their harpoons, as if this might make any bloody difference when the Manihiki warriors reached them.

The *Medes* careered for the end of the detour in the tangle, by caves & hillocks, towards something Caldera had understood & which, in the chaos, Sham had not clocked they were approaching.

With a soundless & utterly important shift, they rushed suddenly past a last set of wrecks, a final knoll & tunnel, out of the railsea, & onto the last, solitary, solo rail.

"Look," breathed Sham. He was there. He was tearing through the picture at which he had stared so many times, his crewmates & friends alongside him.

"I'm looking," Caldera said.

"*Look* at it!" The navy would have Sham soon, but this moment was his.

"You saw the ruins," Caldera said. "The wrecks." He kept his eyes on that one rail. "Sham. What do you think did that? My parents saw this, but they turned back, remember? Why d'you think I took us just where my parents didn't go?"

Good question. Good enough to work through Sham's distraction. He turned to face her. He looked back at Reeth's train, roaring after them, following them onto the last line. "In about fifteen seconds," Caldera whispered, "you're going to know the answer."

Sham narrowed his eyes. "There was something that . . ." Twelve seconds.

"Something that kept people out," Sirocco said. Eight. Seven.

"Something that still does," said Fremlo. "Something . . ."

". . . something big," Sham said.

Three.

Two.

One.

Sound came out of the pit they'd passed.

"Go fast," Caldera said. The noise grew loud. "Really, go fast." It seemed to be everywhere. Everyone on deck was turning to see what made so terrible a sound. Such a bass grinding. Such whining of metal. Officers turned, too, on the deck of the wartrain. A hill shook.

"I think we got close enough," Dero said. Loose stones jumped. A curtain of vines at the hole-entrance trembled. The sky was filled with blaring. & from out of the pit, riding the rails, something came.

An angel. Like no thing they had ever seen.

Everyone made noises of terror.

From under the ground, a train of spiked & spiny metal. It spat steam, dribbled fire. Grey smoke rose from a dorsal ridge of chimneys. How many parts were there to it? Who could count its ways? It slipped by segment into the light. Like a convoy of thorned towers.

How *old* was this bad thing? The birds flew shrieking off. Daybe huddled in Sham's arms. The angel pressed down hard & made its appalling noise. Its front was a wedge-shaped blade. With a blast like low thunder, it came.

It ate up yards. It came so fast. Its weapons glowed. The crew stared like worshippers.

"Welcome," Sham breathed, "to the outposts of Heaven."

"That," Caldera whispered, "is what keeps people from the edge of the world."

"But," Dero said, "it ain't used to facing two of us at once."

The angel howled onto the one true line behind the Manihiki wartrain. They were all, from rear to front—angel, navy & molers—committed to this single rail. All they could do was go fast.

"Will you *move!*" That was Captain Naphi. Staring over the *Pinschon* & the hulking wartrain at the world's-end protector. She was shouting, however, at her crew. They knew it; they obeyed. They managed to make the *Medes* accelerate.

The angel closed impossibly fast. It closed on Reeth's train. Sham could see him, staring at it. Closer. Close. Closed.

Say what you like about those Manihiki officers, they were brave & bolshy souls. They fired & fired. Sent bullets, missiles, lobbed bombs at the incoming angel. It ignored them. Ground through the explosions. It reached the rear carriage.

The angel's wedge split, opened onto a furnace-mouth, the

glowing insides of heavenly cogs & shearing metal. It bit down. It breathed out fire.

An appalling crash, a flash, a spinning maelstrom of metal. & the wartrain was gone.

Just—gone. So fast as to be unbelievable. The molers screamed at the sight of such an act, even committed against an enemy. The wartrain & those aboard were eaten & burnt, or churned under the angel's wheels. Seconds, & all it was, that pride of Manihiki, was litter, scattered in ruins.

Silence fell again across the *Medes*. Sham shivered. The angel flamed through the rubble.

"It stopped them!" someone shouted.

"It stopped them, yes," Sham said. "I wouldn't get too excited though. Because there's nothing between us & it, now. & it's still coming."

Chapter Seventy-Six

ANGELS HAVE a thousand jobs. For each job, a shape. For each task, celestial engineering in the factories of the gods. Not many of us are made according to such most minute & intricate blueprints.

In an angel's philosophy, it was once said, two times two equals thirteen. This is not slander. Angels are not crazy, could not be further from madness. They have, insofar as any theologian understands, absolute purity of purpose. A stiletto-sharp fidelity to the task of keeping Heaven clean.

To messy-minded humans, to *Homo vorago aperientis*, so glass-clear & precise a drive makes no sense at all. It is considerably less comprehensible than the ravings of those we call insane.

Angels, unremittingly & absolutely sane, cannot but seem to poor humanity relentlessly & madly murderous.

Chapter Seventy-Seven

SHAM SWALLOWED. Beyond the captain, behind the train, a flaming & gnashing enormity, came the angel.

Its wheels were many sizes, an irregular flank of them, of interlocking gears. Tusked with weapons. It did not have, nor did it need, windows. There was no seeing out nor in: it was an avenging rail-riding chariot of wrath. It burnt the bushes in its passing.

Even the atheists on the *Medes* whispered prayers. Sham swallowed. *Come on*, he thought. *Don't stop*, he thought. Think *more*.

Ahead was the too-close horizon, the end of the world. The same distance in the other direction, the angel. Moving faster than the *Medes*. The math was simple: the situation was hopeless. It would reach them before they reached whatever was there.

The captain did not move, & she did not, for all its monstrousness, appear to be looking at the angel, but rather through it. Sham looked at the receiver he held. He saw the glowing screen-blob. He had almost forgotten Mocker-Jack.

"All is lost," someone shouted.

"We're shafted," shouted someone else.

Sham felt Daybe strain as he fiddled with the machine. He remembered how the bat had lurched for the captain as she tinkered, & narrowed his eyes. "I'm his philosophy," Naphi had said of the great moldywarpe.

"Sirocco," Sham said. He waved the mechanism. Daybe bobbed as it moved. "Can you make this thing's signal get bigger?"

She looked quizzical. "Might be possible. Need more power."

"So connect it to something." He looked around, pointed at the *Medes* intercom. "That gets power from the engine. Come on, ain't you a salvor? This is what you do."

She pulled tools from her belt, yanked wires from the speakers & stripped them. Unwound some things, wound others together. Hesitated a second before plunging her tools into the guts of the racing *Medes*. There was a great crack, & all the machines on the train went off for an instant & came on again.

"Oh my head!" Sirocco shouted. They all felt it. The crew moaned at the rising, humming, trembling something, in the air, in the substance of the train. Even the captain staggered. Sham winced & grabbed Sirocco's arm, took the receiver. It was wired now to the train's insides.

Daybe was screaming at him. Scrabbling & scratching for the machine. Sham stared. The screen was pouring with light. It was bleating like a sheep. & the glowing blob that was Mocker-Jack was moving faster than he'd ever seen before.

"Oh my hammer & tongs," whispered Vurinam. "What did you even do?"

"Made it stronger," Sirocco said.

"What's the point of that?" Mbenday shouted. "You *sped up* the mole?"

"Much as I hate to undermine this technical achievement," Fremlo said. The doctor looked pointedly behind them, at the roaring angel. The crew stared.

"Mocker-Jack," the captain said dreamily. "Mocker-Jack's

your philosophy now, too, & you belong to it. We're going to have to face it." If the angel concerned her at all, she did not show it. The captain smiled. She walked to her dais. The crew watched her.

"She's right," Sham said.

"What?" hissed Vurinam. "She's lost her mind! Have you seen what's about to get us?" He pointed at the terrible engine. "One thing it ain't is a bloody mole!"

"She's right," Sham insisted. "We're molers. & it's our moling skills we need now."

Chapter Seventy-Eight

No LINES TO EITHER SIDE: they couldn't release jollycarts. The explosive harpoon at the train's front pointed uselessly in the wrong direction. Instead, they gathered at the *Medes*'s stern. Benightly went further, jumped down onto the *Pinschon* that jostled behind them, right to its end. He stood silhouetted against the great angel scant yards behind. Its mouth-clamp opened. It roared.

Light was waning. Below the rumbling of the rails there was another rumbling, of the ground. "What's that?" Caldera said. In the plain behind the chase, the earth trembled. & erupted. Sham gasped as a molehill burst up to huge height. A furrow roared in their direction.

"Stoneface," Sham whispered. Sirocco tugged at the wire-strewing transmitter & squeezed some impossible last drop of power from it. Miles off, through thick earth, Sham heard Mocker-Jack roar.

The *Medes* ploughed through a split in the rock line, followed seconds later by the gaining angel.

His crew watched Benightly. Even so big a man, even tensing all his bulk, he looked tiny in front of the onrushing visitation. He hefted his harpoon. Against the angel. It was laughable. But Benightly drew back his arm & waited & somehow did not look absurd. The angel grew closer.

"What are you doing?" the captain shouted. "Mocker-Jack's

not even here yet." Benightly said not a word. But the world itself answered.

It shook. Rocks quivered. Behind them, at the entrance to the rock chasm, the ground rose. Broke. Bigger than a tidal wave. The dark dirt fell away from a surging yellow something that shook the stones & rails & sent rockfall hurtling down the inclines. As if the earth spat out a new, rearing, fur-clad mountain. With teeth. Impossible ivory talpa, the titan moldy-warpe.

Blood dropped out of Sham's stomach. He staggered. Abacat Naphi howled a welcome.

A pale & shaggy enormity, a glimpse of blind red eyes in a debris plume. The mole roared.

& crashed back through into the dark beneath. Behind the implacable angel, the last line in the railsea shifted uneasily, rucked in segments as the mole burrowed faster than any train towards its summons.

Sham blinked away tears of awe. The crew were open-mouthed, staggered, by the angel, & by what came behind it. There was no time for reflection. The echoes of their passage swept away & changed, & with a rush the *Medes* emerged from between rocks. The angel was closing. Sham turned to look ahead at what was coming, & gasped again.

A bridge. Endless. A bridge into dark, jutting from the end of the world.

They were at the rim of the railsea. Racing towards a final cliff. The world came to a stop. Into the nothing, the void beyond earth, their one true rail continued.

They were hurtling way too fast to stop, & an angel was right behind them. Was grinding in engine triumph.

"You," Benightly said to it, "are close enough."

The angel's metal maw gaped. Benightly sang a hunt-hymn. Sham held out his hand.

Sirocco tugged the receiver free of the wire moorings that had boosted it. She handed it to Sham, stepped between him & the captain.

"No!" shouted Naphi, but the salvor kept her back, while Sham ran forward, whispered a prayer, & hurled the receiver towards the *Pinschon*. Towards Benightly.

It arced. *Too high! Too high oh what have I done?*

But Benightly leapt straight up. He plucked the charged-up receiver from the air with his fingertips. Landed already clipping it to his harpoon. Stood, his throwing arm ready, took aim, & Captain Naphi shouted, & the angel opened its mouth-thing again onto gnashing flaming gears with a blast of scorching triumph, into the gusts of which Benightly threw.

The spear flew. An immense throw. Benightly aimed not at the angel was but at where it would be. The spear slammed into its mouth. Which closed.

With a rush of wind the *Medes*'s wheels rattled on suddenly raised rails, as it careened onto the bridge to nowhere & the land receded. Someone screamed. "Brakes!" someone shouted. To either side was abyss. Sham reeled & stared as the angel bore down.

Behind it something came. A living earthquake. Shaking the edge of the world. Black earth parted, & animal enormity burst forth.

Pale leviathan, shoved up from the under. It gnashed in epic rage. That mouth! A vast slavering, where steeple-fangs jostled. The mole howled. Haunches like overhangs, claws like towers, shoving into light.

The vast harsh velvet beast breached.

Mocker-Jack soared. Cloud-great & ravening.

& twisted in the air, rolling as it came, so in its endless flanks & belly storming towards the angel, Sham saw the stubs of weapons. Snapped-off handles & hafts, a pelt-archaeology of failed hunts, stinging trophies accumulated over the centuries the colossal burrower had taunted & destroyed.

Hunting that unseen salvaged force, the signal now blaring from the angel's mouth, down the giant moldywarpe came. Onto the angel. Slab-teeth bared. With a scream of metal ruination, Mocker-Jack bit.

The angel fired all its weapons. Fire gusted across the behemoth & scorched its yellow hair & it snarled but did not release its mouthgrip even as it smouldered. It ripped, it tore. The crew gaped.

The captain shouted to Mocker-Jack, a loud & wordless greeting, challenge, lamentation.

The godlike mole tore the angel from the rails. The two great presences somersaulted in slow time, skidded, gouged across the last of the land. Mocker-Jack shook its prey apart, strewing heaven-trash & fire.

At the brink of the precipice the angel poised for long seconds straight up, a tower, wheels spinning. As if undecided whether to topple back onto the flat land. Gripping it, Mocker-Jack, on fire, bled & gnawed through steel, stared at the *Medes*.

Sham knew those blood-coloured orbs could barely discern more than light & darkness. Still, he would always swear the moldywarpe looked carefully in their direction. Stared & chewed & *pushed*. Pushed its quarry & itself out of that instant, & over the world's end.

The mole & the angel fell. The angel-train tumbled, & with

it went the great southern moldywarpe, *Talpa ferox rex*, Mocker-Jack the great, the captain's philosophy, into the abyss. & Sham would always swear on the lives of all the people he cared about that as it went, the mole looked with malice & satisfaction into the captain's eyes.

THE ANGEL DISINTEGRATED into shadows, became a shower of burning. The island-sized talpa glowed ghostly as it fell, until the dark that filled the trench beyond the railsea swallowed it, & the *Medes* was left above emptiness, waiting for the sound of impact, a sound that never came.

"Well grubbed," Sham whispered at last, into the silence.

Vurinam repeated it. Fremlo copied him. Fremlo copied him, & Mbenday Fremlo. Then others, & more & more. Even Yashkan cleared his throat & muttered the words. & they carried & grew louder until everyone was shouting, "Well grubbed! Well grubbed, by gods, well grubbed!

"Well grubbed, old mole!"

Part Eight

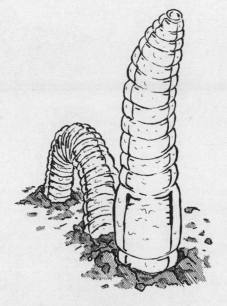

Tundra Worm
Lumbricus frigidinculta

Chapter Seventy-Nine

IT WAS THE NOISES the captain was making that drew attention to her. They were not like any sounds Sham had ever heard any human make before. Naphi was not screaming or crying, she was not howling or complaining. She stood at the train's edge, stared down into the deeps of the air where her philosophy had gone, uttered a succession of phonemes like those that might creep in between proper words. As if she spoke discards & language debris.

"Ah," she said. Her tone was calm. "Fff."

Sham was still dizzy with the abyssward descent he had just seen. He pulled his attention to the captain.

"Asuh," she said. "Mhuh. Enh." Clockwork-stiff, she walked to the edge of the deck. Sham went after her. He watched her with widening eyes. As he passed Sirocco, he grabbed a sharp tool from her salvor's belt.

"Wait!" he said.

Naphi turned, face set. One by one, the trainsfolk on the *Medes* looked at her. Sham sped up. Naphi gripped the railing with her left hand. She drew herself up smartly, & saluted her crew with her right, with the arm they had always known was flesh. She drew her knife, ready for close-quarters hunting, & turned to face the darkness.

"No!" Sham shouted.

Gripping the barrier with her disguised & enhanced limb, the captain braced on it, swung herself up, her legs up & around

& over the edge right out into space. She turned, neat as a gymnast, & began to plummet, to follow the moldywarpe down.

But Sham was there. Even as the captain let go the rail, he stabbed with Sirocco's tool right down into the heavy workings of her fakely artificial arm.

He had no time to aim. Just plunged the blade into pipework. There was an electrical crack, a *phut* of smoke, & the metal glove the captain had worn so long short-circuited, spasmed, snapped shut. Held her still clinging to the side of the *Medes*.

"Help me!" shouted Sham, leaning over. He stared at the captain, dangling over endless nothing, looking back up at him.

"Ah now," she said, in a strange mild voice. Her legs scrabbled & kicked against the train's side. She prodded urgently at her own robotic casing with her dagger, tried to pry it off her, to release herself from her own inadvertent grip & follow her philosophy.

"Help me!" Sham shouted again, as he grabbed for her & tried to avoid her weapon. & here came Sirocco, & Mbenday, & Benightly, who with a hunter's precision batted the knife from her hand. It twirled out of sight. They grabbed her. Together they hauled the captain back up onto the deck.

"Ah now," she kept saying, quietly. "I have something to catch." She did not struggle much.

"Secure her!" Mbenday shouted. They held the captain while Sirocco took pliers & screwdrivers to the snagging arm until with a click it released her. The crew cuffed Naphi's hands behind her back.

"Ah now," she said again, & shook her head. She murmured. She muttered to herself & slumped. She did not fight or cry.

"The bloody angel!" It was Sirocco shouting now. She stood

on the *Pinschon*, hands on hips, staring down like the captain had. She stamped & shook her fists. "It's gone! It went! This is a disaster!"

Was it? Sham was too tired to argue or understand. He kept looking at the Shroakes. Dero looked down into the dark, holding his breath. Caldera looked like she would explode. She was wide-eyed, fast-breathing, shaking with excitement.

The bridge was brick & girders. It arced down to reach the vertical chasm-side, a buttress pushing into the flank of the railsea among suspended pebbles, hard-packed soils, the lines of salvage. The bridge, the track extended into the coming night. Looked endless. "There's no way it should stay up," Sham said.

"It's stuff," Caldera said. Her voice shook. "Material we don't know about."

"Sort of Heaven stuff?" Vurinam said.

Caldera shrugged. "What do you think?" she said.

We are here, Sham thought. *On a bridge over nothing. We got by the guardian angel! We are on our way.*

To Heaven. On a single rail.

"So ..." Fremlo said. Daybe launched into the black, lurched right back, as if even the bat got vertigo. "So we're here." Fremlo said. "Now what?"

The way they had come, the tracks were littered with debris where Mocker-Jack had wrestled the angel into the void. It would take hours to clear.

"'What now?'" Dero shouted. "Duh! Now we go *on*!"

In the quiet that followed, they did not hear the beat of any wings.

No journey had ever been like that one. The *Medes*'s lights were nothing: they shone a few silvered yards of rail in front, while on every other side was black. There were no junctions to negotiate, no points to throw. A single elevated night rail. Sham had no name for the percussion of a train moving over nothing, on brick arches, each arc miles long, each strut descending to whatever floor floored the universe.

The gloom at last began to fade. The sky went as gentle & clear as it did on any other morning, & above that clarity was the must & swirl of the upsky. To their star'd, to their port, empty air. Behind & in front of them, only bridge. Below them cloud, as far below as above. & they on the line in that birdless sky puttered on.

Now we see, thought Sham. Out beyond moles, beyond salvage, past the railsea itself. *We'll just see.* He had made it out.

There was life. They saw scuttling on the tracks. Lizards. & if there were such beasts, there must be bugs, to feed them. Vegetation in the mottles of the wood. A tiny ecosystem between rails, on the approach to Heaven.

The captain did nothing but stare as Sirocco wielded trinkets & expertise & fixed her left arm. The crew cuffed it to the rail, with heavy chains, for Naphi's own protection.

"What if it just goes on forever?" said Sham. "This line."

"If it goes on forever," Caldera said, "then we're in for a long journey."

ON THE EARLY MORNING of the second day, they saw something blocking their way. A lumpy presence. They stared as they approached, at its fly-eye bulbous front, its spiked extrusions, its gnarled barrels, & Mbenday's voice suddenly clicked on in panic from the intercom: "It's another angel! It's *facing* us! Coming for us! Full reverse!"

Chaos! Everyone raced, running to their stations, hauling to turn the engine.

"Wait!" someone shouted. It was, they realised to their shock, Captain Naphi. "Wait." She spoke with enough authority that even unamplified her voice carried. "Look at it," she said. "It is *not* coming. Look at it."

The angel's joints, the cracks between its plates of armour, were verdigrised & overgrown. Built up with calcified exudations, runoff from within. On it & in it grew moss & lichen. The angel was furred with the stuff. Boughs & bushes of it, in frozen gushes.

"It's dead," Dero said.

It was. The angel was dead.

The celestial cadaver was huge. It was on a double- or triple-decker scale. Even long-cold it made the watchers gape. It exuded antiquity. It was absurdly, ostentatiously ancient. Odd machine parts, sigils & script adorned it, like pictograms, like paintings found in caves.

The *Medes* reached it & stopped. The crew regarded it a long time.

Sham reached out with trembling fingers. "Careful, Sham," Vurinam whispered. Sham hesitated. Prepared himself for physical contact with an emissary from beyond the world, in its endless sleep. Before he could touch it, however, a bolt sailed over his head & ricocheted off the front of the angel with a flat clang.

"Are you bloody mad?" he screamed, turning. Caldera stood with her arm still poised from the throw. The crew stared at her.

"What?" she said exuberantly. Before Sham could say anything Dero threw his own missile. Sham yelped, the object clanged & bounced over the side of the bridge, into the endless air.

"Stop throwing rubbish at the dead angel!" Sham shouted.

"What?" Caldera yelled. She was staring at the old engine with a strange expression. "Why?"

Chapter Eighty

"What do you mean, this is where you get off?" Sham said.

"Which bit do you not understand?" Sirocco said. She smiled at him, not meanly.

"You've come this far," Sham said. "You came this far & you, you rescued me! We've only a last bit more to go. Only a little way."

Sham stood at the front of the *Medes*, shouting up to her. Sirocco stood on the tip of the angel. The two trains were pressed up as if in an unequal kiss. Sirocco had leapt onto the angel, hauled herself up its curve & had announced that she was claiming it, for salvage, while the crew stared at her quizzically. She had begun to probe & prod & pry at chinks in the angel's carapace.

Whatever. But there was no way past it. There was only the one rail. & there would be no shifting that corpse. Nor could you haul a jollycart over its landscapey body.

"Well, we'll have to walk," Dero said. & while much of the rest of the crew, still befuddled with everything that had happened, still awesick, you might say, had watched, the Siblings Shroake had strapped on their packs of dried food & water bottles & tools & whatnot, & tripped goatlike up onto the angel. Caldera glanced back more than once, stood at last atop a weather-beaten outcrop of angelback & watched Sham watch her.

"Wait!" Sham shouted. "Where the bloody hell are you going?"

"Oh come on," Caldera shouted back. She shrugged. "You know fine well, Sham. We're farther than they got, but we still ain't there."

"Where's there?"

"I'll know when I see it. Question is what you're going to do?" She walked on, picking her way past copses of antennae, clots of rust, aeons'-worth of grime.

"Will you bloody Shroakes stop!" Sham shouted. Caldera hesitated. "Give us five minutes & stop being melodramatic. We're *all* coming!"

NOT REALLY.

"This is where I get off. What makes you think I want to go to the end of the world?" Sirocco said. She had drilled an opening in the angel's coating, & she was shoving her hand into its cold insides.

"We're way past the end of the world already," Sham said. "& I thought, I mean, you came for me . . ."

"Well now," she said. "What I came for, in fact, is right here." She slapped the engine-corpse flank. Her goggles were lit from within, illuminating her smile with pale grey light.

"Salvage?" Sham said. "You came here for *salvage?*"

"Sham ap darling Soorap," Sirocco said. "I like you, Sham, & I like your friends, but I ain't here for you, & I ain't even here for any old salvage. That I can get anywhere. I'm here for *angel salvage!*"

"How could you know we'd—"

"Meet them? Everyone knows there's angels in the way of Heaven. *Beat* them? I didn't. I made a bet. & you should take that as a vote of confidence."

"Sham," shouted Caldera

"In a *minute!*" he shouted back.

"I knew you'd face 'em when I knew where you wanted to go," said Sirocco, "& I had faith. I couldn't *believe* it when that old mole took it down. Could, not, believe it. But then stick on a few miles & here we are. Do you get what this is? This ain't nu-salvage. This ain't arche-salvage. It ain't alt-salvage even. This is a whole other thing. This is trash from *Heaven*. This is *dei-*salvage! & it is *mine*." Her delight was terrifying.

"We need your help," Sham said.

"No, you don't. & if you do, I'm afraid it ain't yours to have. I wish you well, I really do. But this is what I came for, & this I have. So best of luck to you."

From one of her pockets she pulled out a microphone. Little as it was, the tech in it amplified her voice so all the crew could hear. "Attention please," she said. "You can't get any further. May I propose a business arrangement? I know what I'm doing: you've got a conveyance. We can come to an arrangement.

"I know where to go to do selling. This is my hunting, like that great moldywarpe was yours. Same terms, same shares as if it was molemeat you were bringing back. & you think people pay well for moldywarpe bits? Well, you never dealt in salvage before. & this ain't any salvage. This is *all* our fortunes."

"Fine," Sham interrupted. "But I'm going with the Shroakes. You can keep my bloody share." He raised his voice. "Who's coming with us?"

A silence followed that. *What does it say about me*, Sham thought, *that I'm genuinely surprised no one's putting their hand up? That no one's saying a word?*

"Sham," Mbenday said. "We are not explorers. We're hunters who look after our friends. We came for you. Didn't we?" Some of Sham's comrades were looking avariciously at the dead angel. Some were looking sheepishly, or avoiding looking, at him or the Shroakes. "So let us look out for you. You have no idea where you're going," Mbenday said. He raised his arms & the leather of his coatsleeves creaked. "Or even if there's anything at the other side."

"It's a bridge," Sham said. "Of course there's something on the other side."

"That does not follow," Mbenday said.

"Benightly!" Sham said.

But the harpoonist cleared his throat, & in his deep Norther voice rumbled hesitantly, "Come, Sham. Don't need to do this. You too, Shroakes." Caldera made a rude noise.

"Hob?" Sham said. "Fremlo?" They wouldn't look at him. He could not believe it.

"Walking?" said Fremlo. "Through void? For one knows not what? Sham, I beg you . . ."

"Anyone!" Sham shouted.

"We came for you," Vurinam said. "We came for your Shroakes. We came as far as the angels. There ain't nothing else we want. Now come back with us."

"Tell Troose & Voam I send my love, but I'm following through," said Sham, not looking at him.

"I'll come."

It was Captain Naphi. Everyone stared at her.

Even the Shroakes turned back. Naphi rattled her chains, & looked at them in splendid hauteur until someone ran to undo them.

"I can't have mine," the captain said. She looked at Caldera, at Dero, & at last at Sham ap Soorap. "So someone else's philosophy is better than none."

Chapter Eighty-One

IT FELT STRANGE to walk on tracks, let alone such tracks as these. The Shroakes, the captain & Sham went single file. A terrible short distance to either side the bridge stopped & emptied into the air. Behind them were the clattering & drill-sounds of the crew's salvage, under Sirocco's exasperated supervision. People shouted goodbye, & not the Shroakes, Sham, or the captain answered.

Sham kept his eyes ahead, for hours, focusing on anything but the fall that hemmed them in. He thought of the crew tugging bits & pieces of the old angel out of their housings, teeth from a mouth, filling the rendering cart, the butchery floor, the storage containers, the hold of the *Medes* with unlikely meat. The ceramic, glass & old metal mechanisms.

Daylight went & they continued walking, until even with torches the darkness made it dangerous. They ate together. The Shroakes muttered to each other, & sometimes to Sham. Naphi said nothing. When they slept, they tied themselves to the rails. In case of thrashing, rolling, in their dreams.

They woke before the sun was fully up to the clattering passage of getterbirds overhead. "Maybe we'll feel it when they go," Caldera said, after an inadequate huddled breakfast. "The train I mean. Maybe we'll feel it in the rails."

"Maybe it'll shake us off," Dero said. He made a whistling noise, like something falling.

"We won't feel nothing," Sham said. They had been walking a long time. "What if it rains?"

"Then we'll have to be very bloody careful," Dero said.

Through all the long hours of that day they trudged. Sham kept his eyes mostly down so the trainlines would not mesmerise him, the surrounds not make him dizzy. It meant he didn't see the empty sky, the birdlessness, anything much at all, until Caldera shouted, & he stopped & looked ahead.

They were approaching another cliff face. It loomed out of horizontal haze. The tracks, the bridge dwindled threadlike to invisibility, but beyond the last of it they could see vertical earth. The far side of the chasm.

Sham swallowed. Stonefaces knew how many miles to go. They kept on. & every time he looked up that surface seemed as far away as ever. But then abruptly as the evening grew close he could make out texture. He could see where the struts of the bridge entered it.

In the absolutely dark small hours, exhaustion stopped them a while. But they had walked through much of the night, & it was not very long after that that the sun came up & woke him, & Sham at last could see where they had got to. He gasped.

No more than a mile ahead, the bridge touched land.

Chapter Eighty-Two

SLOWLY, WEAPONS UP, eyes wide, they approached a different kind of rock, a different earth. Heaven was geologically distinct.

It was all rubbly, uneven hillscape, slopes & steepness & crags right up to the sheer. They stepped tie by tie out of the air & under an arch of stone, by hatchways & incomprehensible trackside boxes, onto new land. Heaven had mechanisms.

They were silent, dusty from the crossing. The line took them through a grey gorge. Daybe circled the travellers, never going far. The peaks around them pushed easily into the upsky.

"What's that sound?" Sham said. The first words beyond the world. A repeated rhythm—a subtle, unending hushing beat—came from up ahead.

"Look!" Dero said. A tower.

Above a jawline of stone. It was ancient, windowless, a ruin of strange design. The walkers froze as if it would approach them. It didn't. They continued at last & the landscape slowly lowered. Until the tracks turned, lines of metal running now at last into—Sham gasped—a gusting, cloud-filled, silent city.

Low shacks, blocks in concrete, a town bifurcated by the rail. Destroyed by time. The crumbled remains of houses, empty but for wind. Birdless sky. Sham heard patterings of displaced stone. Daybe went up to investigate, but that empty expanse kept intimidating him, & he returned to Sham's shoulder.

The travellers walked on rails overhung by decrepitude in a

deepening cut. They saw no weeds, no birds, no animals. The sallow clouds of the upsky moved like nothing living. The railway cut through a wreck-town of long-dead concrete, banks of ossified rubbish, dunes of shredded paperdust. Under what looked like vines & were wires sagging with age & thick muck.

"So where's this treasure people keep mentioning?" Dero said at last. No one looked at him.

Their footsteps were slow & unsteady. They walked on. & deep in his mind, staring into all the drifts of ruin, under which the remnants of urban layout were just visible, Sham became aware of something.

Heaven, the world beyond the railsea, was empty, & very long dead. & he, though utterly awed, was not surprised. Everything was made at once clear & meaningless, & his mind felt at once as near-empty & gusted by scrags & stubs of nonsense as this old city—& inhabited by a sly, growing excitement.

& then after Sham had no notion how long of walking, ahead was an impossible thing. Something that did surprise him. That blasted him, in fact, with shock. First he, then the Shroakes, then Captain Naphi gasped.

"What . . . is . . . that?" Dero said at last.

The rail stopped.

It did not double-back to rejoin itself in a loop. Did not tangle aimlessly among a collection of other lines, nor fan out to various sidings which themselves fanned out & eddied into randomness. It was not broken by landslip, explosion or mishap, unfixed yet by any angel.

The track *stopped*.

In a yard, in the shadow of a building, it approached a wall, & ended. Two big piston-looking things extruded from a brace, as if to push back on a train shoving against them, & the railway line,

JUST,

STOPPED.

IT WAS UNHOLY, uncanny. The perversion, the antithesis of what railroads had to be, a tangle without end. & there it was.

"The end of the line," Caldera said at last. Even the words sounded like a transgression. "That's what they were looking for. Mum & Dad. The end of the line."

There were long moments of quiet, of awestruck gawping at the quite impossible flat *stop*. Somewhere, Sham realised, he could still hear an endless sibilant, like a repeated injunction to hush.

"You wouldn't think," said Dero, his voice hollow, "the rails could finish, would you?"

"Maybe they don't," Sham said. "Maybe this is where the railsea begins."

BEYOND THE END of the cut & the rails—the end of the rails!— a crumbling staircase ascended to the city. Dero climbed while Daybe circled him. Caldera, still staring at it, walked past the end of the track towards a hole that had once been a door in what had once been a wall in what had once been the building. She moved with sudden urgency.

"Where you going?" Sham shouted. She shoved inside. Sham swore.

"Come on!" shouted Dero from the top. He ran out of sight. From within the building, Sham heard Caldera gasp.

"Dero, wait!" Sham shouted. He dithered, as Naphi followed Caldera. "Dero, come back!" he shouted, & ran after the older Shroake, into shadow.

Light & gusts of dust-grey wind came slantwise into a half-memory of a room. Staircase stubs rose a few feet in steep zigzags. There had once been many floors in this railside hall. All were gone; the travellers stood at the bottom of a concrete hole, shin-deep in splinters & plastic shapes once desks & ordinators. A maze & dented blocky slope where a building's worth of filing cabinets had piled up. Some were burst open, strewing paperwork become mulch. Some were buried, some wedged shut.

Caldera scrambled up them. She grabbed at handles. Reached into shafts between cabinets. She pried at them. "What are you doing?" Sham said.

Her voice echoed out with the banging of yanked-open drawers. "Take these," she said, handing back ragged papers. "Careful. They're falling apart."

"Come out," Sham said. She handed him more. The metal creaked. She spelunked a scree of drawers, her hands full of folders. She looked lost.

"What is it," Naphi said, "you're looking for?"

"I need to know," Caldera said after a long silence. "About . . . about everything. Everything our Mum & Dad always said." She furrowed her brow & began, manically, to scan the papers she held. "About the railsea."

"Know what?" Sham said. "Come out of there."

"It doesn't . . . I can't . . ." She shook her head, hunting for meaning to it all. "I don't know. Why did we do all this?" The report in her hand disintegrated. Her fingers trailed its muck.

"Mum taught us this old writing. Points . . ." she read. "Oil stores . . ." She went through the sheets, one by mouldy one. "Personnel. Ticket prices. Credit. I can read it, but I can't put it together!"

"You already did," Sham said gently.

"I came here to understand!"

"There's nothing here you don't understand," Sham said. Caldera stared at him. "You've known all this for ages. Things head out from here. You seen which way that dead angel was facing." He spoke slowly. "*You* told *me* all this. What the god-squabble was. Well, this is the town where it happened. The town where the winners were." He raised his hands slowly. "& they're gone. You was never going to find out anything new here. That ain't why you're here, Caldera."

Caldera sniffed. "Really?" she said. "Why am I here?"

"You're here because your parents wouldn't do what they was told. Wouldn't shun anything. They wanted to see what's at the end of the world. & you actually *did*. Do. Are doing." Sham held her gaze.

"Hey." It was Dero. He stood silhouetted in the doorway. Behind him Daybe veered in agitation.

"You Shroakes," said Sham. "Always gallivanting off in all directions . . ."

"You need to see something," Dero said. He spoke in a dreamlike monotone. "There's something you need to see."

Beyond the building & the rails there were yards of paved land, more nothingy concrete-stubbed remains, & then the land, *all* land, abruptly stopped. But not on void this time.

They stood on a pitted coastline road, a raised walkway just like a shore in the railsea. It rose not out of rails, though, as any shoreline must surely, but from miles upon miles, from a giddying, endless expanse of water.

Chapter Eighty-Three

SHAM REELED. The water foamed. It rocked & slapped against the concrete wall. Sham's heart powered. What was this? & what was beyond? A ruined jetty poked above the waves just as normal jetties did above rails. Tentative with wonder, Sham walked to its end.

The enormity of that water. It rose & fell back in lurching swells. It was like nothing he could have imagined.

Above it, the strange deadness of the air ended. Gulls! They wheeled & whooped. Swept curiously past Daybe, who soared in exhilarated aerobatics. This was the source of the repeated noise. The water huffed & shuffled & rocked back & forth against the land.

"The water level's so high," Naphi whispered at last. She looked back the way they had come. "It should be flooding back into that chasm. Even back into the railsea. Should half-fill it."

"You told me they jury-rigged the world," Sham said to Caldera. "Maybe they did something to seal the rock here when they put the water in, so it can't spill out. Can't seep through the sides."

"Yeah," said Caldera. "Only they didn't put the water here: they *left* it here." She was staring too, but dividing her attention, still sifting through the papers she held, frowning as she glanced at the disorganised snips of information. "They drained all the *rest*. To make more rail-ready real estate."

"The world?" Sham said.

"Used to be underwater."

THEY STAYED THERE, said nothing more, for a long time. Sham was too awed to care much that he was cold. The sun dawdled slowly through space, behind the upsky, illuminating it. They could see no beasts up there just then. Only the arcing gulls.

The birds looped & skimmed the surface of the liquid. *There's stuff in there they can eat*, thought Sham. He thought of the stringy fish that lived in the small ponds & pools of the islands & the railsea itself. Looked as far as he could to the horizon. Thought how much bigger such creatures might get in a space so uncramped.

Sham felt something rising through his bones. Daybe felt it too, snuffled in alarm. A rhythm, getting louder. "Getterbirds," Sham said.

Three of them. They came from behind the hills into the downbeat heaven. They veered towards the travellers. They farted smoke, lower than Sham had ever seen them before. The wind from their whirling wings sent up rubbish. They zoomed abruptly off, over the ancient debris, to some out-of-sight nest for old, tired angels.

"What was that?" Dero said. "Curiosity?"

"I don't think so," Sham said quietly. "I think they were giving directions." He pointed.

Figures were emerging from the ash & stubs of the old city.

What were they, these dwellers beyond the world? Rag-clad, hulking & shaggy, creeping, sniffing, they loped out of the dust that announced them. Ten, twelve, fifteen figures. Big women

360

& men, all muscle & sinew, baring their teeth, coming on two limbs & four, apelike, wolflike, fatly feline. Staring as they came.

"We have to go," Dero said, but they could not get past. The newcomers had reached the base of the jetty. & there they stopped. Their dark clothes were so shredded they looked like feathers. They licked their lips; they stared a long time.

"Is it me," Dero said at last, "or do they look excited?"

"It's not you," Sham said.

Something was approaching from the ruins. Seven feet tall, sloped, immense. An ancient, powerful man, of great girth. He wore a repatched dark coat, a tall black hat.

"That costume," Caldera said. "It's like That Apt Ohm."

What looked like a degenerate avatar of the god stepped slowly past his fellows, towards Sham & the others. The jetty shook with his great steps. He licked his face in delight.

"What are we going to do?" whispered Dero.

"Wait," said Sham. He kept his pistol down. The man's eyes were wide. He stopped a few feet away, & gazed at the visitors.

& then, enormously, he bowed. Behind him, the others bayed. It sounded like happiness. Like triumph. The big man bellowed. Snarls & growling, gulping, knotty language.

"That's some weird mix of old Railcreole," Caldera said. "*Really* old."

"Do you understand it?" Sham said. He recognised a few words himself. "Controller," he heard. "Rails." & with a start, a line from an old hymn: "Oh shun!"

"Only a little bit." Caldera squinted with attention. "'Here' . . . 'At last' . . . 'Interest.'"

The enormous figure reached into his coat, & Naphi & Sham stiffened. But what he drew out & offered was a wad of paper. After several motionless seconds, while Naphi kept watch, her gun in her hand, Sham came forward & snatched it. He & the Shroakes leaned over the sheet.

Columns, words, on sheet after sheet, ancient typing that made only a very little sense to Sham. A long preamble, lists, footnotes & observations. "What is this?" he said.

On the last page of the pile was a long string of numbers. Circled in red. Caldera looked at her brother, & up at Sham.

"It's a bill," she said. "They say this is what we owe them."

THINGS FLICKERED through Sham's mind. These figures' feral wanderings in ruins from where once the trains & tracks had been controlled. The man's hat. "He's the leader," Sham said. "The controller."

Caldera stared at the paper. "This is . . . more money than there's ever been in history," she whispered. "It's gibberish."

"Their ancestors must've got lost here," Dero said. "On the wrong side of the gap." The controller snarled strange words.

"He . . ." said Caldera. "He's saying . . . something about *settling up?*"

"You said something about credit," Sham said. "Oh, this lot didn't get lost. They've been *waiting*."

He stared at the massive man. The controller. Who licked his lips again, & bared sharp teeth. "Our ancestors couldn't afford their ancestors' terms," Sham said. "For the use of the rails. The bill's been growing. They've been charging us interest. They think that's why we've come. He thinks we're ready to *pay*."

He sifted through the papers. "How long you been waiting?" Sham said. "How long ago was the godsquabble? The railway wars?" Years. Centuries. Epochs.

The watchers yowled. One or two shook what Sham saw were the scraps of briefcases. They must have grown up with a prophecy. As had their parents, & theirs, & theirs near-endlessly, shuffling through the collapsing city. Waiting in their board-room & in emptiness. A prophecy they thought was coming true.

Abruptly, Sham hated them. He didn't care that they were lost too, in thrall to a remorseless drive, the hunger of a company presiding over ruin. That refused to allow the fall & rise of civilisations, the visitations & transformations & leave-takings & rubbish-pickings of aliens, the fall of waters, the poisonings of skies & the mutation of the things in the earth, because of the very actions for which they charged, to intrude on their patient accounting. Endlessly extending terms to a humanity unaware they were in debt, that they had for millennia been buying travel-passes on the never-never. All in the hopes that at the end of time, economies would be back in place to pay.

"'Ghost money in Heaven,'" Sham said. "Not 'cause it died—ghosts because it weren't born yet." He stared the big man in the face. "We," he said, "owe you nothing."

The controller stared at him. His look of hungry expectation slowly changed. To one of uncertainty. Then slowly to one of misery. & abruptly to one of rage.

He roared. All the Heaven-dwellers roared. They lurched forward. The jetty rocked as they came.

Daybe launched at the huge figure, but the controller batted it away. "Move!" Sham shouted, but before he could even get his pistol up, the controller had snagged his neck & squeezed & smacked the weapon from his hand. Through blood pounding in his ears, Sham heard the gun hit the water.

His vision was darkening as he flailed. He could make out

the Shroakes trying to get away, Captain Naphi firing her pistol twice, before a perfectly flung rock slammed into her hand & disarmed her. & then there was simply not enough blood in his head for Sham to focus.

He shifted in woozy pain. Someone was tying his feet together, his hands behind his back, with manky old rope. He was hustled, tugged, cuffed, dragged to the jetty's edge, the yells & struggles of his fellows behind him, the screeches of impotent daybat rage.

His head spun, he heard Caldera's voice. She was next to him, Dero by her, then Naphi, all tied up but for the captain's enhanced arm, too strong for cord, held instead in the grips of several captors. Who bickered & chattered. Some sobbed, in the epochal disappointment of prophecy unfulfilled. Some hissed. Some busily filled their captives' clothes with stones.

The controller raged. He ground his teeth. Daybe swooped below curious gulls, but the man ignored or smacked it away again.

"Oh, shun!" he whispered. The feral businessman pointed at the water, & snarled some more. He was declaiming for his minions. He was, Sham thought, *announcing sentence*.

"Other people'll come," Sham shouted. "They think there's treasure here! All the fares, the imaginary money you think you've got coming!"

Sham staggered under his weighed-down clothes, & struggled in his captors' grasps, stared out at his attackers & the remnants of this bureaucratic heaven. "No!" he shouted. "This isn't how it ends!"

He looked right at Caldera. She stared at him. She called Sham's name as he was shoved to the walkway's edge.

Sham tried to dig in his toes. He felt the ground shake. For a moment he thought it was his heart thundering his body. But his captors were hesitating too. Something was happening.

Daybe's alarm call changed timbre.

Grinding towards them all, coming backwards along the rails, through the cut in the ruins, towards the buffers at the line's end, was an angel. A huge & age-crusted angel. An oil-fouled angel. The angel over the corpse of which Sham had clambered. Woken & alive again, hauling in reverse back the way, generations before, it must have come.

THE EXECUTIVES OF the factory-town screamed. They howled. They scattered. Sham reeled. It must be very much longer than a lifetime since the angel had died & isolated them. None of them had ever seen a train move, seen any rolling stock on any line.

The angel gusted filthy smoke. Sham heard yells, saw familiar figures riding its rear. Benightly, & Mbenday, & Sirocco the salvor, & Fremlo, &, his coat billowing splendidly despite all its holes, Vurinam. Sham's crew rode towards him on the bum of a backward-moving angel.

Sham shouted mightily in welcome. Benightly shot into the air, & the wild bosses ran. All but the giant controller. The angel's rear-end rivet things pushed into the buffer & it stopped.

"No!" shouted the controller. That word was the same. "No, no! Shun! Oh shun!" With startling speed, he grabbed for the nearest captive. Caldera Shroake. & at that sight, quicker still, without a thought, Sham intervened.

He was a nothing, a silly pipsqueak, next to the huge figure. It was a wonder all of Sham's momentum was sufficient to shift him at all. Perhaps in no other circumstances would it have been. But the man was poised on the very edge of the walkway.

& when Sham slammed into him he wheeled his arms, tottered, his feet slipped, & he pitched roaring towards the waves.

He reached, he raged. He grabbed as he went.

Grabbed Sham. Took Sham over with him, into the water. Took him down.

Chapter Eighty-Four

& THANK YOU. Do you feel it?

We are slowing.

We will soon be done, & at our destination.

It could make a person despair, to dwell on how many parts of everything have been neglected. Have not even been discussed. You might by now have heard of the stretches of eastern & northern rails, far beyond Manihiki or any navy, where there are tribes of wild horses that have learnt so well to stay safe from burrowers, to never stray from the rails & ties, that it is encoded in their bones. So a newborn foal swaying on its sticklegs will not let its hardening hooves fall on the open flatearth. So trainsfolk in that meadowland share the rails with long lines of horses, trotting single file forever, eating the juicy grass between the rails.

In Amman Sun is a cold fortress served by trains made of ice. It's said. The political fiddles between Deggenlache & Mornington could fill many entertaining hours. The drab & isolated lives of those cowed, bored generations of self-styled bosses in that town at the end of the rails, by contrast—they are not uplifting. But there's things to be learned from the stunted venality of the controllers.

On & on. Had you been in charge you would, even had you started & ended in the same places, have described a different figure. A different "&". But nothing's done. If you tell any of this to others, you can drive, & if you wish, go elsewhere on the way. Until then, safe travels & thank you.

&—Sham, you say?

Sham is drowning.

Chapter Eighty-Five

THE WATER TASTED like tears. That was what Sham thought as he went down. This was not like the streams & ponds on the hills of the railsea: it was salt.

Oh shun, tears forever.

He tried to fight his slow descent. No good. He couldn't see a thing or free his limbs. Couldn't hear anything but his own blood.

Somewhere below him in the cold, because it was desperately cold, he could feel a disturbance, the flailing limbs & bulk of the controller, thrashing. *I hope I don't end up on top of him*, Sham thought. *I don't want that to be where . . .*

To be where.

I saw the end of the world, Sham thought, & ceased moving his body, & breathed out in streaming bubbles, & closed his eyes & continued sinking.

& THEN ABRUPTLY STOPPED.

Felt something grip him painfully by the restraints that held his hands. Felt pressure shift. Was moving up again, against the pull of gravity, upside down, away from the huge body of the man, the last of whose motions he could still just feel, receding below.

INTO THE AIR, spluttering, retching, sucking in oxygen. The captain had him. Clutching him with her metal hand. She was held by the rope still wound around her waist, held tug-of-war-style by the crew. At its end was Benightly, bracing & taking the weight. The captain had gone right in for Sham, her metal hand pulling her down.

Naphi gripped Sham's wet & salty waist & delivered him to the dock. Where Caldera reached for him first & grabbed him, hauled him back & slapped his cheek & shouted his name. Where Daybe came down & licked his face. Where he lay on the concrete & coughed, & vomited & wheezed while the Shroakes & Vurinam & Fremlo & Sirocco & everyone applauded in relief.

"So," said Sham. "Changed your minds?"

The crew of the moletrain *Medes*, hitchers of rides on the backsides of celestial dead, had made a fire at the end of the line. They were singing & eating, telling each other stories.

It was night beyond their firelight. More than once they heard what might be people around them, trying to be quiet. They stationed guards, but they were not much concerned.

"The last head controller is currently being dissipated into fish-poo," Fremlo said. "I think the rest of the board is a little disoriented, don't you?"

Sham nodded his damp head. With it wet he had realised how long his hair had grown. "I thought," he said to Sirocco, "that you were going back." He huddled in his towel.

"Know what happened?" Sirocco said. "Funniest thing. There I was, taking the angel apart. We'd hauled out loads of the bloody thing, & it suddenly occurred to me that with a little tugging of this, & a replacement of that with the other, I could start it up again. That's sort of the key to salvaging: you don't need to understand it. Anyway.

"So after a while & a few false starts, we get it moving. & we're thinking about how to back up the moletrain so we can get the angel going forward, move them in tandem, get the angel-chassis back into the railsea. When someone says, I can't even remember who it was . . ."

"It was you," Benightly said to her.

"Can't even remember," Sirocco said. "Someone says, maybe we should just have a little quick look-see check how that lot's getting on over the bridge. Took a vote, easy pass. Backed our way up, through that tunnel, heard a commotion. Here we are." She dusted her hands in a *job-done* motion.

Here you are, Sham thought. *Here you are indeed.*

"Tomorrow," Sirocco said, "we start again. Back again. I mean, forward again—back to the railsea. & now you can come back with us." She pushed her stick into the fire, roasting her supper. Sham took a bite of his own. He looked at the Shroakes in the flickering light. Caldera met his eyes. "Not," Sirocco said, "that you're going to. Come back I mean." She smiled.

"Take a message for me?" Sham said. "To my family?"

"Of course," Sirocco said. "What's *your* plan, Sham?"

Sham stared at the fire.

For the railsea, most things would stay the same. Angels, on automatic, long-ago-programmed loops, would continue to police the rails. A few getterbirds would ply back & forward from the dead HQ, delivering automatic surveillance that would be filed against the end of the universe. The debt that the trainsfolk accrued would rise, owed this fossil company, compounding with interest into a sum ever more meaningless.

But thanks to Mocker-Jack, the angel that guarded the bridge was gone. & with the ministrations of the salvor, so was the corpse-blockage. It might take time—it might take years—but the crew of the *Medes* would not be the last visitors. The way was open.

"I've been thinking," he said. "First I was thinking about updivers. I bet you've got suits, Sirocco? I wonder what's up there." He raised his eyes at the mountain silhouettes around them. "& then I was thinking, if you had suits to go up, you could use them to go down, too." He jerked his thumb behind him, at the water. Sham listened to the huffy repetitive investigations of the water on the shore.

"Then I was thinking. Why change direction? I been heading this way so long." He looked at Caldera. "I want to go where your mum & dad wanted you to go," he said.

"Excuse me?" said Dero.

"What?" said Caldera. "We're here."

"They were so keen to learn from the Bajjer," Sham said. "Their myths & stuff, yeah, but it's a long way to go for stories, no matter how good. So I was thinking, what other sort of thing could you learn from them, & *only* from them, hands on?"

The Shroakes stared. Their eyes grew ever wider & more fascinated.

"You remember that last carriage your parents left behind?" Sham said. "Near the bridge? The one that looked weird? I been thinking about it. Can't get it out of my head. I think that's what they wanted to happen. Seeing this place gives me an idea."

Part Nine

Daybat
Vespertilio diei

Chapter Eighty-Six

NO CLATTERNAMES, no switches, no thud of wheels on rail. No rails nor wheels to thud them. Sham shouts in a new motion.

There have been goodbyes. The last rail of the railsea is long out of sight. Sham revels in crashing splash. He whoops in spray.

It took days & efforts & expertise to return to the senior Shroakes' last carriage, to investigate Sham's hunch, & to finish what, they discovered, had been started.

Its ceiling had been turned into its sealed underside. Its body made to taper, wedge-shaped & streamlined. Full of air-filled chambers. Housing was ready for a stripped-tree mast. Rope & stiff cloth was in a lockbox, at which Sham stared with recently acquired expertise. *Why should sails only work on trains?* he had demanded.

Over the water the upsky is thinner. The sun makes rainbows through the spray. They bob in enormous damp space. Daybe scuds, & Sham staggers. His rail-legs are no help on this new deck. On this floaty upside-down water train. *We have to give this thing a better name*, Sham thinks.

Caldera & Dero look up from where they're working the sail. Sham remembers Bajjer techniques & shouts instructions. Canvas billows, a boom swings, & their vessel rushes through the water. Going they know not where.

Sham lifts the hatch in the deck to the little kitchen & the cabins below, rebuilt upside-down rooms. He pauses at the top of the ladder, watches Naphi.

The captain, last member of the crew, stares over the side at a silver-skinned throng of fish. Stares past them thoughtfully. Stares intently, leaning over to stare deep into the water's dark.

Sham smiles.

Acknowledgements

With hugest thanks to Mark Bould, Nadia Bouzidi, Mic Cheetham, Julie Crisp, Rupa DasGupta, Maria Dahvana Headley, Chloe Healy, Deanna Hoak, Ratna Kamath, Simon Kavanagh, Jemima Miéville, David Moensch, Bella Pagan, Anne Perry, Max Schaefer, Chris Schluep, Jared Shurin, Jane Soodalter, Jesse Soodalter, Mark Tavani, Evan Calder Williams, & all at Macmillan & Del Rey.

As always, I'm indebted to too many writers & artists to list, but particularly important to this book are Joan Aiken, John Antrobus, the Awdrys Sr & Jr, Catherine Besterman, Lucy Lane Clifford, Daniel Defoe, F. Tennyson Jesse, Erich Kästner, Ursula le Guin, John Lester, Penelope Lively, Herman Melville, Spike Milligan, Charles Platt, Robert Louis Stevenson & the Strugatsky Brothers.